The Cybelene Conspiracy

Albert Noyer

THE CYBELENE CONSPIRACY

The Toby Press

First Edition 2005

The Toby Press LLC, 2004
POB 8531, New Milford, CT. 06676-8531, USA
& POB 2455, London W1A 5WY, England
www.tobypress.com

ISBN 1 59264 033 8, *paperback*

A CIP catalogue record for this title is
available from the British Library

Typeset in Garamond by Jerusalem Typesetting

Printed and bound in the United States by
Thomson-Shore Inc., Michigan

With special thanks to the writing group:

Jennifer, Melody, Mary, Frank, Russell
and
Leslie S.B. MacCoull Ph.D.
Coptic Archeological Society (North America)

Res humanas ordine nullo
Fortuna regit spartisque manu
Munera caeca, peiora fovens;
Vincit sanctos dira libido,
Fraus sublime regnat in aula.

Fate without order rules the affairs of men,
Throws about her gifts with a blind hand,
Cherishing the worst; violent desire defeats the virtuous,
Deceit reigns sublime in the palace halls.

Lucius Annaeus Seneca, *Phaedra*

DRAMATIS PERSONAE

Getorius Asterius	Surgeon at Ravenna, Western Roman capital
Arcadia Valeriana Asteria	Wife of Getorius, training with him to be a *medica*
Thecla	Arian Presbytera of the Basilica of the Resurrection
Gaius Quintus Virilo	Master of the merchant galley *Cybele*
Claudia Quinta	Virilo's daughter
Diotar of Pessinus	Archpriest of the cult of Cybele
Adonis	Disciple of Diotar
Leudovald	Investigator for the palace Judicial Magistrate
Flavius Placidus Valentinian III*	Emperor of the Western Roman Empire
Licinia Eudoxia*	Valentinian's wife, Empress
Galla Placidia*	Mother of the emperor, daughter of Theodosius I
Publius Maximin†	Wealthy senator at Ravenna
Giamona and Tigris	A gladiatrix and gladiator
Zhang Chen	Importer from Sina (China)

* Real people recorded in history
† The character Publius Maximin was based on the real person Petronius Maximus but as his role in the novel was largely fictionalized, his name was changed.

GLOSSARY OF PLACES MENTIONED

GERMANY

Mogontiacum—Mainz

Treveri—Trier

FRANCE

Autessiodurum—Auxerre

Lugdunum—Lyon

ITALY

Arminium—Rimini

Ancona—Ancona

Aquileia—near Trieste

Bononia—Bologna

Caesana—Cesena

Classis—Classe

Comum—Como

Forum Livii—Forli

Mutina—Modena

Ravenna—Ravenna (Somewhat
fictionalized)

AUSTRIA

Brigantium—Bregenz

Vindobono—Vienna

BALKANS

Aquincum—Budapest

Epidamnus—Durres

Issus—Vis Island

Olcinium—Olcinj

Scodra—Shkoder

Sirmium—Sremsk-Mitrovka

Siscia—Sisak

Spalato—Split

Risinium—Risan

Viminacium—Kostolc

TURKEY

Constantinople—Istanbul

Pessinus—Balhisar

RIVERS

Bedesis—Montone

Gallus—near Skarya River

Padenna—ancient branch of Po

Padus—Po

Rhenus—Rhine

Rhodanus—Rhone

xi

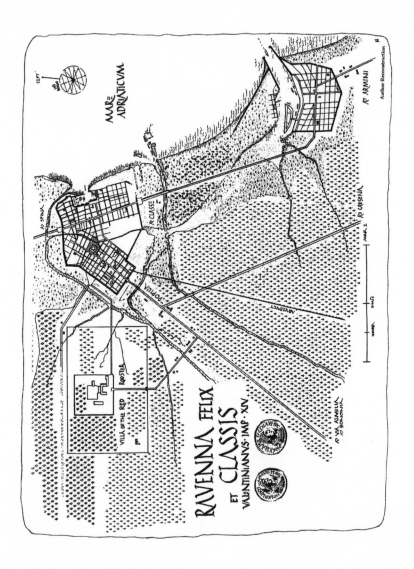

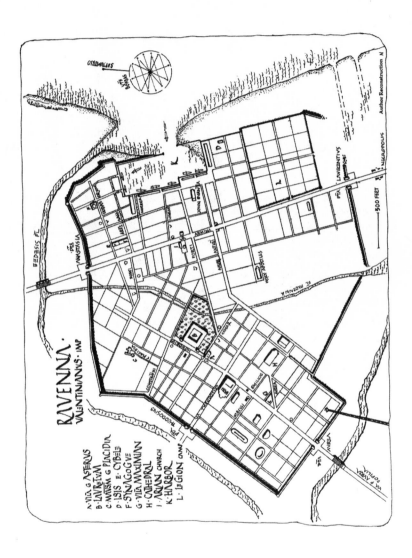

RAVENNA.
VALENTINIANVS· IMP

A · VILLA G· ASTERIVS
B · LAVRETVM
C · MAVSM· G· PLACIDIA
D · ISIS   E · CYBELE
F · SYNAGOGVE
G · VILLA MAXIMINVM
H · CATHEDRAL
I · ARIAN CHVRCH
K · HARBOR
L · LEGION CAMP

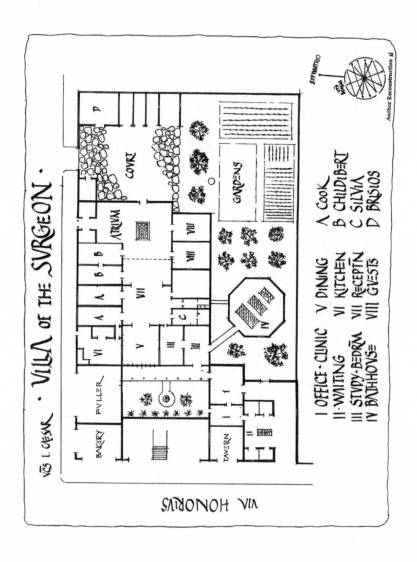

VIA HONORVS

VÕS I. CÆSAR · VILLA of the SVRGEON ·

BAKERY FVLLER

COVRT

ATRIVM

GARDENS

SEPTIMATRIO
VIA WINDS

Author Reconstruction af

TAVERN

I OFFICE · CLINIC   V DINING
II · WAITING   VI KITCHEN
III STVDY · BEDRM   VII RECEPTN
IV BATHHOVSE   VIII GVESTS

A COOK
B CHILDIBERT
C SILVIA
D BRISIOS

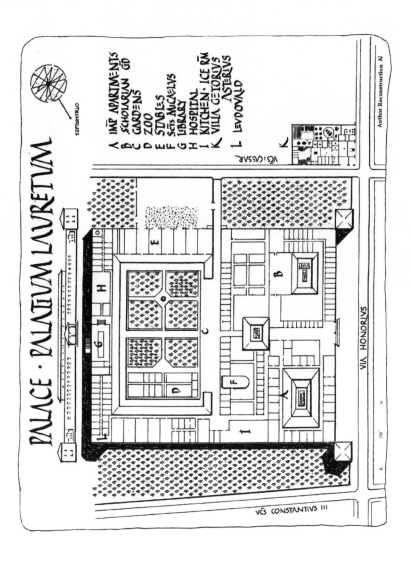

PALACE · PALATIVM LAVRETVM

SEPTEMTRIO

A IMP APARTMENTS
B SCHOLARIAN GD
C GARDENS
D ZOO
E STABLES
F Scts MICAELVS
G LIBRARY
H HOSPITAL
I KITCHEN · ICE RM
K VILLA GETORIVS
ASTERIVS
L LEVDOVALD

VCS CAESAR

VCS CONSTANTIVS III

VIA HONORIVS

Author Reconstruction N

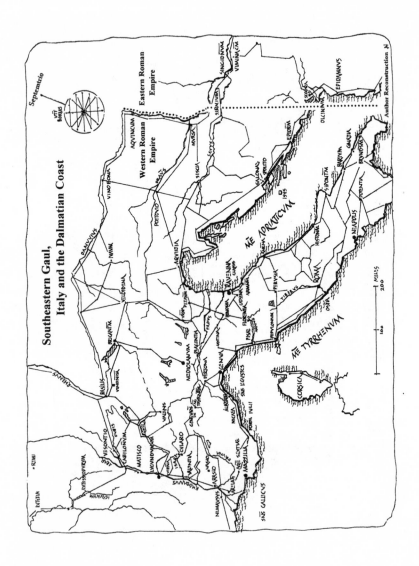

Ravenna

Chapter one

Thecla, the woman presbytera of the Arian-sect Basilica of the Anastasis, repressed a light belch with her hand—a rancid taste of cumin and crayfish—and glanced up at a flight of evening swallows. The darting birds speckled the sunset sky like spatters of black ink on a vermilion manuscript page.

She winced at a persistent dull pain in her abdomen and sighed. "*Hirundines*, how I wish I had your energy. Your…freedom."

Ahead of her, across the Via Armini, the brick bulk of the Anastasis church and its octagonal baptistery were somber silhouettes against the fading afternoon light. Already their bluish shadows stretched out to the curb where she stood. Thecla realized her stomach held a daemon, but she still needed to fill the oil lamps in the basilica for the morning service, before it became too dark. After letting a wagon pass, she made to step off the curb, but then two oxcarts loaded with matting rushes blocked her way as they rumbled slowly along the stone paving. At least because of market day yesterday the street was relatively free of animal droppings. The farmers' slaves would have shoveled up all the manure to take back and add to the steaming piles in their yards.

"Move on, move on," Thecla grumbled at the slow-moving beasts. "It's not as early as I thought. I can't see that well even in daylight, and the lamp openings are small."

The presbytera impatiently tucked a wisp of gray hair back under her veil and touched her cheek. *Wrinkled as the rind on a Calabrian melon. You're old, woman, and you still haven't learned to be patient. Eugenius used to tease you about it. Patience is above learning, he'd say. Strength grows in the garden of patience. Patience wins the argument.* Even though her husband had been dead for fifteen years, Thecla felt a welling of tears and wiped a threadbare sleeve across her eyes.

After the two oxcarts with their load of green fronds finally passed by, Thecla hurried diagonally across the paving toward her church, clenching her jug of olive oil against her chest and skirting around a trail of manure that had dribbled from one of the oxen. She had crossed the Via Armini from her apartment every day for thirty-four years—the street measured exactly fifteen paces wide. The presbytera paused on the curb to catch her breath and watch a group of children playing a noisy hoop game in front of their apartment building. They recalled to her her childhood long ago in Philippi, in the province of Macedonia, far from this north Adriatic port of Ravenna. She had been Euodia Apollonia then, the only child of a pagan father and an Arian Christian mother. After the family moved to Constantinople, she was tutored by a deacon, then ordained an Arian presbytera at the age of twenty-nine, and Euodia became Thecla, named after a female disciple of the Apostle Paul, whose life and martyrdom she had read about in *The Acts of Paul and Thecla*.

After serving eight years as an assistant in the Eastern Roman capital, Thecla had been assigned to Ravenna, with the mandate of resurrecting its declining Arian community. Now, at the age of seventy-one, she was a gray-haired widow who had helplessly watched her responsibilities shrink to one scattered congregation in the decrepit port quarter of the city. Her energy and freedom had gradually diminished along with her flock over the past years, and Thecla's sense of humor recognized the irony of her church being dedicated to the Anastasis—the Greek word meant "Resurrection."

Thecla watched two members of the civic guard light torches at the street corner on the shadowed west side of the road. Near the first evening hour, the Armini was almost deserted. Only a few customers were in shops, and it was still too light for women from the local brothels to begin soliciting for temporary lovers. Although the late afternoon sun softened the port buildings' scarred stucco faces with a clean wash of apricot-colored light, and a faint glow from unshuttered windows gave the area a deceptively well-off look, Thecla mused that if the poor indeed were to inherit the earth, the Kingdom would certainly be inaugurated in the squalor of Ravenna's harbor area.

Apartment blocks along the Armini formed the bulwark of a warren of artisans' workshops and two- or three-story dwellings where dockworker families lived, or slaves were quartered and rented out by their masters. Under arcades and awnings at the sidewalk level, shop owners struggled to make a living selling bread, meat, vegetables and household furnishings. Others held street-corner booths or walk-in taverns that sold cooked food and regional wines. Too many of the shops were vacant, and few of the merchants were in her congregation.

The Via Armini was the unofficial eastern boundary line beyond which Arian Christians in Ravenna could live in relative peace. The Anastasis basilica, set in an open space just west of the road, dated from an earlier time, and its walls were marred by occasional damage from the city's more rowdy youths.

Thecla saw that lamps were gleaming at Videric's food stall on the corner of the Via Porti, outlining a few customers who were buying his lard-fried squid or pork for their evening meal. She inhaled the cool air with a frown. The ever-present smells of animal dung, and salt-and-fish on the Adriatic off-sea breeze, had been overlaid by that of greasy smoke and garlic-laced meals being prepared in port quarter kitchens or taverns. Her stomach reacted to the smells with another gurgle of colic.

A short time earlier she had finished a supper of boiled crayfish. Now, a growing queasiness made her realize that the honey-sweetened sauce of cumin and pepper had probably masked spoilage of the crustaceans. As an unpleasant, acrid after-taste rose in her throat,

Thecla swallowed hard and hoped she would not publicly embarrass herself by vomiting in the street.

"*Christotokos,* Mother of Christ, help me," she muttered, hoping that an upset stomach was not of too little significance to warrant divine attention.

Covering her mouth with the edge of her veil, Thecla walked onto the new grass in the shadow of the basilica and immediately felt the damp chill of the April air seep through her black tunic. In her haste she had forgotten to slip on a cloak. At the same moment, a northeast wind gusted in from the harbor and whipped the veil over her head. As she struggled to pull the tangling folds from her face without dropping the jar, Thecla heard a voice behind her.

"Havin' trouble, Presbyt'ra?"

She turned to see a lanky man dressed in dirty wool trousers and a scuffed leather vest; the son of an invalid parishioner. "Fabius, you…you startled me. How is your mother? Legs still bad?"

"That surgeon in the Julius Caesar makes me treat her with vinegar."

"Good. Oh, do you recall his name, Fabius? I might need a physician to purge my stomach."

"Getorix. Geturios. Somethin' like that." He held his nose and made a face. "I'm sick of th' stink from th' vinegar I rub on mother's legs."

"I'm sure it's not pleasant for Felicitas, either. Are you working, Fabius?"

"Th' port's open again after th' winter, so I been unloadin' here and there. Nothin' steady."

Thecla studied his face. *Gaunt, Germanic, eyes a bit too close together. Untrimmed blondish hair and mustache. Probably handsome once in a barbarian sort of way. No wedding band, so just an old mother to criticize his ways. And from the smell on his breath, he's already made a dent in tavern wine kegs to get away from a tongue that's probably as acid as the vinegar he complained about.* She turned Fabius by the arm and pointed along the straight line of the Armini, to the masts of stone-lifting cranes at the Anastasia Gate, a quarter mile off.

"The Augustus is extending the north wall around to the harbor. You could get employment there."

"Haulin' brick with slaves?" Fabius spat and indicated the nearest building with a toss of his head. "Valentinian ought to spend th' gold fixin' up around here, instead of on his palace. Y' heard that his mother just built herself a fancy tomb?"

Galla Placidia. All of Ravenna gossiped that Valentinian III passed most of his time hunting or drinking with his bodyguards, while his mother ran the government. "Yes, well, Fabius, Bishop Chrysologos is probably advising her that not a *siliqua* be spent in our Arian quarter. Have you thought of moving to Classis? There's work there. Because the Vandals have captured Carthage, the Classis harbor is being dredged, and a fleet of war galleys reconditioned."

"Mother would never go," Fabius mumbled, rubbing a hand across his stubble of blond beard. "Presbyt'ra, they say th' Vandals are Arian Christians, like us. That's good, no?"

Thecla considered the recent Vandal victories in Rome's African provinces to be a mixed fortune for her sect. The tribe's reputation for destruction had already created a new verb, "to vandalize."

"There's a measure to all things, Fabius," she answered, evading his question. "They threaten an invasion of Sicily, even Italy itself. There would be more killing, demands for tribute. Possible retribution against Ravenna." Thecla decided to end speculations that Fabius would report as facts in the next tavern he entered. "Where were you going?"

"Gettin' mother some supper. Y' know how she loves her fried pork."

"I'm bringing oil to fill lamps at the church. Will you be at the Eucharist Meal in the morning?"

"Meal?" Fabius echoed.

"It's the Lord's Day." Thecla scowled. "Or Sunendag, under the Frankish names just adopted. I prefer the old term. Will you be there?"

"Uh…mother might need me." Fabius looked toward the food booth and nervously jingled his belt purse.

"Another time then." *No point in pushing the man, or he'll never come.* "Greet Felicitas for me, tell her I'll look in tomorrow afternoon."

Fabius grunted agreement. Thecla watched him slouch off to Videric's, and then turned back toward the basilica.

The building's unrepaired lower courses of dark brickwork were scarred, parts even chiseled out in places, the result of vandalism by local Christians who professed the Roman creed. The spring rains had not washed off all the charcoaled graffiti that attacked the Arian belief that Christ was not co-eternal with his Father. *Homoiousians,* her people were called—those who believed Christ had a nature that was similar to God's, but not the same, as the Roman Nicenes proclaimed. Still, she was grateful that the two factions generally left each other alone, even while realizing that could change like the sudden fury of an April thunderstorm, now that Carthage was in Arian hands. Danger might make men devout, as the saying went, but it also made them fearful and intolerant.

After a glance at the rounded apse and high dark windows of her basilica, Thecla decided to look into the baptistery. She put her jug down on the sill to unlock the door. Inside, three of the room's eight alabaster-covered windows admitted a final red glare of slanting rays. She shaded her eyes against the brilliant light that illuminated the water in the central pool.

"Mother of Christ!" Thecla exclaimed, startled by its color. For an instant the reddish rays had seemed to tint the pool water the color of blood. "Half my flock would see this as an omen of evil."

The Feast of the Resurrection had been two weeks earlier, yet only three converts, all women, had consented to be immersed in the chill water and emerge as Reborn Souls of the Arian Creed. Thecla wondered if her Nicene rival, Bishop Chrysologos, had fared any better, or if there was general apathy among all of Ravenna's non-baptized citizens. She realized that the sacking of Rome by Visigoths a generation earlier, and the present Vandal victory at Carthage, had shaken people's faith. Other potential catechumens undoubtedly were attracted to the foreign cults seamen brought in on galleys. Last month was an example.

Early in March, she had seen a procession of shaven Egyptian priests from the cult of Isis bless the opening of the navigation season. A good-sized crowd had watched them move from their temple, south of the harbor, to the breakwater wharf. Men dressed in women's tunics acted as escorts for a bear and monkey, which were costumed as demigods and carried in litters as parodies of the human and divine. Women crowned with forsythia blossoms scattered more of the yellow flowers in front of the priests. Behind them, musicians playing flutes and jingling silver sistra preceded a group of men who wore animal masks representing various Egyptian gods.

At the wharf, the priests had floated a statue of Isis in a small boat decorated with pond lilies. Magic spells in their picture writing were painted on the linen sail. After praying, and purifying the hull with sulfur, the dark-skinned priests sprinkled the statue with spices and milk, then set the craft adrift on the blue Adriatic.

A week later, to the jubilation of the worshippers, a grain galley arrived safely from the Nile delta. Thecla realized there were converts to Isis made that day, but feared that other less-benign pagan rituals were being enacted in basements or atria of the port's houses.

She eased herself up to sit on the edge of the pool—the cramp in her stomach was persisting—and noticed flakes of paint scattered on the limestone rim. She glanced up at the dome mural. Already less of the image of Christ being baptized in the Jordan River was visible on the mildewed plaster than the week before. Veiled by the painted translucence of the water, the nude figure of Christ and his rough-clad cousin, John, were only phantom images, yet, curiously, the hoary body of the pagan god who symbolized the river was still clearly depicted. His head was wreathed in green rushes, with one hand raised in a benediction of the ritual. Thecla knew of rumors that Chrysologos planned to replace his deteriorated baptistery paintings with permanent mosaic tiles. Certainly, he had enough funds to do so. What the Arians in Ravenna needed was a larger congregation and their own bishop, but the nearest of either was at the port of Ancona, a three-day journey south, along the coastal stretch of the Via Popilia.

Thecla's assembly was made up of Gothic recruits from the

7

garrison legion, and harbor workers or artisans who lived in the port quarter. Despite Chrysologos's periodic attempts to close her church, the civil authorities refused, unwilling to risk a riot among the dissenting factions. It had come to that kind of fragile standoff between the differing interpretations of Christ's nature.

Thecla occasionally wondered why, in the face of Nicene hostility, she stubbornly remained an Arian. The teaching of the presbyter, Arius, that Christ was not divine, but only a man created by God to participate in His divinity and be His intermediary with mankind, had been twice condemned by Church councils. Arius was dead a hundred years, but his creed and the Testaments of the four Evangelists, translated into Gothic by Bishop Ulfilas, sustained the surviving renegade congregations.

Perhaps a Christ who was more human than divine was easier to imitate, yet Thecla realized that the subtlety of a relationship among the persons of the Trinity, "God the Father and Lord of the Universe, our Redeemer Jesus Christ, and the Sacred Spirit," was of small significance to her illiterate flock. She had enough trouble choosing passages from the Gothic text to serve as examples that might make a difference in their daily less-than-subtle relationships with each other.

Musing on all this, Thecla realized she now felt truly nauseous. She pressed a hand against her abdomen to test its tenderness, and stood up. After relocking the door and taking up her oil jar, she walked across the paving toward the entrance of the basilica. Several pigeons, hopeful for a few morsels of bread, fluttered down nearby, frantically strutting to keep up with her in their comical, bobbing way.

"Poor *columba*," she cooed. "No bread, not even a crumb for you tonight. And if you felt as I do, *columba,* you would never eat again."

The last arc of orange sun slid below the tiled roof of Lauretum Palace in the distance, recasting the reddish-pink brick of the Anastasis into a dull-brown earth tone. Thecla saw the shallow porch and its row of six wooden pillars drop into shadow, and muttered regret at having lingered in the baptistery. It might not be light enough inside the apse to fill the lamps for the morning service. She found the correct key on her ring before noticing that one of the double doors was ajar. Had Odo been there earlier and forgotten to relock the portal? The nearly senile porter had done that before.

A half-smile replaced the presbytera's frown of annoyance. *After seventy-one Aprils, I'm getting forgetful myself.* Thecla pushed open the pine door and felt a shiver ripple through her body. The air in the dim nave was as chilly as that of the outdoors, but something else, some premonition, caused the sensation. Although the basilica was fragrant with the scent of incense and melted beeswax, the pleasant odor was not strong enough to block out the pervading smell of mold coming from the damp walls. A faint light gleamed through the alabaster panes on the clerestory windows, but the chancel was shrouded in a half-gloom. The apse mural of the *Anastasis,* the Glorified Christ standing at the tomb opening, was barely visible.

Thecla had often sat before the fresco and speculated that the ghostly image might have looked just as ephemeral to Mary of Magdala and the two other women on that awesome dawn of the Resurrection. She also marveled that there were females present as witnesses that morning, but no disciples who were men. The risen Christ had shown himself to a trio of Eve's Daughters first, and she had long since forgiven the Apostle Paul for omitting that significant detail in his first letter to the Corinthians. A later writing, the *Testament of Mary of Magdala,* told how the Magdalene stood up to Peter's challenge to her teaching. "Are we to turn around and listen to her? Did he prefer her to us?" Matthew had defended her authority and rebuked Peter for contending against women as adversaries. Even Paul eventually acknowledged women's equality with men in his letter to the Galatians, but Nicene authorities now prohibited both the ordination of women and a married clergy. Thecla felt fortunate that Arian bishops still honored both of the old traditions.

Thecla was just turning back from opening the second door, to admit as much of the fading light as possible, when she heard what sounded like sobs echoing in the dim space, coming from the direction of the chancel area around the altar. She hesitated a moment, then walked along the arcade until she made out the figure of a woman swathed in a white robe, sitting on the stone floor near the pulpit. A veil partially concealed her head and face. The woman's bulky garment rose and fell with each sob.

"Domina? Domina, are you ill?" Thecla whispered, puzzled that someone would be in her basilica at this hour.

Louder sobbing was the only answer. *The robes look vaguely familiar,* Thecla thought, *but I don't believe she's a congregation member.*

"Can I help you, Domina?" she repeated more loudly.

When Thecla moved closer, she noticed a puddle of blood on the floor that was seeping onto the lower part of the woman's tunic. Then, in the half-light, she made out the nude body of a young man lying to one side of the woman. A golden sickle gleamed softly in his limp hand. The dark pool of blood seemed to be coming from between his legs. Thecla bent next to the youth and saw in horror that his scrotum had been severed.

"*Christotokos,*" she gasped, "what happened here? Did...did he...?" Nausea choked off the question. Thecla leaned sideways in a retch that brought bitter bits of crayfish to her throat. She felt the jar she was still carrying slip from hands that were drained of strength, helpless to hold onto the smooth clay. The container smashed on the floor, sending a splash of golden oil flowing over the stones to mingle slowly with the crimson puddle at her feet.

After a moment she recovered enough to wipe a sleeve across her mouth. *Virgin Mother...the man has...has mutilated himself. He needs medical help. What was the name of that physician Fabius mentioned? It sounded Celtic or Gothic...said he lived on the Via Julius Caesar.*

Thecla decided the sobbing woman could wait until a physician came. With another glance at the youth's body, the presbytera staggered to her feet. Dazed, in shock, she supported herself on each nave column in turn, lurching back to the entrance.

A diminishing trail of oily blood from the hem of her tunic had feathered out by the time she reached the front doors. Thecla went out into the shadow of the portico, to gulp in cool evening air until she felt less faint. Gradually, her mind cleared. When she looked around for someone who might help, she saw a small figure walking along her side of the Via Armini.

"Boy!" she called out in a hoarse voice. "Child, wait!"

The boy stopped and looked her way. She fumbled for a bronze *quadrans* in her purse, then half-ran to him, hiking up her tunic to keep from tripping on the folds, thinking that any loss to her dignity was of less importance than finding help for the man in her church—if he was still alive.

Thecla was out of breath when she reached the boy. "Child," she panted, "th…there's a bronze in it…if you…bring that physician…who lives…on the Julius Caesar here quickly."

The urchin stared at the old woman in her black tunic, eyed the coin in her hand, then turned and ran west along the Via Porti.

Mother of Christ, have I frightened the child off? In this twilight I must look like some dark-robed sorceress.

"Quickly," she repeated faintly, although the boy was out of hearing. Then Thecla slid to her knees on the damp grass. The horrifying scene at the church filled her mind again.

Christotokos, eleison. Have mercy, Mother. Who is that young man? Why did he come to my church to…to do that to himself? And the woman. Who is she?

Thecla held back an urge to vomit with a prayer of desperation. "Mother of Christ, now I truly need your help. Let that boy bring back the surgeon who treats Fabius's mother. *Quickly!*"

Chapter two

I was called too late, the young man bled to death." Getorius Asterius straightened up and brushed his black hair forward in a quick gesture of frustration. "Why would he castrate himself?"

"Horrible." His wife Arcadia shuddered, then remarked, "Getorius, that golden sickle looks like a ritual knife. Didn't Pliny describe a druidic rite where one was used to cut mistletoe?"

"I recall the passage. Celts considered it a healing plant, but druid priests didn't castrate victims. Besides, there are none around. Who is...was he, Thecla?"

"I've not seen him before. The unfortunate youth was not of my congregation."

"Your congregation?"—Arcadia's brows arched above her hazel eyes—"What do you mean?"

"I'm the Arian presbytera in Ravenna."

"Sorry. I...I guess I'd heard. When you sent that boy for my husband, I just didn't make the connection."

"You're surprised because I'm a woman?" Thecla's voice was testy. "There were many presbyters in the early Church who were female. Some became bishops."

"I didn't mean to—"

"You treat patients with your husband, my dear?" Thecla asked in a more gentle tone. "Is that why you came with him?"

Arcadia nodded. "Getorius is teaching me to be a medica."

Thecla commented with a mischievous smile, "Not exactly a traditional occupation for a Roman lady, would you say?"

"I understand your point...Presbytera."

"Ladies, could we discuss your work later?" Getorius nodded toward the woman kneeling on the floor. "She hasn't stopped sobbing, nor moved, during my examination of the man. Do you know who *she* is, Thecla?"

"I've not seen her here before either."

"Get her away from the man, Getorius, and out of that blood," Arcadia said.

"Right." He stooped down and lightly touched her shoulder. "You can tell us what happened later on, but come to my clinic now. I'll prescribe a sedative, then we can take you home. Where do you live?"

The girl suddenly pulled aside her veil and looked up. She was younger than Getorius expected. As she stared at him her wet eyes widened in sudden terror.

"What's that horrible smell?" she cried, then her body stiffened and she fell sideways onto the stone flooring before Getorius could catch her. Her slim figure twitched and jerked about in spasms, spreading the bloody puddle further on her tunic and over the floor.

"Christ, she has the Sacred Disease!" Getorius exclaimed. "Arcadia, get that wooden rod from my case. I'll hold her still, while you ease it between her teeth so she won't bite into her tongue."

Getorius pulled the girl's head forward to help her shallow breathing, but before Arcadia could work the thick rod into her mouth, her body stopped twitching. As the girl's breathing returned to normal, she seemed to fall asleep. "Let her relax a moment," he advised. "Some seizures can be of short duration."

"What you call a sacred disease," Thecla remarked, "Christ might have attributed to daemons."

"Would *you*, Presbytera?" Getorius retorted sharply, his blue eyes narrowing under a frown of annoyance. "I've not seen a daemon jump out of anyone I've ever treated."

"Hippocrates considered the illness to be no more divine than any other," Arcadia added. "He thought it originated in the brains of people who had inherited a tendency toward phlegm imbalances. Certainly, this girl has been producing phlegm through her weeping."

"Your husband is teaching you well." Thecla looked back at Getorius. "Daemon or not, Surgeon, can the poor girl be cured?"

"Medically, her sickness is called epilepsia, but sometimes I use the common name," he answered, relieved that his wife's explanation had headed off a confrontation with the old woman. He glanced around the darkened apse. "The girl can be examined at my clinic, but have you something to put over the young man? Until we get a magistrate here."

Thecla nodded toward the altar. "Christ would not object to using a cloth that covered his Agape Table."

"Fine. I'd like to examine his head. Do you have any lamps? It's almost totally dark in here."

"I came in here to fill them with oil for the dawn service, but dropped the jar when I discovered this…this horror."

"Bring me the one burning in the sanctuary. Arcadia, try to revive the girl with my phial of thyme oil, then we'll see if she's able to walk to the clinic."

After Thecla brought the votive lamp and went back for the altar cloth, Getorius stepped around the bloody pool and pottery shards to look at the dead youth's head. He was surprised to find a bronze plaque around his neck, which most likely identified him as a slave. He held it up to the flickering light and read the incised name.

"*Atlos Didymos.*' Greek? In any case the Didymos household has lost a handsome worker." Getorius lifted the youth's head. It was flexible. He felt his chest. "Still warm. Atlos died within this watch period." When his fingers felt a lump beneath the skull, he turned the head to one side. A distinct swelling was evident beneath the glossy matted hair. "That's strange."

"What is it, Getorius?"

"There's a bruise on the back of his head."

"Could it have happened when he fell?"

"I thought of that, but I doubt that he would castrate himself standing up, if that's what happened here. That will be a matter for the magistrate to decide." Moving his fingers around to the face, Getorius noted that the eyes were half open, staring in shock. That would not be unusual. He eased an eyelid up and observed that the pupil was dilated. Thecla came alongside with the linen cloth. "Yes, cover him, Presbytera," he said, standing up. "The judicial magistrate at the palace will send one of his investigators to question you about Atlos."

"I know nothing beyond finding his body," Thecla objected, fidgeting with the hair under her veil. "You and your wife are the only others who have seen him."

"Besides the girl. She'll be questioned too. Could anyone else have been here?"

"Odo, my porter. But it's ridiculous to think that he could be involved. He's barely strong enough to push open the portal doors."

"It's fortunate my husband was home," Arcadia said. "He's palace physician to Galla Placidia."

"What?"—Thecla frowned—"Fabius didn't tell me that. It was presumptuous of me to send for such an important man."

"Important?" Getorius chuckled. "I was appointed in January, hardly long enough to become indispensable to the Augustus's mother."

"I was going to ask you to treat a sudden ailment of mine, Surgeon, but now…"

"Nonsense, Presbytera, I've retained my private practice as well. What can I—" A groan interrupted Getorius. The girl was regaining consciousness. "Good, Arcadia, the thyme was effective." He bent down to wipe spittle from the girl's lips, but she pulled away. She looked to be no more than sixteen or seventeen years old. "My wife will take you to our clinic, to make sure you're all right. How are you called, girl?"

She stared up at him. The fright was still in her eyes and her pale cheeks were wet from tears, but she did not answer.

"My wife would like to know what to call you," Getorius persisted, trying not to sound impatient.

"What is your name?" Arcadia asked softly.

The girl glanced at her. After a pause, she looked down and mumbled a word that was almost inaudible.

"Cybele."

"Sybil?" Getorius misunderstood the like-sounding names. "My wife will give you something to forget all this for awhile, Sybil. But after you've slept, you'll have to tell the magistrate what happened. Understand?"

"Sybil, do you feel well enough to walk four or five blocks to our clinic?" Arcadia asked.

At the girl's slow nod, she supported her under the arm. As she helped her stand up, blood splotched Arcadia's tunic and sandals.

"Let me take her to the front door." Getorius reached out to help, but the girl drew away and a look of fear shadowed her eyes again.

"She's frightened"—Arcadia motioned him back—"I can do it alone."

Getorius shrugged, but stayed alongside. Arcadia held onto Cybele and walked the length of the nave to the entrance. Thecla followed behind them.

Outside, the dusk sky now was well into the last bluish glimmer of twilight. Getorius was grateful that people were eating supper and that darkness would conceal the soiled tunics of the two women. It was better that Arcadia and the girl not be seen—both of them wearing bloodstained clothes would be sure to arouse curious gossip.

"When you get back, Arcadia, send Childibert to the magistrate's office at the palace, to report the death."

She nodded. "I'll clean Sybil, then give her a valerian drink to help her sleep."

After the two women were lost in the darkness of the Via Porti, Getorius turned to Thecla. "I need to go back in once more. I want to examine that sickle in his hand."

"I'm going with you."

"You'd be better off staying here, Presbytera. Away from…from what's inside."

"It's my church, young man," Thecla snapped. "I said I was going in with you."

"As you wish." *Not the time to argue with her. The magistrate can do that tomorrow when he questions her.*

The lone sanctuary lamp flame cast a grotesque flickering shadow of the dead youth on the marble pulpit base. Getorius kneeled beside the body, staining his left boot with blood. He pulled the altar cloth aside and eased the sickle handle out of Atlos's stiffening fingers. The slender, curved blade glinted in the flickering light.

"It's gold all right. Looks new, or isn't used much."

"As your wife observed, possibly a pagan ritual blade. Druid priests used mistletoe sprigs for their solstice rites."

"*Druid priests?*" Getorius scoffed. "Even if Atlos wasn't Christian, there are none here still practicing that ancient religion."

"Surely, he was not. We are opposed to suicide, and certainly castration."

"So Paul was engaging in a bit of irony when he told some Galatians who wanted converts circumcised to go all the way and castrate themselves too?"

Thecla looked at him with a quizzical expression, then a half-smile. "You tease me, Surgeon. The passage is obscure; I see that you read books other than your medical texts. If you recall, Paul also referred to them as, 'you stupid Galatians'."

Getorius grinned. Not many clergy had a sense of humor, yet here was a frail, white-haired, woman presbytera, with a face like wrinkled parchment, whose mind was sharp enough to recognize a gentle jest. In her faded black tunic and ill-fitting square veil, Thecla reminded him of one of the swallows that had swooped low over his head as he was hurrying to the basilica.

A gurgle sounded in Thecla's abdomen, and she turned away, embarrassed.

"Was that the ailment you mentioned?"

"This horror made me forget. Have you something in your case for a stomach that is being tormented by a daemon?"

"Another daemon?" *She is witty.* "I have a purge, but it's too dark to find it in here."

"My rooms are in an apartment across the Armini. If it would not trouble you to go there?"

"No, no. And Arcadia needs time to examine Sybil." Getorius placed the sickle back over Atlos's hand, then wiped a bloody finger and thumb on a corner of the altar linen. "I'll find something that might help you, but lock the front portal after we leave."

"The body can't remain here," Thecla protested. "I celebrate the Eucharist in the morning."

"That's right, tomorrow is Sunendag."

"I prefer to call it the Lord's Day. About Atlos, Surgeon?"

"The investigator won't come tonight, and probably not on Sunen…on the Lord's Day…without a dispensation from the bishop. The floor paving is cold. Atlos's body won't deteriorate too much, but I'm afraid your rites won't take place."

Thecla sighed. "Odo wouldn't be able to clean up all that blood in time anyway. I'm not sure how disappointed my flock will be. After thirty-four years, my sermons aren't exactly as inspired as Saint Paul's." She took Getorius's arm in a firm grip. "And from the way my stomach feels, I'd probably be too ill to preside. Let's go cast out my daemon." As Thecla slid the front door bolt into its retaining bracket, Getorius noticed that the new moon was in its first quarter, a burgeoning crescent again engaged in the monthly struggle to swallow its paler host.

"My apartment is there." Thecla pointed to a two-story building that was on a diagonal across from the basilica. She took his arm again. "Don't walk too rapidly, young man. These old legs feel even weaker after this."

The moonlight and torches on the Via Armini threw only a faint light on the basilica's wall, but Getorius was still able to make out charcoaled graffiti critical of Arian beliefs. GENITOM NON FACTOM, DEVM VEROM DE DEO VERO and GENETOS. Thecla could see what had caught his attention. "'Begotten, not made.' 'True God from true God.' Your bishop's vandalizers paid little attention to their spelling lessons," she commented sarcastically.

"Vandalizers." He chuckled. The tribe's name had recently been used in the theatre as a synonym for destructive activities. "Yes,

'*Genitum,*' '*factum,*' '*verum.*' But I doubt that Bishop Chrysologos sent those who wrote this."

"Perhaps, perhaps not."

Getorius knew Arians differed in their view of Christ's nature, believing the Son had been created after the Father and was not co-eternal with Him. The bishop occasionally preached against the heresy, but no longer took its doctrinal threat very seriously. Arianism kept the Gothic legionaries pacified, and those converts who were not in the army were confined to their quarter of Ravenna. They were usually not harassed by Nicenes, but outbreaks of violence still occurred from time to time. Getorius wondered if Atlos had been a recent convert. He had, after all, come to the Arian church.

Thecla's rooms were on the first floor of a building which once had been handsome. Constructed of long narrow bricks, its arched overhangs gave a measure of shade to the windows that gave air and light to the rooms. The curved lines were repeated in a decorative arcade over the shops and in the twin entranceways of the first level. One door led to the upper floor by way of chipped limestone stairs. The other, which Thecla used to reach her rooms, admitted ground floor tenants.

"Christ with you, boys and girls," she said in greeting to some children who were playing with wooden hoops by the light of a smoking torch set between the apartment entrances.

None responded. The urchins looked dirty and thin to Getorius. Several had hacking coughs. "Isn't it late for them to be out?" he asked Thecla. "Night air is noxious, and their phlegm humors are already upset as it is."

"A risk, but there's not much privacy in the rooms," she explained. "No doubt their parents told them to play outside so that they can snatch a moment's pleasure making new brothers or sisters for them."

It was a situation to which Getorius had not given much thought. His villa had fairly good-sized rooms. These children made him realize that the majority of people who came to his clinic probably lived in places like this.

Beyond the limestone sill, black tiles in a mosaic pavement

of worn white tesserae depicted a merchant galley and lighthouse, a picture framed by a square panel with the name C. MARIVS still visible. Getorius surmised that Gaius Marius had been the owner of a shipping business, and had built the apartment for its rental income. Perhaps his family had occupied the first floor.

A narrow corridor, tracked with dried mud, smelled of onions, fish and sausage fried in rancid lard. Thecla's door was the first one on the right. As she unbolted her lock, the woman gagged again from the food smells. Inside, she lighted the three spouts of a brass lamp from the single one that had been left burning.

"What caused your daemon to misbehave?" Getorius asked, glancing around a small room that looked like both the woman's study and reception area.

"Spoiled crayfish, I believe."

"Not unusual. I'll need hot water and two cups."

"That won't take long"—Thecla indicated a small kitchen that was visible through a door on the left—"I always have a jug on the stove. I'll just revive the charcoal a bit."

"Let me help."

"I'm perfectly capable, Surgeon," she replied with an impish smile. "You find your anti-daemon potions."

Getorius opened his instrument case. He wasn't called out often—sick people came to the clinic if they needed treatment—so his stock of remedies was limited to those most used. For Thecla it would be a purgative herb, cassia, followed by a decoction of mint, rosemary, and lavender, to soothe any stomach spasms she might experience. He set the bottles of herbs and a sieve aside. While he waited for Thecla to bring the water and cups, he looked at several books on her cabinet shelf.

Jerome's Latin vulgate Testament propped up a Gothic translation by Bishop Ulfilas which he had not seen before. Alongside, parchment-bound works by Arius, and the pro-Arian pamphlets of Auxentius, were balanced by *Against Heresies* of Irenaeus, *Against the Pagans* of Arnobius, and a number of works by Clement and Origen of Alexandria. *At least Thecla is unbiased in her reading.* Getorius took down a slim volume titled *Lex Gothica* and flipped through the pages.

Despite the Latin title, it was written in Gothic; he surmised it was a legal code that governed barbarians. After slipping it back in place, he turned to the chipped remnants of a shrine the Marius family must have used for displaying their household gods. Set inside was the portrait of a middle-aged man, painted on a wooden panel.

Thecla returned with a clay jug of steaming water and two cups, and noticed Getorius looking at the picture. "My late husband," she explained. "Eugenius was consecrated a bishop at Constantinople by Ulfilas himself."

"And, of course, Eugenius then ordained you." Getorius immediately regretted the implied slur. "Sorry, Presbytera, I didn't mean to be sarcastic. When did he die?"

"Fifteen years ago, but I came here long before that. Eugenius traveled a lot, visiting Arian communities."

"You were born in the Eastern capital?"

"No, at Philippi, two hundred and fifty miles from there. Father moved to Constantinople when I was thirteen. I was called Euodia then, but I took Blessed Thecla's name after Ordination."

"Who was she?"

"One of Paul's converts. Thecla once described herself as just a mean old woman, to dissuade men who intended to rape her."

"I don't know the story," Getorius admitted, "but that's terrible."

"Oh, don't worry, God intervened and she remained a virgin. Unlike me…" Thecla laughed softly and indicated her husband's portrait. "After I first met Eugenius, any thought of imitating *that* aspect of her life vanished."

"Yes, well…let me prepare your remedy before the water cools." Getorius spooned dried cassia leaves into the cup, added the water, then stirred the mixture and strained the liquid into the other cup. "This should purge your daemon. You, ah, have a latrine nearby?"

"Don't worry, young man. I've managed to take care of my needs for over seventy Aprils."

"Of course. Presbytera, I…I meant nothing by my remark about your ordination. My own wife is flouting tradition by training with me."

"Commendably so. She wishes to cure the body, while I attempt to save ill souls. How old is Arcadia?"

"Twenty-eight next January."

"I was a year away from ordination at that age, but, I don't think quite as beautiful."

"Arcadia's mother died in childbirth. Her father was away a lot of the time, so she was raised by a governess."

"Loneliness made her independent." Thecla drained the cassia and handed back the cup. "Not unpleasant."

"No, and this mint mixture will soothe your stomach and help avoid spasms," Getorius explained, as he prepared the dose.

"How long before—?"

"A watch period."

"Then we have time." Thecla pointed to a wicker chair. "Sit down, Surgeon. We can talk."

Getorius had already developed a fondness for Thecla, so he was reluctant to get into what he expected would be a pointless theological argument. But he grinned, and sat in obedience to the mock forcefulness of her voice.

Thecla asked, "Did you find anything strange about the way that young woman in the church was dressed?"

"A white flowing tunic and veil?" *It seems she doesn't have religious differences in mind after all.* "It did look out of fashion. Why do you ask?"

"I want you to see something." Thecla stood and beckoned him toward a curtained doorway. "Here, in my bedroom."

"What?"

"My bedroom. Where I sleep, Surgeon. There's a mural I want you to look at. Bring the lamp."

Getorius followed her into a small room furnished only with a narrow bed, a table, chair, and clothes chest. A rough wooden cross was fastened to the wall above the bed, with three-week-old branches of willow catkins tucked behind the arms.

"Bring the lamp to the wall and tell me what you think of this." Thecla pointed to a faded mural above the chest. The painting depicted a procession in which a row of veiled women led a small bullock toward an altar. Each wore a white jacket with purple stripes over a long tunic, and a purple mantle that reached to the ground. "Well?"

"Sybil was dressed almost like one of those women," Getorius recalled. "Who are they? Is it some kind of ritual sacrifice?"

"I was told once by the building manager that it shows a procession of Vestal Virgins."

"Vestals? But the priestess cult was abolished under, whom, Constantine?"

"No, after him," Thecla corrected. "By the first Theodosius."

"So about…forty, forty-five years ago? Then there shouldn't be any followers of the cult still around, even among the few pagans who might worship in secret."

"One would think not."

"You think this Sybil is drama-acting?"

"Perhaps. But it wouldn't explain the castrated youth. That was never part of their rituals."

"The girl is ill, Presbytera. She may be experiencing a fantasy."

"Why in my church?" Thecla nervously touched her veil again. "As it is, we Arians are called disciples of the Antichrist. I don't need this kind of scandal."

"I don't know why Atlos went there, but I should get back and see what Arcadia discovered in her examination. And she may have found out where Sybil lives."

"A Vestal Virgin, *any* virgin, lost or not, would be something of an abnormality in this city."

Getorius smiled. "Yes. I really must go. If you're not feeling better tomorrow, come to my clinic. It's on the Vicus Caesar at the corner of the Honorius."

"A moment, physician. Your fee." Thecla searched her purse and held up a bronze *follis.* "Is this enough?"

Getorius closed her gnarled fingers over a coin that would buy a small amount of food, and pressed her hands together. "Use it to replace the oil jug you said you broke. I…I'm glad your 'daemon' brought us together, Presbytera. I enjoyed talking with you."

"As did I, young man, despite the circumstances. Come visit

me again with your wife." Thecla touched his arm and looked at Getorius with an amused smile. "You thought I wanted to speak of our differing theologies, didn't you? Perhaps, next time. Or we could talk about the implications of Paul's reasoning that male and female are equal. One under Christ."

"That would no doubt please Arcadia. I hope my remedy is effective." Getorius repacked the herbs, strapped the leather case shut, and slung it over his shoulder.

"Christ and his mother with you, Getorius."

"And you, Thecla."

When Getorius stepped outside, the children were no longer there. He crossed the Armini to the Via Porti, where taverns were open and members of the civic guard had now joined the drinking. He was only a few blocks from his clinic and the Lauretum Palace, but the difference was obvious in the deteriorated look of these older buildings.

The quarter of Ravenna that bordered the main road through the city had not fared well in the years since a silted ditch which connected with the Padus River to the north was paved over and named the road to Arminum. Four blocks to the east, merchant galleys still unloaded cargoes of grain, oil, wine, cloth, and spices on the wharves, but the harbor's south end was choking up with sand washed in by the relentless Adriatic current and the alluvial deposits of the two rivers that encircled the city walls. In the past, the waterways and ring of swamps had made the city impregnable from invaders, but now each year mud and sand deposits filled in more of the beach, marshes, and harbor areas. Ravenna, capital of the Western Roman Empire, was threatened with being choked off from its link with the sea.

The Via Porti intersected at an angle with the Julius Caesar. Getorius's villa and clinic were at the end of the block. His residence, commonly called "The Villa of the Surgeon," was located next to the palace, and had been willed to him by his mentor, Nicias. The old surgeon had rescued Getorius as a four-year-old child when his parents were killed in a Burgond raid at Mogontiacum in Germania Prima. Nicias had managed to escape with the baby to Ravenna, where the surgeon set up a medical practice and fostered the young

Getorius, teaching him the healing arts. The villa had a separate wing
for treating patients, and the luxury of its own bathhouse, with the
same sequence of hot, tepid and cold pools as the public one.

After being admitted to the atrium from the door on the Vicus
Caesar by Childibert, his housemaster, Getorius slipped off his cloak
and handed him the medical case.

"Is your mistress here with a girl?"

"In clinic with her," Childibert replied, his Latin tinged with
the guttural Germanic of his Frankish origins.

Getorius went through the corridor that connected the medical
area with his living quarters. After he rapped on the door, Arcadia
opened it. He looked past his wife.

"How is she?"

"Asleep. Sybil hasn't had another attack. I gave her a good dose
of valerian, and dressed her in a clean tunic."

"Good. I treated Thecla for an upset stomach, and then we
talked a bit. She believes Sybil may be deluded enough to think she's
a Vestal Virgin."

"A Vestal?" Arcadia shook her head. "Sybil could pretend to
be a priestess, but definitely not a virgin. She's about three months
pregnant."

"Pregnant?"

"And without a wedding band."

"Then that could explain the dead youth. Atlos was a slave, and
I assume Sybil is a freewoman. Her father, brother…someone in her
family…found out and evened the race."

"Getorius…your metaphors! Evened the race that drasti-
cally—with a druid's ritual sickle?"

"I admit that part's a mystery. I mean, druid priests in Ravenna?
Now?"

"Exactly. If there are still a few around, they're in the wilds of
Britannia, not on the Via Armini."

"So my family theory makes more sense," he said.

"Perhaps, but that's for a magistrate to decide. I'll stay with
Sybil in case she wakes up and has another seizure."

"You'll stay all night in the clinic?"

"I'll sleep in the wicker chair," Arcadia replied. "You didn't finish supper. Shall I tell Silvia to get you anything?"

"Only a cup of mulled wine and bath towels. After what we saw, I have no appetite, but a warm soak would be nice." Getorius looked at Arcadia and realized how tired she was. Dark circles surrounded her hazel eyes, and the black hair he loved to nuzzle when they made love framed a complexion that was gray with fatigue. "You look exhausted, *Cara*." He reached up to knead her trapezius muscles, knowing they would be stiff from tension.

"Mmmm, that feels good." Arcadia rolled her neck and shoulders to the rhythm of his massage.

Her sensual motion and closeness was arousing. He kissed the back of her neck and gently nibbled at the nape hair. "How about joining me in the bath house? We don't have to make love. I just want you to soak off some of the horror."

"I should stay here, Getorius, but that felt nice." Arcadia reached back to hold his fingers.

"Your hands are cold. Are you sure you want to stay?"

"I'm fine." Arcadia turned to face her husband. "Getorius, why did Thecla think Sybil looked like an ancient priestess?"

"When I went to the apartment to purge her stomach daemon, she showed me a mural depicting some kind of Vestal ritual. The women were dressed like Sybil."

"Strange. We should know more about her in the morning."

"After we find out where she lives." Getorius pulled Arcadia into a close hug. "I'll miss you in the bath."

"And I on the wicker chair."

He bent and playfully burrowed his face in the front of her tunic. Arcadia laughed and pushed him out the door.

❧

In the tepid water of the pool, Getorius sipped a cup of warm wine mulled with mastic and continued his speculation about the chain of events that could have led to such a hideous death for Atlos. In his mind the sequence gradually became as clear as the water around him.

Simple. A slave impregnates a freewoman. The family finds out and saves the magistrate the trouble of a hearing, trial, and execution.

The girl's pregnancy was proof of the slave's guilt. At a trial, Sybil's illness would have to be revealed and the family would accuse Atlos of raping her while she was helpless. The verdict would be death. As punishment, he would be tied up in a grain sack—with perhaps a poisonous adder thrown in for company—and tossed off the breakwater wharf into the cold Adriatic. Murdering the youth had saved Sybil's family the embarrassment of publicly displaying her infirmity.

Getorius drained his wine and heaved himself onto the edge of the pool to scrape down with a strigil and towel himself dry.

If an investigation did reveal that Sybil's father, or another family member, was responsible for mutilating Atlos, even the bishop's court would agree that the youth's death by castration, however gruesome, was appropriate punishment for a sin of lust. A scribe would record that the matter was closed, settling the problem for Sybil's father.

Getorius slipped on his night tunic. *When we take Sybil to him, how will her father react to his daughter's overnight absence? Sybil was found in a heretic church, next to her lover's dead body. Did she find him there, or was she dragged to the spot as punishment? Technically, her father has* patria potestas, *the power of life and death over his daughter. A magistrate wouldn't enforce it, but just the threat could be enough to bring on one of Sybil's epilepsy attacks.*

"We'll know in the morning," he muttered, throwing the towel aside and slipping into a silk dressing gown that Childibert had laid out on a bench.

Chapter three

A brilliant sun, reborn an hour earlier, cast warm rays of light through the open glass-paned doors that led from the villa's garden to the dining area. Along with the brightness, a faint perfume of apple blossoms wafted into the room, giving a hint of life to the rustic orchard scene painted on the right-side wall.

Getorius heard the chirp of finches above the soft slapping splash of the garden fountain as he walked outside. The startled birds fluttered into a row of poplar trees, whose upswept branches were hazed by light-green leaf buds. On each side of the fountain, blossoms on apple tree branches mimicked a covering of pink winter snow. The wet weather had caused the rosebay—*rhododendron*, "rose tree," the Greeks called the evergreen shrub—to already send out reddish buds. Getorius took a deep breath of cool morning air to shake the lingering image of the dead youth, then went back inside to a table laden with bread, cheese, eggs, olives, and almonds.

He looked at Arcadia with mock surprise. "What, no boiled barley for breakfast this morning?"

"Very funny. Don't you recall this is a special day?"

Special day? Getorius nervously smoothed his hair forward, trying to recall if he had forgotten some event in their courtship or marriage that was important to his wife. Despite the bath, he had not slept well, and the scene of horror at the church had clogged any other memory. He finally shrugged in frustration.

"Sorry, *Cara,* what *is* the occasion?"

"Getorius"—Arcadia reached over to tousle his black hair laced with a few white strands—"it's your birthday."

"April eighteenth? No, I think Nicias had it wrong. I remember being born in May."

Arcadia laughed as she pushed a dish of almonds toward her husband. "You were four years old when he brought you to Ravenna and you remember? He always said in April."

Getorius shrugged and did not contradict her. That was in the past, an unimportant detail in the incredible odyssey of the legion surgeon who had escaped with him from a city in Germania, where Burgondi warriors had killed parents he could not recall.

"Thanks, this is nice, Arcadia," he said, reaching for an almond. "How is Sybil this morning?"

"Still asleep."

When his wife sat down opposite him, he noticed dark areas still shadowed her eyes. "You must have had a bad night."

"I slept a bit. I'll look in on Sybil in a moment, but first, I have something for you." Arcadia went to the dining room cabinet and brought back a flat cedar box.

"What, a Saturnalia gift this early?" he quipped.

"Saturnalia? What dead pagan author have you been reading? No, this is because I love you and I'm glad you were born on this date. Actually, it's for your office."

Getorius felt the grain of the pinkish cedar, and then opened the lid to sniff the scent of the fragrant wood. "Nice. What's wrapped in the cloth?"

"Open it, Husband, and find out."

Getorius slipped a bronze plaque from its woolen cover. He felt the cool, gleaming metal for moment, then ran his fingers over an incised inscription.

"There's writing on this. What does it say?"

"Read, most excellent surgeon."

"Wh…at? All right." He held the plaque up toward the light. "'I swear by Asklepios the Healer that, according to my ability and judgment, I will keep this Oath and this stipulation—to reckon him who taught me this healing art equally dear to me as my parents.'" Getorius looked up at his wife. "The Oath of Hippocrates?"

"A somewhat shorter version, but the sense is there."

He reached over the table and squeezed her hand. "I like it, *Cara*, but…for my office, to make the sick feel better? Most of them couldn't read it."

"But you can. And you did begin to ignore patients a few months ago, during that forged papyrus business."

"Treating the sick in my stead gave you good experience." He knew his excuse sounded defensive and went on to read the plaque's next section. "'While I continue to keep this Oath faithfully, may I enjoy life and the practice of my art, respected by all men at all times. But should I violate this Oath, may the opposite be my fate.'" Getorius paused to wipe at an eye. "Nicias made me memorize this, but I'd forgotten the exact words." He went around the table and squeezed Arcadia in an embrace. "*Cara*, it was very thoughtful of you."

"Yes, and now eat," she ordered. "If Sybil is awake, I'll bring her in for some breakfast. I wonder how much of last night she remembers?"

"Hopefully nothing about her lover's fate."

After Arcadia disappeared around the door panels, Getorius speared a portion of sheep's milk cheese with his knife. It was local, and he thought its brine cure made the taste too salty. The ripe olive he bit into had a rich, nutty flavor.

The *triclinium* was a pleasant area. The three reclining couches that originally gave the dining room its name were no longer in fashion, and Nicias's marble-top table and set of padded chairs had replaced the slanted benches on which diners once lay to eat.

The old surgeon had been in the army of Theodosius, at the carnage of the Battle of Frigidus River almost a half century ago. After the first day's bloody assault, ten thousand Visigoth allies lay dead, prompting the poet Claudian to write that the Alpine snows had grown red with gore. Afterwards, Nicias had gone to the remote Rhine River frontier to forget, and had rarely talked about the battle. Here at Ravenna his room decorations were gentle landscapes, studies of birds, fruit, or flowers, and sunny paintings of fanciful harbor scenes, anything to draw him away from the memory of that horrific slaughter.

Getorius munched a piece of bread while he took up the plaque once more and continued reading the Oath's stipulations. He was to teach the healing art to Nicias's children, but the surgeon had had no offspring. The Oath swore him to abstain from injurious treatments, including prescribing deadly medicines and abortifacients. He chuckled, after realizing that a provision had been left out which forbade the seduction of females and males, free or slave. Arcadia evidently felt it an unnecessary warning for him.

Getorius was at the section that prohibited revealing any personal information he might learn from a patient, when Childibert interrupted him.

"Master. There is a man and woman in wait-room."

"Tell them today is Sunendag and the clinic isn't open."

"I think you will see man," Childibert insisted.

"Not unless he's dying. Tell him to come back in the morning."

"Man has sick arm, but is still strong enough to come in here."

Getorius was about to vent his annoyance at Childibert for the intrusion, when his eye caught the gleam of the bronze plaque next to his plate. "Very well," he relented, "but your Mistress isn't available. You take him into my office."

He finished chewing the bread, then stuffed half a boiled egg in his mouth and went out to the garden portico. Swallowing chunks of yolk, Getorius watched the finches twitter up into the greening poplars as he followed the porch past the clinic and opened an outside door to his office.

The room was lit by north-facing clerestory windows which were set above several shelves that displayed a collection of animal skulls and skeletons. The prize of Getorius's collection was the skeleton of a monkey, which he had dissected after the simian died in Valentinian's palace menagerie. Although the physician Galen had been dead two centuries, his views on medicine and anatomy still dominated the field. Galen had the advantage of having been able to dissect corpses, a practice now banned by Church authorities, but Getorius had defied that ban once and had partially examined the dead body of an indigent stevedore in secret. His discovery that the function of the brain was not to produce phlegm was one of the things that put him at odds with a claim of the ancient physician.

Evidence of other animal dissections were displayed in glass jars—hearts, livers, and lungs. Patients usually avoided going near these reminders of their own mortality.

Getorius looked across the room. Childibert was trying to persuade a well-muscled brute with cropped hair to sit on a stool. The man's left arm was wrapped in a dirty length of wool. A loincloth covered his groin, and his bare chest displayed a number of white and pink scars. Although Childibert had abandoned Latin to cajole the man in Frankish, he only glared at the steward and showed no sign of cooperating.

A stocky, blonde-haired woman stood beside him, her tunic cut short enough to show more of her muscular arms and legs than a Roman matron would think proper. She turned when Getorius entered and frowned at him with eyes that were the cold tint of a winter sky.

"Were you in the latrine all this time, Surgeon?"

"I…sorry you had to wait," Getorius found himself apologizing. "We're not open today." Childibert slipped out the door, leaving the man standing to glower his defiance at Getorius.

"What happened to your arm? What's your name?"

"Tigris," the woman responded.

"Tigris? The animal or the river?" Getorius immediately regretted his feeble jest. "Ah, what's *his* name?"

"I just told you," she snapped. "And I'm called Giamona."

"Yes. Well, tell Tigris to sit down so I can look at his injury."

Giamona turned to the man, but he slumped onto the stool before she could tell him to do so.

"That's better." Getorius bent down to undo the makeshift bandage, but the man pulled away with a savage grunt. "Steady there, Tigris. What happened to him?"

"An accident at…at the port." Giamona glanced away toward the shelf of animal skeletons.

"He's a stevedore? What kind of accident?"

"Cure his arm," she snarled, the winter sky in her eyes turning to blue ice. "Isn't that what you do?"

Great Asclepius, where did these two come from? "I…I'll have to unwrap the cloth to examine the wound."

"Tigris, let him look at your arm."

He glowered at Giamona, but supported the arm in his right hand and slowly extended it with a grimace of pain. Getorius noticed that several of the man's teeth were missing, and his nose had been broken at one time. The smell of his perspiration was strong. Getorius sucked in his breath when he unwrapped the wool binding and saw the extent of Tigris's wound.

Gore glistened in flesh laid open by a slash that exposed part of the humerus bone. The wound extended from the deltoid muscle to just below his biceps. A flap of swollen flesh from the deltoid dangled downward, held on by a mere shred of skin.

"Christ, what hoisting machine did this to you?" Getorius blurted out in outrage that he couldn't hide. "If it was a winch, it should be tossed into the sea." He knew that the extent of flesh here exposed to air assured the formation of black bile in a few days. The arm was lost. "How did this happen?"

Tigris's narrowed brown eyes reflected pain and fright, but he did not answer. Giamona was also silent, looking down and tracing the floor tile grouting with the toe of a sandal.

Getorius reexamined the wound and studied Tigris. The man was well built, with his hair cut unusually short. A nail-studded leather band circled his right wrist. The skin on his left arm up to the elbow where the slash ended was pale, as if shielded from the sun, yet his thighs and chest were tanned. He noticed that the skin around Tigris's neck was chafed to a pinkish smoothness, and guessed that it was the result of once wearing a slave collar. He glanced at Giamona. She displayed the same pale areas on her arms as Tigris, as well as on her legs up to the knees. She, too, was scarred. The reason struck him with the force of a boxer's blow: the limbs had been covered by arm guards, or leg greaves, as protection against an opponent's weapon.

"You...you're gladiators!" Getorius exclaimed. "But how? The games are illegal now."

Tigris jumped up into a crouch. Giamona scowled at him and shook her head. He sat down again.

"Illegal? You are child-like, Surgeon," she chided. "Where men are willing to wager gold, there will be bouts. You'd have us enter a monastic order and shovel dung for our bread?"

"Of...of course not."

"Then cure his arm."

Getorius exhaled, pondering the dilemma. He could be arrested for failing to report renegade gladiators, and Tigris also might be someone's runaway slave. Yet the man needed help. Getorius examined the damaged area again. The deep wound was inflamed, and noxious air had been entering the exposed flesh for at least a day. He looked back at Giamona and shook his head.

"I can't save his arm. Muscle and tendon damage are too severe. It's a miracle that arteries weren't severed. Amputation is the best I can do."

"Cut it off?" The woman fixed him with the flat stare of a marble statue in the old senate house. "No, Surgeon. You will cure the arm."

Getorius hesitated. *How can she sound casual and threatening at the same time? Where in Hades' name is Arcadia? Perhaps she can reason with this...this wild Amazon.* Tigris had suffered a deep slash, probably from a sword. No way could severed muscles and tendons be reattached, but even if they could, the wound would soon become corrupt from an overbalance of black bile. Amputation and cauterization of the stump were the only ways he could save the gladiator's life.

"Giamona, wounds of this kind attract noxious bile," he explained. "I could try to suture the skin back together, but—"

"Suture?"

"Sew the wound closed."

"Then begin your needlework, Surgeon."

"I…I've never worked on an injury this deep," he protested.

"In the arena we're taught that the first blow is half the bout. Begin sewing."

Getorius shook his head, trying to recall the comments of Hippocrates on the treatment of an injury caused by bone protruding from the skin. It was to be cleansed with compresses dipped in hot wine, then covered with a warm salve of achillea leaves in a thick beeswax base. More leaves were to be applied, and the area loosely covered with unwashed wool. A poultice or tight bandage was not recommended.

He had treated a deep cut on a fisherman's hand with achillea a few months ago, but the wound had succumbed to black bile and not healed.

Arcadia opened the door from the clinic and looked in. "I thought I heard someone."

"My wife assists me," Getorius told Giamona, who had begun to stand up. "Arcadia, this man was hurt in an…an accident. I'll need your help."

"Of course. Sybil hasn't awakened yet."

"We'll give Tigris a strong opion sedative. Get the medium silk thread and a gold needle. And despite what Hippocrates recommends, I'll apply a poultice of moldy bread over the sutures, yet keep the bandaging loose."

Giamona stood up. "Then start. I'll bring mud from the riverbank."

Getorius frowned. "Mud? What for?"

"You think this is his first injury?" Giamona asked sharply. "Look at the scars on him. Our arena may not have the services of a surgeon, but we know about some methods of healing wounds." She looked around. "I need a container."

"Let her bring it, Getorius," Arcadia said, "I'll get her a basket. I've read that Egyptian physicians treat wounds with Nile mud."

"We won't argue the matter. Take Tigris into the clinic for the suturing, but put up the sailcloth screen between him and the girl. I don't need her waking up and seeing this. I'll prepare the opion."

Giamona ordered Tigris to drink the papaver juice sedative, then left the clinic to go and collect mud along the banks of the Padenna River, which ran through Ravenna.

After Arcadia persuaded Tigris to lie down on the examining table, Getorius gently arranged the man's arm on a board. He began a gentle probing while his wife watched.

"The brachial artery seems intact, Getorius."

"Fortunately. Otherwise he would have bled to death before getting here. But the flexor muscles and tendons are severed. Get me the sketches I made when I dissected the monkey arm. No, wait. It's useless. Those tendons can't be reattached. Tigris will never fight again."

"Perhaps it's just as well. If he was caught he wouldn't take well to working in a mine."

"I'm sure Tigris would have taken that chance."

"He's asleep."

"Good." Getorius sifted achillea powder over the swollen tissues, then pulled the shred of deltoid muscle as close to its original position as he could. He sutured the skin over it, then repeated the procedure with the lower part of the arm, certain that despite the achillea, black bile would fill the wound. The putrefying limb would have to come off at the shoulder joint. *Tigris can face that prospect later...if he comes back here.*

Getorius was slathering on the last layer of beeswax, and Arcadia was standing by with the wool bandage, when Tigris groaned and opened his eyes. He gazed around at the unfamiliar room with confusion. After he saw his arm, it changed to one of alarm.

"Steady, man, I'm helping you," Getorius said.

Tigris eyed him a moment, then jumped off the table with a feline snarl that must have given him his name. The board supporting his arm clattered to the floor. He swung out with his good arm, catching Getorius on the cheek with the bronze studs of his wrist guard and flinging him back against the canvas screen shielding Sybil. The pot of beeswax shattered against the floor, sending the salve flying out to smear the tiles and stick to the broken pottery shards. Getorius slipped on the ointment and tumbled to the floor.

Arcadia leaped back and grabbed at the lightweight barrier to keep it from falling on the sleeping girl behind it. Still growling, Tigris crouched low in a stance he used in the arena, then cradled his stiff left arm with the other hand and loped toward the office door. He was only a pace away when Giamona returned with the basket of mud. The gladiator shoved her and the container of wet earth roughly aside. Mud spattered against the wall and oozed down to settle on the floor tiles.

"*Caco!*" she spat out. "Shit! Where do you think you're going, Tigris?"

Without answering he ran past her, into the office.

"He'll get out through the waiting room door," Arcadia cried.

"*Caco!*" Giamona raced after her friend.

"The fool," Getorius muttered, staggering to one knee. "I was almost through."

Arcadia caught his arm and helped him stand. "Are you hurt?"

"No…" Getorius touched his bruised cheek and winced. "That brute was strong as Hercules. I almost hope he doesn't come back."

"If he does, it will be for the amputation." Arcadia blotted at the blood oozing from her husband's injury. "Nasty. I'll make a conferva poultice. I'll get Primus. The child can clean up the mud." She glanced around at Sybil. "I can't believe the girl slept through it all. Where do we start looking for her family, Getorius?"

"Give me a little time to think about that—it's been a hectic morning. I'll be in my study."

⁊

The shadow on the sundial in the garden fell between III and IV when Getorius passed it on his way to his study. He rummaged through the shelves of a cabinet, then pulled out the manuscript with the sketches of the Rhesus monkey arm he had made while dissecting the limb.

Longer and thinner than that of Tigris, he mused. Galen believed that God had formed every part of a body perfectly, and the physician had devoted a large part of one book to explaining the action of the human hand. Certainly, the long arms of the Rhesus were adapted

38

to swinging from trees, but the thumbs were set at an awkward angle, making it more difficult for the creature to grasp objects than for a man. Why were there animals that resembled humans so closely? God had almost duplicated His effort, yet, in a sense, made one creation superior and another inferior. Man was his most perfect creation.

Getorius was wondering about how to obtain another human body for dissection when Childibert interrupted him again.

"Master, two men at Julius door."

"Childibert, I've given you and your wife freedom. I've told you that you needn't call me master."

"Yes, Master."

"Never mind. Tell them the clinic is closed today."

"One man asks about girl."

"Sybil? That's different, send them in." Getorius laid the drawing aside. *Could he be Sybil's father? If so, how did he find out she was here?*

Childibert ushered in the two men. One was a stocky man whose ruddy complexion suggested that he spent much of his time outdoors. An unkempt mop of receding brown hair above square brows and squinting eyes combined with a fleshy chin gave him the look of a clerk, yet the unmistakable smell of fish came from his leather jerkin. His companion was taller, with a swarthy complexion that Getorius thought somewhat inconsistent with his soft, effeminate look. The man's black hair was swept back like a woman's and concealed under a turban. The brocade tunic he wore looked expensive.

After Getorius stood to greet the two visitors, he noticed that the taller man wore a necklace of ivory beads framing a medallion of a woman, or ancient goddess, who wore a turreted headdress. *The personification of a town?* There were traces of rouge and eye make-up on the man. *Perhaps an actor, but the theater season hasn't begun, and the bishop is working to see that it doesn't open.*

"I was told you had my daughter here," the red-faced man claimed. "I've come for her."

Getorius recognized his rough Latin as the local Flaminian dialect. "And you are?"

"Gaius Quintus Virilo, master of a merchant galley in the harbor." His small eyes glanced around the study. "Where is she, Surgeon?"

"Sybil is with my wife."

"Cybele? My daughter's name isn't Cybele. It's Claudia Quinta."

"She told me it was Sybil," Getorius countered. "I assumed she was named after a seeress. She—"

"Perhaps I have an explanation," the swarthy man interrupted. "I am Diotar, a family…confidant."

Getorius recognized that the man's accent was not local, Greek perhaps, but not as refined as the classical style his tutor had taught. Diotar's voice was high-pitched, like that of a male actor onstage imitating a female.

"Virilo's galley is named after Cybele, the goddess called Great Mother," Diotar continued with a womanish giggle. "The names are similar. Claudia may have been invoking the goddess after seeing Atlos like that."

"Atlos?" *How can he know about the dead slave?* "Yes, I examined him. Horrible. Please, take chairs. I'll have my steward bring the girl."

After summoning Childibert and sending him to the clinic, Getorius sat across from Virilo. "Your daughter is quite ill, sir."

"The Sacred Disease," Diotar murmured.

"Sacred?" Getorius scoffed. "Epilepsia is no more sacred than a…a broken leg. Hippocrates writes that those who call it that and try to cure the symptoms with incantations or sacrifices are frauds. I agree completely."

"But Surgeon," Diotar sneered, "you must also agree that there are mysteries beyond the scope of your medicines."

"Only because we haven't yet found their causes…" Getorius turned back to Virilo. "Do you suffer from the affliction, sir? It can be transmitted."

Arcadia came into the room before the galleymaster could respond. She was holding a bowl with the poultice for Getorius's cheek. Claudia was with her, dressed in the night tunic Arcadia had given her.

"Arcadia"—Getorius stood up—"this is Gaius Virilo. The girl is his daughter."

"What have you been doing, Claudia?" Virilo asked in a gruff tone. "I been looking for you all night."

"Claudia?" Arcadia looked puzzled. "I don't understand."

"It seems her name is really Claudia Quinta," Getorius explained. "How is she?"

"You've seen how she is," Virilo snapped. "Her mind is like a child's."

Arcadia glanced at her husband and touched her stomach.

Getorius understood her signal. "But her body isn't a child's, sir. Are you aware that your daughter is pregnant?"

Virilo looked down at the floor and shuffled his feet, but Diotar reacted enthusiastically, holding up his gold medallion over Claudia in a benediction. "And Cybele be praised! The child is a gift of the Mother Goddess."

Getorius instinctively disliked Diotar. Now he felt anger at the actor's absurd assertion. "Cybele? Pagan goddesses aside, who was Atlos, other than the earthly father? How did you get into Thecla's church? Who told you Sybil...Claudia...was here?"

"I understand someone from the palace will be investigating the death?" Diotar asked, deflecting the questions with one of his own.

"Tomorrow. This is still the Lord's Day," Getorius replied, still irritated, "but I hope Bishop Chrysologos gives the magistrate permission to move the body out of Thecla's basilica today."

"You were the one who found Atlos?" Diotar asked.

"No. I was called by Thecla."

"The Arian priestess."

"Priestess?" Getorius reddened, but held his temper. "If you wish to call her that. Thecla called me to help, but Atlos was already dead. Emasculated with a sickle."

"Sickle?" Diotar raised his painted eyebrows in surprise. "Surely, the castration was done with a knife."

"I saw a golden sickle in his hand," Getorius contradicted, "even held it."

"Surgeon, you're mistaken," Diotar insisted, fingering his necklace. "Was it not dark in the church?"

Arcadia moved between Diotar and her husband. "I should apply this medication to your bruise, Getorius."

He waved her off. "In a moment." This woman impersonator was trying to tell him what he had seen. The nave had been dim, but the blade had gleamed in an unmistakable curve by the light of the sanctuary lamp. Getorius turned back to Virilo. "Perhaps I can help your daughter's illness. Hippocrates suggested specific examinations to locate the cause of the imbalance…moist, dry, hot, cold…then diet and other countermeasures."

"The galleymaster will take Claudia home," Diotar said quickly. "Familiar surroundings are the best cures."

"Virilo, is that what you want?" Getorius asked.

"Home." The man looked away. "I just got back from a run across the Adriatic a couple days ago, but I'm at my house now."

"As you wish, you're her father, but Claudia may need a sedative to help deal with her lover's death."

"And you know where our clinic is," Arcadia said. "Send one of your slaves." She took the girl's hand. "*Vale*, Claudia, goodbye. May you soon feel better."

"Cybele," the girl mumbled without looking up, and walked toward the door.

⁂

After the three were shown out, Arcadia sat her husband down to apply the conferva poultice. "So her name is really Claudia?" she asked, dabbing at the swelling with a cotton packet of the water plant's moistened leaves.

"Claudia Quinta."

"Hold still, Husband. I didn't care for that Diotar."

"Nor I. And I didn't like the way he was speaking for Virilo. He's probably an actor…an unlikely friendship."

42

"There's something effeminate about Diotar that reminds me of Heraclius."

Getorius chuckled. "The emperor's eunuch procurer?"

"Stop that. Heraclius is in charge of Valentinian's quarters."

"And finding him pubescent slave girls."

"Getorius!"

"Sorry, *Cara,* but it's true. You were saying?"

"Perhaps Diotar works in the palace. We just haven't seen him."

"It didn't take this Virilo long to find out where his daughter was."

"I sent Primus to the magistrate's office with a sealed note, just as you asked me to do."

"Primus? Arcadia, I said to send Childibert. If a child brought it, any palace secretary would read it first and gossip."

"'Even whispered words are heard in Rome,' they say."

"And written ones in Ravenna." Getorius thought back to his conversation with the actor. "Why would Diotar insist there was a knife at the scene? How would he know what was there? I watched Thecla lock the door."

"That *is* strange, but I'm more worried about the girl." Arcadia put down the bowl. "Hold the cloth against your cheek a while longer." She wiped her hands on a towel, then came to sit down. "Claudia may not come back. I'll have her bloody tunic washed at the fuller's, but we don't even know where she and her father live."

"I'd guess somewhere in the harbor area. You know, I might have been able to persuade Claudia's father to bring her in for treatment, except for that actor. What kind of hold does Diotar have on Virilo?"

"I don't think he is an actor," Arcadia said. "Did you see the tunic and turban he was wearing? Silk, possibly from Constantinople. And that ivory and gold necklace? No actor could afford those, even if theater subsidies hadn't been cut off."

"Whoever he is, I hope it's the last we've seen of him." Getorius tossed the medicated pouch into the bowl, muttering in disgust, "'Gift of the Mother Goddess.' Atlos was the baby's father."

"The poor child."

"Born of a slave and a freewoman. Claudia's baby may well end up being thrown off the breakwater wharf on some dark night in October."

"Don't even *think* that." Arcadia stood to take the bowl back to the kitchen. "Getorius, what will happen to Thecla?"

"Nothing. It's impossible that she could have had anything to do with Atlos's death." He reached back for the Rhesus arm sketches and spread the parchment on his lap. "A few questions by someone from the magistrate's office, and she can go back to trying to bring salvation to her stubborn flock of Arians."

Chapter four

On Sunendag? I didn't expect anyone until tomorrow." Getorius was puzzled when his steward interrupted supper to announce that a man from the Judicial Magistrate had come to see him and Arcadia. "All right. Take him to my study, Childibert."

"And have Silvia bring us mulled wine, hot," Arcadia ordered. "The air is chilly tonight."

Getorius finished sopping a chunk of bread in the sauce of dates, honey and wine in which Ursina had served slices of lamb shoulder. "Whoever was assigned to investigate the death evidently couldn't wait until tomorrow," he speculated, wiping his fingers on a napkin. "Well, it shouldn't take long to answer his questions."

"I hope you're right," Arcadia said. "I had nice plans for us."

In the study Getorius saw a man who looked vaguely familiar and extended a hand. "I'm Surgeon Getorius Asterius. My wife Arcadia."

"Yes, you're physician to the Empress Mother." The man's return grasp was limp as he introduced himself. "Leudovald, interrogator for the Augustus's magistrate."

A Frank, Getorius thought, *but his Latin is educated, less tainted by Germanic than Childibert's.* The Franks had been allies of Rome for eighty years, with the sons of chieftains brought up at the emperor's court. Had Leudovald's father been one of the favored youths? "I've seen you before…" Getorius thought a moment. "Of course. At the last Nativity Vigil Mass I noticed you talking to the records clerk."

"Protasius."

"Yes. Senator Maximin told me who you were."

"Please, sit down," Arcadia offered, indicating a chair.

Leudovald ignored the wicker seat in favor of a folding stool. He wore his blondish hair longer than a fashionable Roman might, but shorter than barbarians in the legions. Getorius thought his drooping mustache had more of a comical effect than the manliness Leudovald might have intended. If Virilo, Claudia's father, had the look of a clerk, this man might have been his colorless assistant; taller, but unassuming.

When Leudovald looked around the study without beginning a conversation, Arcadia said, "That young man's death was a terrible one."

"Terrible, Domina." Instead of looking at her, he leaned forward to examine Getorius's bruise. "What happened to your cheek, Surgeon?"

I'd forgotten about Tigris's blow. "Ah…an accident with a patient. How can I help you, Leudovald?"

"I can't officially question you until tomorrow."

"I understand. This is Sunendag."

"Sunendag." Leudovald glanced around the room again, then back at Getorius. "Perhaps we could merely…socialize."

"Christ taught that the Sabbath was made for man," Arcadia pointed out. "That would apply to social calls."

"To social calls," Leudovald repeated, allowing a thin smile to pucker his mustache.

"Were you given permission to remove the youth's body from the basilica?" Getorius asked. "Thecla was concerned."

Leudovald hesitated an answer, looking down and rubbing the wooden cover of a wax slate he had brought to take notes.

"Just social conversation," Getorius reminded him.

"Conversation." Leudovald's wan smile returned. "The body is at the palace, surgeon. In the ice room—"

Silvia entered carrying three silver cups decorated with chased olive branches, and a matching flagon. As she poured out the hot wine, a scent of laurel leaves rose from the steam. Getorius studied Leudovald. *A few years younger than I am...he has a boyish, innocent look for a man who investigates crime. That probably helps the guilty lower their shields. He has a funny habit of repeating the last words you've said.*

Leudovald accepted his wine without comment, put it down on the floor instead of a table, then flipped open the cover of his slate. "A social call of pleasant talk," he murmured, incising a few words in the wax. "Surgeon, how did you come to discover the body?"

"Thecla sent a boy for me."

"The heretic presbytera?"

"Arians do have a different creed, but—"

"Why didn't she send for a magistrate?" Leudovald interrupted, looking up from his tablet with a hard stare.

"Thecla may have thought the boy was still alive," Arcadia volunteered.

"Alive. But he was not, Domina." Leudovald frowned, then an amused expression hovered beneath his mustache. "You work with your husband?"

"Yes. He's training me to be a medica."

"A medica, so you went with him. What did *you* find?"

"Atlos bled to death," Getorius snapped. The man had a way of making his questions sound like accusations—Arcadia's presence at the church, the comment about his bruised cheek.

"Bled...to...death," Leudovald repeated slowly, as he wrote in the wax. "Exactly how, Surgeon?"

"A wound in the scrotal area generally severs the testicular vein."

"And the knife was next to the dead slave?"

"Knife?" *Has he been talking to Diotar?* "It wasn't a knife," Getorius corrected, flushing. "And it wasn't next to him. Atlos was holding a golden sickle."

Leudovald's light-green eyes darkened to a jade color as they focused again on the raw wound at Getorius's cheek. "You're mistaken, Surgeon. I found a fisherman's saw-toothed knife at the side of the body."

Getorius felt a shudder of uneasiness spill into his stomach. *Is he trying to implicate me in Atlos's murder? I was accused of illegally dissecting a monk's body this past December and placed under arrest. Now this Leudovald is looking at my injury as if he suspected I might have gotten it in a quarrel with the dead youth.*

"My husband is correct," Arcadia said, to break the embarrassing silence. "It was a golden sickle."

"Thecla saw it too," Getorius added. "She thought it might be some kind of ritual instrument."

"Ritual instrument. So. I have a loving wife's testimony, indeed, almost a colleague, and that of a heretic." When Leudovald paused, Getorius surmised that it was to leave the conclusion up to him. Then the investigator's stare softened and his boyish look returned. "There was a girl kneeling beside the body?"

"We thought her name was Sybil, but it's evidently Claudia Quinta. Her father came for her this morning."

"This morning. His name, Surgeon?"

"Gaius Virilo. Said he was master of a merchant galley at the harbor." Leudovald looked up from his notes at the same instant that Getorius caught the connection with a sailor's tool. "But it *wasn't* a fishing knife. I saw a golden sickle, even handled it."

"Surgeon, there were blood smears on the edge of the cloth covering the youth," Leudovald continued.

"I wiped my fingers on it after handling the sickle."

When Arcadia saw Leudovald's blond eyebrows arch in renewed astonishment at the admission, she explained, "My husband asked Thecla to cover the body out of respect."

"Of course, Domina. 'Covered…body…'" Leudovald's stylus traced the words in the wax. "This Claudia. What happened to her?"

Getorius hesitated. The Oath on his plaque forbade him to reveal a patient's infirmity without a compelling reason. Let Leudovald provide that first.

"What happened to her, Surgeon?" Leudovald repeated more firmly. "You seem unsure."

"No. Obviously, Claudia was quite upset. I sent her back here with my wife, so she could examine the girl and give her a sedative."

"Well?" Leudovald turned a cold gaze to Arcadia.

"The…the girl is pregnant," she admitted.

"This Claudia is with child?" Leudovald slammed the wooden covers of his tablet together and stood up. "Then there's the answer to this crime's riddle. Violated daughter…furious father…handy fishing knife. And this Atlos was a slave, I have his collar."

"It's still murder," Getorius pointed out.

"Murder? At best, destruction of someone's property," Leudovald contradicted. "Under the Lex Aquilia, Virilo would pay damages to the owner. Except, in this case, the magistrate might find that the galley master's property had been damaged by the slave and dismiss the claim."

"You're treating Claudia as property, and her pregnancy as 'damage'?" Arcadia demanded, her complexion reddening.

"Retribution the Hebrews might call 'an eye for an eye,' Domina." Leudovald walked to the doorway, then turned and repeated, "A furious father and his knife, but I'll talk to this heretic presbytera, and certainly with you again, Surgeon."

"You haven't tasted your wine," Arcadia said. "It's still standing on the floor."

"Another time, Domina. Don't bother seeing me to the door. I recall the way out."

Arcadia shivered after he was gone. "Icy little man."

"Indeed. I'd wager he'd have his grandmother decapitated and make her sharpen the sword," Getorius quipped, but his voice was weak. As he gulped the last dregs of warm wine in his cup, his hand trembled.

"Relax, Husband. That last remark sounded like Leudovald was trying to convince himself." Arcadia rubbed at creases in Getorius's forehead. "Are you afraid he thought you weren't telling the truth?"

"*Cara,* the magistrate believed that I was lying last December."

Getorius caught at Arcadia's fingers and held them over his eyes. His head had begun to host a dull ache and her touch was cool. "The question is…two questions…how did the sickle get replaced with a fishing knife, and why was it replaced?"

"There's a third puzzle, Getorius."

"Oh?"

"How could Diotar know that the dead boy's name was Atlos? You said Thecla locked the door when you left."

"Or, for that matter, that he'd been castrated."

"Supposedly only Leudovald knew those things," Arcadia said. "Somehow, Diotar must have gotten into the basilica."

"Or any curious servant brave enough to enter the ice room where they put Atlos's body might find that out. It's unlikely one did, but it's said that when gold asks the question, even pigs are eager to answer."

"You think that Leudovald was bribed by Diotar?"

"Arcadia, how else would the actor…or whatever he is…even know there had been a death?"

"Diotar did avoid answering when you asked him how he knew Claudia was here."

"I had come to the same conclusion as Leudovald, that a family member killed Atlos," Getorius recalled. "Perhaps I was seduced, by what seemed most obvious."

"Speaking of seduced." Arcadia's hand slipped down the neck of Getorius's tunic and toyed with a nipple. "Didn't you try to lure me into the bath for a bit of lovemaking last night?"

Getorius pressed her hand against his chest. "Tonight, I think that just might cure my headache."

"I could read you some Ovid."

"Please. Not about deceiving the deceivers again."

Arcadia smiled at the recollection. "All right. How about a love story from his *Metamorphoses*? You can choose which one. I'll have Silvia bring more wine to the bathhouse."

❧

Getorius was lying half-awake when he heard the entrance *tintin-*

nabulum start to jingle incessantly. The high-toned echoes of the small bell announcing that someone was at the door on the Vicus Caesar reached into the bedroom, along with the muffled barking of the watchdog belonging to the gateman, Brisios.

"What hour is it?" Getorius mumbled, rolling away from Arcadia's scented warmth and fully opening his eyes. "Dark as the pit of Tartarus. Who could be here at this hour?" The movement had not awakened his wife. Getorius lay still to gather his thoughts, recalling that immediately after making love in the bath and getting in bed he had fallen asleep, a leg thrown over Arcadia's thigh and his face nuzzled into the rose smell of her hair. But he had awakened a few hours later, his mind clogged by images of the dead youth in Thecla's church, the visit of Claudia's father and that capon of a man with him, then Leudovald, he of the boyish face, but with eyes and manner that were accusatory even in ordinary conversation.

Someone's talking to Childibert. Getorius swung his feet out from under the covers, onto the cool tile floor. The last patient to come in the night had been a sick vagrant, brought by a friend. The man suffered from an irreversible phlegm imbalance, and had died on the examining table. Getorius had partially dissected the corpse before becoming nauseous and ending the experiment.

"What is it, Getorius?" Arcadia murmured in a voice thick with sleep.

"Someone at the door." He fumbled in the dark for his sandals. "Stay warm, I'm going out to Childibert before he comes in here."

Getorius managed to locate his sandals under the bed and slipped them on without fastening the straps. After groping for a cloak in the wardrobe, he crossed through his study and the reception room, into the atrium.

The night air outside was warmly damp, smelling of the rain that had fallen earlier. No stars showed through the roof opening above a central pool now filled to its marble rim with rainwater. The floor tiles around the small cistern glistened in orange wetness, reflecting the light of a single torch. Getorius saw his steward at the front entrance, arguing in loud whispers with a man.

"Who is it, Childibert?"

"Master, slave of Senator." He handed Getorius a wax tablet with the imprint of a ring seal.

"Publius Maximin?" In the dim light Getorius made out the deep intaglio image of a rooster and the letters P. MAXM, emblems of the most influential senator in Ravenna. He was not too surprised. The man had inconvenienced him several times asking for medical services. "Is the Senator's mother worse?"

"His niece, Master. Faustina."

Getorius did not recognize the name. "What's wrong with her?"

"Midwife asks that you come. Delivered niece of a child."

"Then it must be serious. Midwives don't usually call in a physician unless things are desperate."

"Slave has a carriage."

"Good. Tell him to wait while I put on trousers and get my medical case."

When Getorius returned to the bedroom, Arcadia had lighted a lamp. She was sitting on the bed, knees tucked to her chin, black hair tumbling loose over bare shoulders. He leaned down to kiss an ivory shoulder.

"*Cara,* how can you look so beautiful any time of the day or night?"

"Enough of your Celtic honeyed words," she retorted. "Who was it?"

"Senator Maximin's niece, Faustina, has given birth. There are evidently complications that the midwife can't handle. He wants me to come."

"I'm going with you."

"No, it's late and I want you to stay here," Getorius told her, even while knowing that his wife would ignore his order.

"I need to see the problem." Arcadia slid off the bed and searched in the wardrobe. "You know it's my dream to open a clinic for women," she reminded him, selecting a full-length light wool tunic. "And I still have the book on gynecology that Theokritos had lent me. It might be helpful for Faustina."

Getorius pulled on wool trousers and belted a short tunic over them. While he put on waxed leather boots as protection against rain puddles, he thought of something that might dissuade his wife from coming with him.

"You know, you'll have to convince that midwife to let you help her. They're a pretty independent lot."

"But they aren't physicians. Blessed Cosmas only knows what she may have done to the woman."

"Arcadia, that's unfair," Getorius chided as he straightened up. "Most midwives are competent, and Maximin could certainly afford the best."

"Then, according to Soranus, she'd be Greek."

"Latin-speaking, hopefully. My Greek is, ah, *sta cripia*, in ruins."

"*Gnorízo hellenikó eph' homileín autē. Biazometha! Tachy, tachy!*"

"I think you said that you know enough Greek to talk to the midwife? Fine, Arcadia, get dressed and we'll go."

Getorius gulped a drink from the washbasin pitcher as Arcadia finished fastening a hooded cloak over her gray tunic. "Ready?" he asked. "I'll get my case from the clinic and meet you at the door."

"All right. Just let me put a band around my hair and get something."

❧

At that hour, the Vicus Julius Caesar was deserted, and shrouded in mist from the evening rain. Torches on the corner of the Via Honorius appeared in the distance as flickering islands of dim yellow light. Maximin's carriage was an elegant black covered rig, drawn by an equally beautiful ebony mare. When the driver turned around to help Arcadia onto the back seat, Getorius caught a glimpse of the words MVTVS SVRDVS engraved on a silver plaque dangling from his neck. *Mute and deaf. Not bad limitations for a driver who sees everything that goes on at Maximin's and might be tempted to sell the information.*

Arcadia put down the leather pouch she was carrying and caught her husband's arm when he followed her onto the seat. "It's the same deaf-mute who picked me up that time I was invited to the senator's villa," she whispered.

"While I was under arrest, I recall."

Arcadia looked away. "It all worked out."

"Not for that dead Hibernian abbot."

"Let's not bring that up now." She gestured toward the slave, who had clambered up alongside the driver. "Go."

The axle suspension's leather hinges creaked in protest as the carriage pulled away from the curb. At the corner, the wheels jostled left onto the smoother paving stones of the Honorius. Getorius saw that the driver was heading toward the old Oppidum quarter, where Maximin and the wealthy families of Ravenna had villas. The area dated back to the last decades of the Roman Republic, when a military camp was constructed to protect the small town.

The Via Honorius was empty of cart traffic and pedestrians, but watchdogs in shuttered homes and shops occasionally snarled or barked an alarm at the rhythmic clip-clop of the mare's hooves.

An unpleasant smell of fish and sewage was heavy on the damp air, and a soft gurgle of water came from sewer openings in the squared lava paving stones. Some of the torches on street corners were burned out, even though Getorius estimated there might still be three or four hours until dawn. Galla Placidia and her emperor son would not be out to inspect the lights, and the men hired by the city to maintain them were undoubtedly asleep somewhere. God only knew where the night civic guard was—either already at home or bedding the taverns' serving girls they had flattered earlier in the evening.

"I wonder where this Faustina lives?"

"You've gone to the senator's villa, Getorius."

"His is on the Via Aurea. She may live nearby."

"Maximin hasn't had you in to treat his mother since December," Arcadia recalled. "Agnes must be better."

"Or has died. We don't socialize, so he wouldn't bother to tell me. I mean, he's obscenely wealthy, twice been Prefect of both Rome *and* Italy. A term as consul a few years ago."

"I don't really trust him," Arcadia admitted. "Too smooth. He even managed to convince the magistrate that he knew nothing about that abbot who died inside his country villa."

The carriage passed the Cardo I intersection, recently renamed the Via Theodosius, then clattered past the Milarium, a tall column with a golden milestone at the base. Distances from Ravenna to other cities in the empire were measured from there. Rome lay a relatively manageable one hundred forty miles to the southwest. Mogontiacum, from which Getorius had been rescued as a child, was in Germania, over three hundred grueling miles to the north, far beyond the Alps.

A block past the old forum, the dark front of the Basilica of Hercules acted as the backdrop for a colossal statue of the demigod. The giant stooped on one knee, supporting a globe whose upper surface was a solar and lunar timekeeper, where twin markers recorded the passing hours. One dial gnomon cast the shadow of the sun from its rising to its setting. On nights when enough light from the moon cast the companion dial's crisp shadow on numerals, the night hours were recorded.

The black carriage lurched right at the Via Herculis, onto a narrow street bordered by umbrella pines. The houses along the sidewalk had no shops on the first level, rather, their stucco facades were only broken by wooden doors and a few high windows that were barred by thick cast iron grilles.

Getorius noticed someone waving a lantern from the doorway of a house in the center of the block. "That must be Faustina's."

After the deaf-mute halted the mare in front of the open door, the senator's slave clambered down from the carriage, took the lantern from a boy, and ushered Getorius and Arcadia through a narrow entrance hall toward the right side of the villa's atrium. As they started across, Publius Maximin hurried from a side door to intercept the trio.

An orange glow reflecting from the torch tinted the white strands that flecked the man's well-groomed hair. He wore an expensive tunic of fine-spun wool, banded with the twin purple stripes of a senator, and red-dyed leather boots. A scent of bay oil wafted from him.

"I appreciate your coming, Surgeon," Maximin said, nervously twisting the carnelian signet ring with which he had stamped the wax. "If anything happens to Faustina, I'll exile that cursed midwife to a godforsaken Dalmatian island for the rest of her worthless life."

"Where is your niece, Senator?" Getorius asked.

"In a room across the atrium." Maximin bowed to Arcadia and smiled. "My dear, how lovely you look, even at this ungodly hour. I didn't expect you to come."

"I assist my husband, Senator."

"Of course, of course. I'd forgot—"

A hysterical scream from Faustina's room cut him off. It was followed by her shrill voice threatening the midwife.

"You fat sow! If you don't give me something for this pain, I'll have my uncle rip your furcing ears off."

Maximin chuckled weakly. "Headstrong girl. Picked up legionary slang when her husband put in his tour as tribune."

Getorius understood. The furca was an X-cross to which legionaries were tied as punishment. The men used the hated name as a derogatory verb or adjective.

"Go in and calm her," Maximin demanded.

Faustina's bedroom was large, brightly lit—and overheated—by several lamps and candles. A sweet smell of camphor hung on the stuffy air. The girl, who looked to be only a little older than Claudia, was propped up against pillows, her face and arms bathed with perspiration. The short, blood-stained tunic she wore revealed a body that was thin to the point of anorexia. Bloody cloths littered the floor. A blanket-wrapped bundle lay in a wicker basket on a nearby chair seat.

"Midwife, I've brought the surgeon," Maximin growled at a stocky woman standing next to the bed.

Getorius thought she looked relieved to see him.

"*Onomazome Calliste.*" The midwife gave her name in Greek, then asked, "*Milate elenike?*"

"*Mono lighos.* I speak only a little Greek," Getorius replied. "Calliste, you'll have to talk in Latin."

"The sow butchered my baby," Faustina bawled, "and now she's trying to furcing bleed me to death."

"Niece, try to stay quiet," Maximin urged in a weary voice. "The surgeon is here to help you."

"I don't want him looking up my Venus love hole. Just have him give me something for the furcing pain."

Getorius glanced at his wife. Arcadia nodded in understanding and went to the girl's bedside. "Faustina, my name is Arcadia. Perhaps you'll let me examine you, then I'll give you an opion sedative."

"Opion?" Getorius shook his head. "I didn't bring any of the drug, only valerian."

"I did. And acacia extract." Arcadia unfastened the leather pouch she had brought. "I also have wool suppositories and that copy of Soranus."

"Will you two quit blabbing?" Faustina shrieked. "And give me that narcotic!"

While Arcadia mixed the drug in a cup that Calliste handed her, Getorius motioned the midwife outdoors.

"What happened?"

"*Moro*...baby...was too small, born dead. I...I think the girl self-aborted the child."

Getorius noted that Calliste's Latin was good. Had she wanted to speak Greek as a foil against the senator's anger? Or, perhaps, to lie about Faustina's condition? If the girl died, the midwife would want to absolve herself of blame. "Why do you think she did that?" he asked her.

"Child's size," Calliste explained. "It is observed that women who are...pampered, who do not exert themselves, have poor deliveries. Also those who are very thin. In this case the *chorion*—"

"*Chorion?*"

"Placenta, Surgeon. Afterbirth. The girl retained the *chorion* in her uterus. I tried to draw out the umbilical, but her humors of blood are unbalanced. The vaginal area is inflamed."

"I have no experience in this," Getorius admitted. "What do you advise?"

Calliste shook her head. "The girl is stubborn. I can do nothing for her. *Tipota*. Nothing."

"Where's her husband? He could order her to cooperate."

"From Thessalonika?" Calliste scoffed. "Or perhaps Constantinople? He attends to his business."

"I see. Let's go back in. My wife may have been able to calm the girl."

Faustina was quiet, exhausted from the trauma and on the verge of falling asleep. Maximin was slumped in a corner chair, still toying with his ring and staring at the bloody rags.

Arcadia turned when the two entered, and brought a finger to her lips. "The papaver extract is taking effect."

"Calliste thinks the placenta has been retained."

"Yes, I've read a section in Soranus that deals with that. I inserted a wool suppository soaked in acacia juice to control bleeding. Once inflammation is less severe, we can try to remove the placenta before black bile forms."

"I'm…amazed at what you've done," Getorius stammered. "Good…excellent, Arcadia."

She nodded acknowledgement, then suggested, "Let the girl sleep. Perhaps Calliste could stay with Faustina until the sedative wears off."

"No!" Maximin hissed, bolting up. "I want that Greek out of this house. I'll have the cook stay with my niece."

"There are other treatments, Senator," Arcadia said. "Soranus recommends heated cupping vessels."

"Fine, fine. Let's talk about that over some mulled wine." Maximin glowered at Calliste. "Now get out, you infernal sorceress!"

Calliste dashed through the door. After a glance at his niece, Maximin escorted Getorius and Arcadia outside.

The slave who had summoned Getorius was lounging against a wall. Maximin paused to whisper to him, then led the way across the atrium to a reception room in his villa.

"Faustina's husband is Marcus Cossus, from Mutina," he volunteered. "Away a lot. Poor girl gets lonely."

"I'll look in on her again in a few hours," Getorius promised. "That is, my wife will."

"Yes, thank you my dear." Maximin leaned forward to pat Arcadia's hand, then looked back at Getorius. "Damnable business, Surgeon, that castrated slave found in the heretic church. I heard you examined his body. Did you find out who his owner was?"

"N…no, sir." Getorius was surprised by the unexpected comment about Atlos. In the light of Faustina's condition, it was the last subject he expected to be asked about. He glanced at Arcadia. A slight lift of her eyebrows indicated that she thought the same thing.

"There was a girl with the dead youth?"

How could the senator know that? "She's named Claudia, sir. Her father came for her today."

Maximin nodded. "Gaius Virilo. I use his galley, *Cybele,* for importing and shipping out some of my commodities."

Getorius thought this might be a good time to find out more about Diotar. "There was a strange man with him. An actor I think. Called himself Diotar."

"Diotar an *actor*?" Maximin gave a mocking chuckle. "I suppose he could be pretending to be a man."

"Sir?"

"He's reportedly the leader of a Phrygian sect whose priests castrate themselves, but there's nothing to the rumor. The law prohibits castration, even of slaves—"

A servant interrupted Maximin by coming in with cups of mulled wine. Getorius touched his stomach and shook his head hoping that Arcadia would understand the signal—he didn't want her to mention Claudia's pregnancy.

After taking a gulp of wine, Maximin continued, "Oh, there *are* eunuchs around, like that Heraclius the Augustus uses to, ah, service his bedroom." He stifled a yawn with the cup. "It must be well after the tenth night hour."

"We should go, Senator." Getorius stood and motioned to Arcadia. "I'd like to look in on Faustina once more."

"Fine," Maximin agreed. "I'll have one of her servants send your fee in the morning."

"There's no hurry, Senator. We'll still be treating her."

"Yes, well, I'll have Ankios bring the carriage around."

"I'd like to walk back," Arcadia said quickly. "Wouldn't you, Getorius?"

"Ah...certainly, *Cara.* We'll walk back, Senator."

When the couple looked in on her, Faustina was asleep. An older woman dozed in the chair where the wicker basket with the blanket-wrapped fetus had been set earlier. It was gone.

Outside, the mist was lifting. To the east a light wash of blue-gray began to reveal a silhouette of warehouses and the masts of merchant galleys moored in the harbor. Birds chirped tentatively in the pines along the Honorius, while in the distant countryside roosters crowed a lusty greeting to the new day.

Across from the public baths, in Ravenna's main market square, fires blazed in iron braziers, giving light to early vendors who were helping to unload carts of produce brought in from local farms.

Arcadia grasped her husband's hand to cross the busy road. "I don't know if I'm more sorry about Faustina or that poor midwife."

"Calliste. Did you notice the fetus...the baby...had been taken away?"

Arcadia nodded. "Faustina has a fever and isn't out of danger yet. Soranus prescribes a treatment of rest and soft foods like porridge, along with the cupping I mentioned."

"She wants nothing to do with me, but perhaps she'll respond to you." Getorius walked in silence for a while before commenting, "I can't believe that Maximin knew all about the death of Atlos."

"It may be palace gossip by now," Arcadia said, "but he did seem to be probing."

"What possible interest could the senator have in a slave that wasn't even his?"

"If he knows Virilo, he must know Claudia," Arcadia pointed out. "Unless her father keeps her isolated."

"He seemed to know all about Diotar, too, probably through Virilo. Diotar may run a private club for men with tendencies for 'Greek love.' Bishop Chrysologos doesn't take kindly to open homosexuality."

"There must be all kinds of Eastern cults that come and go in the port area," Arcadia said. "Remember last month? We watched a procession of Isis worshippers bless the opening of the navigation season."

"The bishop opposed that too, but people want to be entertained, if nothing else." As Getorius guided his wife onto the Vicus Caesar, the savory smell of freshly baked bread drifted out from the shop on the corner. "I suppose you're right, Arcadia, about the short life of these cults. Diotar's club…sect…whatever it is, will undoubtedly melt away as fast as…as snow would on one of the ovens in that bakery."

Chapter five

"Filthy scavengers," Diotar muttered, eyeing the row of gray-white gulls preening themselves on the wall that surrounded Gaius Virilo's house and the Temple of Cybele. Other sea birds circled before landing in raucous flappings to squabble with their shabby neighbors and stain the ancient brickwork with yet another layer of chalky droppings.

As they descended, the gulls' ashen plumage was abruptly transformed into a beautiful pale-rose tint. A scarlet morning sun had cleared the flat Adriatic horizon in the east and thrown its warming rays on the quarreling birds, coloring their plumage the same pinkish shade as the stucco portico on the front of Cybele's temple. The gleaming metamorphosis lasted a scant moment before the gulls' feathers again reverted to a dirty white.

Diotar turned away, pulled shut the gate to the villa's garden, and secured a bolt that locked it against the awakening residents of the crowded streets in this northeast quarter of Ravenna's port area.

The flush of newborn light had summoned yawning slave and freeman artisans to their workshops near the Anastasia Gate. Shutters banged open in silver and gold workers' shops, from which craftsmen emerged to eye the weather and stretch briefly in the mild breeze, before going back into cramped spaces to hammer out or cast their metal wares. Potters began the daily, back-bending chore of wheel-throwing dishes and pitchers in workrooms clogged with barrels of stagnant clay. A faint, sweet smell of lumber came from pine and oak shavings in carpenters' shops, but it was not strong enough to cover the sour smell of sewage and decay pervading the air.

Beyond the wall, Diotar heard the wail of infants and the sporadic coughs of workers. The daily pall of acrid smoke from iron forges and bitumen ovens had already begun to smudge the pale blue of the sky with a sickly yellow-gray. He brought a linen cloth from his sleeve to cover his mouth, reminded again that this was not an area he would have chosen for a temple in which to worship Cybele. The house Virilo owned was located in the noisy artisans' quarter, but the property was a secluded enclave among the narrow alleyways and crowded shops that clustered around its wall. The high brick barrier effectively enclosed an area that had once been a marketplace—Virilo's land went from the Street of the Artisans to that of the Judean quarter just north of it.

Surrounded as he was by dirty shops and unending noise, Diotar consoled himself by remembering that living in the city was a temporary arrangement, an expedience. Once he had recruited enough wealthy patrons he would move the shrine of Cybele to a quiet place in the countryside. A temple in the Apennine foothills, perhaps around Forum Livii, fifteen miles to the west, would be a pleasant location in which to carry out rites to the Great Mother. As ArchGallus—Chief Priest of the cult—he felt that he deserved a better site for Cybele's devotions, and was determined to have one soon.

As Diotar crossed the garden, his musing was interrupted when a handsome youth ran out from one of the villa's rooms. He wore his hair as long as a girl might, and his short tunic was also styled like a woman's. His cheeks were lightly rouged. Dark make-up outlined his brown eyes.

"Kastor is sick, ArchGallus," the young man called out. "There's a terrible pain in his back."

Diotar gave a grunt of annoyance. Kastor was always complaining. "Nevertheless, Adonis, you will bring him to morning services. The Great Mother shall hear his cry and heal him."

"But ArchGallus," Adonis protested, "Kastor can't get out of bed because of the pain."

Diotar reached out to caress the youth's smooth, rouged cheeks. "Soon you will be one of Cybele's priests, Adonis," he said more gently. "Finish your make-up and put on your jewelry. I will pray to Cybele for Kastor, but he must join us and the others. This is the last ritual to the Great Mother before we leave in the morning, to celebrate her festival in the temple outside Olcinium."

"The Megalensia?"

Diotar nodded. "The feast that commemorates the arrival of Cybele's statue in Rome during the city's ancient war with Carthage. Poor weather prevented us from celebrating on April fourth, the proper date, but the goddess will forgive us for being a few days late. Go now, but bring Kastor back with you."

"Atlos was…was not in his room this morning."

"Strange. Your twin was to be initiated at the Megalensia. I'll look into it." Diotar waved him off with a limp gesture of dismissal, and then turned toward his quarters. "Good," he murmured to himself, "none of the novices yet knows of Atlos's death. The young fool had to go and impregnate Claudia, then bungle his castration. I can't have the girl give birth to the child. Perhaps that surgeon can prescribe something to abort the fetus."

Diotar stopped and looked across at Claudia's room. *Is she there or still with her father?* He squinted at the eastern sky. The sun's rays had not yet reached the window opening that illuminated Cybele's statue inside her temple. There was time to speak to Virilo before the morning service.

A slave answered his knock on the door that separated the quarters for cult members from Virilo's area of the villa. Claudia was in the dining room with her father, sitting, head lowered, absently stirring a bowl of millet porridge with a silver spoon. Virilo looked furious.

"Never should have allowed you into that cult," he was shouting. "What will happen now, with the bastard and all?"

"Enough, Galleymaster," Diotar commanded, coming up behind Claudia and putting an arm around her shoulder. "The girl has suffered already in seeing Atlos…liberate himself from the prison of the flesh."

"He took advantage of her while she was in the Disease."

"No doubt. And he has repented in kind." Diotar lifted Claudia's chin and shook it gently, until she looked up at him. "Child," he murmured, "it's almost time for our morning devotion to Cybele. Go put on your vestal robes."

Claudia sniffled and wiped her eyes on a sleeve, then nodded obediently. After Diotar watched her leave, he turned to Virilo. "You'll bring on an attack, scolding her like that. According to the surgeon, Claudia's pregnancy is a fact, yet no one else need know just yet. We will deal with it after our return from Olcinium."

"The surgeon and his wife know," Virilo reminded him.

"Then ask them on the Oath to keep Claudia's condition secret. Tell them it's for your daughter's sake. The penalty for a Vestal Virgin who violates her chastity is to be buried alive."

"Claudia's no Vestal, except in your mind."

Diotar ignored Virilo's scoffing comment and sat down. He selected a piece of bread with a delicate gesture, and dipped it into a dish of honey, before asking, "We've been associates how long, Galleymaster?"

"About two years. Since you happened on me in Olcinium. My boat was named *Aurora* back then."

"And well known to customs officials at Olcinium."

"That bunch of thieving extortionists."

"Virilo, spare me your righteousness." Diotar licked honey off a fleshy index finger. "You put in at that run-down Dalmatian port, instead of Epidamnus, because you found that the maxim, 'A bribe will enter without knocking,' was well known to customs inspectors at Olcinium. In fact, their door was always conveniently left open."

"And the door of that swindling provincial governor at Scodra," Virilo growled.

"Even with that, costs are less and our profits high. The province of Prevalitana is on the far western edge of the Eastern Empire, barely under the control of Emperor Theodosius. It's well known that most of the tax officials he sends to Olcinium from Constantinople have a way of being mysteriously swallowed up in the mountain valleys of the interior."

"Meanwhile, my daughter is pregnant and you still want to take her to that infernal temple?"

"I need her for the rites." Diotar wondered if Virilo was going to be difficult again. It was reasonable for him to be upset, but the matter with Claudia's lover was at an end. "The magistrate will declare Atlos's death to be a particularly gruesome suicide, but he won't fail to see the irony of the method. The bishop won't allow Christian burial for an unknown slave who killed himself, but I'll have Atlos buried in the old pagan necropolis outside the Lawrence Gate."

"We can't have palace interrogators coming here to investigate," Virilo warned.

Suddenly alarmed, Diotar countered, "Why would they come here? The body was found in the heretic's church."

"Claudia was with Atlos."

"The girl is blameless, she has the Sacred Disease. The surgeon will attest to that." Diotar helped himself to an olive. "The cult of Cybele is growing, Virilo. I'm forced to celebrate the Megalensia elsewhere this year, but I plan on holding the September procession here."

"In Ravenna?" Virilo gave a dry laugh. "The bishop will have you arrested and exiled."

Diotar reddened beneath his pale make-up. "You doubt my intelligence, Galleymaster? I realize the last thing palace authorities want is a riot in the streets by Christians, so I'll get permission to stage one of Rome's oldest rituals, purely as an historical pageant."

"What historical pageant?"

"The Megalensia commemorates the arrival of Cybele's statue in Rome at the time of the Republic," Diotar told him. "The goddess was credited with the Roman victory over Hannibal in the wars with ancient Carthage."

"So?"

"*So?*" Diotar shook his head and exhaled a long breath of frustration. "The Vandals captured Roman Carthage six months ago. Can't you see the parallel? Our time to act is now."

Virilo shoved his plate of olive pits aside with a curt thrust. "I still wish my daughter wasn't involved."

"Then you wish against Fate," Diotar retorted. "Your Claudia is the reincarnation of the Vestal, Claudia Quinta, who pulled the barge with Cybele's statue up the Tiber."

"Reincarnated only in your pagan mind."

"Like Christians, the followers of Cybele believe in immortality, an afterlife," Diotar said evenly, controlling his temper. "We celebrate with a ritual meal. Even atonement through suffering."

"Castration," Virilo scoffed, "is hardly a penance the bishop would assign sinners."

The ArchGallus thought it better to change the subject to the next day's journey. "Is your galley loaded for the run to Olcinium?"

"The last of Maximin's pepper will be brought ashore today. His wool bales, oil and wine amphorae will be stowed in the *Cybele*'s hold by morning."

"Northwest winds?"

"Probably favorable. Be on board with your novices by the first hour watch."

Diotar noticed a shaft of sunlight illuminate the tiles in the hallway. It was time to begin the morning ritual. "I must conduct prayers for our safe journey," he said, wiping his fingers on a damp napkin as he stood. "Will you join me, Galleymaster?"

"You have my daughter for that"—Virilo pushed back his chair—"I need to get to the dock and take care of my own *Cybele*."

"A partnership between galley and goddess that works to our mutual benefit."

Virilo glared at Diotar, but stalked out of the room without further comment.

⁂

In his quarters, Diotar selected a pink linen tunic and small gold crown studded with gems. After dressing, he slipped a golden bracelet on his arm, then arranged a long necklace of ivory beads around his neck. As he squinted in a polished silver mirror to finish applying rouge and eye liner, Diotar thought back to his own initiation at Pessinus, in the Asian province of Phrygia.

His uncle, Sebastos, who had conducted the ritual, taught that castration was an entrance into the blessed Nature of beings who were above the world, a method of gaining access to an immortal life where there were neither male nor female genders. He had said that *Magna Mater*, the Great Mother, was the image of Matter, the recipient of the higher forms of the visible world, but sterile, like the eunuchs who served her. It was all a bit confusing for a ten-year-old, but his uncle had promised that those who broke with the material world would be rewarded with immortal life.

After a final glance in the mirror at his smooth, fleshy face, Diotar went through the door that connected his quarters with Cybele's temple.

The two-story room smelled of incense. Sunlight entering through a high window was still centered on the ceiling, just above the statue of Cybele. Diotar saw that Adonis had placed a vase of violets and field wildflowers at the base of the goddess's image. A few flies buzzed round a silver dish of *moretum,* an offering of soft cheese laced with herbs that was set next to a clutter of terracotta images; votive offerings to the goddess that spread over the base.

Cybele was represented as a smiling, full-breasted, pregnant Earth Mother, who gave fertility alike to men and beasts and vegetation. She sat on a throne, her sandaled feet resting on a footstool symbolizing the stability of the earth. A turreted crown on her head represented the goddess's protection over towns. Adonis had placed a mother-of-pearl pendant on her forehead, carved with the June sign of the Zodiac, the Crab, to suggest the renewed summer fruitfulness growing in her womb.

Diotar glanced at a mural painted on the shrine's right hand wall. It depicted the Megalensia procession he had mentioned to Virilo, that first entrance of Cybele's cult statue into Rome over six hundred years ago. The image of the Phrygian goddess showed her sitting on a dais, holding a scepter and the drum that called worshippers to her, while priests and attendants formed a line behind the platform. Some held cymbals, others sprigs of greenery. Four carriers leaned on canes, waiting for the signal to lift the statue and lead the procession.

The tranquil scene was a marked contrast to the painting on the opposite wall, which Diotar used to instruct novices about the cosmology of the Cybelene cult. He had ordered the artist to show the goddess and her lover, Attis, ascending heavenward in a chariot pulled by four charging lions. The self-castrated yet resurrected Attis held a pan-pipe and shepherd's crook as he gazed at Cybele, seated alongside him. The couple was attended by three armed and helmeted Beings who were posed in the gyrations of a wild dance. These were protective Daemons, who, through Attis's sacrifice, channeled creative forces into the world below. In the path of the chariot, another figure also holding a scepter of authority, represented the New Age that was to follow the present one of Atlantis.

Attis's creative powers, and his periodic withdrawal of them through voluntary castration, symbolized the recurring creation and destruction of civilizations. Now, just as Cybele had resurrected Attis to live with her until the cycle of fertility began again, the goddess would initiate a New Age for her followers.

Looking at the scene again, Diotar became excited, realizing how soon that might be. As he reckoned it, four hundred and forty years had passed since the birth of the Resurrected Galilean whom Christians venerated, yet the Roman worship of Cybele predated that event by two hundred and fifty-four years. The goddess had waited patiently in the interval, but in six years, seven centuries would have passed. Nature ordained balance, symmetry. The mystical number seven hundred obviously signified the end of the Male Age of Rome and the beginning of a new cycle in which Cybele would inaugurate a Female Age. Just as Christians presently controlled power in the twin Roman Empires, so the castrated priests of Cybele, symbols of the Female Principle, would supplant them as stewards of Gaia, the Earth Mother.

Diotar knew it would take money to set up this rule of androgynous Cybelene priests, but his home city of Pessinus was on the Via Regalis, the trade route to the country of Sina, lying at the far eastern edge of maps he had seen. Glossy silk thread, rumored to be spun from the cocoons of worms, was not the only precious commodity the orient had to offer. Other fantastic goods could be brought across the Adriatic to Ravenna and sold at enormous profit. Diotar smoothed his tunic and half-smiled. If Virilo's daughter constituted only the means to an immediate end, the master and his galley would be of more long-range usefulness.

The front door opened and sunlight flooded across the tile floor. Diotar turned to see a group of his initiates filing in. There were also faces he did not recognize. Good...new recruits curious to know about the cult. Kastor was there, half bent over in pain and supported by a companion. In a niche underneath the floor, at the statue's base, Adonis was at his post as Keeper of the Flame.

When Claudia entered, dressed in her white Vestal robes, and moved slowly toward a chair set on the right side of Cybele's statue, Diotar masked his irritation with a stiff smile. *Foolish girl, her pregnancy can't be allowed to come to term. Burying her alive is out of the question, of course, but aborting the fetus before anyone finds out is not. If the surgeon won't agree, there are midwives who will supervise the procedure for a silver coin.* He glanced around for Calliste, the midwife who was a Cybelene follower, but she was not at the service.

Diotar faced the circle of worshipers. "The Great Mother welcomes guests who have come to learn about her rites," he said in a high-pitched, accented voice, trying to sound kindly. "To those proud of their Roman ancestry, I say that Cybele's cult was celebrated at Troy, whose son Aeneas founded Rome itself. Can those who worship the Galilean make such an ancient claim to Roman tradition?

"Does the Galilean offer immortality? So does our Great Mother. Is there a ritual meal and redemption for Cybele's followers? Yes, and more, for those of us who have shed our blood in imitation of her consort Attis, resurrection into the New Age will soon be upon us.

"Why do we priests glory in what outsiders call 'our mutilation'? By imitating Attis, we gain immortality and acquire a place alongside Cybele in her New Age."

Diotar saw several newcomers glance down and shuffle their feet. Others coughed nervously. As usually happened, some in the group were becoming restless at an explanation they either did not understand, or found offensive. His recruiters had gotten them there by promising a meal and some wondrous display of the goddess's power. It was time to distract them. Diotar turned to face the statue and raised his hands in supplication.

"Cybele, Mother of the gods, we ask your blessing. You who control the winds, grant that they may be favorable tomorrow for our voyage to your temple at Olcinium. Protect us, as you did long ago, but now from the fury of the Vandals, who seek to imitate the Carthaginian Hannibal and attempt to destroy Rome. Great Mother, give us a sign."

As Diotar finished his invocation, the ritual flame at the base of Cybele's statue suddenly spurted up in a flash of multicolored hues. A dove materialized from the fire. Amid the gasps of onlookers, the white bird circled to the ceiling, then flew toward light coming from the high window. It fluttered against the glass pane, struggling to get outside, before finally settling on the narrow ledge.

"The Great Mother looks with favor on my prayer," Diotar called out in an excited voice. "I—"

Claudia's scream interrupted him. She clutched her stomach and slumped in the chair, then slid to the tile floor. Her body twitched and stiffened in an epileptic seizure. Diotar strode to her side, but, rather than helping the fallen girl, he raised his hands over her.

"The girl is blessed with the Sacred Disease," he intoned. "A sign of Cybele's pleasure."

The onlookers stood immobile, stunned by the spurt of colored flames, the materialization of a dove from fire, and now the girl's supernatural possession. Two women broke away and ran toward the entrance, to escape this frightening combination of sorcery and daemonic power.

"Cybele has given me her signs," Diotar announced to the remaining onlookers. "I must prepare for the voyage to the goddess's temple. Your meal is in the dining hall."

He clapped his hands and motioned the group out of the shrine. After the last person had passed through the door, Adonis stepped out from behind the statue. He saw Claudia lying on the floor and ran to her.

"The girl is well," Diotar remarked. "An ecstasy induced by the goddess is short."

Claudia whimpered as she regained consciousness. Adonis helped her sit up and lean against the chair.

Diotar glanced at the girl, then up at the dove. The bird was still on the window ledge, calm now. "Adonis, you did well with the flame and bird," he praised, with a womanish giggle. "Had I not known about the small opening behind the votive flame, I, too, would have been convinced that the dove rose out of the fire."

Adonis brushed strands of damp hair away from Claudia's face. "Is she well enough to go with us to Olcinium for the Megalensia?"

Diotar hesitated a moment. "It will not be the processional rite, Adonis. We will celebrate Sanguis, the spring equinox 'Day of Blood.'" He reached down to touch the youth's head. "Now, instead of Atlos, *you* will be privileged to shed the blood of your manhood for the Great Mother. To become 'Adonis-Attis,' a priest of Cybele."

"ArchGallus, am...am I worthy?" Adonis stammered, standing up.

Diotar stroked his cheek. "Atlos succumbed to the flesh, but you will be free of such temptation after the Day of Blood."

"What will happen, ArchGallus?"

"The sea run to Olcinium takes four days," Diotar replied softly, noticing the fear in Adonis's eyes. "During that time, I will instruct you about the ritual. Now, help Claudia back to her room, and then pack clothes for the journey. You and Kastor must be aboard *Cybele* by dawn."

"Kastor is coming with us?"

"He must. Go now."

Diotar watched Adonis help Claudia to her feet and support her as she slowly shuffled to the front door. Then he turned back to the statue of Cybele and took up the dish of *moretum,* reflecting on the forthcoming ritual. The Day of Blood, normally held on March twenty-fourth, was the culmination of nine days of ritual penance.

The prolonged fasting and devotions of the worshippers induced an ecstasy that was expressed by self-flagellation with knucklebone whips, slashing of arms and legs during unrestrained dancing to the sounds of panpipes and cymbals, and finally, the frenzied mutilation by some men of their testicles with a flint blade.

Diotar winced, feeling a sharp pain in his groin. The sensation had become as physical as it was emotional each time he recalled his own castration at the hands of his uncle. That could not be undone, Diotar thought, half-limping toward the door to his quarters. Neither could the suicide of Atlos. His initiation as a priest of Cybele would have been important for the cult. There was Adonis now, but his twin brother had been the more outspoken of the two, and might have brought in other rebellious young slaves desperate for any kind of asylum.

As he opened the door to his quarters, Diotar recalled a matter that could prove to be more fortunate than the sad fact of Atlos's suicide. He had learned from his contact at Olcinium that the goods he and Senator Maximin were expecting from distant Sina had finally arrived at the port.

Chapter six

As the morning sun slowly warmed the port quarter, Arcadia stood in the shade of an arched warehouse portico and searched among the confusion of brightly painted boats anchored in the harbor for a glimpse of the merchant galley *Cybele*.

With the end of the ice storms that had come out of Gothiscandza, and the return of the sun from its winter sojourn in the land of the Ethiopians, Ravenna's inner waterway had once again become an aroused anthill of shipping activity. Docks swarmed with freemen and slave stevedores, unloading cargoes for masters who had risked March storms to be the first in port with the Egyptian winter harvest of wheat, barley, cotton and figs. Other galleys, equally fortunate, had safely brought in Dalmatian timber, or wine and oil from the Greek mainland. More luxurious cargoes of amber, ivory, incense, spices, and fabrics from the Orient had been transshipped from ports on the island of Rhodes.

Because of a threat from the Vandal fleet at Carthage, Emperor Valentinian had ordered the repair of the rusted hoisting mechanism and iron chain that barred access to Ravenna's harbor from the Adriatic Sea. Beyond that barrier, currently lowered, to the right of the

breakwater lighthouse, Arcadia saw an immense galley of the grain
fleet lying at anchor, waiting for the harbormaster's pennant signal to
enter and unload. She made out the name HORVS on the bow, above
the painted all-seeing eye of the falcon god who had guided the vessel
from the Nile delta. It was an encouraging sign, now that wheat from
the African provinces was in Vandal hands. Emperor Theodosius at
Constantinople seemed willing to divert part of the Egyptian harvest
to the West, but she guessed that brokers in the Eastern capital had
bought up most of the grain to monopolize the supply. The price of
bread was sure to increase, and fewer tokens for free loaves would be
issued to citizens. Food riots could result.

Arcadia turned away to look for the *Cybele* again. She finally
spotted Virilo's galley at a berthing on the south end of the wharf. A
bronze plaque at the bow, with the name ΚΥΒΗΛΗ in Greek, identified
the boat, as well as a sculpted head of the Phrygian goddess. The hull
was painted a dull brown, with a contrasting stripe of sea-green along
the upper strake. *A subdued color scheme*, Arcadia reflected, *compared to
the bright yellow and blue of some of the other galleys*. She walked closer,
noting that the smooth sweep of curve from bow to stern contradicted
the reputation for clumsiness that dogged merchant galleys. Under
full sail, and with oarsmen pulling at the six ports in the hull, she
guessed the *Cybele* might even be able to outrun a war galley.

A large passenger cabin structure on the aft deck indicated that
Virilo collected additional fees by taking travelers to the Dalmatian
mainland opposite Italy.

Cybele. *Why did Virilo use that pagan name for his galley?*
Arcadia's tutor had taught her that the Asian goddess was popular
in Rome long ago, but she recalled nothing about the cult. It was
surely prohibited now, like that of Isis, but Bishop Chrysologos had
trouble enforcing the ban on pagan rites in the port quarter. Just as
the Isis priests had done, those of Cybele might be attempting to
revive worship of the goddess. Strange. Virilo had not seemed to be
the type of man who would have nostalgia for pagan deities.

At the wharfside, stevedores had finished unloading *Cybele's*
cargo of wine amphorae from one gangplank. At the other, workers
carried bales of wool or slim clay jars into the hold for the outbound

journey. As Arcadia approached she noticed that the air was overly fragrant with a pungent spicy smell, then saw that it came from a load of peppercorns scattered on the paving, amid the shards of a broken amphora. Virilo, red-faced, was angrily trying to block two urchins who were working as a team to scoop up as many of the black pellets as they could.

A loud whimper of pain came from the shadow of the warehouse portico. Arcadia looked in that direction and saw one man beating another with his fists, a slave probably. The blows seemed to be viciously out of proportion to the value of the cheap broken jar, and despite what the boys might be able to filch, most of the spilled peppercorns could be recovered. Her anger flared, but she hesitated to interfere. Although the bishop occasionally asked for donations to replenish a fund that bought freedom for old or sick slaves, she knew the Church accepted slavery as part of the social order. In one of his letters, Paul advised slaves to obey their masters as a way of serving Christ, yet had also warned owners to give up using violence against them.

Her remembrance of the Apostle's admonition prompted Arcadia to finally protest. "Stop that man from hitting the slave," she called out to Virilo. "*Stop him!*"

The two boys paused to watch this potential confrontation between a woman and the galley owner. Virilo scowled at Arcadia, but evidently remembered her as the surgeon's wife and signaled his cargo master to halt the beating.

"Quite right, my dear," someone behind her agreed. "No man should treat another that way. Not even a slave."

Arcadia recognized the voice and turned to Publius Maximin. "Senator. I…I suppose I shouldn't have interfered, but—"

"No, no. I don't allow such mistreatment in my warehouse." Maximin pulled Arcadia back by the arm to let two men carrying a broom and empty amphora pass. "Get all the corns," he ordered them without releasing his hold on her.

"I remember now," Arcadia said. "The other night, at Faustina's, you told us you leased the *Cybele*."

"Indeed." Maximin released her arm to bend down and picked

up a lead seal from the broken jar. "P. MAXM, my mark. Pepper, sweet Macedonian wine, and oil shipped from Dalmatia in exchange for wool and Tuscan wines."

"I thought you raised chickens on your farm," Arcadia said, recalling the few days she had spent there in December, and the unending smell of chicken dung.

"My dear," Maximin said with an indulgent smirk, "pepper prices have soared ever since Alaric demanded four thousand pounds of the spice as part of a bribe not to attack Rome. The market has been depleted since then, and I've contracted to be the only supplier to Ravenna. *Enormous* profits to be made." He edged closer and chuckled. "And the smell is nicer than that of a chicken yard. Perhaps I could let that husband of yours in on the investment possibilities."

"Getorius is happy with his medicines, Senator."

"Then he misses an opportunity." Maximin beckoned her away from the clean up. "What brings you to this sordid part of Ravenna, my dear? Is someone ill?"

How much could she tell him? The senator had been indirectly connected with the death of a visiting abbot in December but, through his influence in the court of Valentinian, had avoided serious questioning at the time. The matter had been dropped.

"I'm looking for Claudia, Virilo's daughter," she told him. "The poor girl suffers from epilepsia."

"The falling sickness? I didn't know."

"Virilo has probably kept it secret, but my husband wants his permission to treat her."

"I have seen Claudia," he said. "The mind of a child. A nurse is always with her at his villa."

Not all the time. He obviously doesn't know Claudia is pregnant. The man sweeping the peppercorns was prodding the two boys away when they suddenly looked beyond him, bolted up, and scampered to the end of the warehouse. Arcadia heard the rhythmic clack of nail-studded boot soles on the paving stones and turned. Four guards, led by a tribune, halted at his command on the edge of the spilled pepper. Leudovald was with them.

"Galleymaster," he called to Virilo, "this tribune wants a word with you."

The officer unrolled a small scroll and read, "'To Gaius Quintus Virilo, Master of the galley *Cybele*.'"

"Yes, th…that's who I am."

"By order of the Judicial Magistrate you are ordered to come with us for questioning in the death of the slave Atlos."

"I had nothing to do with that," Virilo protested.

"My orders are to bring you to the magistrate," the tribune replied, rolling up the parchment.

"Tribune, this is ridiculous," Maximin intervened. "I lease this man's galley. The *Cybele* is to leave for Dalmatia in the morning."

"Senator, I…I have my orders," the officer stammered. "It's not my decision." Arcadia guessed that the tribune had recognized Maximin and knew that his senatorial influence could have him transferred from the capital to the most distant outpost on any of the Roman frontiers.

"Of course, Tribune." Maximin softened his tone. "Virilo, I'll speak to the magistrate. *Cybele* will hoist anchor on schedule, with you as master. Very well, Tribune, do your duty."

After Virilo was marched away in the custody of the guards, Leudovald sauntered toward Arcadia. "Domina," he said with a measure of sarcasm in his voice, "I thought slaves, not mistresses, soiled their hands at the marketplace."

"I came to look for Claudia."

"For Claudia. Not for a golden sickle?"

Arcadia ignored his taunt. "My husband thinks he can help her epilepsia."

"Epilepsia. You obviously don't know that your husband was called to the palace. One of the pigment makers in the bookbindery is ill. Why are you missing an important part of your medica training?"

"I…I'll see if he needs help," Arcadia mumbled. When no one had come to the clinic that morning, she had decided to look for Claudia. She turned back to Maximin. "Senator, my husband and I are looking in on Faustina during the fifth hour. How was she this morning?"

"I haven't been over there yet," he admitted.

"She should have been able to sleep. I'd better see if my husband needs me."

"Then, *vale*, farewell for now." Maximin squeezed Arcadia's hands between his. "I'm still trying to convince my wife Prisca to let you examine her."

"I…it would be an honor, Senator." With a glance at Leudovald, who stood by with a smirk beneath his mustache, Arcadia turned toward the Vicus Longus to reach the Via Honorius and the palace. *Strange that the senator isn't more concerned about his niece*, she thought. *For all his outward charm it seems he's merely a self-centered opportunist. Could…could he have called Getorius to treat his niece just to find out what he knew about the dead youth in the church?*

The narrow street was filled with the noise and smells of shops and vendors' stalls. Cackling poultry stared in their stupid, wide-eyed way from wicker cages, next to fish vendors hoping to sell the night's catch before the day became too warm. At the Via Armini, Arcadia skirted a crew of slaves in a pit of foul, stinking water. They were struggling to repair a clay sewer line, which connected to the main culvert that emptied into the harbor. Further on, near the wooden bridge that spanned the Padenna River, she paused to watch children playing in the street, dodging around carts and chasing hoops or tossing leather balls. But it was the nearby women who interested her most, especially those who looked pregnant or nursed infants at their breasts. She knew there were competent midwives available for those who could afford to hire them, yet too many pregnant women had to rely on friends when it was time for the delivery of their child. After discovering the shocking number of children who died in childbirth, or during their first year, Arcadia had approached Getorius about setting up a clinic to treat only women. Even though she had argued that she would hire the best midwives in Ravenna, he had put her off by saying that she was not experienced enough. He was undoubtedly correct, yet he also constantly found himself coming up against diseases or injuries he had never treated before. She wondered if he might not be facing such a case at that moment with the sick pigment maker.

Arcadia turned left into the Via Honorius and saw the twin corner towers of Lauretum Palace three blocks distant. The foundations of the emperors' residence had been laid out thirty-eight years earlier by Valentinian's half-uncle Honorius, after he had made Ravenna the capital of the Western empire. Honorius had ordered a forest of laurel trees planted around the building, perhaps hoping that the sweet-smelling leaves, long associated with victory wreaths, would help restore the harried fortunes of the Romans in the West.

Arcadia had heard that the architect had been influenced by Diocletian's palace at Spalato in Dalmatia, but adapting the grand scale of the late emperor's building to what he could build using Honorius's shrunken revenues had challenged his design skills. Like Spalato, the front of Lauretum was divided into arcades, but they were only half the length of those on Diocletian's palace and made of brick instead of stone. Valentinian had begun to face the brick with Travertine marble, but Galla Placidia ordered the work stopped, to concentrate funds on embellishing the interior apartments with mosaic works similar to those she had seen at Constantinople.

Arcadia approached the front entrance, which led past reception rooms into an atrium with a central pool for collecting rainwater. The Imperial apartments were on the north side, and the state dining room, tax office, and Scholarian guard barracks were on the other. Citizens on business were quickly escorted through the corridor, although many hoped to catch a glimpse of the emperor or his mother in a side hallway.

Arcadia had been in Galla Placidia's private reception room, but few citizens saw the family quarters. Those fortunate enough to have done so returned with descriptions of the splendid mosaics. Scenes from Valentinian's life depicted him being proclaimed Caesar at age five, Augustus at six, and being married in Constantinople to Eudoxia when he was eighteen. He was also shown at state functions with his mother, his sister, Justa Honoria, and his cousin Theodosius, the Eastern emperor.

At the entrance steps, Arcadia waved to one of the Frankish sentries she knew. Charadric nodded her in. After Getorius was appointed palace physician, entering Lauretum had not been a problem.

She found her husband in the office of the Library Master. The previous librarian had died in December and a new curator had not yet been appointed. Getorius was standing in front of a seated worker whose leather apron was stained with vomit. When Arcadia entered, the pale man glanced up with a listless stare. Getorius turned.

"Arcadia. I'm glad you're here. This man…Maros…makes the white pigment used in painting designs on manuscripts. He's been experimenting with different concentrations of vinegar to transform the lead into powder." Getorius looked toward a gaunt man standing well away from the sick man. "Ursio, isn't that what you told me?"

The pigment shop master nodded. Getorius checked Maros's sallow skin condition again, recalling what he had been shown of the pigment-making process when he was under house arrest in December. Coils of lead were suspended over vinegar inside a pot that was buried in manure. Heat and acrid fumes converted the metal into a white powder.

"Can you feel this?" Getorius asked, pinching Maros's knobby fingers.

Maros gave a non-committal shrug.

"I've seen these symptoms in workers at the foundry where lead water pipes are made," Getorius recalled. "Ursio, you'll have to give Maros other work. He won't get any better if he stays here."

"Is…is it like the plague?"

"An excess of acid caused an imbalance in his body," Arcadia broke in. "It won't affect you."

Getorius said nothing. His wife was sometimes given to a hasty diagnosis, but she was probably correct this time.

"Can't you treat the acid imbalance with honey?" Ursio asked. "Don't you have a lot of sick vinegar makers?"

"No," Getorius admitted, "and that's the puzzling thing. In fact, they seem unusually healthy."

"Yet you said Maros won't get better," Ursio insisted.

Getorius shrugged. "Let me see where he works."

After Ursio led the way to a corner of the pigment shop, his stained workers gathered around to watch. "Take the top off that barrel," he ordered the nearest man. After the lid was removed, the putrid odor of manure and acrid vinegar fumes filled the air.

"Last winter, when it got so cold," Ursio explained, "Maros wanted to bring his dung barrel out of a courtyard shed and inside."

"The stink made us all sick," the lid-lifter said, holding his nose and making a face.

"I can see why." Getorius indicated a perforated clay lid jutting out of the slimy mass. "Let me look inside that pot."

Ursio nodded to the worker, who muttered under his breath but pushed away the manure with one hand until the top was clear, and opened the jar.

When Getorius bent down, the strong fumes made him gag and his eyes sting. Through tears he made out a coil of whitish powder lying on a shelf molded into the pot's side. Vinegar glistened with a metallic sheen on the bottom.

"That's our white pigment," Ursio said, pointing to the powder inside the jar.

Getorius wet an index finger, dipped it into the whiteness and tasted the residue. It was neither bitter nor sweet, but did leave a metallic taste in his mouth, as if he had pressed his tongue against a copper dish. Someone handed him a cup of watered wine. He rinsed his mouth and spit into the manure.

"Put the barrel back outside, and send Maros home. I'll try to help him, but he must stay away from here."

After Ursio grunted agreement, his men broke into smiles. The obnoxious barrel and the sick man were no longer a problem.

❧

On the way out Getorius paused in the palace garden with Arcadia to breathe in some fresh air and dispel the aftertaste of metal and vinegar in his throat.

"It will take all day to clear that out of my humors," he complained. "What did you think?"

"After you said the powder tasted metallic, I had second thoughts."

"*Not* a vinegar imbalance? You smelled the fumes, and the white lead residue was relatively tasteless."

"But that's the only other component," Arcadia contended. "You said yourself that vinegar makers are healthy, while lead workers exhibit similar symptoms."

Getorius sighed. "Perhaps I can learn something from treating Maros. Where were you earlier?"

"At the port." Arcadia grasped his sleeve. "Virilo has been brought in for questioning, and Leudovald implied that you would be next."

"The sickle versus the fishing knife." Getorius pointed across the garden to the room in the palace where he had been confined in December. "If Leudovald decides I'm lying and arrests me, I won't have those quarters this time. What were you doing at the port?"

"Don't be upset. I was looking for Claudia."

"Claudia? I don't think we should interfere in the affair. Examining Atlos should have been the end of it."

"I thought I might convince Claudia's father to let you treat her. I ran into Senator Maximin. Remember he told us he leases Virilo's galley? He imports pepper through Dalmatia."

"Pepper is worth more than its weight in gold these days."

"So the Senator told me. He's going to use his influence to get Virilo released because the *Cybele* is to sail in the morning."

Getorius frowned. "That will leave Leudovald free to question me. Even if he thinks the galleymaster killed Atlos, he must realize that Virilo wouldn't commit the murder by himself. He'd pay someone to do it. I wonder if Leudovald has questioned Thecla yet?"

"I'd almost forgotten about her. Poor old woman."

"She—or I—will be next on his list. And even Claudia." Getorius fell silent. Leudovald seemed the kind of man who would bring charges against a suspect just to impress the magistrate, and then let lawyers sort out accusations afterwards. That could take months. *In December*, Getorius recalled, *after I was charged with illegally dissecting a corpse, the evidence of my innocence was almost buried by the two deacons who were witnesses against me. Claudia is guiltless. Perhaps if I could board the* Cybele *and talk to Virilo, I might find out something that would prove Atlos killed himself. And an explanation for that fishing knife. I can't do that if I'm held in a cell. Still, I don't want to alarm Arcadia.* Getorius stood and took her by the hand. "I don't much care to be imprisoned again, *Cara.* After we look in on Faustina, I'll take care of anyone who has come to the clinic. You pack up a few clothes and tell Childibert we'll be away for a few days."

"What do you mean, Getorius?"

"I mean I hear that the Dalmatian coast is quite beautiful in springtime."

⁂

It was dark, into the third night hour, when Getorius escorted Arcadia along the Via Porti to the warehouse shed near where she had told him *Cybele* was docked. One of the boarding planks was still in place. No light showed through the portside cabin windows. At sea the crew would be berthed below deck, but Getorius assumed that the men were now spending their last evening ashore in port taverns and brothels. None would return at the earliest until the midnight watch.

A single sentry was on duty, huddled inside the shed portico, away from a chill sea breeze. He warmed himself at a fire, idly throwing dice on the ground to pass the time until his relief came. Getorius guessed that by the dawn watch, when the galley departed, another guard would have taken this man's place. He fished a small silver coin out of his belt purse, held up the traveling bag Arcadia had packed, and strolled over to the guard.

"We're passengers on the *Cybele.*" Getorius let a half siliqua reflect the firelight, then pressed it into the man's hand and leaned close to him. "My wife doesn't think I'd get here on time in the morning," he whispered in a confidential tone. "She'd like us to sleep on board."

The guard eyed Arcadia a moment, winked, palmed the coin, and motioned the couple toward the gangplank with his spear.

A waxing first-quarter moon had risen, giving just enough light on the deck area to show it had been cleared of cargo for sailing. Six rowing oars were secured against the inner strakes. Behind the prow, a tile roof protected a brick stove where meals were cooked.

Silhouetted against the undulating sparkles of moonlight on the sea behind, the aft cabin house loomed beyond the mast as a black, angular shape.

"We can't go into a cabin," Arcadia whispered.

"No, it might be occupied, or will be by morning."

"Where *can* we hide?"

Getorius glanced around and spotted a dark rectangle in front of the mast. "The hatch to the cargo space is open. We'll have to make ourselves comfortable in the hold, at least until we're well out to sea. We can deal with Virilo then. Be careful as you follow me down."

At the bottom of the ladder the air smelled partly of bitumen, but even more strongly of wine. A single lamp toward the prow gave enough light to make out the source—clay amphorae stored in racks that were set against the curve of the hull. The center of the hold was stacked with the bales Arcadia had seen being loaded on board. She pinched a tuft of white, fingered it, then smelled a sample.

"Wool. At least we'll be warm down here."

"Good. I'll loosen the ropes on two bales far in the back. We can crawl inside for the night."

"Where does the crew sleep?" she asked.

"Probably in the bow, beyond that curtain. I image there's a crude latrine up there, too."

"Good, I—Shh, listen." Arcadia held three fingers to his lips. "I heard something scurrying over there. Getorius, would there be rats down here?"

He hedged, "I…ah…have never been on a galley before."

"Getorius"—she tugged at his sleeve—"Are there?"

"Probably, *Cara*, but…" He paused as a soft but insistent mewing sound came closer. A small gray form appeared, slinking toward them from between the bales. Getorius grinned. "Catkin there can probably answer your question about rodents."

"Thank Blessed Cosmas!" Arcadia slumped against a bale and

fumbled in the dim light to undo the straps of her traveling bag. "If I can find the cheese I brought, I'll give it some."

"I wouldn't," Getorius cautioned. "Feed our little friend and catkin might give us away by coming back for more, once the crew is on board."

"I suppose you're right. Poor thing."

"Let's get settled in the stern. I suspect catkin will get bored and go away."

Getorius selected two of the lower bales. He picked at the knots until they loosened, puzzled that they were tied differently from each other, then pulled apart an opening in the packed wool.

"Sorry," he mumbled. "It's not exactly the kind of sea journey I had planned for us some day, to go, say, to Constantinople."

"But this is exciting," Arcadia commented, wriggling into the soft material. "Certainly better for you than a cold prison cell some-where under the palace."

Getorius leaned over to kiss her. "That's why I love you, *Cara*, even though you can be exasperating at times." His face dropped down to nuzzle her breasts. "I suppose a little lovemaking…quietly of course…is out of the question?"

"With catkin watching? Out of the question," Arcadia mur-mured, and turned to nestle more deeply into the wool. The cat nosed in after her to explore the dark, warm new space.

Getorius crept into his bale. *She's right, this isn't a pleasure cruise. All we need is for a crew member to come back early and find us.* He settled into the pleasant softness and thought back to Leudovald's questions. *Someone had a reason for substituting the knife he said he found for the sickle. And he knows that it would be my word and a heretic woman's against that of a palace official. Arcadia's right…a small, makeshift cocoon and the prospect of being found and interrogated by the magistrate on a murder charge are not ideal elements for fervent lovemaking.*

⁂

On the deck above the hold, Diotar sat at a small table in a cramped

87

cabin on the starboard side and scowled at the sleeping form of Adonis in the upper bunk. The youth had refused to stay in the cabin he was to share with Kastor because his ill companion had begun vomiting. Now, Adonis said, Kastor's urine was tinted a light red. If he was coming down with plague, he wanted to be as far from the sick man as possible.

That was one problem. Diotar recalled his morning conversation with Virilo. He seemed to be having second thoughts about allowing his daughter to remain in the cult. Claudia was crucial in recruiting members. The most useful person Cybele had. Witnessing an attack of the Sacred Disease for the first time frightened people, but the susceptible ones came back again to view this direct experience of the goddess's power.

That fool Atlos stirred up a wasp's nest with his fornication, but he at least used the Arian church for his suicide. Leudovald has not had to come to the temple compound to investigate. The woman priest will have to prove that she was not involved. By the time the Cybele *returns from Dalmatia, the magistrate will have satisfied himself with a verdict of self-inflicted death.*

Diotar drained the dregs of watered wine in his ashwood cup. There was still the problem of the pregnancy of a Vestal Virgin, yet there might even be an alternative to abortion. Claudia was three months along, the surgeon's wife had said, so the child should be due in September. There might be a way of relating the birth to the pageant he was planning for then.

Adonis moaned in the bunk and kicked off part of his blanket. When Diotar noticed the youth's erect penis, presumably the result of an erotic dream, he stood and roughly pulled the covering back over him, then lay down on the bottom bunk. The sight brought back to Diotar thoughts of his uncle Sebastos.

Sebastos had been the ArchGallus at Pessinus when he ordered his nephew's castration, after he caught him in a storage shed showing curiosity about a neighbor girl's genitals. Diotar guessed it would have happened in any event. Sebastos was already teaching him that priests of Cybele freed themselves from the body's sexual prison by imitating the sacrifice of the goddess's consort, Attis. At a spring ritual they voluntarily castrated themselves, then affected women's clothing and mannerisms.

Galli, these eunuch priests called themselves, after the Gallus River, whose sacred water induced their frenzied visions and dancing. But the name in Latin translated as "cocks," an ironic jest, Diotar realized, since the sex organ of the same vulgar nickname had been rendered useless to the men.

Let the fools snicker, he thought. *In the New Age Cybele is about to inaugurate the goddess will assure that her pet cocks prosper from their mutilation. Let Augustine, the African bishop, ridicule us in his* City of God. *He wrote about how we perfume our hair, cover our faces with make-up and affect a woman's walk as we swish through Carthage, begging.*

Begging! Diotar choked with resentment and anger whenever he thought of the indignity the old state-supported Roman cult priests had never had to undergo. *After I bring back my cargo from Olcinium, I'll be wealthier than Publius Maximin...*

Diotar heard Adonis moan in his sleep again, then gagged at the smell of semen coming from the youth's bunk.

Let him have his disgusting dreams now. After the Day of Blood, as Adonis-Attis, a priest of Cybele, he will no longer be affected by the fleshly temptations that were the downfall of his twin.

Olcinium

Chapter seven

Getorius awoke to the sound of oars splashing in water, the steady rhythmic creak of wooden timbers, and a gentle rocking of the dim cargo space. He saw that the crew's lamp had been put out. Only a pale bluish light showed at the hatch opening through which he and Arcadia had entered. "*Cara,*" he whispered, "are you awake?"

"For quite a while." Arcadia sat up, brushing wool tufts from her tunic. "Catkin scampered off about a watch period ago, at the time I heard people walking on deck. Now it feels like we're moving."

"The crew must be rowing *Cybele* through the harbor basin into the Adriatic. Did you sleep at all?"

"Not that well. Something hard kept prodding my back."

"Sorry, I was over here," he quipped with exaggerated innocence. "It couldn't have been me."

"No, this was much harder—" Arcadia realized what he was joking about and laughed. "I didn't mean it that way." She groped inside the wool and pulled out a leather sack. "Here's what it was."

"Let's see my rival." Getorius hefted the small bag. "It feels like it's full of coins and it's certainly heavy enough to be." He untied a thong securing the neck and pulled out several bronze disks. "I was right, it is money." He held one of the coins up to catch the feeble light and made out the inscription D.N. PLA. VALENTINIANVS P.F. AVG., surrounding a portrait of the current emperor. "Something's not right. The Augustus issues very little bronze coinage. Arcadia, get me one of the gold *solidi* we brought along."

She searched a purse in the clothing bag, then handed Getorius the coin. He compared it to the one in his hand. "The designs are identical, except this is bronze and the emperor's features are more crudely tooled. The reverse shows Valentinian holding a cross staff, with a Victory figure in his right hand, and the initials RV at the bottom to identify Ravenna as the location of the mint. Christ! It looks like Virilo is counterfeiting Valentinian's gold coins in bronze and smuggling them to Dalmatia."

"But Maximin leases the galley," Arcadia reminded him, "and they're hidden inside the senator's wool…look, I found a silver one."

Getorius took the coin and scratched it with a thumbnail. "It's only a silver wash." He stood up and looked around the hold at the rest of the cargo of wine amphorae. "I wonder what other contraband the *Cybele* might be hauling? Arcadia, let's keep three of these bronzes out. Put them in your purse and stash that coin sack back inside the wool. I'll tie up the bales again."

After the bag was replaced and the wool secured, Arcadia leaned against a bale and closed her eyes to minimize an incipient feeling of nausea caused by the swaying motion of the galley. Getorius wondered about the smuggled coins. Why would Maximin—or Virilo, for that matter—be bringing forged money into Dalmatia? Yet it might be neither man. A government official at the mint could be involved. Western coins were legitimate in the Eastern Empire, yet counterfeit bronze money bearing the image of Emperor Theodosius, not Valentinian, would have attracted less attention.

Arcadia had begun to feel worse after the odor of roasting meat wafted through the hatch from on deck. At the same time, the hold began a violent pitching motion. She sat up, sure she must look pale because her skin felt clammy. A queasy feeling settled in her stomach, then rose to her throat. The smell of food, sour wine, and bitumen in the close space became overwhelming.

"Getorius, I feel sick," she murmured weakly. "I've got to get out of here…find some fresh air before I throw up."

"I was worried about seasickness. We'll have to go on deck earlier than I'd hoped."

After Getorius helped his wife stand up, she frantically clambered over the bales to the hatch ladder. He followed her up the rungs to the outer deck, thinking that in any event Virilo would have soon found out they were on board.

The galleymaster was talking to his helmsman when Arcadia stumbled out of the hatch opening and ran toward the rail. While she retched over the side in dry heaves, Virilo went over to the hold and peered inside.

Getorius looked back up at him.

"What the furc—" Virilo blurted, sounding more surprised than angry. "Surgeon, how did you and your woman get aboard?"

"We'll pay for our food," Getorius said amiably, climbing off the ladder onto deck. "I've brought money."

"Passengers take along their own rations. I asked why you were here."

"Virilo, weren't you were just questioned by Leudovald?"

"He let me go free."

"Yes, on Senator Maximin's order. I was arrested last year when someone tried to blame me for something I didn't do. I want to let this affair about Atlos cool down."

"Leudovald's a prick. He—"

"A moment, my wife." Getorius noticed that Arcadia had straightened up. When he went to the rail, her complexion was the pale color of bread dough. "Are you feeling any better, *Cara?*" Arcadia slowly wiped spittle from her mouth and shook her head.

"Can I get you something? A little water?"

In answer she leaned over the rail and retched again, just as Diotar came out of the forward starboard cabin, followed by someone wearing a hooded cloak. The priest looked at the couple, clearly surprised, then beckoned his companion back inside. Getorius held onto Arcadia's shoulder and glanced at Virilo, but decided not to question him about what business Diotar had at the *Cybele*'s destination. Instead, he called out, "Is your daughter, Claudia, on board?"

Virilo's scowl softened. Without answering, he pointed to the sun-washed outline of Ravenna and its dark-green line of pine forest receding in the distance. "*Cybele*'s running with the tide, I'll not turn her back. You'll stay aboard."

"Fine. Then, do you have cabin bunks that are more comfortable than the wool bales we slept in last night?" Getorius watched Virilo's expression for some sign that he knew about the coin bag concealed inside the wool, but saw no change.

"The crew can set up cots for you near their quarters," he replied gruffly, starting to turn back to the helmsman.

"Getorius, I need to use a latrine," Arcadia muttered loud enough for Virilo to hear.

"Do you have one?" Getorius asked him.

"Star side, aft of the helm deck."

"Privacy?"

"None." Virilo chuckled. "Crew'll probably watch."

"How about an *olla cubiculi*?"

"A pisspot? Maranatha," Virilo called out to the cook, who was lighting charcoal in a stove near the prow, "give the surgeon one of your cracked pitchers."

Getorius again asked about a better place for his wife to spend the voyage. "You don't have a spare cabin? I said I had money."

"The hold," Virilo insisted. "And take your woman below to piss after she's through vomiting on my railing."

❧

Arcadia nursed her seasickness by lying in *Cybele*'s rolling belly with a wet cloth on her forehead and not moving. It was an imbalance similar to one she had experienced as a young girl, when she had whirled around and around, arms outstretched, until she felt dizzy and nauseous. Getorius was less affected, but at noon ate only bread and drank a little watered wine. In mid-afternoon, he told Arcadia he was going to talk to the helmsman and try to find out where their destination was in Dalmatia.

Getorius stumbled and had to brace himself against the mast when he stepped onto the deck, caught off-balance by the slanting pitch of the *Cybele* as she nosed through the blue-green waves. Overhead, a stiff northwest wind flapped the square linen mainsail with a sharp snapping sound. The oars had been secured against the strakes. Now four crewmembers struggled with brail ropes to raise a triangular topsail into place above the main sheet.

Getorius found the helmsman at the sternpost, on a platform that was high enough for him to look over the cabins and see the bow. An awning fluttered above as protection against the sun and rainsqualls. He was dressed in a hooded, sleeveless leather jerkin and wool trousers. The greasy hood framed a beefy face and strands of scruffy blond hair. The man's brawny arms controlled two massive steering oars, which angled back on either side into the galley's wake.

"*Salus,* Helmsman," Getorius called up pleasantly in greeting. "Health to you. I'm Getorius Asterius, surgeon to the Empress Mother."

"Sigeric," the man replied, glancing briefly away from the bow to look down and see who was speaking.

"Your name's Sigeric?" Getorius asked. "From which tribe? My father was Treveri."

"Burgond."

"Ah." *The Burgondi were the tribesmen who raided Mogontiacum and killed my parents. It's past time I met one of them.* "Mind if I keep you company?"

Sigeric shrugged a muscular shoulder without looking away from the prow. "Might be good t' have a surgeon on board, if we run into *piratae.*"

"Pirates?"

"One of th' risks. Y' can climb up, Surgeon."

As Getorius mounted the short ladder, climbing to an opening in the railing that surrounded the platform, he took in his surroundings. Another crewman was standing at an angle behind Sigeric. A cabinet built into the rail in front of the helm was fastened to the deck.

In the center of its top, a silver figurine of the sea god Neptune gazed toward the prow. A small flag, attached to a dowel that was pegged into a hole on a bronze disk, whipped noisily in the same direction. Next to it, protected by glass in a frame sealed with bitumen, was a stained navigational map.

Getorius wiped a film of salt spray off the glass and read titles that identified the coasts of Italy and Dalmatia, from Aquileia in the north down to the island of Corcyra off the Greek mainland. A red line traced a crude zig-zag from Ravenna to a port in southern Dalmatia.

"I never knew my father, but I was told he made maps, probably like this one," Getorius said, trying to establish a common interest with Sigeric. "What port are we headed for?" When he saw the helmsman's brow knit in a puzzled frown, Getorius quickly added, "That is, how long will it take us to get there?"

Sigeric motioned to the crewman, who came to take over the steering oars.

Standing next to Getorius, the helmsman placed a callused forefinger on the glass. "This here red line shows our route t' Olcinium."

Olcinium. "What are the four numerals along it?"

"Our position at sunrise each day." Sigeric chuckled and stroked the silver statue. "That's if Neptune here is busy fooling around with sea nymphs and can't brew up a storm. This band across th' top shows stars in Aries and Taurus."

"March and April skies. The diagram along the bottom?"

"Height of the sun at each hour. Sunup t' sunset."

"So, it will take four days to reach…Olcinium?"

"Like I said, if Neptune behaves. Th' flag shows wind direction. Northwest Caurus. What I need."

"You've marked places along both coasts in red."

"Landfalls. Help me know my position. First day and night we'll be running with th' Adria Current, should make about a hundred twenty miles. We'll sight Ancona lighthouse off the star rail around th' eighth night hour." Sigeric shifted his finger to an island. "*Cybele* will bear by Issa, about half way t' Olcinium, but she'll start bucking a north Ionian Current near there. Slow her up a bit."

"Fascinating." Getorius looked into Sigeric's gray-blue eyes as he reached to shake his hand. The man's own relatives might well have taken part in the Mogontiacum raid, yet, Fate had placed the son of two of their victims in the helmsman's safekeeping. "I hope we don't meet those pirates you mentioned, but if I can be of help, do call on me."

Sigeric grunted. "Y'd better give Neptune a friendly pat, Surgeon, and ask for calm seas. We'll have no sight of land all of tomorrow."

Getorius reached over and touched the metal god. The statue felt oddly warm, at body temperature, but of course it was the afternoon sun that was responsible. He moved to leave, but at the top of the ladder turned back to Sigeric. "I hope to learn more about *Cybele*."

Sigeric pushed strands of hair back into the leather hood. "I liked her better as *Aurora,* not named after that Stygian goddess. But she's still a stout lady."

Stygian goddess? What does he mean? Getorius climbed down and walked to the center of the port rail to try and get a deeper sense of being at sea. He had seen the blue, flat line of seemingly endless horizon from the beaches around Ravenna, but to be surrounded by water on all sides would be an exhilarating—if slightly unsettling—experience.

Pushed southeast by the Caurus wind and Adria Current, *Cybele* dipped in and out of the rolling Adriatic swells almost playfully, a creaking companion to the dolphins which had sidled alongside and now frolicked in leaping zig-zags across her prow. To the right, on the mainland, Getorius could still make out the flat coastline of Picenum, backed by the jagged bluish summits of the Apennines, and estimated the galley was about twelve miles offshore. Mount Conero, overlooking the Via Flaminia, was a slightly higher, hazy crest. He looked seaward again. In essence, on the most dangerous part of the voyage on the following day, his and Arcadia's universe would be reduced to a fifteen-by-sixty-foot curved wooden box, pitching on a seemingly infinite expanse of water. The intimidating thought combined with a freshening afternoon breeze to make Getorius shiver and wish he had put on a cloak.

Two stocky crewmen with curly black hair and swarthy, pock-marked complexions came on deck from below. Getorius guessed they could have been recruited from any of the coastal villages south of Ravenna, hoping to find life aboard a merchant galley more adventurous than tedious days of bobbing in a fishing boat, and exhausting nights cleaning slimy seaweed from broken nets. The men knelt to separate a coil of cord from two-foot square blocks of red-painted oak which had silver busts of human heads attached to the top. Curious, Getorius approached them.

"I'm a surgeon," he said as an introduction. "Never been on a galley before. What are you doing?"

One of the men glanced up. "Getting ready to gauge *Cybele*'s speed," he replied, then went back to unwinding the cord.

Getorius noticed that the sailor's accent was provincial, yet certainly better than Sigeric's guttural Germanic pronunciation. Virilo was evidently shrewd enough to recruit crewmen who were above the average naval war galley standards. "How will you do that?" he asked, hoping the man, like Sigeric, would be humored enough by the interest to explain. "You are…?"

"Gaius."

"How is that done, Gaius?"

The man stood and held up one of the red blocks. "This log has Jupiter on top. Weighted with lead to make him float upright. I'll drop him in the sea at the bow, call out 'One' when I see the god pass the stern. While I pull Jupiter back, Victor, on the port side, will throw in Mercury and yell out 'Two.' We'll keep this up until Sigeric tells us his sandglass has recorded a quarter of an equinoctial hour."

"And?"

"*And?*" Gaius snorted. "*Cybele*'s sixty feet long, Surgeon. I figure she's making five miles every hour. If we end around number one hundred, I'll be right."

"I see. Thanks." Getorius turned back to watch the sea, wishing he had paid better attention to his mathematics tutor. *A legionary mile is about four thousand, eight hundred feet long. During the sandglass quarter-hour interval, one hundred times the length of the hull, multiplied four times, evidently adds up to* Cybele's *speed.* He glanced up at the sun, estimating there were less than three hours until sunset, then went down the ladder to see how his wife felt. *I'll figure it out later.*

The cargo space was damp from salt spray blowing in through the open hatch. Arcadia was lying under a blanket on one of the two folding cots the crew had set up in the center of the hold. A wet cloth covered her eyes.

"Are you feeling any better?" Getorius asked, dropping down onto one of the bales.

"No, but I may survive if I never look at food again."

"I know, I'm a bit queasy myself. But it should pass in a day or so, and we're fortunate the sea is calm. I talked to the helmsman, a Burgond named Sigeric. Our destination is the port of Olcinium."

"I've not heard of it."

"Nor had I. He said it was four days from Ravenna, *if* we don't offend Neptune and run into a storm." Getorius picked absently at the bale's rope knot, deciding not to mention what Sigeric had said about the possibility of a pirate attack.

"Getorius, while I was being sick, wasn't that Diotar who came out of a cabin?"

"With someone else who was wearing a hooded cape, so I couldn't see who it was."

"Is Claudia on board?"

"I asked Virilo about that, but he avoided answering."

"Why would he be taking Diotar to Dalmatia? The priest seems to have some hold on Virilo, and knows more about Atlos than he should." Arcadia lifted the cloth from her eyes and sat up. "Getorius, what have we gotten into? A few days ago things were going well. Now, we're practically fugitives, running away to an unknown town—"

"We? *Cara*, you're not involved in this."

"I certainly am. Leudovald suspects you and knows I was at Thecla's basilica when you found Atlos."

"He wouldn't arrest a woman."

"Getorius, we don't know how the man's mind works. Even you joked about him being capable of beheading his own grandmother."

"It was just that, Arcadia, a jest." Getorius held a hand up to shield his eyes from a ray of sunlight that had slanted through the hatch opening. The hull's yaw gave the shaft movement as the square of brightness swept over the bales of wool, then back again. A moment later, a smell of grilled fish wafted in with the light. "The crew is preparing supper already."

"Not for me."

"No"—Getorius brushed a hand against her cheek—"Arcadia, we can't change anything that happened in Ravenna, but we mustn't let Virilo even suspect that we've discovered those counterfeit coins."

"Did he react when you told him we slept in the bales?"

"He didn't. Either he doesn't know about the coins, or he should have been an actor." Getorius looked toward the hatch opening. "I think I might eat a little. Sure I can't get you anything? Watered wine? Bread?"

"Nothing. I'm not moving from this cot."

Getorius leaned over to kiss her. "By this time tomorrow, *Cara*, you'll be back to feeling normal."

"I hope so. I'm going to lie back again."

On deck the crew was being served wooden plates of red mullet, liberally sprinkled with pepper filched from Maximin's import supply. The cook, nicknamed Maranatha—"Come, Lord,"—by the crew, a jesting reference to being poisoned by his food, was a short, wiry Greek tending a grill set over glowing charcoal. The stove area was shielded from the wind and sea spray by the curve of the prow.

When Maranatha turned to hand Getorius a bowl of bread chunks soaked in fish broth, he saw that the left side of the cook's face was disfigured by pink burn scars. The man's sightless eye was a milky sphere resembling those found on statuary. What had caused such a hideous injury? Had a careless assistant spilled water onto a pan of hot olive oil and caused a terrible accident?

The crew, except for Victor, who stood, squatted on deck to eat their mullet and help themselves from a keg of green olives. Getorius joined them, hunkering down next to Gaius. He tried a spoonful of the broth and found it delicious, flavored with onion, laurel and coriander. Maranatha handed a crewman a pan of the fish, and three plates, and Getorius watched him take it toward Diotar's cabin. *Three? There must be someone else with the priest and that person I saw.*

The sailor returned, smirking and clutching his crotch while making jokes in Greek. Getorius caught the words *eunoukhoi* and *hermaphroditos*, and guessed that the men's snickers related to comments about Diotar's womanly manner.

"They're laughing at the priest?" he asked Gaius.

"And about what goes on at his temple outside Olcinium," Gaius replied, picking a mullet bone from his teeth.

"Diotar has a temple? Have you seen it?"

"Only the outside. Rumor is Diotar's sorceresses change men into women in there." Gaius tossed the bone away and winked. "Neptune knows what else they might do to a man."

"Sorceresses?" Getorius probed. "Don't you mean a priestess, like Claudia?" Perhaps the crewman would tell him if she was on board.

"Sorceresses," Gaius repeated.

Before Getorius could ask about Claudia, Maranatha leaned down in front of him with a plate of the mullet. Getorius slurped down the rest of his broth, then handed the bowl to the cook in exchange for the pinkish fish.

"I'm sure this will be as good as your soup."

Maranatha cocked his head to look at Getorius with the good eye. "Tell that to the bilge scum, Surgeon," he commented loudly, nodding toward the crew.

In response the men hooted and threw fish bones at the cook. Getorius took a bite of mullet, but saw Victor suddenly fling his uneaten fish over the side and come to kneel in front of him.

"Y' said y' were a surgeon?" the crewman asked.

"Yes."

"My gut's hanging out my ass," Victor complained. "Would y' take a look?" He turned and hiked his tunic up over a bare, swollen rectum.

Getorius's bite of mullet stuck in his throat as he recognized the raw symptoms of hemorrhoids. Hippocrates had described the condition as an excess of bile in the anal veins leading to a heating of the blood. This attracted more blood from nearby veins and forced the bowel outward. Getorius spit fish bits into his hand.

"There are…several treatments," he told Victor. "Perhaps we could talk about them tomorrow, when you're not on watch?"

"Fourth hour." Victor flipped the tunic down and reached for a handful of olives.

"Fourth hour." Getorius looked at the reddish mullet chunks on his plate and felt his already-queasy stomach rebel. He stood slowly and scraped the fish over the rail, grateful that Arcadia was not well enough to join in the crew's evening meal—even though she had missed an opportunity to gain an intimate, if disgusting, bit of knowledge about yet another medical problem.

Chapter eight

That evening Getorius tried to recall as much as he could about the methods that Hippocrates had recommended for treating Victor's condition. The most drastic was to purge the patient, and then cauterize the pile with a red-hot oblong iron until the swelling dried up. Since this also involved several days of applying poultices and suppositories to the area, he decided against such a painful and lengthy procedure. Excising the hemorrhoid was somewhat less drastic, but utilized medicines in the healing poultice that he did not have, such as calcined flower of bronze. He finally decided to wash the man's anus with hot water and administer a suppository composed of what was available on board; alum and boiled honey from Maranatha's stores, ground cuttlefish shell, the bitumen used in caulking the hull, and verdigris scraped from the galley's weathered bronze fittings. There was plenty of wool in the bales for making the insert itself.

❧

By mid-afternoon of the next day, after the odors of fish, garlic, and onion from the noon meal had dissipated on the wind, Arcadia felt well enough to come up on deck for some air. Getorius had just finished treating Victor when he saw her emerge.

"Arcadia, you're better? That's wonderful." He turned from watching the dolphins that were still racing the *Cybele* to take her arm and bring her to the railing. "I was about to go below and tell you to come see this."

"I do feel weak, but less nauseous."

"Good. Come look. The dolphins seem to be enjoying our company. It's like a game for them."

Arcadia tentatively walked to the railing and peered over the side. Getorius put his arm around her waist, and was just pointing out the frolicking mammals when he saw Diotar come out of his cabin and stand at the stern rail.

"I still wonder what Diotar is doing on board. This is only the second time he's been outside, that I've seen."

"Even creatures in Ravenna's swamps come up for air," Arcadia commented dryly.

"You really *don't* like Diotar."

"I told you that the first time I saw him," she reminded her husband. "He's undoubtedly a eunuch, like the Augustus's steward, but that isn't the reason. There's something…sinister about him."

"I'd like to talk to him. Find out more about his cult."

"Now would be the time. Let me try."

The Cybelene ArchGallus was dressed in a full-length wool tunic, hooded cloak, and tight-fitting felt boots. A glint of gold at his throat came from a neck torc. His face was pale under the light make-up he had put on. Getorius noticed him draw back as Arcadia walked over to start a conversation. He followed her.

"Has the sea upset your humor balance as it has mine?" she asked pleasantly.

Diotar looked past her at Getorius. "Surgeon. I had not expected you on this journey."

"I…decided rather quickly. We've always wanted to visit Olcinium."

"That minor port?" Diotar's painted eyebrows rose in surprise. "It's not to be compared with Dyrrhachium in Macedonia."

"Perhaps import duties are less strictly collected?"

"A concern of the galleymaster, not mine."

"Are you an associate of Senator Maximin's?" Arcadia asked. "One of his investors in pepper?"

"Each man knows his own business best." Diotar evaded her question and looked past Arcadia again to ask Getorius, "Are you familiar with the worship of *Magna Mater*, Surgeon?"

"Great Mother? Not really."

"The goddess is not unlike the Christians' Maria."

"We don't worship her," Arcadia corrected. "She's only honored as the mother of Christ."

"The cult of the Great Mother, of Cybele, is centuries older," Diotar sneered.

Arcadia tried to place the man's accent. She was certain he knew Greek, but there was also a Celtic lilt to his pronunciation. Diotar might try to ignore her, but she was determined to know more about him and his cult. "You've not come to our clinic," she probed. "Have you been in Ravenna long?"

Diotar hesitated a moment before replying, "I went there from Pessinus."

"That's in which province?" Getorius asked.

"Galatia." Diotar abruptly turned toward the door of his cabin. "I must go inside. This wind is chilling."

"So much for finding out more." Arcadia led her husband to the stove area in the shelter of the bow. "He said he lived in Galatia. I *thought* he knew some Celtic."

"As they speak it in the East, corrupted by local dialects and Greek. If I remember Polybius's history, the original Celtic tribes settled there some seven hundred years ago."

"Yet Jerome wrote recently that he could understand the people," Arcadia recalled. "He said they sounded like those who live at Treveri in Gaul."

"Where my father was born."

"Yes." Arcadia moved away from the stove. The sight of the swiftly moving sea had made her feel nauseous again. "Getorius, I...I think I'll lie down again."

"*Cara*, you should eat something. At least drink watered wine."

"Not quite yet." Arcadia walked back to the hatch opening. "Perhaps in the morning," she called back before starting down the ladder.

"Fine, I'll come check on you in a bit." Getorius turned back to the sea, thinking of what Diotar had said. He had called the cult goddess Cybele, the same name as the galley. Sigeric had referred to her as Stygian, an infernal deity. *Let's see what she looks like.*

Getorius held onto the rail as he went to examine the carving of Cybele at the bow, leaning far over the graceful curve of the prow to glimpse her profile. The carving was crude and gaudily decorated with encaustic colors that resembled stage make-up on an actress. Still, the goddess's features hosted a benign smile. Why had Sigeric described her as a dark entity?

Pulling back, Getorius gazed at the sea around him. As the helmsman had predicted, the galley was alone on a vast expanse of water that blended eerily into a curtain of hazy horizon. The effect was of being at the world's unknown edge. No land was in sight, no distant beaches or mountains in Picenum to establish a link with *terra firma*. Only a few mewing gulls did that, soaring in the galley's wake as they searched below for scraps of anything edible that might have been thrown overboard. Getorius thought of a trusting, yet undoubtedly worried Noah, with his zoo of animals drifting on such a waterscape, and chuckled. The *Cybele's* cargo smelled much better.

⁊

By early morning of the third day at sea, Arcadia felt well enough to eat a small portion of barley bread for breakfast, without oil or honey. When she came up on deck, she saw Maranatha reviving the glow of the stove charcoal. She nodded to him, noticing that the roofed space he worked in, enclosed on three sides, was larger and better equipped with cooking utensils than most of the kitchens she had seen in Ravenna's crowded apartments.

A light rain had fallen during the night, making the air misty and speckling the galley's surfaces with beads of water. She sucked moisture off her lip, aware that her balance of Wet and Dry Humors had suffered during the time when she had felt too sick to drink. Looking east from the port rail, to where a timid sun valiantly tried to push through the remnants of gray rain clouds, Arcadia made out the shapes of several islands. Three were little more than low, pine-studded rocks, but the furthest looked to be several miles wide. Behind them rose the soft bluish tint of mountains on the Dalmatian mainland. The largest island seemed to be only a few miles off.

"Getorius, come up," Arcadia called down to her husband. "I can see land."

He joined her on deck a moment later, and looked toward where she pointed. "That may be the island of Issa that Sigeric told me about."

Arcadia squinted at a white squarish shape that seemed to detach itself from the green-blue silhouette of the island. "Getorius, does that look like a sail?"

"It does." He watched the vessel until he could make out a red emblem on the sail. "The upright line with two arms looks like a Patriarchal cross...I think I see a staff and gourd painted on it. Let me ask Sigeric." He ran back and called up to the helmsman, "Would that be a boatload of pilgrims going to the Holy Land?"

Sigeric wiped moisture from his eyebrows and peered into the distance. "More likely pirates than pilgrims," he muttered. "*Caco!* Almost caught us off guard." He reached into his cloak for a flute and blew a high-pitched signal, then shouted, "*Piratae! Piratae!* Aft portside."

As the rest of the crew stumbled on deck from below, Virilo opened his cabin door and looked to where Sigeric pointed. "Thieving scum," he growled. "We'll try to outrun them. Let out the topsail and bowsprit artemon sail."

As the crew worked the brails, the two auxiliary sheets sluggishly caught the wind. The morning breeze was light, and the *Cybele* made only a slight gain in speed.

In the distance, the lighter corsair's sail billowed out, then eight oars started working in rhythm to try and close the gap with the *Cybele*.

Getorius noticed a second galley that had come out from behind the south end of the island. "Virilo!" he yelled. "There are two boats. It's an ambush!"

"I see the scurfy sons of Satan. They're going to work us like two wolves chasing a lone calf."

Getorius could see that the second, swifter corsair would cross *Cybele's* bow and try and slow her down. That would allow the other galley to sail in until she was near enough for the crew to throw grappling hooks and drag her quarry alongside to be boarded.

Virilo sputtered another vulgarity when the low sun suddenly burst through the clouds in a flash of dazzling rays that blinded him and Sigeric. The glare gave a new advantage to the pirates, who had the sunrise brightness behind them.

Shading his eyes as the first vessel drew closer, low in the water from the weight of all the men she bore, Getorius could see grins on the bearded faces of the marauder crew—brigands, probably, or deserters from barbarian and Roman armies. He counted about twenty-five men, who looked as disreputable as the motley collection of looted armor they wore. There was no name on the vessel.

A glinting shower of arrows arced toward *Cybele.* Getorius pulled Arcadia down behind the shelter of the strake. The shafts slid harmlessly into the waves, some three hundred paces short of the galley.

"Surgeon, get below with your woman," Virilo ordered.

Getorius shook his head. "I'll be needed if someone's wounded. Arcadia, you go back down into the hold."

"I'm staying too," she said without looking at him.

"Furcing idiots," Virilo growled. "Then get behind the stern strake, by the cabins. I don't have time to argue with two stowaways."

Getorius pulled Arcadia back along the deck. He had heard that piracy was largely suppressed along the Adriatic coasts by the Roman fleet at Classis, south of Ravenna, but the unsettled situation caused by the recent Vandal capture of Carthage had emboldened the corsairs once again. The Dalmatian coast was a labyrinth of islands that gave them almost-limitless hiding places.

Virilo called his crew to the shelter of the kitchen. "*Cybele* hasn't been attacked before," he reminded them, "but you know of other merchantmen that never returned to Ravenna. We practiced a defense tactic with wooden blocks, but didn't consider a second galley…" He ducked down when an arrow glanced off the tile roof of the enclosure and skipped into the sea. "*Caco!* They're getting close. Crew stations, double pace!"

As the men ran to stand by for the defensive maneuver, other random arrows thudded into the port strake. They were supposed to unnerve the crew, Getorius assumed, since there was little chance of hitting anyone on the pitching deck. The bandits were undoubtedly after money, food, wine, and slaves, not the bulky cargo of wool bales the galley carried.

A series of sharp raps rattled off *Cybele*'s hull. Lead balls arced through the air, a few of them punching holes in the mainsail.

"Stay down," Virilo yelled, "their slingers are finding our range! One of them lead balls can crack open a head like it's a muskmelon."

The red Patriarch's Cross—an upright bar with two unequal arms extending from it—was now clearly visible; a crudely painted decoy for pilgrims travelling under the sponsorship of a bishop. Now, the raiding galley was close enough for the *Cybele*'s crew to hear the steady hammer beat of the hortator, the timekeeper who signaled the rowing speed of his eight oarsmen.

"Trim main to half-sail. Lower ram." Virilo shouted the orders, and then sprinted up the stern platform ladder to help Sigeric with the steering oars.

Getorius was surprised at the twin commands. Trimming sail would slow them down, yet Virilo had said he wanted to outrun the pirates. And merchant galleys were not equipped with a ram, nor had he seen one extending from *Cybele*'s prow.

As three crewmen hoisted on the brails and the mainsail slowly furled upward, Gaius sledged away the ratchet on a winch at the prow. The harsh grating rattle of a chain sliding through a scupper sounded, as a bronze ram was lowered into a horizontal position from its hidden berthing.

Clever, Getorius thought, *a ram was tucked into the prow.* Simultaneously, he felt *Cybele* lose the wind and lurch, protesting with a creak of timbers and shifting of cargo as she yawed and lost headway. The galley with the Patriarch's Cross, still aft of Virilo's portside, began to draw abreast, but the second corsair now would overshoot the *Cybele's* bow and be forced to haul about and tack into the wind to regain position.

Virilo eyed the red emblem. It was slightly behind and about sixty paces off. "Mainsail down! Hard port rudder!" he yelled, and helped Sigeric force back the long-bladed steering oar into a tight turn to the left. *Cybele* groaned again, but slowly hauled about toward the pirate vessel.

Since Patriarch's Cross had been intent on closing to starboard with her prey, the unexpected maneuver took her helmsman by surprise. He desperately tried to steer to port, away from the onrushing, deadly beak. When the pirate hortator realized what was happening, he hammered a frantic signal for the oars to be stroked in reverse, hoping the oncoming galley would glide harmlessly past his prow.

Getorius carefully raised his head above the strake and saw that each man's action had cancelled the other out. The pirate vessel was almost stopped. A few archers tried to hit Sigeric and Virilo at the steering oars, but their shafts thudded harmlessly into the cabin wall beneath the two men. Frantic now at the imminent ramming, the other pirates on deck tried to unbuckle their bulky armor and save themselves by diving overboard.

None succeeded. In a grinding screech of triumph, *Cybele's* ram crunched through the corsair's bank of oars, aft of the mast, and penetrated the hull in a shower of splintered ribs and planking shards. Virilo and his crew had braced themselves, but Getorius and Arcadia were unprepared, and the impact threw them forward. He grabbed for the railing and held on. She slammed hard against the strake and fell back on deck, bleeding from a forehead gash.

Although dazed, Getorius was aware of men on the pirate galley being flung overboard into a mass of floating wood scraps from their smashed hull. In moments, thrashing helplessly and wild-eyed with terror, the weight of their armor had sunk them beneath the green foam.

When the lighter hull of Patriarch's Cross heeled back from the ram's impact, two of Virilo's crewmen worked the mainsail to swing the *Cybele* back into the wind. Gaius and Victor grappled long, iron-tipped poles from their holders and pushed hard against the pirate vessel to separate themselves from the foundering galley.

The pirate helmsman had been the only crewman not wearing armor, and his grip on the steering oar had saved him from being flung into the sea. As the *Cybele* slowly pushed away from his sinking galley, he dove off and swam alongside, looking for a handhold.

Virilo spotted the man. To batter him away, he ran down the ladder and snatched a pole from Victor. Getorius scrambled to his feet and intercepted the master.

"You can't, Virilo," he shouted. "That's murder!"

He glared at Getorius a moment, then looked past him and threw down the pole. "Surgeon, I got other furcing troubles to deal with."

Getorius turned. The crew of the second corsair was still tacking into the wind to heave about, when the unexpected action had distracted them. He knew their master had to have been impressed with maneuverability, which he would not have expected in a merchantman. The second vessel took a hard port turn to catch the wind and escape.

Getorius took up the pole and extended it over the side for the enemy helmsman to grasp, but saw the man now clinging to the bronze beak that had destroyed his vessel. He ran to Arcadia. She was unconscious. Splotches of blood from the gash stained her hair and oozed down her face. Getorius cradled his wife's head and looked around for help in taking her into the hold.

Smashed pottery and bits of glowing charcoal from the stove were scattered on deck. Maranatha was trying to douse live embers with water from the drinking bucket. Gaius and Victor leaned over the prow, assessing any damage that might have been caused by the ramming. One of the bronze plaques identifying the *Cybele* had been .

torn loose, and the goddess's gaudy head was broken off, floating back somewhere amid the debris of the sinking raider. Paint had been scraped off the bow, and wood around the ram housing was splintered, but the hull planking was intact.

"Help me carry my wife below deck," Getorius called out to the two men. "I need to find my medical case in our travel bag."

Gaius and Victor brought her into the hold, and stood by to watch. Getorius rummaged through the leather bag, guessing that his wife had packed the smaller of his surgical cases. Hippocrates had written a treatise that dealt with head injuries. The second mode described contusions where the bone was not fractured. This, fortunately, seemed to be the case with Arcadia.

"Gaius, bring me a cup of vinegar and a jug of seawater," he ordered. "Victor, press this cloth over her wound."

He found the case, a stiff leather box with a shoulder strap, holding a minimum of instruments and medical supplies. After Gaius returned, Getorius washed away the blood with a seawater and vinegar solution. When the sting of the vinegar brought Arcadia squirming back to consciousness, the two crewmen said they were going on deck to haul the pirate helmsman aboard.

"I know, Arcadia, it's painful," Getorius commiserated, "but I'll need to stop the bleeding with a styptic."

"Is it very bad?"

"Nothing worse than some nasty swelling and I expect an enormous headache."

"What happened, Husband?" Arcadia murmured, closing her eyes again.

"After we rammed the pirate galley, the helmsman was the only survivor. His mates went down in their looted armor." Arcadia nodded slowly and reached up to touch her wound, but Getorius pulled her hand away. "I can make a plantago poultice for the bruise and a decoction of spirea leaves to minimize your headache."

"I love you, Getorius," she whispered.

"Yes, but this wouldn't have happ…" Getorius caught himself as he was about to criticize his wife for refusing to go below deck at the start of the action. *No point. Arcadia won't listen next time either.* "I love you, too, *Cara*," he murmured instead, and kissed her forehead next to the gash.

❧

The hold reeked of the sharp smell of new wine. In the ramming, two amphorae had been dislodged from their rack and broken. Arcadia spent an uncomfortable night; her wound throbbed, and a spirea extract did little to relieve the headache. Getorius lay sleepless for a long time, pondering what might have happened if the pirates had been successful in capturing *Cybele*. At best, Arcadia's father would have received a ransom demand and succeeded in getting his daughter back. At worse, she might have been made the concubine of one or more quarreling pirate chiefs. As a valued physician, Getorius knew he might have been smuggled north, to an area beyond the Danube River that was not under Roman control, and sold to some barbarian king. Except for Virilo's seamanship, it might have been so.

❧

At midmorning of the next day Arcadia felt well enough to go on deck and join her husband in watching the playful antics of a school of dolphins. Their sleek, dark shapes leaped alongside, parallel to the galley's sides, mimicking *Cybele's* prow as it pitched in and out of the waves. In the distance, a hazy outline of mountains marked the Dalmatian mainland, a bluish background for a few colorful fishing boats gently bobbing on a calm sea.

"How far are we from shore?" Arcadia asked.

"I'd estimate less than twenty miles. Sigeric said the *Cybele* would be slowed by a current flowing from the south, but we should arrive at Olcinium by late afternoon."

The door to Diotar's cabin abruptly opened and he stepped out. Getorius thought Diotar looked worried as he hurried toward him. "Wonder what the priest wants? With the ramming and your injury, I'd forgotten he was on board."

115

"Surgeon," Diotar called out in his womanish voice. "One of my priests is ill."

"Oh? What are his symptoms?"

"Fever. Nausea. You must look at Kastor."

"I don't have many medicaments."

"You treated Victor."

Word gets around. "Yes, mostly with what I found on board. All right, I'll get my medical case."

When Getorius returned, Arcadia accompanied him to the end cabin. Diotar, who stood just inside the door, held up a restraining hand. "The woman may not enter," he stated coldly.

"My wife trains with me. I want her to observe as many illnesses as possible."

"Nevertheless, she must remain outside."

"Look here—"

Arcadia touched her husband's arm. "Getorius, it's all right. You can describe his symptoms to me later on."

He shrugged and followed the priest into a small cabin about five feet wide and seven feet long. It was furnished with two narrow bunk beds, one above the other, a hinged wall table, a folding chair, and a low clothing chest that doubled as additional seating. The single window was closed and covered with a heavy fabric. The lack of fresh air together with flames from a broad-based oil lamp made the room uncomfortably stuffy. Getorius found the heavy scent of incense in the close space oppressive, and it did not completely mask a smell of vomit and urine.

Another man, the one he had seen on the first day, Getorius guessed, lounged in the shadows of the upper bunk. He looked vaguely familiar. A youth lay moaning on the lower bed, covered with a blanket despite the heat.

Getorius drew the chair over to him and sat down. "I'll need more light. Pull that window curtain away." Diotar flipped the drape aside. "Better. Where do you hurt, young man?"

"Kastor speaks only Galatian," Diotar said. "I will answer your questions for him."

"Galatian? What does Kastor complain about?"

"A pain suddenly appeared in his back a few days before we left Ravenna."

"This pain is located exactly where?"

"Just above his waist," Diotar replied. "Kastor proclaimed it worse on the left side, then that it spread downwards. He vomited after we sailed, but I thought it was the effect of the sea's motion."

When Getorius bent closer to feel the youth's face, he was surprised. By his slight body, Kastor had seemed no more than fifteen or sixteen years old, yet faint wrinkles around his eyes and mouth indicated he was far older. His brow was hot. "I'll need a urine sample. Diotar, do you have a small glass vase or bottle?"

After Diotar said something to the person in the upper bunk, in Galatian, he slid down and started rummaging in the storage chest. While the man searched, Getorius rolled down the blanket, gagging at the stale smell of vomit, sweat, and urine. Kastor was nude. Small white slit-like scars dotted his torso, and a few of them had not healed and were festering. His lower abdomen was terribly inflamed.

"Will this do?" Diotar handed Getorius an empty, short-necked perfume flask.

"Fine. Help him sit up." After Kastor was positioned on the edge of the bunk, Getorius held the bottle to Kastor's flaccid penis, then sucked in a breath of horror. The man's scrotum was a shriveled sack of loose flesh, from which the testes had been removed. "This man's been castrated!" Getorius cried. "What's going on, Diotar?"

"Kastor bears the voluntary sign of Cybele's cult."

"Voluntary or not, castration is a criminal offense. Even on a slave, if that's what this man is."

"Not if performed outside Roman jurisdiction," Diotar replied smugly.

"*Roman* jurisdiction? I'm going on deck. Bring the urine to me." Getorius lurched out the door, shaken, and saw Arcadia standing at the nearby railing. "The sick man has been castrated," he told her, "probably also the other one in there. Some kind of perverse cult practice."

Arcadia pulled him away from the door. "That's the second castration we've encountered in a week."

"Atlos? His was suicide, or a revenge murder, not a ritual gelding. I want no part of this. Let his Cybele goddess heal Kastor."

"Getorius, remember your Oath. What were the man's symptoms?"

Getorius watched the dolphins for a moment before replying, "Vomiting, fever. There were scars on his body, probably from some kind of self-mutilation. The unhealed ones on his abdomen have—"

The cabin door opened. Adonis, his face again concealed by the hood, handed over the bottle and went back inside.

"Kastor's urine." Getorius held the specimen to the sky and saw a pinkish caste to the cloudy yellow liquid. "There's blood in it. His kidney humors are terribly out of balance."

Arcadia took the bottle and sniffed the contents. "Foul smelling. Hippocrates held that the kidneys attract urine."

"Any pig butcher could tell you that."

"Getorius, I know you're upset, but listen to me. Hippocrates also believed that veins were responsible for propelling the urine into the kidneys. An imbalance might cause blood to mingle with it."

"Possibly."

"What will you prescribe?"

"His abdomen was hot, distended, so Kastor's bladder must be in the same imbalance. Extended bed rest. I'll tell Diotar that his eunuch disciple can't go ashore."

"A purgative to expel the imbalance?" Arcadia suggested.

"It would help. Hot euphorbia juice poured over figs is a mild laxative. After that, watered white wine for the fever. Boiled barley meal to keep up Kastor's strength. A little fish, again boiled, when he feels better."

"Would weak hydromel be helpful?"

"Good, Arcadia. Honey-water should relieve his thirst and help the fever."

"I'll write out instructions for Diotar. The medications should be available in Olcinium."

"Thanks, *Cara*." Getorius moved his wife away from the cabins, toward the center of the railing. "Sorry I barked at you like that," he apologized, watching her empty the urine bottle through a scupper.

"What I saw made *me* sick. Diotar implied he could buy castrated slaves who were outside Ravenna's control. Could the counterfeit bronzes be his? A frontier slave trader might not notice the difference."

"Why would he hide them in the bales, when he has a cabin?"

"To avoid customs inspectors?"

"The wool belongs to Maximin," Arcadia recalled. "If either is involved with the coins, then, along with murder, Leudovald has a case of treason on his hands."

Getorius put an arm around her. On the distant shore the square gray outline of stone buildings in Olcinium began to separate themselves from their dull-green mountain backdrop. Gaudy fishing boats dotted the sea between the *Cybele* and port. He watched clumps of stringy seaweed float by a moment, then released Arcadia and turned her to him. "Treason?" he repeated, more as a comment than a question. "Looking back to where we slept the first night…the wool bales…you and I are quite literally in the middle of it."

"Very funny. Getorius, with all that's happened, I'd forgotten about Thecla. I'm worried about what Leudovald might do to her."

"Arcadia, the woman is over seventy years old. He may question her, but that's all." Getorius shaded his eyes and scanned the stony hills behind Olcinium. "Gaius told me that Diotar has a Cybelene temple outside the port. I may find out more about his cult there, and whether or not he's the one smuggling counterfeits into Dalmatia."

The early evening air was cooling rapidly. Arcadia nestled against her husband's warmth. "I…I'm a little apprehensive at being here, Getorius. The furthest I've ever traveled is Caesena in the Apennine foothills."

He hugged her shoulder in reassurance. "*Cara*, you'll be fine. Virilo will unload Maximin's cargo and take on his imports. Now, let's go below and decide on what to take ashore. I'm getting us a real bed to sleep in tonight."

"Thanks, Husband. I couldn't stand another hour in that hold. Because of the broken wine jars, it smells like the aftermath of a Bacchanalia."

As Getorius followed his wife down the ladder, he realized that he actually had no idea of what they might find in Olcinium. Or even when they would leave.

Chapter nine

The rays of a low afternoon sun washed the distant stone walls and houses of Olcinium with a golden hue, giving the Dalmatian port a gilded haze of undeserved magnificence.

Getorius held the leather traveling case and stood with Arcadia, watching Sigeric maneuver the *Cybele* between a maze of fishing boats that bobbed on the waves as the men returned to sell their day's catch at the wharf. Virilo climbed the platform and stood beside his helmsman when the galley neared the breakwater pier, a right-angle stone barrier that protected the harbor against seas rolling in from the northwest. Stonework on a five-story lighthouse at the pier's end was crumbling, and the eastern end of the harbor basin was silting up with sand deposited by both the Ionian Current and a river flowing a short distance beyond. To the left of the port, a loaf-shaped mountain rose abruptly from an expanse of sandy beach, then tapered down toward the river. Getorius estimated its summit to be about a mile high. Beyond the river, a lower hill, about a third as tall, began a gradual ascent to the east. A few miles behind the shoreline, the rugged mountains of southern Dalmatia rose as a guardian barrier for the crowded port town.

After Virilo ordered a tack into the wind to round the shorter angle of the breakwater, the *Cybele* slowly slipped into the calm waters of Olcinium's harbor.

"I was impressed at your handling of the pirates," Getorius called up to him. "Was it your idea to have a hidden ram?"

Virilo spit leeward of the deck, then looked down. "I had *Aurora...Cybele*...built at Classis for Maximin. She's slimmer than a merchant galley, length to beam. His wine and pepper cargos don't take up much room, and he wants speed."

"You said this was your first run-in with bandits?"

He nodded. "But if our fleet leaves Classis to blockade the Vandals in Carthage, they'll get bold as Bacchus's balls. The authorities here will cut a thumb off that helmsman, maybe squeeze out an eye, then let him go free so he can spread the word to the pirates to stay clear of this end of the coast."

The breakwater dock area was close enough now to pick out details of warehouse sheds and the buildings around them, melon-colored for another instant before the sun dropped below the horizon and the aura of golden light faded. Getorius could see that most of the homes and apartments were deteriorating and in need of repair.

"The port's seen better times," Virilo commented, as if reading his mind. "Epidamnus to the south gets most of the trade that's going to Macedonia." He eyed a signal pennant fluttering over the harbormaster's building on the pier. "We're cleared. Why doesn't that furcing Greek send out a boat to tow us to a berth?"

One other galley, a grain carrier with the Hellene name *Demeter,* was being unloaded at the nearest wharf. Two well-dressed customs officials supervised the slaves, one giving each man a token as he carried his sack of wheat into the warehouse, while the other recorded the tally in a ledger. Getorius saw a mosaic design on the harbormaster's building; twin eagles standing on a *fascis,* a bundle of rods enclosing an axe, with the name PREVALITANA underneath. One of the Imperial birds looked toward its left and the other to its right.

"Virilo. What's that emblem?"

"Jupiter's eagles watching east and west. We're in the province of Prevalitana, in the eastern lands of Theodosius at Constantinople. We crossed the boundary meridian half a watch period ago."

"The Eastern Empire?" Arcadia glanced at her husband. He understood—the counterfeit coins of a Western emperor were being smuggled into the East. If they were Maximin's, or Virilo's—even Diotar's—whom were the men planning to cheat? "How long will we be here?" she asked Virilo.

He gave a non-committal shrug. "We'll unload our wool and wine in the morning. I'm picking up pepper for Maximin, Macedonian wine, and some other cargo."

"What other cargo?"

Instead of answering, Virilo turned away to eye his position with respect to the wharf. "Furl mainsail," he shouted to the crew. "That furcing harbormaster must be off eating dinner. We'll anchor *Cybele* here in mid-harbor for the night."

"Virilo, my wife would like to sleep in a bed tonight," Getorius called up. "Is there an inn at Olcinium you could recommend?"

"The Emilianus, across from the church that has the saint's name. I'm staying on board, but the crew wants to scout the bazaar and *Lupanar*...and a few other places."

"Does Diotar stay at Emilianus?"

"His cult has a temple north of town, on the Via Scodrae." Virilo hesitated a moment, then asked, "Surgeon, why did you really stow away aboard my galley?"

"I told you. Leudovald suspects me in Atlos's death and I didn't want to submit to his questions. What did he ask you about?"

"The fishing knife he said he found, but he didn't show it to me."

"No, he'd first produce it at your trial. And I found a ritual sickle with the body, not a knife."

"Did you already know your daughter was pregnant?" Arcadia asked.

Virilo looked away. "Claudia lives in Diotar's half of my villa."

"I see. Getorius, before we go ashore you should look in on that sick man again."

"Right. I'll give Diotar the treatment you wrote out."

Getorius knocked on the cabin door, then held up the parchment note when Diotar opened it a crack. "This is what you must do for Kastor. How is he?"

The priest snatched the slip. "Much better, Surgeon."

"On no account must he go ashore."

Diotar glared at him and slammed the door shut.

⁂

The *Cybele* had towed a skiff in her wake during the voyage to Olcinium. When the crew pulled the small boat alongside, Virilo ordered that his two stowaways be rowed ashore with them.

On the wharf, Getorius guided Arcadia past warehouses and shipping offices with mosaic pavement designs that advertised the ports to which they sent cargo. At the marketplace beyond, stalls whose awnings covered crates of spring greens and last winter's vegetables were scattered among other booth vendors hawking fish, mussels, and squid. In open butcher shops along the main street that led north, flies and wasps buzzed around hanging links of sausage or sheep and pig carcasses skewered on hooks.

Arcadia noticed that the bakeshops sold the round loaves familiar to her, but also a thin flatter bread that she had not seen in Ravenna. Taverns and corner booths selling hot food were beginning to fill with supper customers. A few women in bright tunics and heavy make-up already lounged outside *Lupanarae*, the brothels that Virilo had presumably thought better not to mention. Many of the shop signs were in Greek, and the language was heard as often as Latin in the babble of conversation. Both tongues were harsh with the accents of local dialects.

Ravenna had its share of mixed Roman, Germanic, and Asiatic peoples, but Arcadia marveled at the polyglot makeup of the crowded street. Tall, blond barbarians from Gothic or Germanic tribes mingled with swarthy Macedonian Greeks and traders from Syria, Judea, Parthia—God only knew where. Even a few flattish oriental faces stood out, similar to those of the Army Commander's elite guard

124

at Ravenna; Hunnic deserters to the Eastern Empire who had no stomach for the wars of their kings, Bleda and Attila.

The shops and houses were made of the grayish local stone, most without a stucco finish, and only crumbling patches of the coating remained on those that once had been plastered. The grayness extended to the roofs, which were covered with flat slabs of slate, rather than the reddish terracotta tiles of Italic structures. The effect was drab, and one that would probably be echoed in the surrounding mountains once the green grass that sprouted from the winter rains had withered in the summer heat.

Just past the center of town the busy main street opened up into a small square. A temple stood at the north end. The green-stained letters on its bronze entablature still bore the original dedication to Mercurius, god of commerce, but a Christian cross had been mounted on top of the pediment.

"Would that be the church of Holy Emilianus?" Getorius wondered aloud.

"Reconsecrated from a pagan temple," Arcadia surmised.

A moment later he saw the name confirmed on the wall of a two-story building to his right. Flaking letters spelled out AD SCTI EMILIANI, above the crude painting of a beheaded legionary. An incongruous halo framed the gory head that was lying on the ground next to the body.

"I've never heard of that saint, but we know how he was martyred," Getorius remarked. "The inn that Virilo recommended doesn't look too hospitable, but I'd rather not wander around a strange town looking for another one. *Cara*, that's our home for tonight."

"Fine, as long as it doesn't pitch and yaw." Arcadia laughed. "I even feel like eating a full meal again."

The sound of applause from a crowd gathered at the temple stairs drew her attention back to the building. A troupe of actors was performing a scene from a drama. After listening for a moment, Arcadia said, "That's *The Pot of Gold* by Plautus. Let's watch—it's almost over."

The performers were dressed in shabby fur costumes evidently intended to represent barbarians. A scarred wooden board on the side lettered MOGONTIACVM GERMANIAE set the scene.

"Mogontiacum? That's where you were born," Arcadia said. "I don't understand."

"Nor I. Why set a Greek play in Germania? Let's go closer."

An old man in exaggerated white make-up, playing the part of the miser, Euclio, was speaking. "...or my feet. I can't even give orders in my own house now."

His neighbor, Megadorus, answered, "Cheer up, Euclio. We'll soon have good news for you. My nephew Lyconides is here."

A younger man came out from behind one of the portico columns, followed by his slave, a wrinkled, white-haired dwarf, who waddled onstage. A smattering of applause, and titters at the dwarf's exaggerated comic walk, greeted the two. Lyconides winked and showed the audience a clay jar that was half-concealed in his cloak.

Euclio frowned. "Your nephew is insolent and shameless. The last person in Mogontiacum I want to see."

"I can understand that, you old miser," Lyconides retorted. "But even if you don't want to look at me, you *will* want to see what I've brought."

Euclio turned his back. "I don't want to see, touch, hear, smell, and certainly not *taste* you."

After the bystanders finished hooting at the vulgar insinuation, Lyconides handed the jar to Megadorus. "Then my uncle must convince you to at least take a look."

"Yes," Megadorus agreed. "We have something that belongs to you."

"What is it?" Euclio asked, turning. "What do you have? Great Thunor! It's my jar of gold come back to me. Where did you find it?"

Megadorus beamed. "My nephew can tell you."

Euclio slipped an arm around Lyconides. "So, it's you I must thank for finding my treasure? Let me give you an *as,* no, half an *as* as a reward."

The spectators groaned at the miserly sum. One of them threw a cabbage that rolled toward the dwarf. "Ah, we eat tonight," the dwarf quipped, looking at the audience. "Perhaps a sausage, too. Anyone? Even a small sausage?"

"Y' already *got* a small sausage," someone in the audience shouted.

Lyconides waited for the laughter to end, then pointed to the dwarf. "The credit is also due to this old slave of mine. I rewarded him with his freedom."

"Your slave, you say? Come here, slave." Euclio handed him a sausage from the folds of his cloak. "Good fortune on your new freedom." As the dwarf toddled up to grab the link, Euclio bent down and peered at him. "Haven't I seen you before, slave...er...former slave? Didn't I catch you loitering around here?"

"Y...y...yes," he mumbled.

"And didn't I think you stole my jar?"

"You did? I mean you *did*, sir."

"But you hadn't touched it?" Euclio asked.

The dwarf took an exaggerated posture of defiance and squeaked. "No, I hadn't."

"And then you found it by chance somewhere else. On the banks of the Rhine, perhaps."

The dwarf winked at the audience. "No, but I...found...it by chance."

"And you thought it might be mine and gave it to your master?"

"I told my master."

Euclio smiled. "You asked him to return it to me?"

"Oh, no, he...," the dwarf began, but Lyconides glared at him and coughed a warning. "That is, *yes*, I asked him to return it to you."

Euclio turned to Megadorus. "By Thunor's Beard! How easy life would be if all Germani were this honest. Here, former slave. Another half *as* for you."

"Does this mean I have to give back the cabbage?" the dwarf whined.

Lyconides took his uncle aside. "Now's the time to ask Euclio about my marriage to Phaedria."

"A worthy idea. Well, Euclio, we're all happy that you have your gold back. But have you changed your mind about my nephew marrying your daughter?"

"Eh? What? Daughter? By all means, let them marry."

Lyconides waited for the hoots and applause to subside, then continued. "Thank you, sir. Your generosity is more than I can ever repay."

"First I must see that my gold is safely put away and…" Euclio stopped. "But what can I do with it? Oh, balls! You take it, Lyconides. Spend it on my daughter."

Megadorus grasped his sleeve. "My friend, how generous of you."

"Nothing of the sort," Euclio protested. "If that gold can do some good, I'd be the happiest man in the world, instead of the most miserable. I've not had a moment's peace with it on my mind. Now I'll be able to sleep again."

"There's a wise man," Megadorus cooed. "To be able to sleep, and be content in a cesspool like Mogontiacum, is worth more than ten jars of gold. Let's go in and celebrate the happiness of our two young lovers."

"Yes, yes, come in," Euclio urged. "I'll have my cook prepare a feast of bear meat, barley, and beer."

"Wait, uncle. Aren't you forgetting something?" Lyconides winked at the audience.

Megadorus looked puzzled, then turned to the crowd with a helpless gesture. "Ah, yes. We would gladly invite all our friends here, but what would be a barbarian feast for six would be poor fare for sixty. So, let us wish you better eating at home, and ask only your thanks in return."

The dwarf chuckled and held up the cabbage. "Your thanks in gold, that is."

He tucked his two bronzes and a slightly larger gold coin into the cabbage's top leaves, then waddled into the audience and held it out to them. Most turned away, but a few slipped small coins between the leaves.

Getorius watched a moment, and then pulled Arcadia by the hand toward the stairs. "I'm going to ask the old man if he's ever been in Mogontiacum."

Euclio began wiping make-up from his face. When he approached him, Getorius was startled to see that the actor's pale wrinkled complexion was not painted on, and his eyes had a pinkish cast. The man was not only old, but an albino.

After Getorius pressed a gold *tremissis* into Euclio's hand, the actor stared at it a moment, then looked up. "Very generous, sir," he said with a touch of suspicion in his voice. "You wish to hire us?"

"No, I wanted to ask you about Mogontiacum. Have you been there or is this just part of your play?"

"Why do you want to know?"

"I was born there. I wondered if you might have known my parents."

The albino looked surprised, but before he could answer, the dwarf returned, pulling the last coin out of a cabbage leaf. Arcadia noticed that he paused when he looked up at Getorius, as if he somehow recognized her husband.

"A *siliqua* of Theodosius," the dwarf squeaked, holding up the silver coin. "At least we eat this week, Albino."

"Pumilio, this man says he was born in Mogontiacum."

"Germania?" He studied Getorius. "How…how long ago?"

"About thirty years ago. I wondered if you were there at the time and perhaps knew my parents. Treverius and Blandina Asterius."

Albino wiped his neck and coughed nervously. "And…and now you live in Olcinium?"

"No, no, at Ravenna. I'm a physician. I was taken there by the garrison surgeon at Mogontiacum, after my parents were killed."

Albino suddenly began to tremble and sat down unsteadily on the top stair.

"As my husband said, he was an infant when Nicias brought him to Ravenna," Arcadia explained.

"He told me a little about my father," Getorius continued, "but there were some murders he and a Judean friend helped solve. I was curious."

"Murders?" Pumilio whined. "We know nothing about any murders, do we Albino?"

"Easy," Getorius soothed. "I'm not from a magistrate's office. Why did you set your play in Germania?"

"We…we get more laughs if we parody barbarians."

"Why perform on the church steps?" Arcadia asked. "Isn't there a theater here?"

Albino shook his head. "They've all been closed. We perform where we can. We were in Dyrrhachium last week."

"We'll move up the coast," Pumilio explained. "Risinium, Epidaurum, Spalato, and be in Aquileia by fall."

Getorius returned to his question. "Again, I know it's unlikely, but were you in Mogontiacum about thirty years ago, at the same time as my parents? Nicias said there was a theater in the city."

Albino looked away across the square, then replied in a voice so low that Getorius had to lean toward him to hear. "No. No. We were never in Germania. It's all make-believe. All acting."

"Too bad. Well, I wish you good fortune for the summer." Getorius took Arcadia's hand. "We're going over to the 'headless soldier' to rent a room for the night."

As Albino watched the couple cross to the inn, he wiped the last smudge of dark paint from around his eyes. It was slippery with a tear. "Pumilio," he commented hoarsely, "as sure as Clotho spins the thread of life, that was the son of Treverius Asterius."

"Yet you didn't tell him we knew his father."

"A sleeping wolf is not to be feared, Pumilio. Should we poor actors awaken one unnecessarily?" He tossed the towel at the dwarf. "Now give me those coins, you little turd. Tonight we eat at the Golden Stag."

⁊

Vidimir, the proprietor of the Emilianus, was a stocky man with a limp and a scar that ran the length of his right cheek. Getorius identified his accent as Gothic, guessing he might be one of Alaric's Visigoths who, years earlier, had devastated the area to the north. After the man was wounded, he had probably been left behind, but found his way to the coast and settled in Olcinium.

Because the summer trade routes were not yet fully open, Vidimir had rooms available. He showed Arcadia one she found acceptable. Supper, he told them, would be served at the beginning of the first evening watch.

Getorius used the interim time to change the bandage on Arcadia's forehead. He was pleased that the gash was healing cleanly. Arcadia told him that the bruise on his own cheek, from Tigris's blow, was now almost invisible.

The inn's cook prepared meals on a clay stove set at one end of the dining room. For the evening meal she offered a fish stew simmered in wine and seasoned with bay and pepper, or a second choice of grilled tuna served with a green sauce of anchovies, mustard and cucumbers. These were accompanied by flat bread, hard sheep's milk cheese, and a somewhat harsh local red wine.

Getorius tasted his tuna. "Quite good. Even that poor vintage won't spoil the meal. How's your stew?"

"Excellent." She held a spoonful towards him. "Try it."

"If you taste the tuna." He skewered a piece on his knife and handed it to her.

"Mmm. Nice tart sauce, too."

Getorius glanced around at the other diners. "I'd guess these are local merchants who risked mountain snows to be the first to ship Macedonian goods to the west."

"I noticed the two men at that corner table," she said. "They look a bit like Aetius's Huns."

Getorius looked around, then back at Arcadia. "But smaller and with more delicate features. The robes they're wearing look like the silk tunics from Constantinople that Galla Placidia owns. I wouldn't be surprised if the men came from Sina."

"Exciting! That's the eastern limit of Roman trade routes. I'd like to hear about their country."

"I doubt that they speak much Latin, but I wonder if they're involved in this extra cargo Virilo said he was picking up for Maximin."

"You think the senator is importing silk?"

"Probably not. Silk cloth goes to Constantinople and its importation is strictly controlled. Maximin's agents may have discovered some other exotic product."

Vidimir brought out a last course of honey-sweetened cheese, raisins, and dates. Getorius noticed the two Orientals leave immediately after finishing their meal. He winced at a last swallow of the harsh wine, then wiped his mouth on a napkin.

"It's still light out, Arcadia. Let's take a walk along the Via Scodrae and find this temple Virilo mentioned."

"Fine. I need to unlimber after being cramped up on that galley for four days."

Vidimir was carrying dishes into the scullery when Getorius went to pay for the meal. "How far along the Scodrae is the Cybelene cult temple?"

The proprietor eyed him suspiciously. "Why would you want to visit that den of eunuchs?"

"Eunuchs? We met someone on the galley named Diotar and—"

"Their archpriest. I know him."

"He mentioned a cult of *Magna Mater*."

"The Great Mother?" Vidimir scoffed. "She's called Kybele here. You don't look like part of that gang, yet you say you know Diotar?"

"We don't actually know him," Arcadia corrected. "He was travelling on the galley with us."

Vidimir spat on the tile floor. "He'll be at the slave market in the morning, looking for calves to geld."

Does the man's metaphor mean what I think it does? "Geld?" Getorius asked.

"The slavemaster's not neutering slaves anymore before they're sold. The priests might not like their looks and refuse to buy."

"Where exactly is this temple? We're going for a walk before bedtime."

"Stay on this road. Out beyond the Scodra Gate…big stone building on the right."

Getorius felt a rising outrage as he dropped an extra *half-siliqua* in the man's hand. "The porridge indeed thickens," he muttered to Arcadia as they started along the rising street that led to Olcinium's north gate. "The name Cybele is cropping up much too often."

"Virilo's galley and now this temple. Diotar said *Magna Mater* is another name for the goddess."

"And if Diotar is her archpriest, he must have a following we're not aware of in Ravenna."

Arcadia shuddered. "The emperor's steward is a eunuch, but to have a religious cult advocating castration is unthinkable. I wonder if Bishop Chrysologos knows of it?"

"He can't do much about what goes on in the port area."

When Getorius and Arcadia reached the Porta Scodrae, the sentries warned them that the gates would be closed at the second evening watch. They had about two hours until then, and less than another hour before full dark.

The road was lined with ancient mausolea and tombstones, many of the latter fallen over. Earthquakes in the past, Getorius thought. Most of the monuments were so badly weathered that the inscriptions could not be read, but fragments of the names LEGIO IV FLAVIA and XIII GEMINA recurred several times. The units had been stationed there before Emperor Aurelian abandoned the area.

The temple was further away than Getorius expected, almost two miles along the road, and situated on a low hill that overlooked a lake. By the time the dark shape of the twin-towered building appeared on the crest, a last reddish tint of sunset was coloring the western horizon.

The star Hesperus shone brightly in a pale greenish firmament, awaiting the rise of his companion moon. A low wall and residential building were visible in the twilight, but they were dominated by the ominous stone bulk of the main temple. An iron entrance gate was set beneath an arch in the wall, with the inscription, AEDES MAGNAE MATRIS, centered on the keystone.

"The Temple of the Great Mother," Getorius read, giving the gate a slight push. It creaked partway open. "Let's find out exactly who this goddess is, who wants to be served only by neutered priests."

Chapter ten

Six rusty hinges creaked in nerve-grating protest as Getorius pushed the gates open far enough to enter the sacred compound. Cybele's temple stood some seventy paces distant, along a stone walkway. It was different from any he had seen in Ravenna. Unlike the brick basilican churches there, or the surviving marble Roman temples, the sanctuary of the Great Mother was constructed of blocks of dark stone. On each side of the massive front, squat towers were pierced by small double windows and connected by a colonnaded gallery. Beneath this, the entrance portal was sheltered in an arched, deep-set porch reached by a flight of stairs.

Flickering torches on either side of the entry gave bizarre motion to a head of the goddess Cybele sculpted on the arch keystone. She wore a mantle and turreted headdress surrounded by the twelve signs of the Zodiac, symbols of her power over the visible universe. The deity's Phrygian name, ΚΥΒΗΛΗ, was chiseled in Greek letters underneath.

Arcadia peered at the woman's image in the dim light. "She looks amiable enough, like her figurehead on the galley. Do you suppose only cult members are allowed in the temple?"

"There's one way to find out." Getorius led the way up seven steps and into the porch entranceway. "These wooden doors look like they might have replaced ones of bronze. See the massive size of those hinges?"

When he pulled on an iron ring, one of the twin portals slowly swung forward. Arcadia followed him through the opening. Inside, the nave was chilly, a dim, gloomy space that still retained its winter cold and smelled of stale ceremonial incense. Square stone piers supported the upper walls and defined shallow side aisles, which were curtained with heavy draperies. Three oil lamps hanging from a center ceiling beam gave the space a dingy light. At the far end, another lamp in the apse threw feeble rays on the statue of a seated figure. No one seemed to be in the temple, but the sound of drums, cymbals, and high-pitched reed pipes could be heard through window openings behind the image.

"That statue must be of *Magna Mater,* or Cybele, or whomever she's called," Getorius whispered. "Let's take a closer look."

As they approached they could see that the figure was of a woman, shown in frontal pose with her feet resting on a stool. Jars, pitchers, and baskets of offerings—oil, wine, and grain—surrounded the base of the statue. A relief carving on this platform depicted a youth wearing a floppy Phrygian cap and shepherd's cloak. He lay beneath a pine tree, his right hand clutching his genitals, and his left a shepherd's crook.

"Who is that supposed to represent?" Getorius bent to examine the sculpted details.

Arcadia looked up at the statue's head, then cried out in a shocked voice, "Mother of God! Look, Getorius!"

"What is it?" He stood and followed her gaze. Instead of the benign features that were on the face of the sculpture over the entrance, those of this statue were blank; the rough, pitted surface of a dark-brown triangular stone. "Wh…what kind of…of joke is this?" he stammered. "Now I see why Sigeric called Cybele a Stygian goddess—"

"Neither a jest, Surgeon, nor a goddess from the Underworld." Diotar's womanish voice echoed from behind one of the pilasters.

The priest stepped out of the shadows, silver bracelets on his arms jingling musically as he came forward. He was dressed in a pink robe elaborately decorated with a golden leaf pattern. A serpentine gorget in gold circled his throat. His headdress depicted Cybele flanked by two men in Phrygian caps, like that of the man on the footstool sculpture. Heavily made up as he was with cosmetics, anyone who had not seen Diotar before would have mistaken the eunuch for a woman. "The stone is a gift of the Great Mother from the Cosmos," he continued. "From heaven itself."

"Gift of the Cosmos?" Getorius scoffed. "What *is* that…that grotesque face?"

"Our cult tradition," Diotar explained, "tells of a sacred stone… an aerolith…that fell from the sky before Cybele went to save Rome from her Carthaginian invaders."

"A meteorite?" Getorius half-laughed. "This is pure idol worship."

"Yet, Surgeon," Diotar taunted, "you Christians also worship a symbolic Christ. Bread, wine, water."

"But not a black stone."

"And like your own priests," he went on, "I offer baptism, but one of blood." Diotar pointed to the right of the statue. "Over there, stairs lead to a pit covered by a marble slab pierced with holes. Our initiates enter the Cribolium, where they are purified by the blood of a ram sacrificed above them. One of your own mystics, John, had a vision of men washed in the blood of a lamb."

"It's not meant literally."

"Who is the person on the footstool?" Arcadia asked, suppressing her revulsion.

"The foolish, yet deified, Attis. He betrayed Cybele's love for him by coupling with a wood nymph, then castrated himself in remorse."

"And so your priests imitate his example? How…how horrible."

"Woman," Diotar retorted, "the Great Mother resurrected him. Augustine, one of your own bishops, declared that man through his nature is forever damned by sexual desire."

"Augustine recommended continence, not castration," Getorius reminded him.

"A half measure," Diotar sneered, then turned toward the window. "The music outside has stopped. Our 'Day of Blood' is celebrated in March, at the spring equinox, but I was unable to come then. As ArchGallus—"

"ArchGallus?" Vidimir had called him an archpriest.

"Our priests are called Galli."

"Cocks?" *How ironically inappropriate*, Getorius thought, suppressing an impulse to laugh.

"Galli," Diotar went on, "not from the Latin word, or its vulgarism. The Gallus is a sacred river near Pessinus. But I hear that the dance has ended. Come witness our fertility ritual. One of your poets even immortalized it." In a swish of expensive fabric and perfume, Diotar started toward a door at the left side of the apse.

Getorius hesitated, wondering what further repellent surprises were ahead, but then considered that he had in fact come to find out more about the cult of the Great Mother.

"Surgeon," Diotar called back, "few are privileged to actually experience what your poet only read about."

"My wife?"

"The woman may watch."

"Lead the way, then."

Arcadia came alongside her husband. "Do you remember which poet he was talking about?"

"No. My tutor evidently didn't cover that arcane an aspect of my education."

The door opened onto a walled garden, where smoky, pine-pitch torches gave light to a field of trampled grass. Black earth at one end was mounded into a low hillock and planted with young evergreens, to resemble a miniature mountain. The tallest pine at the near edge was draped with purple cloth. A group of spectators stood to one side of the mound; the people who had brought the offerings, Getorius assumed. Directly ahead, at the back wall, a booth covered with pine boughs displayed a smaller statue of Cybele, but this image bore the benign aspect of the goddess. Two priests dressed in a manner similar to Diotar flanked the shrine, holding silver bowls. To their right, water gushed into a basin from the mouth of a leering stone face, identified as that of a river god by the wreath of marsh reeds in his flowing hair.

"That's probably a personification of this Gallus River that Diotar mentioned," Getorius muttered.

On the other side of Cybele's shrine, sat a woman wearing a full white tunic and a mantle that hid her face. She was holding the tether of a white ram.

"Could that be Claudia?" Arcadia whispered.

"We didn't see her on the galley, but she could have been in Virilo's cabin."

Several young men and women wearing short white tunics stood near the fountain, still catching their breath after the dance. Some of the women had small hand cymbals, and the men held round drums.

As Diotar approached the Cybelene shrine, a youth and girl, who had been waiting at the edge of the pine trees, walked out to the center of the grassy area. The youth, whom Getorius thought looked somewhat familiar, wore the same soft cap as the Attis figure on the footstool of the temple statue, and also held a shepherd's crook and set of pan pipes. He was dressed in tight-fitting trousers that were buttoned down the legs, but with the front left open to uncover his lower abdomen, to make it evident that his genitals were not mutilated. The girl wore a forest nymph's short tunic made of a transparent material, which even by the wavering torchlight revealed her small breasts and dark pubic triangle.

Diotar motioned for Getorius and Arcadia to stand by the fountain, then stood in front of the statue and raised his hands. "*Magna Mater*, both mother and consort of Attis," he intoned, "your son will not consummate his love for you, nor you for him, thus he offers you his blood. May it seep into the earth and revive its dead vegetation, even as we hope to be reborn, like Attis, and ascend with him into the sky until the coming of the new world cycle that will follow our Atlantis.

"Grant your Galli the courage to release themselves from worldly pleasures and thus rise to you in spiritual ecstasy."

After the two priests scooped water from the fountain into their bowls and passed it around for the dancers to drink, the young man began playing the high-pitched notes of a melody on his panpipes. Getorius recognized the shrill Phrygian mode of music, recalling his tutor had said that the emotional frenzy the instrument evoked had been used in pagan religious rites. The youth's female companion began to sway around him in a teasing, erotic dance. The other women imitated her, softly tinkling their cymbals in time with her steps. One added the piercing notes of a twin-reed aulos. The men joined in by tapping the hide on their drums. Swaying in cadence with the rhythm, the group began to sing.

> Dance on Cybele's ground, where the cymbals tinkle.
> Dance where the drums thump, and the pipes shrill.
> Where Maenads wildly toss ivy-crowned heads,
> And robins flit restlessly above the thicket.
> Where the holy scream signals the emasculating rite.

It was soon obvious from his erection that the youth was responding to the nymph's teasing movements. He joined in the dance with her for a time, then threw down the pipes with a cry of passion and pulled the girl into the shadows of the pine trees.

The aulos player stopped. Other women slowed the rhythm of their dance and lowered their voices so the sound of the couple's lovemaking could be heard. In moments a climactic gasp was followed by an interval of silence, which was timed to a repetition of the last verse of the song.

"And the holy scream signals the emasculating rite."

After a rending shriek sounded from the pine grove, the youth staggered out of the darkness. His left hand clutched his bleeding scrotum, and the other held a red-stained golden sickle. He threw something down, looked around in a daze, then collapsed beneath the pine tree.

"Christ," Getorius blurted, "that's what Diotar implied! The boy has ritually castrated himself!" He started over to help the youth, but the male drummers blocked his way, their eyes fixed in an ecstatic trance. "I'm a physician," he told the closest one. "Let me examine him."

"Surgeon, I wouldn't interfere," Diotar called out in warning. "The hypnotic waters of the Gallus River have 'trapped them in a snarl of frenzy,' as your poet put it. They'll offer you an unwelcome gift of chastity with that sickle."

"Getorius, come back!" Arcadia screamed.

He retreated and put an arm around her, watching, helpless, as the mutilated youth writhed on the ground.

Getorius became aware that the chirping of night insects had suddenly stopped. Watchdogs somewhere in the residential compound began to bark. Other dogs in the night blackness beyond the temple took up their yelping. The ram bleated in panic, then began to struggle at its tether.

"What's happening, Getorius?" Arcadia asked, puzzled.

"I...I don't know. This satanic ritual..." His voice trailed off as he glanced around. The woman holding the ram's leash dropped it, stood up from the chair and tried to tear off her head covering, as if she had trouble breathing.

Arcadia saw there was something familiar about her movements, then the shawl fell back to reveal the girl's face. "It *is* Claudia Quinta! Getorius, she's about to have another epileptic seizure."

Getorius ran to help the girl. He had just loosened the shawl around her neck when a roar, louder than any he had heard before, came from beyond the wall. It was a deafening sound he could only compare to the din that a thousand farm wagons might make, rumbling along the rough paving of the Via Honorius in Ravenna.

Arcadia, kneeling alongside him, stood and looked up at the dark mountains beyond the wall. Then the roar became louder and the ground rolled beneath her feet. She lost her balance and fell. Claudia's body arched with the sickening motion, stiffened and lay still.

"My God, we...we're in...an earthquake!" Getorius shouted, finally realizing what was taking place.

One of the woman dancers screamed, then cried out the name of Gallus and pointed to the fountain. The river god's mouth spewed a stream of mud that oozed down to cloud the clear water. As the wall behind the head rippled and cracked, the stone basin fractured, spilling its contents onto the flattened grass. Cybele's shrine collapsed onto her cult image in a tangle of support poles and pine branches.

The ram, now released, darted onto the wooded mountain to butt at the trees in frantic terror.

"Everyone get away from the temple!" Getorius yelled, seeing a thick cloud of black dust roll out of the building's apse door and into the garden. "Part of the ceiling must have collapsed."

Despite his warning, the two priests, with several men and women, ran coughing through the doorway, and into the building. Getorius was aware of someone dropping beside him.

"How is she?" a youth asked. "How is Claudia?"

Getorius looked up into Atlos's—or his ghost's—concerned expression. "Atlos? H…how did you—?"

"He was my brother," Adonis snapped. "Will Claudia be all right?"

"Your brother?" Getorius realized this was the man he had seen dancing with the girl. "I don't understand…you…you just castrated yourself."

"Never mind that. What about Claudia?"

"She's had an epileptic attack. We've got to get her…everyone…into open space, away from the temple. Weren't you on the galley? Who *are* you?"

"I'm called Adonis."

"Take her feet." Getorius was on one knee, supporting Claudia's shoulders, and Adonis was ready to lift her legs, when the second shockwave shook the earth.

As the ground buckled in another series of nauseating ripples, a crack split the temple apse masonry. Roof tiles slid to the ground in a crash of dust and broken slate shards. The statue of Cybele inside was heard toppling to the floor, smashing the marble around her meteorite face. Through the settling dust, orange light appeared at window openings. The lamps had spilled their flaming fuel onto the floor paving, where it oozed, burning, into the side aisles and ignited the draperies. Offerings of olive oil, spreading from broken jars, caught the blaze.

Diotar stood clutching a pole from the goddess's shrine, immobilized by fear. Arcadia grabbed him by the sleeve. "My husband wants everyone out the front gate. If the temple collapses we'll be trapped in this yard."

Getorius pushed Adonis aside, then scooped Claudia up in his arms and followed his wife around the side of the temple. He stumbled on the uneven ground, but had reached the center of the buckled stones on the front pathway when the front nave piers and right-hand tower gave way in a deadly shower of mortar bits and blocks of ashlar. After the sickening sound of the impact, a momentary silence was broken by the muffled screams of cult members trapped inside the temple and the coughing of those fortunate ones who had managed to stagger out the front entrance. They were still only black silhouettes against the light of the flaming interior when a third, less intense, tremor hit.

Arcadia, outside the wall gate, screamed as she saw Getorius fall under Claudia's weight on the shattered paving. He staggered up again and ran with the girl. The warped gate hinges shrieked like a malevolent daemon when he pushed through them. Once outside the wall, he ran across the roadway to lay the girl in an open field beyond. Arcadia raced after him.

Panting, Getorius sucked in gulps of dusty air as he watched the shattered, burning temple in horrified fascination. Three of the women dancers shoved through the gate, just before the arch above it collapsed and the smashed letters of the Great Mother's name were strewn among the rubble of her temple entrance.

Getorius turned to Arcadia, sitting next to him as she cradled Claudia's head in her lap. "Where's Atlos, or, rather, this Adonis? Did he escape?"

"Atlos? Adonis? What are you talking about?"

"You didn't see him? Atlos, or his shade, came from Avernus to ask about Claudia."

"Getorius, this has been a horrifying experience—"

"I'm not insane, woman, I know who I saw." He noticed Diotar a few paces away. The ArchGallus had recovered and was evidently trying to rationalize the destruction of Cybele's temple to the surviving spectators and his followers. Atlos-Adonis was not with him. Getorius looked along the road and saw a glow to the south. "The earthquake must have set fires in Olcinium. We should take Claudia to the galley…if it's still afloat…and see if we can help with anyone who's injured in the port."

Diotar detached himself from the group and came to where Claudia lay. The light from the flames gave his sagging face an uncharacteristic ruddy glow, and his powdered, rouged cheeks were smudged with dirt.

Getorius faced him in anger. "It's criminal to use the girl's epilepsia to promote your cult."

"I believe Claudia's illness is a sacred one. Even your Christian priests believe daemons are responsible for sickness."

"I'm not a theologian. Some may teach that, but all the illnesses I've seen have a physical cause."

Arcadia heard Claudia moan as she stirred into consciousness and looked slowly around. "You're safe, child," she murmured to reassure the girl. "Do you remember me? I examined you in the clinic a few days ago."

Claudia did not respond. Getorius looked past Diotar to the orange light in the sky over Olcinium. Heavy smoke was visible now, drifting in from the port. How much harm had been done to the buildings? Perhaps the harbor and Virilo's galley were damaged, even destroyed.

"Surgeon, I'll take charge of Claudia," Diotar said, bending to pull the girl up by the hand.

"We should take her back to her father."

Diotar ignored Getorius. "Come, girl," he ordered. "We'll see if your room in the temple annex is undamaged."

"It's too dangerous," Arcadia protested. "You can't take her in there."

"We'll deal with our injured," Diotar snarled, as Claudia slowly stood up. "Disciples of Cybele," he called to the others, "follow me to the annex."

Getorius watched the group walk around the remains of the wall, toward the low buildings at the right of the burning temple ruins. "I still don't see this Adonis. I pushed him aside when I picked up Claudia and ran with her. Was he killed by falling roof tiles when the tower collapsed?"

"Adonis? Getorius, you babbled something about seeing Atlos."

"It wasn't babble. He *was* there."

"It was dark, confused."

"Arcadia. Either he, his ghost, or his twin, knelt down to ask me about Claudia."

"His *twin?*" Arcadia echoed. "Wasn't the sick youth on the galley named Kastor? Like Castor and Pollux in Roman mythology. When one of the brothers was killed, the other begged Jupiter to be allowed to share immortality with him."

"Resurrection and immortality…like Attis." Getorius smacked a fist into his palm. "Of course! That slave collar around Atlos's neck said 'Didymos.' I thought it was a family name, but now I remember that it means 'twin' in Greek. That wasn't Kastor I saw, Arcadia, but I smell a hoax, a conspiracy to deceive the gullible. It would have to happen at a big event, where Diotar could recruit converts. One twin publicly castrates himself, then the brother appears, unmutilated and 'resurrected.'"

"But Atlos killed himself, or was murdered."

"True, Arcadia, undoubtedly upsetting the plan. But Diotar is shrewd. If that youth who pretended to castrate himself under the pine tree *is* the Adonis who asked me about Claudia, he's no eunuch."

"We both saw the testes he threw on the ground."

"Probably some organ from another ram, and the blood too. Kastor may once have been the unlucky twin in a previous ritual."

"To think this could be going on in Ravenna." Arcadia winced. "Getorius, what kind of people are these?"

"Pagan fanatics, far more dangerous than the Isis priests we saw last month." He looked toward Olcinium again. "We'd better get down to the port. If Cybele allowed her stone sanctuary to be destroyed, perhaps the goddess was as careless with the wooden galley that's named after her."

"Now you're thinking like a pagan."

"To understand Diotar. Yet even Christ pointed out the inexplicable mystery of God allowing rain to fall equally on the just and unjust."

"You mean Christians who might have been killed in the port, along with pagans here?"

He nodded. "How many of the people we treat still use magic amulets as protection?"

With a final glance at the burning hulk of the Great Mother's temple, Getorius took Arcadia's arm and guided her onto the road, toward the light in the sky that mimicked a reversed sunrise. Somewhere in the distance a rooster, deceived by the false dawn, crowed a faint, pitiful "*ehr er-er ehrrrr.*"

Chapter eleven

Nearing Olcinium, Getorius and Arcadia encountered groups of panicked citizens fleeing to the open fields north of the port. Some brought bundles of salvaged clothing, others carried articles of furniture, even terrified household pets—whimpering puppies or frightened birds in wooden cages.

Closer in, they saw that a wall section north of the Scodrae Gate had been thrown down by the earth tremors. Water leaking from a nearby aqueduct was rapidly turning the road and fields into an impassable marsh, and was threatening to run down and flood the main street that led back into the port.

Holding Arcadia's hand while wading through the icy water, Getorius guessed that the earthquake had moved in a southwesterly direction and had caused the most damage in this northern quadrant of Olcinium.

No guards were at the gate, whose massive twin portals hung dangerously by only their upper hinges. In places along the street beyond, chunks of roofing slate, fallen cornice blocks, and stone rubble almost blocked the narrow sidewalks. Many of the buildings' door and window lintels were cracked, and ceilings in several lower-level shops had collapsed into the rooms. The smell of wine from smashed storage barrels issued from the smoking ruins of a tavern identified as "The Golden Stag" by a wood sign dangling over its damaged entrance.

Getorius glanced in at the rubble, but saw no bodies. "Anyone injured has probably been taken to some open space, like the temple square."

Smoke swirled from nearby structures where fires still smoldered. The earth tremors had struck at a late hour, after lamps and the glowing charcoal in most of the cooking stoves would have been put out or banked for the night, minimizing the danger from burning oil and coals. Even so, one of the apartment blocks on a side street was on fire, and the low water pressure in the street fountains caused by the leaking aqueduct was hampering efforts to control the flames.

After picking his way through the rubble and being roughly jostled by citizens hurrying in the opposite direction, Getorius reached the temple church with Arcadia. The portico had collapsed, sending its marble columns and ceiling tumbling down onto the stairs. Only a few hours earlier they and more than fifty citizens had been watching the actors' drama. Arcadia murmured a prayer to Cosmas, the patron of surgeons, since she did not know enough about the headless Saint Emilianus to thank him.

Members of the civic watch were laying the dead out on the side of the square nearest the inn. A few men, whom Getorius assumed were surgeons and presbyters, were treating or comforting the wounded.

"Shall we help them?" Arcadia asked her husband.

He looked across at the Emilianus. "It seems that the inn was damaged. Since surgeons have this area covered, let's find out if anyone was hurt at Vidimir's."

He led the way across the square, skirting his way through crowds of injured citizens and their helpers. Arcadia paused at the row of dead on the far edge of the square.

"Wait, Getorius." Arcadia noticed a body that was the size of a child's, then recognized Pumilio. "It…it's the dwarf we saw in the play."

"Sad. I wonder if his albino companion or any of the other actors survived?"

Getorius noticed Vidimir standing near his front entrance, staring at the damage to his inn. Smoke was curling from the first level. "I'm afraid we can't wait to find out. Let's see what happened to the Emilianus." He crossed the street and called to the innkeeper. "Was anyone hurt?"

Vidimir rubbed numbly at his old scar, still visibly stunned by the damage. "Most of th…the other men were visiting *Lupanarae*, but one of the two Orientals was killed."

Ironic, Getorius thought, that men fornicating in the brothel were saved. "What about the other one? Is he injured?"

He shook his head. "A child of Fortuna. He was downstairs checking on the wooden crates he brought with him. She smiled on you, too, Surgeon, when you decided to go to that temple. The ceiling of your room fell in."

"That smoke?"

"Charcoal from the kitchen stove."

"Had the Orientals spoken Latin to you?" Getorius asked.

"The one who survived did…but not too good. He was translating for the other."

"Do you know anything about him?"

Vidimir looked away to the crowded square. "I just rent rooms, Surgeon."

Getorius chose a gold *tremissis* from his belt purse and pressed it into the innkeeper's grimy hand. "This will help pay for the damage to our room."

Vidimir palmed the coin and cleared his throat. "Come to think of it, he was asking about a galley called the *Cybele*. When she'd arrive."

"We came in on the *Cybele*."

"Then he and his crates will be going back with you."

"Crates? Do you know what's in them?"

"The two big ones are heavy." Vidimir glanced around, then leaned close. "Probably smuggling in some of that shiny fabric."

"Silk?"

"That's it, for some rich landowner in Ravenna. Customs officers here are more open-palmed than hawk-eyed."

Getorius realized it made sense. He had heard from a patient that at Ravenna the usual two or three percent import duty had recently been increased to pay for Valentinian's new walls. If the port of embarkation tariff at Olcinium was less, even with paying bribes, a profit could still be made on expensive commodities. That must be the reason Maximin shipped his pepper from this isolated port, rather than larger ones like Dyrrhachium or Salonae.

Getorius looked back at Arcadia. "Where can my wife and I stay tonight?"

"Outdoors." Vidimir pointed to the open square. It was filling with people, mothers with whimpering children, others carrying swaddled infants, or men bringing straw mattresses, blankets, and a few salvaged possessions. "Everyone who's stayed in Olcinium will sleep outside tonight. If that earth daemon comes back, they don't want a wall falling in on them."

"Our travel case?"

"Pulled it out of the rubble. I'll get you blankets."

⁂

Getorius and Arcadia spent part of the night helping the injured, then, exhausted, slept for about three hours on the stone paving. By morning the fires were out, and the city prefect sent council members to assess damage and begin relief measures. The main street to the wharves was wet, but not flooded—evidently the aqueduct had been diverted or repaired. By the time the morning sun had cleared the rugged summits to the east, Getorius and Arcadia had reached the docking area.

Waves generated by the quake had moved lengthwise across the harbor, allowing most of the galleys and fishing boats at anchor to ride the crest of the swells. A few had been hit broadside and capsized, but the *Cybele* was undamaged, and now tied up at a dock. The air smelled of smoke, musty earth, and the raw sewage that seeped out from ruptured pipelines. Toward the sea, a sickly ochre haze of pulverized dust, slowly settling back to earth, screened the horizon.

Some damage had occurred at the north end of the warehouses, breaking or cracking many of the clay amphorae stored there, but most of the harbor buildings and merchandise in them had escaped serious harm.

At the *Cybele,* a gang of port slaves was carrying her cargo of wine, oil, and pepper amphorae aboard. Getorius saw the bales of wool that the galley had brought being stacked in a warehouse, and was puzzled by the fact that a customs official was ordering them sorted into two different piles.

"I wonder who gets the counterfeit coins, and what they're really for?" he muttered to Arcadia. "A half-blind merchant could tell they aren't genuine."

"But someone illiterate might not."

Her remark surprised him. "What are you getting at, Arcadia?"

"How far north are the Danube River frontier garrisons?"

"I...I'm not sure. Why?"

"Could someone be planning to pay legionaries with them? Almost all of them are barbarians."

"Unlikely. This is Theodosius's territory, remember?"

"To Goths, one emperor's portrait looks like another's," Arcadia pointed out, "and the inscription would be so many bird tracks to them."

"You've really thought about this, haven't you? I...I'd like to be impressed with your theory, Arcadia, but a few of their officers can read, you know."

"Exactly, Getorius. And will report back to Constantinople that hundreds, perhaps thousands, of worthless silvered 'Valentinians' are flooding the Eastern provinces."

"Now I *am* impressed with your theory. That would destabilize the currency, the economy, of the entire area. Legionaries largely are paid in local goods. Those could be difficult to trade for other things they want, so the coins would be welcome." Getorius thought a moment. "The bronzes would have to be silvered somewhere near here. I wonder if there's an imperial mint close by? Perhaps in Scodra, the provincial capital."

"If so, the governor probably would be involved."

"Christ! This could lead to legion rebellions, or even civil war between the empires. But…no, Arcadia. Valentinian is Theodosius's cousin and married to his daughter. Why would he foment a war with the Eastern emperor?"

"It doesn't have to be the Augustus, does it? Someone else who would benefit from the turmoil could be responsible."

"Someone with ambitions like that abbot who came to Ravenna… Wait, look. There's the Oriental we saw at dinner."

The man was at the second gangplank, helping supervise some slaves who were trying to maneuver six wooden crates on board. Two of the boxes were flat, about a half cubit deep by two and a half cubits wide on top, and obviously heavy. The other four were smaller, encased in thick quilted jackets. All were sizes that could fit on the flanks of pack mules. The Oriental seemed especially concerned about the four padded crates, lapsing from broken Latin into excited sing-song orders in his native tongue.

"Those red angular markings on the sides must be writing in the Sinese language," Getorius guessed. "You know, the flat crates look too heavy to contain silk, and all of them are too large to be smuggled in, as Vidimir thought. Let's go aboard. I want to talk to Virilo about Claudia, and I'd like to get to know our new passenger."

On deck Virilo admitted to Getorius that Diotar had brought his daughter back during the night, and she was in a cabin. With the excuse that he was too busy loading cargo and wanted to push off into the open sea, he refused to discuss Claudia further.

The Oriental directed the slaves in lashing the crates securely below deck, then came back up and went inside Virilo's cabin.

"So much for talking to him. I wonder if Diotar and the twin came back during the night?"

"Or Kastor. I'm sure Diotar took him ashore, despite being told not to do so." Arcadia pulled her husband toward the hatch. "Before we leave, I want you to hang a sheet or something between us and the crew. I need better privacy on the voyage back."

With the bales of wool gone there was more space available in the hold. The slanting wooden racks built between the hull ribs that had held wine amphorae were now loaded with smaller clay jars filled with pepper. Each bore Maximin's lead seal. Other racks on the lower deck propped up amphorae of sweet Macedonian wine or Thessalonian olive oil. The pervasive and unpleasant smell of bitumen caulking was nicely tempered now by the spicy odor of the pepper and the fruity scent of the sweetened vintage.

Getorius paid Victor and Gaius to partition off a small area for Arcadia with a spare sail. While working, the two men gossiped to him that the "*Orientalis,*" as they called their new passenger, would be quartered in Virilo's cabin. The man had to be important to merit sharing the galleymaster's berth.

⁊⋲

After the partition was finished, Arcadia admired her new enclosed space. "Thanks for the bit of privacy, Husband," she said, hugging Getorius. "I hope I don't get as seasick this time."

He squeezed her closer. "Not private enough, though," he whispered. "We haven't made love in…in half a month."

Arcadia laughed and pushed him away. "You satyr. We'll be home shortly." She sat down on her cot. "Seriously, Getorius, I'm looking forward to sea air clearing my mind of what we saw in that horrible temple."

"And what the quake did to Olcinium. When we left, didn't I foolishly say something about this being a vacation?"

"What causes those tremors, Getorius?"

"Aristotle thought that underground hot air and gases trying to escape to the earth's surface were responsible."

"I didn't notice any hot springs near that temple. Which reminds me. *I need a bath!*"

"You smell good to me, *Cara.*"

"Another of your Celtic lies, but thanks anyway. And I mean in a bathtub, so I can relax."

"It will still be a few days before you can do that. I'd suggest a swim, but the earthquake muddied the harbor and brought up

153

Neptune-knows-what from the bottom. Did you see that slime float-ing on the surface?"

She puckered her nose. "I did, and it smelled as bad as it looked." Arcadia thought of the arrowhead scars on the galley's hull and kitchen. "Hopefully, we won't have to worry about those pirates on the return voyage."

※

Virilo told his crew that he wanted to reach open sea before further earth tremors endangered the galley in the enclosed harbor. Also, the strong summer Etesians soon would blow from the north. Unless other winds shifted in from the southwest, the return voyage would take longer, even though *Cybele* would pick up the Ionian Current that flowed north through the strait between Italy's eastern tip and the Greek mainland.

※

By early afternoon, the last of the cargo, food, and freshwater casks had been secured. Virilo ordered his galley rowed out past the breakwater, into the rolling swells of the Adriatic.

A mile offshore, Sigeric easily found the sea current by follow-ing a stream of mud and seaweed that the quake had shaken loose. No dolphins came to crisscross the bow after he steered the *Cybele* into a trail of yellow-gray water that soiled the azure sea around it—the sea creatures had fled to cleaner haunts.

The breeze held from the northwest, forcing the crew to tack against the wind. Once the galley began to pitch into the swells Arcadia felt nauseous again, but was grateful that she would at least be able to be sick in relative privacy.

※

The next morning Getorius was on deck, watching the diminishing trail of mud and floating weeds in the sea, when the door to Virilo's cabin was pushed open. The Oriental lurched out to the rail and faced the wind. He looked pale as he hung his head out over the side, but he did not vomit. Getorius waited awhile, then decided to open a conversation. "Not much you can do, it's the motion." He demonstrated with a rocking movement of his hand and wondered if the man had understood.

He looked up and replied in a weak voice, "I take clovus."

"Clove oil? Good."

Since being appointed to the palace, Getorius had gained access to the expensive spice that was shaped like miniature griffin feet. He had prescribed it to Galla Placidia for an upset stomach. If the man had come from the east, it was logical he would have the remedy.

The Oriental's face was similar to that of a Hun's, yet smaller-boned and with more delicate features.

"My name is Getorius Asterius," he said, extending his hand.

"As-t'us?" The man looked at the open palm. Westerners grasped each other's hand or forearm when they met, but he only bowed slightly. "Greetings…As-t'us. I Zhang Chen."

"Chen. Good, we can communicate. Where are you from, Chen?"

Chen glanced at the sun and pointed to the east.

"From Sina?"

"As you in West call my home."

"Yes, Rome has trade routes there. You have another name for your country?"

"Sina is good name, As-t'us."

Getorius wanted to correct his pronunciation, but decided not to confuse Chen. "Are you staying in Ravenna?"

"Yes, Rav'enn. Where Val-tan is emperor god."

"Val-tan? Ah, *Valentinian.*" Getorius chuckled. "But the Augustus isn't exactly a god. He—"

Getorius heard another cabin door open and turned to see Virilo step out. The galleymaster glanced at him and Chen, then started toward the bow.

"Excuse me, Chen…" Getorius caught up with Virilo. "How is Claudia today?"

"She's well. Needs to be home."

"Can I do anything for her?"

"Nothing, Surgeon."

"Call me if she has another attack."

Virilo grunted and brushed past to inspect the ram winch. When Getorius turned back, Zhang Chen was no longer standing at the rail.

❧

That evening the sea rose in broad swells that rolled in from the south, and the wind smelled of rain. Sigeric predicted a storm later that night.

Getorius ate a little of the tuna that Maranatha cooked for supper, then went below. The long twilight showing through the open hatch gave a soft glow to the hold.

"*Cara,* how are you feeling?" he asked his wife. "Is that head gash bothering you?"

"No, and I'm getting a little more used to the galley's motion."

"Perhaps I can get some clove oil from Chen."

"Chen is the Oriental's name?" At Getorius's nod, she asked, "Did he tell you what was in his crates?"

"I didn't ask him."

"You thought they looked too heavy to contain silk cloth."

"Yes, but I have no idea what could be inside. It must be the extra cargo Virilo said he was picking up for Senator Maximin."

"Getorius, are you worried about going back to Ravenna?"

"A little. After what happened last December I'm not looking forward to Leudovald's questions. Back then it would have been my word against those deacons who accused me of dissecting a body, which would have been buried before the trial. My scalpel would be presented as evidence against me. Court cases are usually won by the best orators, and I didn't know any lawyers."

"We couldn't have stayed in Olcinium."

"I know." He lay down on his cot and laid a forearm over his eyes. "I just wanted to get away when I heard that Virilo had been taken in for questioning."

❧

156

Getorius was dozing, and Arcadia had closed her eyes, when the galley gave a sudden lurch. She heard a loud crack, then a softer sound, like a rain of tiny pebbles falling onto the deck. The smell of pepper intensified.

Arcadia sat up and looked toward the storage rack nearest her, from where the sound seemed to be coming. Peppercorns dribbled out of a triangular hole in the body of one of the clay jars. She looked at her husband. He seemed to be fast asleep.

"Getorius," she called out, "an amphora broke. Pepper is spilling out all over the decking."

"Wha...? Oh." He got up and went with her to look. "It must have cracked in the quake and the dock workers didn't notice."

"Or didn't want to be blamed." She cupped her hands under the flow and tried to keep her balance on the swaying deck. "What can we catch these in?"

"One of the cook's bowls?" He looked around. "Use one of our towels to stopper the hole while I get one."

"Hand it to me." Arcadia had wadded the towel and was about to insert it in the opening, when the flow of black pellets suddenly stopped. She poked a finger inside and felt the break plugged by a small bundle. "There's something in there, Getorius." Prying the package loose, Arcadia held it up. "A leather pouch."

"Not *more* counterfeit coins."

"It isn't heavy enough." She unfastened the thongs and spilled out several small dull-blue stones into her palm.

Getorius picked up one. "What is it, lapis lazuli?"

Arcadia sorted through the stones, and then held one that had been polished up to the light. Its sparkling cobalt brilliance was unmistakable. "No," she said in a whisper, "these are...these are sapphires."

"What? Maximin is smuggling gemstones back in his pepper amphorae?"

"Lower your voice," she hissed. "And you don't know it's him. It could be Virilo."

"Why do you always defend the senator? Just because he fawned all over you after I was arrested in December—"

"Husband, don't bring that up now," she interrupted, with an icy glare. "We don't know how honest the crew is. One or more of them could have hidden the stones there for safekeeping."

Getorius thought it unlikely, but forced himself not to say so and further upset her. "Yes, and Apollo couldn't play the lyre," he muttered to himself. "We have to put the gems back, Arcadia. Whoever did hide them wouldn't be too pleased to know they've been found."

Arcadia pushed the bag as far into the jar as she could and stuffed the opening with the towel. "Shall we tell a crewman, Getorius?"

"No, I'll just let Virilo know we sealed the break before too many corns spilled out."

⁂

The rainsquall signaled by the lurching of the *Cybele* was a mild one that swept in from the southwest, yet the galley's motion during the night bothered Getorius. He only fell asleep toward morning, and it was daylight when he helped Arcadia up the ladder, onto the main deck. The air still felt clammy from the rain, but the ochre dust cloud was gone. A bluish haze hugged what was visible of the horizon.

While Victor worked the steering oar, Sigeric was at the port rail with Virilo, straining to identify three square sails to the southwest, beyond the *Cybele*'s wake. The white shapes were barely discernable through the haze.

Concerned, Getorius followed the men's gaze. "Pirates again, Sigeric?"

"Too big, and those scum don't usually hunt in packs of three."

"Who, then? They can't be Vandals already coming up from Carthage, can they?"

Neither man answered Getorius. The rectangular sails were quickly drawing closer. After a moment, a crewman who had shinnied up the mast to the yard top shouted down in an alarmed voice.

"War galleys aft!"

"War galleys?" Getorius echoed. "Whose?"

"Hopefully ours, or Eastern," Virilo speculated, "but they could

158

be barbarian. If the Vandals captured the Carthaginian fleet, they've had since October to learn how to use it."

"And they're bearing in from th' south." Sigeric climbed the ladder to take over the steering oars.

"*Could* they be coming from Africa?" Arcadia asked.

Virilo shrugged. "Rumors been circulating in Ravenna all winter that the Vandals' Arian friends would welcome them in Sicilia. That's less than a day's sail north of Carthage. If they invaded the island, the port at Tauromenium is about two days from the entrance to the Adriatic."

The trio of galleys was now close enough to be identified by class.

"Th' aft two are triremes," Sigeric called down, "but th' closest has only two banks of oars and a mainsail. That bireme is even faster than th' pirate galleys we met off Issa."

Arcadia pointed to the painting of a man visible on the billowing linen of the nearest ship. "What's that emblem on the sail?"

Virilo squinted at the figure of a bearded man in a presbyter's tunic, surmounted by his name SCS APOLLONARIS. "Apollonarius, patron of Ravenna and Classis. One of ours…unless she's another decoy."

The *Apollonaris* had the same following wind as *Cybele,* and her twin banks of oars were being rowed in smooth unison, adding to her speed. Getorius counted thirteen shields of various shapes and colors lining the star rail, and made out the helmets and bows of two rows of archers kneeling behind them. Doubled by those from the portside bowmen, any concentrated hail of arrows was sure to find a mark. He saw two crewmen set fire to a pot of bitumen, then hoist it forward with pulleys until it dangled over the prow. One man hunched down near a rope that he could yank to spill the flaming pitch onto *Cybele's* deck once his galley maneuvered close enough.

Apollonaris was near enough now for the hortator's dull, steady hammer beat to be heard.

"She's almost at ramming speed," Sigeric yelled. "*Caco,* they must think we're pirates. Galleymaster, I told you to put an RV on our sail for Ravenna."

"The senator didn't want that—"

"Can't you lower our own ram?" Getorius shouted, cutting off Virilo. "We could at least defend ourselves."

"Couldn't heave about fast enough. And *Cybele*'d bounce off that hull like a furcing slinger's lead on one of them shields." Virilo spat overboard, then bounded up the ladder to help with the steering oars.

Getorius pulled Arcadia close to him. Even with Virilo's help, there was little Sigeric could do to maneuver out of the way of the faster bireme. From the angle the *Apollonaris* was approaching, it was clear that *Cybele* would be rammed at a diagonal, on her port side.

The stroke of the timebeater's hammer quickened its interval to ram speed. Oarsmen strained to keep up with the cadence, their groans and sporadic curses loud enough to carry on the wind. As the warship surged closer, the grinning faces of the master and his watch officer appeared above the prow rail. Clearly visible below them, a three-pronged bronze ram on their war galley slid just beneath the foam toward the *Cybele*, about a hundred paces off now.

Zhang Chen evidently heard the commotion on deck and came to the door of his cabin. Diotar, who had not yet shown himself on deck, peered out his window at the approaching galley. A look of terror froze on his pale face. Getorius thought he saw Claudia in the darkness behind the priest.

"*Apollonaris* is going to hit us!" Arcadia cried.

"Down!" Virilo yelled. "Brace yourselves!"

Getorius hugged Arcadia tightly, mesmerized by the oncoming prow, thinking absurdly that it resembled the head and beak of some giant predatory bird.

A moment after Virilo gave his warning, the master of the *Apollonaris* shouted his own command. As his crew sprang to furl the mainsail, and the two helmsmen strained their steering oars into a tight port turn, the hortator's hammer beat suddenly changed to a new cadence. One hundred and four oarsmen shoved the tip of their blades at right angles under the surface, throwing up geysers of seawater and straining to bring the galley to a halt. At a second order the hammer signaled again. Oars stroked in reverse. After the

Apollonaris shuddered to a reluctant stop, the bireme and her deadly ram slowly backed away.

When the master looked toward *Cybele* again, he grinned and waved. His mocking laughter wafted over clearly on the wind, even as the distance between the two boats widened.

Virilo spit toward him. "Furcing bastard was playing cat and bird with us," he snarled, wiping a sleeve across his face. "She must be one of our patrol galleys out of Classis."

"Thank God…" Getorius kissed Arcadia's face, then released her and ran to Chen. "Are you all right? That was frightening."

"Zhang Chen good, As-t'us. Go back inside now."

"Fine." When Getorius glanced at Diotar's cabin, the priest had pulled the curtain completely across the window.

Virilo watched the three warships fall astern. "Only good out of this," he commented, "is pirates hiding out along the coast probably know about the *Apollonaris* and her twin triremes. We won't be ambushed this trip."

"Thank Saint Cosmas for that, too," Arcadia murmured, thinking that worry about the sapphires, counterfeit coins, and what Leudovald would do to her husband after he returned to Ravenna already gave her enough to pray for.

Ravenna

Chapter twelve

Scanning the horizon at midday on April twenty-ninth, Arcadia gave a squeal of delight and grasped her husband's arm. "I see our lighthouse and breakwater! We're back home."

Getorius squeezed her hand. "And except for that jack mule of a master on the *Apollonaris,* the return was fairly pleasant."

"I didn't get as sick. I am exhausted, though."

He kissed her hair, which smelled slightly rank. "You can finally take that bath you wanted in Olcinium, *Cara,* then a long nap."

"Only if you join me."

Getorius held her tightly in answer—there might be Leudovald to face before that could happen.

As the *Cybele* was towed to her berth at the center wharf, stevedores sprang to ready gangplanks for unloading.

Arcadia recognized Publius Maximin's black rig at the end of the warehouse portico. Two men stood next to it, watching the galley dock. "Getorius, that's the senator's carriage. One of the men is his driver, the deaf-mute who took us to treat Faustina."

"I wonder if he's here to meet Chen?" Getorius saw Leudovald step out of the portico shadows, flanked by two palace guards. *The harbormaster must have reported* Cybele's *return to him.* "Time to face a one-headed Cerberus," he quipped, "but with all that's happened this trip, even the guardian of Avernus doesn't seem so intimidating right now."

"I know how you must feel, but he only wants to question you," Arcadia reminded him. "I'm sure I could speak to the senator and—"

"*Forget* Maximin," he snapped. "Did you bring our clothes?" Arcadia indicated the leather bag next to her on the deck with the toe of a sandal. "Good. Have Brisios take them to the fuller's to be cleaned, then look in on the clinic. I'll join you after I explain myself to Leudovald."

Once stevedores had secured the galley against stone wharf dogs with hawsers, the gangplank was lifted into place. Getorius took the carrying case and walked ahead of Arcadia down the wooden ramp. Leudovald met the couple at the bottom.

"Ah, my wandering Ulysses returns," he smirked. "And *with* his Penelope."

"I prescribed some sea air for us," Getorius said, returning the man's sarcasm.

"Sea air indeed, Surgeon." Leudovald nodded toward the case. "What is in your bag?"

"Mostly soiled clothes," Arcadia told him.

"Soiled clothes, Domina? Come with me, you two." Leudovald led the way into the warehouse portico, then signaled to one of the guards. "Search their bag."

"Wait a moment. We—"

"Surgeon"—Leudovald cut off Getorius's objection—"you have some explaining to do. Your sudden exodus disturbed me."

The soldier rummaged through the bag and Getorius's medical case, and shook his head.

"Nothing irregular there? Look in their purses."

Getorius clutched at his money pouch. "This is an outrage! What is he supposed to be looking for?"

The guard hesitated and glanced toward Leudovald for confirmation. At the investigator's nod, he unslung the soft leather cases from around Getorius's and Arcadia's necks. Leudovald opened her purse first.

Getorius knew she had not kept any of the sapphires, but felt his face flush at the indignity of Arcadia being treated like a criminal. He thought of trying to intimidate, or at least impress Leudovald by reminding him that he was Galla Placidia's physician, but he held back, fearing that might only increase the man's antagonism. Instead, he asked, "What do you expect my wife to be hiding, Leudovald?"

Without replying, the investigator poked among Arcadia's coins, then feigned surprise as he held up three bronzes, "What have we here?" Arcadia blanched, realizing she had forgotten about the counterfeit coins Getorius had told her to keep. "A trinity of false 'Valentinians.'" The innocently quizzical look in Leudovald's eyes changed to a cold stare at Arcadia. "The Augustus only issues this denomination in gold, Domina. Where did you get these? No matter," he added before she could explain. "Guard, place this woman under arrest. She can keep company with the Arian presbytera."

"Arrest my wife?" Getorius objected, realizing that what he feared would happen to Thecla had come about. "And on what grounds are you detaining the old woman?"

"The Bishop wants the heretic tried for the mutilation of the dead youth you found. The magistrate has charged her with his murder." Leudovald returned Arcadia's purse to Getorius and softened his tone. "Your wife will be well, Surgeon. We don't confine women with common bandits until their trial. You can bring her clean clothes and some food later this evening."

"I can explain the coins."

"As indeed you shall, Surgeon. At the proper time."

"What will happen to my wife?"

"There will be an inquiry into this whole affair," Leudovald said, almost casually. "At that time I also will question the girl who was at the murder scene. I'll want you there, Surgeon, since I understand she has the Sacred Disease."

"Do you think the counterfeit 'Valentinians' are connected to Atlos's death?"

Leudovald ignored the question. "Surgeon, bid your wife farewell for now."

Getorius embraced Arcadia. "*Cara*, I'll come, or send Brisios with a clean tunic and nightwear as soon I can. And some supper."

"I'll be all right," she reassured him. "And I am anxious to see how Thecla is doing."

Getorius watched his wife and the three men turn into the Via Longa, then picked up the traveling bag and walked past the portico to the end of the warehouse. One of Maximin's men had escorted Zhang Chen to the carriage, where the deaf-mute sat ready to drive off. The six crates were in the back seat. *I was right. That extra cargo is for the senator, and the Oriental must be his associate.*

Chen's business with Publius Maximin was only one of the questions Getorius pondered as he turned onto the Via Porti toward his villa. He still had not discovered what hold Diotar had on Virilo that would make him allow his epileptic daughter to be part of such vicious rites. Pagan cults were forbidden, even if no one had bothered the Isis priests, and Diotar's rituals were surely practiced in secret. There had to be a temple to *Magna Mater*, Cybele, somewhere in Ravenna. Diotar was too well organized to be a leader of one of the many short-lived cells the authorities had nicknamed "mushroom cults." Getorius realized now that he had been wrong to think that Cybele's worshippers would melt away like snow on a bakery oven.

The false coins. Leudovald had said the denomination was issued only in gold. If Arcadia's hunch was correct and silvered counterfeits went to pay Danube legions, a massive rebellion could result once the men realized they had been cheated. An unstable frontier could be the excuse for either Valentinian or Theodosius to attack each other's territory, as well as for unknown barbarian tribes in the north to move in. An ambitious governor or legion commander could be involved. The rule of the three Valentinian family emperors in the West had begun some seventy-five years earlier, after the death—some believed assassination—of Julian ii, the nephew of Constantine. Valentinian iii was a weak, erratic emperor who was overly influenced by astrologers and his mother, Galla Placidia. She distrusted Aetius, the Western army commander, perhaps with reason—for many years, legions had been creating emperors from popular army officers.

Getorius had not been arrested with his wife because, under the Theodosian Code, Arcadia was still under the legal control of her father, not her husband. Still, Leudovald might have let him go in order to have him watched, to find out if he was involved in the counterfeiting.

Getorius reached the Arian church on the Via Armini. He saw guards on duty, both there and at Thecla's apartment across the street. The murder charge against the old woman was laughable. Even Leudovald must realize that! Could Bishop Chrysologos have become involved in her arrest because of her sect's heretical teachings about Christ?

Getorius started sneezing as he continued down the Via Porti and a cold west wind penetrated his tunic. His throat felt raw and his nose was clogged with mucus, the first signs of a possible phlegm imbalance. He realized that anxiety, as much as a sudden chill, could be responsible. In his concern over Leudovald's discovery of the coins in Arcadia's bag, he had forgotten about the sapphires. Either Maximin was smuggling them in, or Virilo was using the senator's pepper cargo as a convenient hiding place for his own illegal imports. If so, it would help explain the vicious beating Arcadia had seen when a slave broke an amphora. Of course, not all of them could hold gems. Customs inspectors might take a sample from one or two of the jars, then weigh the others to calculate import duties. And if a bag was accidentally discovered, Maximin could deny involvement, or no doubt bribe his way clear.

Publius Maximin. What was his connection to the mysterious crates Chen had guarded so carefully? Something valuable had to be in them, and yet it wouldn't be contraband. Customs officials had not even looked inside the containers. Senatorial privilege or bribe money?

Getorius was shivering, and walked faster when he turned into the Via Caesar and saw his villa at the far end. *It will be good to soak off this chill in the bathhouse, but I'll miss Arcadia.*

Brisios let Getorius in through the carriage gate. After he called for Childibert, the housemaster came into the atrium.

"Tell Silvia to get her mistress's night tunic and some other personal things together," Getorius ordered, throwing down the carrying case. "She'll know what. Perfumed oil too. Put my medical things in the clinic. The clothes are to be washed. Have any patients come while I was away?"

"Woman and two men come today. They say they will stay until you return."

"Stay here? Where are they, in the clinic?"

"In bathhouse, Master."

"My bathhouse? Why would you let them in there? Never mind, I'll go." Annoyed at the intrusion, Getorius stalked through the corridor past the furnace room to a side entrance. When he entered the tepidarium room, he saw two well-built men lounging in the warm water. A completely nude, muscular woman sat on the edge of the pool, scraping her oiled thigh with a curved bronze strigil. He was stunned to recognize the gladiatrix, Giamona, and instinctively clutched his left arm. *Christ! Her friend lost the arm and she's come to take a tooth for a tooth, or rather an arm for an arm!*

After Giamona looked up, she chuckled at his stare of surprise. "What's the matter, Surgeon, you've seen tits before, haven't you? Mine aren't very big, but they're the last nice thing a lot of men in the arena saw before they went to meet whatever god they believed in."

"Forget your tits, Gia," one of the men called over gruffly. "Now that the bone-cutter is back, we got more important things to do."

"*Ita*," she agreed. Her look of amusement vanished. "Surgeon, Tigris is waiting for you at our camp. Bring all the medical instruments you have."

"I knew that his arm could only get worse. He shouldn't have bolted from me that day—"

"We're losing furcing time!" Giamona snapped. "Get what you'll need."

The two men heaved themselves out of the pool to towel water off their bodies and dress. When Getorius came back with his medical case, Giamona was wiping her legs and feet dry. He saw the ugly white scars on her arms, upper chest, and the curve of one breast. Her remark about men she had fought in the arena was not an exaggerated boast. Undoubtedly the gladiatrix had killed opponents.

"Tigris's arm didn't heal well," Giamona said, picking a narrow cloth band off the bench where she had left her tunic. "That's why he needs you."

"I warned him. The damage was severe."

"You did what you could. Tigris shouldn't have run, but his fear was different from the one he feels facing an opponent on the sand." She wrapped the band around her breasts, then slipped a short tunic over her head and arranged a hair net on short blond curls.

She's attractive in a sort of hard, muscular way, Getorius thought, *and certainly healthier looking than the prostitutes who work the street by the Theodosius Gate.*

"Ah, where is this gladiator camp of yours?" he asked after Giamona looked back at him.

"Where's your woman?" she hedged, bending to lace a sandal cord around her ankle.

"In Lauretum Palace. Leudovald arrested her."

"The bastard. He's been trying to track down our camp..." She gave the lace a final tug and straightened up. "Arrested her for what?"

"I'd rather not say just now, but it was a mistake. Look, Giamona. Am I going to fight Tigris, or treat his arm?"

"Treat him."

"Then it would be better if he came here, where I have the proper implements." Getorius avoided mentioning anything about amputating the limb, although he felt sure the woman realized it might be necessary.

"I told you to get what you need." Giamona turned to the two men, who had finished dressing. "He'll tell you what to bring with us."

"Leudovald said I could take clothing to Arcadia."

"Her house slave can do that, and also tell her that you went somewhere to treat a patient. Let Bellelus know what you want."

After Getorius directed the man in packing a small surgical

saw, scalpels, cotton dressings, and a cauterizing iron, he went to tell Childibert that Brisios should take the clothes Silvia selected, together with some food, to Arcadia.

Giamona led the way to a narrow alley off the Via Honorius. A boy held the reins of two horses which were harnessed to a wagon with enclosed wooden sides and a door to admit passengers. Its curved top was covered in heavy waxed sailcloth.

"Go home," she ordered the child, tossing him a bronze coin. "Bellelus will drive. Surgeon, sit in back."

As Getorius climbed in, he saw the second man walk on through the alleyway. "Isn't he coming with us?"

Giamona ignored his question to call up to Bellelus, "Get us there by sunset."

Getorius helped her up through the door. Arcadia's perfumed oil on the woman's body made her smell teasingly like his wife. When Giamona sat opposite him on the leather seat, her short tunic revealed more scars on her legs, white against the tanned skin. He reached to push aside a curtain over the window on his right side, to see where they were going.

Giamona pulled his hand away and looked hard into his eyes. "Leave it covered." Getorius shrugged and sat back, with the medical case on his lap. *She's keeping the location of this camp secret.* In a moment he heard the wheels clatter through the alleyway and onto paving stones, then felt the wagon sway and himself being squeezed against the right side. *Turning left onto the Honorius. We could be going to the Via Popilia and either Bononia or Arminum, or out the Theodosius Gate.* Bononia, the next large town north along the Popilia, had been known for its gladiatorial games before the ban.

When Getorius heard the vendors' shouts and breathed the mingled smells of the market square at the Via Theodosius, yet did not feel the carriage turn in, he knew they were headed for the Porta Aurea and the Popilia. He had lost all sense of time in the confusion after disembarking from the galley—Arcadia's arrest, the report of Thecla's imprisonment, this unexpected appearance of Giamona and her companions. The drawn curtains dimmed the light inside the carriage, but he guessed it was around the ninth hour. If so, there were another three hours until sunset, and a fairly long twilight, but Bononia was a good fifty miles inland from Ravenna. Arminum, on the coast, was at least thirty. The camp would have to be closer, within a ten-mile distance, probably along some little-used trail that led into the Pines.

Getorius fidgeted with the cover of his medical case. The prospect of amputating a putrefying limb alone was not a pleasant one, even less so if done in a camp of renegade, possibly hostile, gladiators.

And neither Arcadia nor anyone else knew where he had gone.

Forum Livii

Chapter thirteen

Early afternoon cart traffic on the road was light. The heavy wagon swayed along the paving stones to the clomping of horses' hooves, a jingle of harness equipment, and the creaking of leather straps.

Getorius noticed that, despite the jostling, Giamona had settled back to doze. He slowly pushed the curtain aside and looked out at marshes swollen by winter rains, where wildfowl were returning to establish nesting sites. A few hunters with nets were standing at pond edges, trying to snare ducks. Glancing to the far right, he noticed the buildings of Maximin's chicken farm shimmering in the glare of the afternoon sun, and recalled that the Villa of the Red Rooster was where the Hibernian abbot had been found dead in a supposed accident. A case strapped to his body had contained the apocalyptic charter of a fanatic sect named the Gallican League. Had they disbanded after the abbot's death?

He thought of Arcadia. *It's the wrong time to be away from her. Leudovald already knows about the counterfeit 'Valentinians,' since he recognized the three in her purse. When he questions her, she'll have to tell him where they were found. That will move the suspicion onto Virilo and Maximin, but Leudovald will go after the galleymaster before implicating a powerful senator.*

Getorius pushed the curtain open further. Now the marshes had receded and he was surrounded by level farmland of a peculiar yellow-colored earth. Newly plowed fields, whose furrows glittered with pools of standing rain, were dotted with tile-roofed stone buildings of the same ochre hue. In a few farmsteads where vineyards were planted, high trelliswork supported the pink-budded gray canes. In others, orchards of almond and plum trees were in bloom, their pink blossoms mimicking sunlit patches of winter snow on the Apennine Mountain foothills in the far distance.

Lining the sides of the road, tall greening poplar trees and dark cypresses were the only vertical elements on a horizon that looked as flat as that of the Adriatic Sea. Getorius inhaled the clean smell of plowed earth and the blossoms' perfume—a welcome change from the stench of Ravenna's sewers.

The wagon jolted, and Giamona started awake. Getorius dropped the curtain back in place. Her body had slid down on the seat until her knees touched his. She had not put on a loincloth; with her tunic hiked up, he noticed her pubic blondeness and felt an involuntary stirring in his loins. The woman straightened, tugged her tunic lower, and moved the curtain aside to look out the window.

Getorius wondered if it was the glamor—if that was the correct term—of her profession, that made him find her closeness arousing, despite his concern about Arcadia.

Giamona might not be willing to tell him where they were going, but several hours of total silence would be unbearable. To add to the discomfort of the lurching ride, his head ached, his throat was still raw, and his nose was running. Trying to suppress his sniffling, he decided to try and start a conversation.

"Giamona isn't a Roman name, is it?"

"Celtic." She did not glance away from the landscape.

"Does it have a meaning in that language?"

Giamona turned to look at him with eyes that were as blue

as the late April sky outside. "I was named after one of our months. Some say the first summer one, or the first month of winter. At those seasons you can find either the blue color of gentian blossoms, or of lake ice."

"I see." *Named for the color of her eyes. I opt for ice at the moment.* "How…how do you gladiators survive, now that the contests are illegal?"

The blue eyes flashed contempt. "You'll be paid your fee, Surgeon."

"No, no, I didn't mean that. It's just that it must be difficult for you."

"We manage."

"Do you use actual weapons? Short swords, tridents, and the like?"

Giamona straightened her legs and hiked the tunic back up to show her scars. "Do these look like they were made by wooden swords? Did Tigris's slash?"

"Of course not," he mumbled. "A stupid question." Getorius decided to keep quiet before he made a total fool of himself with this obstinate blue-eyed woman warrior.

❦

The farm villas and their cultivated fields became sparser, replaced by a forest of oak and pine that stretched to the west until the trees disappeared into the golden haze of foothills.

After jolting along in silence for a time, Getorius risked another question. "Have you considered fighting with blunted weapons? Putting on exhibitions? That might be legal."

Giamona flipped the curtain over the window again, then tucked her legs beneath herself, leaned against the wagon side, and closed her eyes without answering.

So much for helpful ideas. Getorius lay back, feeling feverish now, and aware that his stress had been exacerbated by fatigue. The combination had probably brought on his body's wet humor imbalance. *Can I trust that Giamona isn't lying about Tigris? I'm being taken to an*

179

undisclosed location, by an uncooperative woman, to treat an untreatable wound, or perhaps take part in an unwinnable contest.

⁂

A rough careening of the wagon shook Getorius awake. He glanced at Giamona. She was still asleep, so he chanced looking outside again. Roadside trees now cast blue shadows, and the sun had lowered to about three finger-widths above the Apennine crests. Bellelus had turned off into a narrow path that was rutted from the spring rains, and overgrown with newly sprouted weeds. The wagon passed the yawning ruins of an abandoned walled villa. Its entrance gate hung off the hinges, marked by a sign painted with a crude skull and the warning, PESTILENCIA.

At another jolt, Giamona stirred and glanced out her window. "We're here. Bellelus made good time."

"That ruined villa back there. Is there plague?" Getorius asked.

"Intruders don't stay around long enough to find out."

One good way to insure privacy. This must be where her troupe hides out.

The path led through a grove of trees that screened an open space a short distance on. In the center of the clearing, a sunken hollow had been enlarged into an arena set with wooden benches on opposite slopes. Two wooden barracks, deteriorated, but with covered porches like the ones in the legion camp at Ravenna, were at the far end, in the first shadows of a dense pine forest that continued on behind them. A few women tended children, while others cooked the evening meal over open fires near a butchered deer hanging from a branch.

Several men were in the arena, watching three contestants who seemed ready to stage a mock fight.

Giamona scowled. "What the furc...one of them is Sabatis. He's on my team, but who are those two strangers? Spies?"

Sabatis was armed with an arm and shoulder guard, a blunted practice trident, and a rope net, and was facing a pair of brawny, dark-skinned men who confronted him with padded lances.

"Stop here, Bellelus," Giamona ordered. She jumped from the door and called out, "Pluto's Prick, Sabatis, who are they?"

He looked toward her. "Numidians from around Carthage. Got away before the Vandals made them slaves."

"Are they any good? Why aren't they using shields?"

"Didn't want them. I thought I'd give them some *retiarius*... 'netter'...experience. They're lance-horsemen."

"Sabatis, give me your net and trident." Giamona gave a throaty chuckle. "Let's see if they're man enough to stick *me*."

The Numidians laughed. Getorius guessed they understood enough Latin to catch the sexual pun, but undoubtedly it was the thought of a woman challenging them that spawned their amusement.

"Gia," Sabatis protested, "my arm and shoulder protectors are too big for you."

"Shit, we're only playing. Help me put them on."

Sabatis slipped the leather bands over Giamona's left arm and hand. The top end was fixed with a curved bronze plate, so the woman could duck down behind it and protect her head from a sword stroke.

"*Galea?*" the Numidian asked, patting his helmet.

"A 'netter' doesn't wear a helmet," she replied. "And I'm not using a dagger in this game either."

After she pulled the top of her tunic down below her breasts, Giamona undid the retaining band and retied it around her waist, then crouched low, net and trident at the ready position.

One of the men spoke to the other in Berber, then turned to Sabatis and said in accented Latin, "We not fight woman."

Giamona heard him and flipped the spear he was holding out of his hand with her trident. The other gladiators laughed, but the second tribesman scowled and leveled his own lance at her.

She grinned. "Good, you have spirit. What's your name?"

"He said it was Aspar," Sabatis told her.

"Well, Aspar," she taunted, "how about a lesson in what a Celtic woman can do besides screw you senseless?"

While she was talking, Giamona had used feints with the

trident to maneuver her opponent around until the low sun was at her back, and in his eyes. As Aspar crouched, squinting, with the padded point of his lance leveled at her, she let her rope net unfold to the ground and kicked it behind her. A novice intent on avoiding the three deadly prongs of a trident often forgot that the entangling mesh was there. She would use that knowledge, the distraction of her breasts, and the sun's brightness to overcome the advantage of Aspar's long spear. Even padded, it could inflict a disabling injury.

Bending forward to make herself as small a target as possible, Giamona kept her three-pronged weapon at the level of Aspar's throat. She knew he would be impatient to make the first move, both to avenge the ridicule he had heard when she challenged his manhood, and to move out of the sun's glare. Her trident thrusts at Aspar's neck kept him in position, yet she knew her advantage of sunlight was only for a short time longer, and his lance was almost twice as tall as she was. She provoked him with a quick jab that scraped the Numidian's shoulder.

Squinting at the brightness in his eyes, Aspar clenched his teeth and thrust out at her with his lance. Giamona side-stepped, caught the long handle between the prongs of her weapon, and pushed it into the ground in a spray of sand. He easily pulled it out and repeated the maneuver several times, but Giamona kept deflecting the weapon away from her body, and teased his groin with flicks of the net.

The man's companion was calling out to him in Berber, what sounded like mockery. Aspar's nostrils were flared from frustration, and sweat glistened on his blue-black skin.

Getorius realized that Giamona's tactics were to spare the man direct attack, but goad him into a reckless move. Since he had decided to not use a shield, she could easily have disarmed him by sliding the trident up the lance shaft and into his hand.

Aspar tried another strategy. Feinting with his usual thrust, suddenly he crossed over his hands and swung the lance sideways, to his opponent's right. The unexpected blow hit Giamona on the shoulder and staggered her around until she was facing the low sun, but instead of following through, the Numidian only stood grinning at his success.

Fool. Giamona's ice-blue eyes were expressionless as they fixed on his brown ones. *Time to end the game. Now that he thinks he's found my weakness, his next swing will be twice as hard. If that shaft hits me in the head, Bellelus and Sabatis will have to perform as a duo. After my funeral.*

A slight movement of Aspar's eyes betrayed his imminent blow. When his lance flailed to the right again, Giamona caught it in the prongs of the trident and pushed it up, away from her head. At the same instant her other hand swung the net out toward Aspar's legs. As his limbs became entangled in the mesh, she jerked the rope toward her. He tumbled heavily to the sand. Before his eyes had lost their look of surprise, she had thrust the trident at his neck, to feint a kill, then stepped back.

Giamona noticed the other Numidian applauding her move, along with her comrades. Good. She wanted fighters who respected their opponents, not those whose pride or recklessness made them underestimate the skills of the other contestants. She decided not to further injure Aspar's pride by extending a hand to help him up, and went over to his companion instead.

"What's your name?"

"Juba."

"Well, Juba, your friend did what I expected. Thrusting is a standard tactic for lancemen. Maybe he felt overconfident because I'm a woman, and these tits probably distracted him"—Giamona paused to allow herself a smile as the other men hooted and clapped—"but he underestimated the net, and my scars should have warned him that I've fought many times and survived."

"If he'd taken the shield," Sabatis added, "Aspar could have broken your jaw when you stepped up to him."

"Yes." Giamona demonstrated with her hands. "A quick upward thrust."

Aspar stood up, brushing sand from his legs. When Giamona reached out a hand to him, he only glared at her with narrowed eyes, but after Juba spat out a command in Berber, he lightly touched her forearm in a reluctant gesture of conciliation.

"Good. Come and eat with us," she offered, pulling her tunic back up to cover her breasts. "Sabatis, where's Tigris?"

"In his barrack."

"Help Bellelus bring the surgeon's instruments."

Getorius looked at the raw bruise on Giamona's shoulder, which was oozing a bloody lymph fluid. "You should let me take care of your injury."

"After you've seen Tigris." She turned and walked quickly toward one of the buildings.

As Getorius followed her, the sun dropped behind the rugged summits in a final blinding flash of brilliance. A savory smell of stewing venison was issuing from an iron pot tended by two women. They looked up at him curiously. Three young girls, who were stacking loaves of bread and setting out wooden bowls and pewter spoons on one of the long tables, smiled. One waved. Getorius nodded to acknowledge them.

Tigris was on the last cot of the nearest barracks, his face florid and glistening with perspiration. Getorius could smell his diseased arm even before he pulled back the covers and saw what he had expected. The limb was black with a putrid bile excess, which indicated that the flesh and underlying bone were dead. The withered remains of a poultice of sumac leaves, with clay votive offerings tucked among them, had fallen aside. "Who knows about sumac here?" Getorius asked, surprised at the dressing.

Giamona hesitated then said, "Sa…Sabatis. Was that the right thing for him to apply?"

"He didn't do anything wrong. Is…was he a surgeon?"

"*Capsillarius*. Legion medical orderly, somewhere in the north."

"That's good, I'll need his help after he brings my instruments. But I'm afraid Tigris will have to trade his arm for his life. Assuming he survives the fever."

The dead flesh reached almost to the shoulder joint. Getorius knew he would have to amputate at that point, then cauterize the wound to stop bleeding from two major veins and the subclavian artery.

Sabatis came in with the driver, carrying the cases.

"Bellelus, stay here. You'll have to help hold Tigris down," Getorius ordered. "Sabatis, have you ever assisted at an amputation?"

He shook his head. "Cutting out arrow heads. Treating sword slashes."

Getorius grunted. He searched among his instruments and selected the surgical saw and a scalpel, then a flattish cauterizing iron. "Have someone heat this in the cookfire. I'll prepare a strong dose of opion to put Tigris to sleep, but I'm concerned about his fever."

"I gave him a brew of rumex leaves."

"Good, Sabatis, but arctium would be better. Can you find some young roots this early in the year?"

"I think so."

"Crush them in wine. It will take all three of us to get him to drink it, and then the opion on top of that."

※

Following the amputation procedure, Getorius pulled the flaps of Tigris's skin together and sutured them over the seared stump of shoulder. After applying another poultice of fresh sumac leaves he judged the amputation itself a success, but the question of the fever remained. Sabatis could probably monitor the healing of the wound, but the next day or two would be crucial to the gladiator's recovery.

※

During the long twilight, Getorius ate a little bread and stew outdoors with the others, listening to harrowing stories about their narrow escapes in the arena, or myths about legendary gladiators of the past with unfamiliar foreign names—Purpurio, Rodan, Filematio. Giamona sat beside him. Despite her exertion in the arena, the scent of Arcadia's oil was still evident, mingled with the slight smell of the woman's perspiration. Several times, as Giamona reacted with laughter to the stories, Getorius noticed that she playfully pushed her leg against his for emphasis. He thought she might be drinking too much in order to forget Tigris's ordeal, but was also aware that her blue eyes were often fixed on him, instead of the man telling the story. He felt in turn embarrassed and flattered, and then aroused, when he recalled the glimpse of her loins in the wagon.

At a lull in the conversations, while wine cups were being refilled, Giamona suddenly turned her injured shoulder to Getorius and leaned against him.

"Y' said y'd treat my arm," she reminded him in slurred words, an odor of wine strong on her breath.

"I did, I did," he replied, grinning foolishly. He had not refused the serving women's refills in his own cup and felt a little giddy. *Name of Hades…I think I'm getting drunk.*

Giamona lurched to her feet with as much dignity as possible. "Bring your case t' my room," she mumbled. "I don't need these wine-soaked pig stickers watchin' y' put a band'ge on me."

The men clanged their cups on the table and hooted as she stepped over the bench and weaved her way toward the second barracks. Getorius muttered an embarrassed thanks to them and walked unsteadily after her, to find his medical bag.

Women and children lived in a separate section of the building. Getorius brought his case to the door that Giamona had entered and found her sitting on the edge of a bed. She had pulled the tunic high above her muscular thighs; her pubic blondeness, now more prominent, triggered an erection in him.

She looked up from examining a scar. "Took y' long enough, Get'rix."

"I'm here." Getorius grinned foolishly as he fumbled to pull the stopper off a jar of plantain salve. "I'll just spread some of this on you," he babbled hoarsely, conscious of the pressure in his groin as he smeared on the ointment. "Then I'll bandage your shoulder, even if old Hippocrates wrote that—"

"Screw Hipp…Hippocr'tes." Giamona slipped the tunic over her head, pushed Getorius back onto the bed and wriggled her nude body on top of him. "And screw spreadin' that glop…spread these." She giggled and clamped muscular legs around his waist.

Wine was strong on her breath as she bent to thrust her tongue into his mouth. At the same time she tightened her leg grip, until Getorius felt as if an iron barrel hoop had circled his body. He had guessed this might happen, even as he followed her, grinning like an idiot.

Her tongue was drunk-sloppy, like a warm sponge washing his mouth. Giamona moved her head alongside his and reached under his tunic to fondle his hardness. "Wan' do it regular 'dog-dog,' or some other way?" She tittered to herself again. "I know lots o' good Greek an' 'Gyptian tricks."

Her short blonde hair was tangled in Getorius's face. As he blew it aside and tried to breathe, the odor of Arcadia's perfume on the woman's skin became overwhelming. He remembered the plaque his wife had given him on his birthday.

*The Oath. I did smear a little salve on her, so Giamona is technically my patient. Arcadia left out the part of the Oath about seducing females because she didn't think it was necessary. But who's seducing whom here? Still...*He tried to slip out from the tight vise of her thighs, and moved to push her hand from his groin. But when he reached down, it was her fingers that went limp. Her leg hold on him abruptly relaxed.

Getorius worked himself free of her weight and rolled an unresisting Giamona to one side of the bed, where she lay on her back, mouth open, snoring in spurts.

Giamona, the Celtic woman gladiatrix whose jiggling bosom had lured hapless opponents to their deaths, and whose iron thighs had trapped other undoubtedly happier living ones, was asleep.

Getorius eased her body all the way to the mattress's center, then covered her with the gray army blanket on the foot of the bed, his Oath to Hippocrates and Arcadia still intact.

※

In the morning Getorius felt nauseous. Drinking had not helped his unbalanced wet humor. After he looked in on Tigris, he saw Giamona come out of her barracks door. She was pale and looked tired, but did not indicate by her manner that she remembered anything about the previous night. He guessed that if she did, the woman considered it an incident not worth recalling, much like a bout she had survived in the arena and would not think about until facing her next opponent.

"How is Tigris?" she asked.

"Still feverish, but not any worse. The crisis could come today or tomorrow. How long do you want me here?"

"Can Sabatis take care of Tigris?"

"If he follows my instructions about continuing the poultices and arctium…wean him off the opion. There's nothing more I would do."

Giamona shrugged her shoulders. "Bellelus is driving a wagon to Ravenna to pick up the supplies Atrax bought. You're free to go with him."

"I'll tell Sabatis what to do."

She grunted and reached into her purse, then handed Getorius two silver coins. "*Siliquae.* If your fee is more I'll get you the money after our next bout."

"No, no…please," he declined, closing her hand over the coins. "If you insist on still fighting, use the money to…ah…perhaps have an armorer make breast protectors for you."

"And hide my best advantage?" Giamona laughed and kissed his mouth hard. She tasted fresh from mint leaves she had chewed. She pressed his hands against her tunic top and frowned. "Are my tits beginning to sag? Maybe I'll think about that armor."

"Giamona, if…I mean *when* Tigris recovers, perhaps a wood-worker, or sculptor, could fit him with an artificial arm. Cedar, and a hollow silver hand."

"Perhaps." She looked toward Tigris's barrack, then back at Getorius. "Come to one of our bouts next month."

"I don't even know where we are."

"Outside Forum Livii. I'll send Bellelus for you."

"Who comes? The bouts are illegal."

"Not when you have the wealthiest senator in Ravenna back-ing your team."

"Publius Maximin? I should have realized. He already wagers on the fighting cocks he raises."

Giamona winked at him. "Maybe, after awhile, raising the same old cock isn't good enough."

Is she propositioning me again or telling me something about the senator? Getorius bent down to pick up his medical case, knowing his face was not flushed solely from fever. "When is Bellelus leaving?"

"Go ask him. I'm going to teach those two barbarians the finer points of avoiding a sudden meeting with *Dis Pater*, Father Death."

❧

On his way back to Ravenna, Getorius began to feel even worse. His head and eyes ached, and overdrinking had aggravated his phlegm imbalance. He thought of this latest venture of Maximin's, sponsoring a team of illegal gladiators. Money seemed to roll in for the senator like breakers on the Adriatic shore. Pepper, high quality wine and oil, possibly smuggled sapphires, and now a cryptic cargo from the Orient. That, too, had to be an investment that would make him even wealthier. A more important concern was to get Arcadia back home, then find the origin of the counterfeit coins, in case she was indicted. And prove Thecla innocent of the death of Atlos.

Once at his villa, Getorius asked Childibert about Arcadia. Told she was well and had been brought clothing and food, he went directly to his bed, dropped onto it fully clothed and slept as if in a feverish trance the rest of that day and into the night.

❧

Getorius arose the next morning, still tired, his nose clogged, and without an appetite. Food would be tasteless anyway. His delirious sleep had been haunted by worry about his wife and the remembrance of the amputation still vivid in his mind; the putrid stink of Tigris's arm, the rush of black bile as he had cut away the last shred of muscle, the searing sound and sickening smell of burned flesh as Sabatis applied the cauterizing iron. Realizing there was no way he could treat patients in his present state, Getorius ordered Brisios to take Arcadia breakfast and tell her he would visit, after he had done some reading at the palace library.

⁂

Since the death of the library master in December, no one had been put in charge of the scroll and book storage bins, but Getorius knew Lucius, the chief copyist. Getorius questioned him about the location of information about the cult of Cybele. Lucius thought the earliest reports were probably by the historian Livius, and sorted through the collection until he located a passage in Codex xxxvi.

Getorius read with growing concern, taking notes in a small vellum tablet he had made, about the first entrance of the goddess into Rome. After he finished he went to find Arcadia. A guard told him she was being held in the third reception room off the atrium corridor.

Arcadia had finished the meal Brisios brought when Getorius entered.

"*Cara,* I missed you. Are you well?"

"Well enough," she replied, standing up. "I'm glad you came, Getorius."

He hugged her tightly and buried his face in her hair, smelling her perfume, and grateful that Giamona had fallen asleep before he could violate the Oath. She pulled away and brushed at the lines on his forehead.

"You look exhausted, Husband. And ill."

"A touch of fever."

"Brisios told me you had been called away. Where?"

"I…I'll tell you later." He sat on her cot and pulled his note tablet from a sleeve. "I went to the library to find out what I could about this Cybelene cult."

"And?"

He flipped open the wooden cover. "It began in the province of Galatia, called Phrygia back then, and settled by Celtic mercenaries after their defeat by a local king."

"Didn't I say Diotar might know Celtic?"

"You were right. Clan chieftains continued to rule over the local population as a Celtic aristocracy."

"What about Cybele?"

"Her cult started in the town of Pessinus."

"Where Diotar said he was born!" she exclaimed.

"Exactly, Arcadia. The goddess was depicted with the body of a woman, but...get this...her face was a sacred black stone thrown down by some sky god or other."

"The meteorite face we saw on that temple statue."

"Yes. Her rites included music and dancing, but also flagellation and ritual self-mutilation...like the cuts I saw on Kastor."

"Castration?"

He nodded. "We saw, or thought we saw, how central to the rite the practice is. After you drank from this Gallus River that Diotar mentioned, you supposedly went mad for a time."

"*Alucinari* in the water?"

"More likely the visions were from chewing plants that grew on the banks. The cult was brought to Rome on the advice of a Sibylline Oracle, at the time of the Carthaginian wars, when the Republic was fighting Hannibal. The story goes that Cybele's statue was taken from Pessinus and hauled up the Tiber on a barge pulled by a Vestal Virgin. Can you guess her name?"

"Don't tell me it was Claudia Quinta?"

"On target, Arcadia! *That's* the connection with our epileptic Claudia."

"Getorius, Diotar is using her. We've got to get the girl away from whatever illegal Cybelene cult is in Ravenna. Who would worship a...a meteorite in our enlightened age?"

"Don't mock. A scribe's notation on the text margin mentioned the *Historia Augusta*. I looked it up. About two hundred years ago an emperor wanted to revive the worship of Cybele in Rome."

"Two centuries past, Getorius."

"Yes, but less than fifty years ago a fanatic named Flavianus tried to restore the cult's March and September festivals. We saw the first one at that temple, the 'Day of Blood.' A man representing

Attis castrates himself, then is 'resurrected' under a pine tree the next day."

"Horrible."

"Another thing. I found a map that locates Pessinus on the Silk Road."

"From Sina? You think Zhang Chen is connected with Diotar too?"

"I don't know, but I'm more interested in the priest's connection with Carthage. He may exploit the disastrous Vandal occupation to revive a cult that began during the old wars against Hannibal. In times of uncertainty people will believe anything they think might help them."

Getorius fell silent, pondering the extent of his discoveries, wondering how they could be connected to the dead youth Thecla found in her church, or even the smuggled items and Chen's mysterious crates.

Arcadia broke the quiet. "Getorius, I don't think that Atlos mutilated himself."

"No. That lump on his head told me he had been hit from behind. Virilo, or someone he hired, is likely responsible."

"And they left the sickle-turned-knife behind?"

"That's harder to diagnose. Have you seen Thecla?"

"Only once. She's very depressed."

"Understandably," he said. "I'll try to talk with her, but you ask her if the church door was still locked when Leudovald went there. If it was, that could mean there's a hidden entrance somewhere inside her basilica."

"And that makes sense, Husband. Arians haven't been all that secure in the past either. If a mob decided to enforce the ban on my sect, I'd certainly make sure I had an escape route."

Getorius looked around the small room. "I'm going to get you out of here. I'll…" He paused at the sound of footsteps and a jingling of metal equipment in the corridor.

A moment later the tribune who had arrested Virilo on the wharf, the day before his galley sailed, came into the room.

"Surgeon. Your housemaster told me you were here," the officer said. "The Empress Mother is ill and orders you to come to her apartment immediately."

"Galla Placidia? I…I don't have my medical case here."

"Nevertheless," he insisted, "you will return with me to the Imperial Quarters."

"Arcadia, I'll come back after I see what's wrong with her."

"Ask Placidia if I could see Thecla again soon. I'm worried about her."

"*Now*, Surgeon." The tribune grasped Getorius's arm and escorted him roughly out the door.

Ravenna

Chapter fourteen

Getorius was surprised when Publius Maximin answered the Tribune's knock on the door of Galla Placidia's private reception room.

"Senator. How is the Empress Mother?"

"Not actually ill, Fortuna be thanked," Maximin said in a confidential whisper. "She wanted you to come on that pretext."

"Come for what?"

"Ah, my Surgeon," Placidia called out from a couch across the room. "I'm pleased that you're here."

"I understood you were not feeling well."

"Do I look ill?"

"No, no. Thankfully, not at all."

Galla Placidia, the headstrong daughter of the late emperor Theodosius, was just past fifty years of age. Getorius had examined her in January, after being appointed to the palace staff as physician. Considering her adventurous life, the woman was in remarkably good health. Captured at Rome thirty years ago by invading Visigoths, Placidia had married one of their kings, been ransomed back after his murder, then became the reluctant wife of Constantius III, the then Western army commander. She had borne him two children. Getorius's train of thought was interrupted when he heard the empress speaking.

"…And so, Surgeon, I'm grateful that you came."

"I'm honored," he said, "but I also wanted to see you about my wife. Arcadia has been arrested."

"The Senator told me. Ridiculous. Tribune…Lucullus…isn't it?"

"Yes, Empress."

"Lucullus, bring the surgeon's wife here immediately. Let Leudovald begin investigating the origin of those false coins attributed to my son, and only then may he question her."

"I'm grateful," Getorius said.

Maximin stepped between the two. "Surgeon, the Empress Mother wants you to witness something. She feels you can be trusted, because of your help in exposing that business about the forged will."

"Senator, I don't want that brought up," Placidia ordered curtly. "Germanus, the bishop at Autessiodurum, where that dead abbot came from, will visit Ravenna in the summer. I'm sure it has nothing to do with the affair, yet I'll deny knowing anything, except that I was assured the abbot's death was accidental."

"As indeed it *was* an unfortunate accident, Empress," Maximin emphasized. "I regret I was not there to prevent it."

"Enough, then." Placida turned to Getorius. "I understand you met a native of Sina on your, ah, impromptu voyage to Dalmatia."

"Chen? Yes." *What is she getting at? I barely spoke with him. What has the senator been telling her?*

A knock sounded. Maximin admitted Lucullus and Arcadia, then he dismissed the officer.

"My dear," Placidia greeted Arcadia warmly, "I hope you haven't been mistreated."

"No, not at all. But Leudovald insists on questioning me in the morning."

"Nevertheless, you shall sleep at home tonight." Placidia stood up and walked over to her desk, behind which a mosaic monogram of her name was inlaid on the wall. "I wanted your husband here...and you." She ran a hand over the golden initials representing her name. "Senator Maximin's contact in the pepper trade has apprised him of an amazing Sinese product whose manufacture is secret. Death is said to be the penalty for betraying the process, but this Chen evidently is willing to risk that for reasons I won't ask about."

"Death?" Getorius asked. "What product would warrant such a penalty?"

"That's what I intend to find out." Placidia unsnapped a key from the ring at her belt and handed it to Maximin. "Senator."

Maximin opened the door to one of her anterooms. Inside, Zhang Chen sat behind a table. He rose and bowed, then cast a glance of recognition at Getorius and Arcadia. Getorius thought the man seemed pleased to see them, although he said nothing.

"You're both sworn to secrecy about what you see here as if...as if on your surgeons' Hippocratic oaths," Placidia warned the couple. "Chen wanted witnesses to this disclosure."

"I ask you come, As-t'us," Chen said.

"You've evidently made a good impression on him," Placidia remarked.

Getorius was unsure of why he and Arcadia were being made privy to what this product was, but could guess the reason why the Augustus was not included. Valentinian was better known for hunting, consulting astrologers, and bedding young slave girls, than for his interest in ruling the Western Empire. His mother, however, had showed no hesitation in taking up her son's duties.

Chen was translating into Latin a vertical scroll covered with the unfamiliar writing of his country. The characters resembled the ones on the crate.

"Are you almost finished?" Placidia asked him.

"Soon finish," Chen replied in his sing-song accent.

On the floor next to the Oriental, Getorius noticed the flat crates that had been taken aboard the *Cybele*, but the four smaller ones were not with them.

"Chen, show us the...what did you call it?" Placidia asked.

"You would pronounce it '*Chih*' in your language."

"Open the top crate, man," Maximin ordered brusquely. "The Empress is waiting."

Chen frowned at him, but began to pry open boards that had already been loosened from their securing dowels. Getorius put a hand on Arcadia's shoulder and led her closer to see what the crate contained. *What precious commodity can Maximin have found? A new variety of gemstone, or a fabric that surpasses the beauty of silk? Some exotic spice or wood? A different kind of incense?*

As Chen unwrapped a waxed silk cloth that had protected the box's contents from moisture, stiff sheets of a tannish-color material became visible.

Placidia stared at the bland material without commenting, but her expression changed from one of anticipation to a glower of displeasure.

Getorius was also puzzled. After expecting shimmering fabrics, or jewels, even sweet-smelling condiments, there were only rectangles of a dull material that had no obvious purpose. "It just looks like stiff cloth," he said, through his own disappointment. "What is it for, Chen?"

"Yes, tell us," Placidia demanded. "What nonsense is this you bring me, Senator? Explain yourself."

Maximin smiled thinly. "With respect Empress, I intend to do so. Surgeon, you spend time in the library. Examine a piece of the material in that crate."

Chen pulled out the top sheet and handed it to Getorius. Arcadia fingered the texture with him, then held it up to the light. "It's almost like manuscript parchment, but smoother," she noted. "It resembles a fine vellum."

Getorius smelled the sheet. "It's not animal hide, but I'll concede that it would make an excellent writing surface."

"*Exactly*, Surgeon!" Maximin burst out. "This *Chih*, or whatever the Oriental calls it, has been used as a writing material in his country for three hundred years. And it's incredibly simple and inexpensive to make. Old cotton or linen garments, hemp waste…any material like that…is mashed to a pulp and the sheet formed on a bronze screen.

Chen is writing down the exact method. After he's constructed a mould, he'll demonstrate the process for us."

"But why all the secrecy?" Arcadia asked. "It seems this would benefit scribes and make manuscript or book copies much less expensive."

"Because, my dear," Placidia explained, "the Senator tells me we'll have the papyrus, vellum, and parchment manufacturers to contend with. Also butchers who provide skins to tanners, even farmers who raise the sheep and calves."

Maximin elaborated, "Entire industries would be destroyed, and the artisans' livelihoods with it. To say nothing of riots provoked by papyrus and parchment workers' associations. No, this will have to be accepted gradually. We can't even hint to anyone of the material's existence."

And since you're the one who brought it here, when it is manufactured, all the profits will go to you and the Imperial family. "Senator, there were four smaller crates," Getorius recalled. "Are they part of this process too?"

Placidia looked up sharply at Maximin. "What other crates, Senator? These two are all you brought here."

"Th…they are…my own property, Empress," Maximin stammered, flushing. "Nothing to do with this. Nothing at all."

"Is that true, Chen?" she demanded.

"Belong sen-t'or. Thing different from *Chih.*"

"Very well. Chen, I want you to finish translating the instructions for making this…this. Mother of God! What did you call it?

"*Chih,* Empress."

"No"—Placidia made a gesture of annoyance with her hand—"I want a Latin word for the material, but one that won't arouse curiosity. Getorius, you said it looked like papyrus. We'll call it that."

"Or 'papir,'" he suggested. "To distinguish between the two."

"Yes, that's close enough, and I can pronounce it. Understand, Chen? We'll call this 'papir' from now on."

He bowed. "Pap-ir, Empress."

Arcadia wanted to know more about Chen and his country,

and a quiet place to do so would be at home, over supper. "Chen, my husband and I would like to invite you to have your evening meal with us. Our villa is at the corner of the Vicus Caesar, not far from here at all."

Hearing the invitation, Maximin glanced toward Placidia, but she gave no sign of disapproving. "How kind of you, my dear," she said instead. "Of course you may go, Chen, once you've finished translating. That probably won't be for several hours."

"I'll have one of my guards escort him," Maximin offered. "Chen is staying at my country villa. No point in his getting lost."

Chen bowed to Arcadia again. "Zhang Chen be happy eat with you Ar-cad'a, As-t'us."

"Good." Getorius hoped that he might also learn something about medicine in Chen's country. "Senator, if he's there by the tenth hour I could show him my clinic."

"You hear, Chen?" Maximin held up ten fingers. "Tenth hour, at the surgeon's. Now finish translating that scroll of yours so I can have the moulding screen made."

※

When she reached home, Arcadia consulted with Ursina on the dinner menu, then persuaded Getorius to join her in the warm pool of the bath. After soaking in the tepid water, they went to the bedroom to relax for a short while.

Getorius had decided not to tell his wife about finding Giamona nude in the bathhouse, nor about the incident in her barracks room, but he did talk about being taken to the hidden gladiator camp and amputating Tigris's arm. Despite her interest, Arcadia dozed off from the strain of her palace detention.

Later, after dressing, Getorius went to the clinic to see if anyone was there, and to check on how well his specimens were being preserved now that warm weather was approaching.

Arcadia joined Ursina in the kitchen to supervise the meal.

※

One of Maximin's guards brought Zhang Chen to the surgeon's villa in the late afternoon. The sun was still high, but the day was cool, so Getorius led him into his study rather than to the garden. He could take him to see the clinic later. Arcadia came in with Silvia, who was carrying a silver pitcher of wine steeped in herbs, and three matching goblets.

Chen wore a high-necked tunic of orange silk, belted with an embroidered flower-pattern sash. The garment's flowing sleeves were decorated with black bands at the cuff. Black silk shoes with curved toes protected his feet. When he took off his squarish hat, his glossy black hair was tied in a topknot. He smelled of jasmine.

Arcadia thought Chen looked strained, almost unhappy. Getorius had also noticed that he seemed ill at ease, but attributed it to awkwardness in unfamiliar surroundings, and language difficulties. Chen's first words confirmed the latter suspicion.

"As-t'us. I will not know words in your language."

"We don't know *any* in yours," Getorius pointed out to relax Chen's fears. "You're doing remarkably well."

"When we have guests," Arcadia said, "we start with absinthium, an herbed wine that's a little bitter tasting. It's supposed to improve your appetite."

"No," Chen declined with a shake of his head. "Your wine can make one act fool. Rule of Lao Tzu forbid us to drink it."

"Laho Tsoo? What is that?" Getorius asked.

Chen smiled. "As your language is difficult to me, so that of Sina is to you. Lao Tzu is teacher, like your Ge-es-Kr'st."

"Jesus Christ? I see. But you must drink something. I'll send Primus for a pitcher of corma. It's a sweetened beer."

"No, As-t'us." Chen pulled a finely crafted sandalwood box, inscribed with red characters, from his sleeve and held it up. "I bring drink for you." He slid open the cover and filtered dried black leaves through his fingers. "We call this *D'a.*"

"How is it prepared?" Arcadia asked. "Do you soak the leaves overnight?"

"Have slave boil water, three cup, then put four spoon *D'a* in...in...I do not know how you name it. Pyramid pan with small holes."

"A sieve?"

"Perhaps that is word. After *D'a* leaves have soaked, we drink hot."

"Hot? Interesting," Arcadia commented. "I'll take the box to Silvia and give her instructions. Thank you for letting us know about a custom of your country." It would be strange to have a hot drink with the meal, but she did not want to make Chen feel any more uncomfortable than he already was by declining his offer.

After Arcadia left, Getorius asked Chen about the man he had mentioned. "Did this teacher give you other precepts...other rules?"

"Rule? To follow Tao, the Way, we are forbid to kill, to steal, to not tell truth. Be with other man's wife."

"Amazing, Chen. It's almost as if Moses spoke to your people as well as the Hebrews."

"But there are things we must do," Chen continued. "Honor parents. Be loyal to the *Ti* and teachers—"

"Tee?"

"*Ti* is like your emperor, As-t'us. And we must not harm living beings." Chen hesitated before adding, "There are other rules, but many of my people find it easier to honor sky daemons. They make gods of rain, snow. Even of Lao Tzu. At the beginning of our year, *Ti* order that we must believe in these daemons. Worship them. I not like."

That's why Chen may have left, Getorius thought. "Tell me about your country. Where were you born?"

"Zhangan. Town on big river we call Huang."

"How did you happen to come west to Roman lands?"

"To Ta-ts'in, as we call your country? When I was boy, my father take me with him in caravan that bring serica, what you call silk...to Pes-in'us."

"Pessinus, in Galatia?"

"Yes, As-t'us. When my father die in Zhangan, I go back to Pes-in'us."

Getorius realized what the man's connection with Diotar might be. "So you became a merchant, a trader, in Pessinus?"

Before Chen could answer, Arcadia and Silvia came into the

study. Silvia poured out three cups of steaming, amber liquid from a silver pitcher. Getorius sniffed the fragrant drink.

"It's good, Chen," Arcadia commented, after taking a sip. "Very delicate flavor."

Getorius tasted his. "Nice, but bland. Romans would want a spice like pepper or cinnamon added to it."

"Don't be critical," Arcadia murmured. "Chen, our dinner is ready. Getorius, will you show our guest to the dining room, while I tell Ursina? Silvia and Primus can serve."

The glass-paned doors of the dining room faced west. They were closed against the cool weather, but a shaft of sunlight angled in to give the area brightness and a little warmth. Getorius directed Chen to sit next to him at Nicias's old marbletop table. Ursina came in with the first course, setting the dishes on a side table that Arcadia's father had given her as part of her dowry.

Arcadia had chosen a first course of early asparagus cooked in an egg custard, and a similar dish with anchovies. Both were served with olives and thin bread.

Chen was familiar with Roman cooking, but did not particularly like it. In Pessinus he had lived in a large community of merchants from his own country, who had continued their own food traditions. Nevertheless, he ate everything Silvia and her small son put on his plate. He found the strong taste of the anchovies a novelty, since Pessinus was not located near a sea. The river fish he was used to eating had a milder flavor.

For the second course Ursina grilled sea bream and served the fish with a sauce of pepper, lovage, caraway, and onion. A salad of dandelion and chicory greens accompanied the fish. By then the lees in Chen's cup were cold, and Silvia had not come in with a fresh brew. In order not to dishonor his host, he agreed to accept a little of the watered Faventia wine that Getorius offered.

After the bream, a dish of lamb stew flavored with onion, coriander, and cumin was accompanied by chopped beans seasoned with asafoetida and the pungent fish sauce that Ursina used to salt every dish. Arcadia explained that it was called *garum*, a seasoning since ancient times.

Conversation lagged during the meal because of Chen's difficulty with the language and his custom of concentrating on the food to please his host. Getorius wanted to ask him about the friend who had been killed in the earthquake, and about the contents of the four padded crates still at Maximin's, but felt the questioning might be too personal. He was curious, especially, about the smaller boxes. What startling product, other than the writing material, had the man brought, which needed to be protected with quilted padding?

Before the last course was served, Getorius signaled for Silvia to serve Chen an undiluted, honey-sweetened wine.

"Let's drink to the success of your papir project," he suggested when all three cups were full.

Chen bowed. "Thank you, As-t'us."

"Would you like to see my clinic now?"

"Cl-in'c?"

"Where I treat people who are ill."

"Yes, see cl-in'c."

Getorius thought that Chen walked a bit unsteadily when he was brought in and shown the collection of animal bones and organ specimens preserved in glass jars. He gazed at the curious animal parts, then the array of medical instruments. As Getorius wondered how to explain their use in simple terms, Chen picked up a long, thin needle.

"You use to help balance *chi?*"

"Chee?" Getorius was unsure of what he meant. "I use needles to remove splinters, probe boils. What is this Chee?"

"Our healers teach that body is balance of two forces call *yin* and *yang*. They put needle in certain body points to adjust flow of *chi*."

"What if there is a diseased organ like…like the kidney in that man I treated in Diotar's cabin?"

"Zhang Chen not like Dio-t'r very much."

"I agree. There is something sinister about him."

"Sin-st'r? What mean?"

"Ah…ominous, evil."

"Bad?"

"Yes, bad. Did you know him in Pessinus?" Getorius probed.

Perhaps Chen could throw more light on the eunuch priest's background.

"Not talk of Dio-t'r."

"No." Getorius decided it would be too difficult to discuss any more medicine with Chen. "Let's go see if the sweet course is ready."

When the two men came back into the dining room, Silvia had set each place with a dish of dates cooked in honey, and refilled the wine cups.

Arcadia noticed that Chen seemed pleased with the simple dessert, and that the wine had made him more relaxed.

Getorius felt a bit lightheaded himself as he finished a last sticky date and thought again about the smaller crates. They might hold another food that was, hopefully, more exotic than Chen's black leaves. Perhaps he could cajole the nature of the contents from his guest.

"Chen, what else does your country have that we Romans don't know about?" Getorius asked with a slight slurring of the words.

"But no more papir," Arcadia objected in a good-natured petulance that was a result of the wine. "I want to hear more about where Chen was born."

"*Cara,* he lives in Pessinus now. He may not remember much. Chen, tell us about another product we don't have here in Ravenna. Would it be in those other crates?"

Chen hesitated. The inside of his head had an unfamiliar spinning sensation that was making him nauseous, and he was no longer in total control of his thoughts. Was this why Lao Tzu had prohibited the drinking of wine? Now As-t'us was asking about what was inside the padded containers. The wealthy sen-t'or had warned him not to talk about it, yet this As-t'us and his wife were new friends, perhaps the only ones he would make in Ravenna.

"My friend at Ol-cin'um—"

"The man who was killed in the earthquake?"

Chen nodded to Arcadia. "Qin Shi own mine of what Greeks call nitron. He have new thing he make himself."

"Egyptians used nitron to preserve bodies for embalming," Getorius recalled. "You say he discovered another use for it?"

Chen stood up, swaying a little, and pointed through the door windows. "You have garden?"

"Yes, would you like to see it?" Arcadia asked. "It's still light outside."

"We go there. Zhang Chen show 'Dragon Cough.'"

"The cough of what?" Getorius was puzzled.

"Draco, Husband. A mystical creature something like a grith-ffin," Arcadia explained, stumbling over the last word.

"A griffin? All right, lead us to the garden so we can hear this creature's mighty roar."

Chen stood up, already regretting that the wine had made him boast of having something that Val-tan, the Western *Ti*, did not. But not to honor his promise would be a dishonor to his new friends. "Good, As-t'us. You bring hot coal from cook stove."

Getorius thought it a strange request, but complied. While he went to the kitchen, Arcadia unlatched one of the panels and led Chen outside. The cool evening air was fragrant from blossoms on the fruit trees and the fresh earth that Brisios had turned in the vegetable garden. In a nearby plot the perennial herbs grown for the clinic were sending out new green growths and a spicy fragrance.

Arcadia watched Chen unlace his purse and take out two thick red cylinders the length of her index finger. They looked as if they were wrapped in a dyed piece of the tan material she had seen earlier. A candlewick extended from one end.

"What are they for, Chen?" she asked. "They're too small to give off much light."

"Not candle. Qin Shi and I use to celebrate New Year. Much noise."

Getorius returned, holding a red coal in a pair of tongs. "What do I do with this?"

"Give me." Chen touched the end of the coal to one of the wicks. After it began to sparkle, he threw the tube to the ground.

"How pretty…" Arcadia bent down to pick up the fizzling object, but Chen pulled her back, crying, "No touch! No touch!"

A moment later the cylinder burst apart in a loud sound

amid a shower of sparks, smoke, and bits of wrapping. Getorius was reminded of the snap of a released catapult cord against the frame. Arcadia likened it to the pop of pinewood on a fire, only much more sharp and intense.

A sulfurous smell came from a smoking, shallow hole in the ground. The force of whatever happened had thrown bits of grass and dirt into a circle around it.

Brisios's dog Nivello howled at the sudden noise. The guard who had brought Chen, lounging outside the carriage gate, rattled the portal for entrance. Brisios came running into the garden to see what had happened.

"It's nothing, Brisios. Go tell that guard," Getorius ordered. "Our friend showed us a…a toy from his country." Bending to inspect the hole, he hoped the garden trees had helped muffle the sound. Getorius smelled the soil and fingered a few tufts of grass that had been thrown a distance of three paces away. "Amazing," he muttered, straightening up. "Chen, can we use the other one? I'd like to try something."

Zhang Chen's mind was clearing a bit, but he had now experienced firsthand why Lao Tzu had ordered abstention from wine. Friend or not, he regretted showing As-t'us the Dragon Cough.

Getorius brought a chipped pitcher that Brisios used to fill the birdbath dish. "Let me put the other one under here so it won't sound so loud," he said, taking the cylinder from Chen, before he could object.

He propped it up at an angle on a small branch, then laid the pitcher top-down so the lip rested on the twig. Getorius blew on the coal and touched it to the wick, then moved Arcadia back to the other side of the herbs. Chen also stood well away.

An instant later the cylinder exploded, shattering the pitcher and flinging ceramic shards in a wide circle around the spot where it had stood. One struck the bottom of Arcadia's tunic. Getorius picked up the shard and found it was slightly blackened and smelled of the same sulfurous odor as the hole.

"Christ! Enough of these bigger Dragon things could destroy a house. Is that what you brought in the four crates?"

"Zhang Chen…" Instead of finishing the sentence, Chen ran to a corner of the garden and vomited. He returned moments later, wiping his mouth. He bowed. "Zhang Chen must go back. Good meal. Thank you."

Arcadia grasped his sleeve. "Chen, I'm so sorry. Come in and rinse your mouth, wash up—"

"Zhang Chen must go," he insisted, shrugging out of her hold. Getorius walked him toward the gate. Brisios was trying to quiet the dog again, and the guard was straining to peer through the board cracks. Getorius unlatched and swung open the portals.

"Everything is all right," he assured the man, pressing a silvered *follis* into his hand. "Chen showed us a harmless plaything. Take him back to Maximin's, but don't tell the senator we saw the toy. He…he wants to surprise us." Getorius felt that might be half true, yet he knew it was not a surgeon whom the senator wanted to impress with the dragon's powerful cough.

※

Later, in the bedroom with Arcadia, Getorius thought about the astonishing things they had both seen that day. One, the writing material, had been shown at the order of Galla Placidia, but the Dragon Cough was clearly an inadvertent display by a man who was not used to the effects of drinking.

"I feel sorry for Chen," Arcadia remarked, slipping on a night tunic over her head. "We really shouldn't have insisted that he take the wine."

"A headache in the morning, then he'll be fine. And without it he might not have shown us that coughing dragon."

"It was loud enough to be heard inside Lauretum."

"What interests me is its potential for destruction. That small amount of nitron, and whatever was mixed with it, smashed that jug as if it had fallen from the roof."

"Frightening. What did you think of his writing material?"

Getorius watched Arcadia run an ivory comb through her hair, a ritual he always found sensual, before replying, "If this papir is as simple to make as Maximin implied, he'll surely become the richest senator in Roman history."

Arcadia put down the comb and took up a mirror to check her hair. "He could also become wealthy without manufacturing it."

"I'm not sure what you mean. Why do you think he wouldn't put it on the market?"

"You heard what Maximin said about opposition, even rioting, from parchment and papyrus makers and their suppliers."

"*Cara*, the poet Horace once quipped that the prizes of life are never acquired without trouble."

"And, Husband"—she tilted the mirror to look at his reflection—"wasn't he the one who also said that bribes enter without knocking?"

"Bribes? You're suggesting papyrus and parchment makers would pay Maximin to keep the process a secret? Really, Arcadia, how much wine did *you* drink?"

"I'm probably wrong, yet he'd make money either way."

"Actually, when I think about it, you're not necessarily off target. How much would it be worth to the industry to avoid ruined businesses?" Getorius got up and came behind his wife to kiss her neck. "You need to sleep well tonight, and be fresh for Leudovald's questioning in the morning. I'll go with you, of course."

"No, you have to keep the clinic open. And I don't want you telling him that you knew about the 'Valentinians.'"

"Leudovald's not stupid. He realizes that I know."

"I'll simply tell him the truth. That I found the coins in a bale of wool."

"And implicate Maximin? Do we want someone as influential as the senator for an enemy?"

Arcadia turned to him. "Then what should I do? Flutter my eyelashes and tell him they must have gotten into my purse through sorcery? You just said he wasn't stupid."

Getorius's jaw clenched. *I keep forgetting how stubborn Arcadia can be.* "Would you like a valerian drink to help you sleep?"

"*No!* Getorius, I just don't want you imprisoned again."

"I'll be fine. Let me pull the covers up for you. I'm going to sit awhile in the study."

❧

With Arcadia settled in bed, Getorius went to his favorite room to think. Presumably, only five people knew about the writing material—Chen, Galla Placidia, Senator Maximin, Arcadia, and he. It could have been only three persons. Why had the Oriental insisted on having two other witnesses present? Had Chen been concerned that after the manufacturing process was written down he might no longer be needed?

Certainly, Maximin must have paid him an enormous sum to bring in the crates. Perhaps Chen would try to withhold the formula for making this Dragon's Cough as a guarantee of his safety. Maximin must surely have seen it demonstrated, and fully realized its destructive power.

Getorius yawned and got up to join his wife. Time enough after Arcadia was questioned to speculate about the new products. He was also anxious to see Thecla again, find out if she was well, and ask her if she knew of any hidden entrances in her church. If Leudovald objected to a visit, he would, as Galla Placidia's physician, insist on checking the old woman's health.

Chapter fifteen

J ust before the third hour, Getorius walked with Arcadia across the palace garden toward Leudovald's wing of the building. His office and the adjacent rooms for interrogating suspects were located at the far northeast corner of Lauretum Palace—probably to muffle any cries that might be heard if, as rumored, suspects were tortured to obtain information.

One of the Gothic guards at the entrance escorted the couple through the garden and past the menagerie of exotic animals that Valentinian kept in his zoo. Arcadia paused to look at the emperor's newest prize, a pair of ostriches she heard had been brought from Egypt on the grain ship *Horus*. In the light of her own predicament, she empathized with the frantic look and nervous pacing of the birds in their bamboo pole cage.

As Getorius brought his wife into Leudovald's office, the investigator glanced at the sandglass on his desk.

"Good, Domina," he observed amiably. "You are here exactly on the hour."

"We want this cleared up," Getorius told him. "Neither Arcadia nor I know anything about the origin of those coins."

"Coins. Of course not, Surgeon, but we have a more pressing matter. You and your wife are here as witnesses."

"Witnesses to what? I came to help defend Arcadia against your accusation."

"Accusation. Yes, we'll come to that, but the murder of the castrated youth is of more importance." Leudovald stood up from his desk and indicated the door to an adjacent room. "We have the Arian priestess and the others in there."

"Others?" Getorius asked

"The galleymaster and his daughter."

"Why them?"

"Them? You shall see, Surgeon."

The interrogation area was divided into four cramped sections by curtain partitions. A high window was the only source of light. Hanging from wall pegs were leather whips, hand and leg irons, and devices that were used to extract information from suspects, or frighten them into talking.

Getorius saw Thecla sitting on a bench below the window. Although she looked tired, he saw no signs of mistreatment. "Presbytera, we've been concerned about you"—he grasped bony hands that felt cold—"are you well? Is your stomach pain gone?"

"The daemon still—"

"Surgeon, stay away from the prisoner," Leudovald ordered before Thecla could finish her answer. "I'll not have poison slipped to this heretic."

"Poison?" Getorius took a deep breath to control his anger. "Leudovald, I've taken an oath not to administer anything harmful to people."

"People. And how many rebellious legion commanders have broken their oath to the Augustus?" he scoffed, then nodded toward two people in the room. "You already know Virilo and his daughter."

"Yes. How are you feeling, Claudia?"

The girl did not look up at Getorius from playing with the folds of her tunic.

"She's fine," Virilo answered gruffly.

"The man with them at the table is Deacon Dagalaif," Leudovald continued. "Since the priestess belongs to an heretic sect, he's here representing the archbishop."

Dagalaif, a pale, nervous-looking man, opened a wax tablet and asked Getorius, "You're the surgeon who discovered the dead youth?"

"I was called to the Arian church."

"Then tell me—"

"Deacon, this isn't an ecclesiastical court," Leudovald reminded the man sharply. "I will ask the questions."

Dagalaif flushed to the unhealthy color of a drunkard, and incised a notation on his tablet.

Leudovald motioned Getorius and Arcadia to a bench opposite Claudia and her father, then slid a short whip off its peg. Standing a few paces from Thecla, he caressed the leather strands and fingered the lead barbs on their tips, as if lost in thought, then looked down at her.

"Priestess, you told me that you discovered the youth Atlos and the girl in your basilica when you went to fill oil lamps. What did you do then?"

Thecla replied in a voice that was barely audible, "I saw a boy outside and sent him to bring a surgeon."

"A surgeon. Getorius Asterius, here?"

"Yes."

"And why him in particular?"

"A parishioner I met on the Armini had mentioned that Getor...the Surgeon...was treating his mother. I thought to send for him."

Dagalaif tapped the flat erasing end of his stylus on the tabletop and spoke up. "Was the youth dead?"

When Leudovald did not protest the question, Getorius guessed that he had seen the deacon taking notes, comments that would undoubtedly be passed on to Archbishop Chrysologos.

"I'm not a physician," Thecla answered.

"Woman, don't be impertinent," Dagalaif snapped. "Surely, you've buried enough of your heretics to know a dead person when you see one."

"Deacon, that will do…" Leudovald turned to Getorius. "Surgeon, what did you find?"

"The young man bled to death. His testicles had been severed."

"Severed. With *what?*" Leudovald cracked the questions as he might the whip.

"There was a sickle in Atlos's hand."

"A sickle? You still insist on that, Surgeon, despite the fact that I found a fish knife next to the body."

"I'm sure of it."

Leudovald dawdled with a lead barb for a moment. "Tell me about Claudia, the girl who was there."

"I…my wife and I…thought she said her name was Sybil, the name of the ancient oracle. She was actually saying 'Cybele.' C-y-b-e—"

"The name of my galley," Virilo interrupted. "You know all that. Why the questions? My daughter had nothing to do with that slave's death."

"No, Galleymaster?" Leudovald flicked the whip toward the floor. "What I discover will be presented to a magistrate. Surgeon. Why did your wife go to the church with you?"

"She's training to be a medica. And I didn't know what I'd find. The boy Thecla sent said only that I was to come with him."

"And your wife later examined the girl?"

"In my clinic. I've told you all this, Leudovald."

"Answer again, Surgeon. What did she determine?"

Getorius wanted to tell Leudovald to ask Arcadia, since she had done the examination, but held back. "She found that Claudia was about three months pregnant."

"And this Atlos was responsible?"

"How would my wife know? Ask the girl."

Leudovald's whip snapped the floor in a gesture of impatience. "Galleymaster. Did you know your daughter was with child, or who the father might be?"

"No."

"Then I'll question her about the matter."

"No! She isn't well," Arcadia protested. "It would be like reliving a frightening dream."

"Woman, you're not to speak," Leudovald reprimanded. "You also are here as a prisoner accused of a crime, and certainly not as an advocate for the girl."

"But my wife is correct," Getorius broke in. "Questioning Claudia could bring on an epileptic seizure."

Leudovald ignored his advice and leaned on the table in front of Claudia, who was absently tracing the folds of her tunic with a finger. "Child," he asked with studied softness, "tell us what happened that evening."

Claudia did not look up, nor answer, and only continued to pleat and unpleat her tunic folds.

"Child?"

"She doesn't talk much," Virilo said. "A god touched her mind when she was born."

"A god." Leudovald straightened to repeat his question more forcefully and shook his whip at the girl. "Child, I'm warning you to—"

"Atlos wanted to marry me," Claudia suddenly remarked in a low, girlish voice. "We went to the church to talk to...to her." She nodded toward Thecla without looking up. "After Atlos told her that I...I was carrying his baby, she became angry and killed him."

"N...no!" Thecla gasped out her protest. "That's not true!"

Dagalaif leaned forward. "Girl, you're saying the presbytera cas...castrated your lover?"

"She said he had done an evil thing in God's eyes."

"That's ridiculous," Getorius objected. "Thecla hasn't the strength to commit such an act."

"She...she gave him something to drink," Claudia mumbled. "Yes...wine. He was asleep when she did it."

Getorius forced himself not to laugh at the girl's accusation. "You're saying Thecla brought the sickle, or, if you will, a knife with her, and murdered Atlos?"

"I'll ask the questions, Surgeon." Leudovald hit the whip handle hard on the table and scowled at Claudia. "Child, are you telling us that this priestess killed Atlos? Who was he, anyway? No one has come to claim his body. And a slave can't marry a freewoman." When Claudia did not reply, he slammed the end of the whip handle against the tabletop. "Look up at me," he shouted. *"Answer me, girl!"*

Claudia suddenly clutched her hands to her stomach and began to sway back and forth.

"Getorius," Arcadia cried, "she's about to have an attack."

As Claudia's body stiffened, Getorius ducked around the table corner and caught her before she fell. He eased the girl off the bench and laid her on the floor, then loosened a shawl around her head. As she jerked uncontrollably, a dark splotch of urine stained her tunic.

Dagalaif signed himself over his heart with a cross and moved away, murmuring, "Father...deliver us from evil."

Getorius glared up at him. "It's all right, Deacon, she won't transmute into a pig and run squealing around the room."

Virilo stood and looked down at his daughter. "She's cursed. Always been like that."

"It's an illness, not a curse," Arcadia retorted. "My husband has told you that it can be treated."

Claudia slowly stopped trembling and her body relaxed. In a moment she was still, seemingly asleep.

"Take...take your daughter home now," Leudovald ordered Virilo, obviously shaken by the incident. "She'll have to testify at the priestess's trial, but...take her home until then."

"He can't just take Claudia back," Getorius intervened. "At the least she should be in the hospital ward here at the palace. There are treatments for her condition."

"She's my daughter," Virilo insisted. "I'm taking her home."

Leudovald held up a hand. "A moment, Galleymaster. Perhaps the surgeon has a point. Let her stay here for a few days under the care of the sisters."

"No!" Virilo grabbed Claudia's hand. "I invoke *patria potestas*. I'm taking her home now."

"*Potestas?* Your legal right as a father?" Leudovald looked at Getorius and spread his hands in a gesture of helplessness. "There's nothing I can do."

After Virilo pulled his daughter out of the room, Getorius went to Thecla. "Presbytera, that was a sick girl who made the accusation."

"Yes, but I was too surprised, too shocked, to respond sensibly. Nothing like that happened. I hadn't seen either one of them before."

"You look exhausted. Leudovald, could Arcadia examine Thecla...prescribe a diet? I'm afraid this stress might put her humors out of balance."

Thecla stood up and smoothed down her tunic. "Thank you, Surgeon, but I'm quite well."

"Then, if you're not ill, priestess," Leudovald said, "the guard will take you back to your room. Claudia's accusation clinches the charge of murder."

"You can't take the word of an epileptic girl," Getorius objected. "Claudia's mind is unstable."

"Unstable and touched either by God or Satan. A magistrate will decide which." Leudovald turned to Arcadia. "You, woman, are free to go home with your husband for now."

"Despite the coins?"

"We'll deal with them in good time." Leudovald replaced the whip on its peg, then opened the door. "Guard! Take the old woman back to confinement."

"May I walk that far with her?" Arcadia asked.

Leudovald hesitated, and then nodded permission. Getorius walked a step behind the two women as they crossed the garden toward the corridor anteroom where Thecla was confined. At the zoo, the ostriches were nervously pacing the perimeter of their temporary cage.

"Poor frightened creatures." Arcadia tried to calm them with soothing clucks, but they hissed viciously in reply, and pecked at her through the bars.

"Their ancestors must have given Noah quite a problem on the ark," Thecla joked.

Arcadia smiled and took her arm. "Thecla, I'm puzzled at what Claudia hopes to gain by accusing you."

"The child is mistaken."

"More likely, she's lying to protect her father," Getorius said. "Of course he knew about her pregnancy. We found that out when he came to us with Diotar. He's the logical person to avenge her."

"By using a ritual sickle?"

"To blame someone in that Cybelene cult, Arcadia."

"Is Virilo that clever?"

"Mastering the *Cybele* and outfoxing pirates takes a measure of shrewdness." Getorius lowered his voice below the guard's hearing. "And don't forget the smuggled coins and sapphires."

"Coins?" Thecla repeated as a question. "What do you mean?"

"Nothing," he said quickly. "Do you need anything, Presbytera?"

"No, they brought me my Gothic Testament and a few sheets of papyrus. Pen, ink."

"We'll try to come and see you tomorrow afternoon," Arcadia promised. "Senator Maximin once offered my husband his lawyer. I'm sure the man will defend you, if it comes to that."

"Thank you, dear, but the Son who is subject to the Father will protect me." She stopped at a door and chuckled. "Here's my hermit's cell. Until tomorrow, then."

※

Virilo was angry, grasping Claudia tightly by the arm as he strode along back alleys toward his home on the Vicus Judaeorum.

"Father, you're hurting me," she complained when he paused for a cart at the Via Fossi.

"You little fool," he snarled without looking at her. "Leudovald realizes the old woman couldn't have killed someone as young as that slave."

"I said it to protect you, Father. He would have blamed you, because of the knife he found."

"I didn't kill Atlos. I don't know how my knife got inside that church."

"You lied," Claudia retorted. "You knew I was pregnant."

"That's none of Leudovald's business. There'll be more questions at the trial, and the magistrate isn't stupid. Diotar will be furious when they ask about your connection with him in the cult. If you hadn't gone whoring around with that slave, none of this would be happening."

"Father, he raped me in the temple while I was touched by the god."

"So you say."

"He did, Father. And Atlos broke his oath to Diotar about becoming a priest of Attis at the Megalensia."

"Megalensia," Virilo muttered, but relaxed the grip on his daughter. A solution occurred to him as he guided Claudia south along the street to the port area. "Maybe that woman surgeon can give you something to get rid of the baby." When Claudia did not reply, he shook her arm. "Did you hear me?"

She pulled away. "I heard you, Father."

"Good. I'll take you there tomorrow."

Virilo felt somewhat better as he crossed the Via Armini. No one else need know about his daughter's shame. Claudia's pregnancy wasn't yet showing, and the surgeon's clinic would have whatever it was they gave a woman who wanted to abort a fetus. He would bring Claudia back to Leudovald, have her recant the accusation, and say that Atlos had killed himself in remorse. The medica would back his daughter by testifying that she had spoken nonsense as a result of her Disease. There would not have to be a trial.

Yet how had Atlos gotten hold of his knife? Perhaps Claudia had let him inside the villa during the day, and that had given him the opportunity to steal the fish-gutting tool. But why did the surgeon keep insisting he had found a sickle in the dead slave's hand?

⁂

On the afternoon of her release, Arcadia found a man in the clinic's waiting room, complaining of a sharp pain in his lower abdomen. Since he had brought a jug of urine, she took it to her husband, thinking he might want to evaluate the patient's symptoms before talking to him.

Getorius poured some of the urine into a glass vial and held it up against the light of the clerestory window.

"Looks pinkish, and there are specks of sand on the bottom of the container."

"What does that indicate?"

"Get me our copy of Galen."

Arcadia pulled down the volume by the long-dead physician whose views still dominated medical practice. She knew Getorius disagreed with Galen on several points, yet he was worth consulting, if only to posit an opposing diagnosis.

"'On the Natural Faculties,'" Getorius murmured, searching the pages. He stopped at information about the bladder. "Here, Section Thirteen. Galen is disagreeing with Asclepiades about the function of the kidneys. His rival agrees that they process the water we drink into urine, but thinks it's changed to a vapor, then recondensed into a liquid before entering the bladder."

"But it would be an unnecessary step."

"Exactly. Nature designed our bodies more perfectly than that." Getorius looked at the discolored urine again. "Let me talk to...what's his name?"

"Decimus Cordus. I'll bring him in."

Cordus was a balding, red-faced man with dark circles of loose flesh below his eyes, an indication of lack of sleep, Getorius surmised, because of the abdominal pain. The man's full-length tunic was made of finely woven wool, decorated at the sleeves and neck by green and blue stripes. His boots were tanned leather, dyed green to match the case slung around his neck. Getorius thought him likely to be an import merchant, well able to pay for treatment. *Good. Being palace physician might be an honor, but it carries no retainer. I'm paid for each service weeks afterwards. This Cordus can help balance the cost of patients I treat without a fee.*

"I'm sorry you're having a problem with your bladder, sir," Getorius said, after the man was seated.

"Drop the polite manure, call me Cordus," he responded gruffly. "And it's my gut that hurts."

"Ah…yes." *Wealthy, perhaps, but not born to it.* "Exactly where do you hurt, Cordus?"

He made a vague circular motion with one hand, which indicated his entire lower body.

"I've looked at your urine. Sometimes the kidneys secrete hard stones that can cause pain."

"What, rocks inside my gut? That's lunacy."

Getorius ignored his outburst. "Are you uncomfortable when urinating?"

"What?"

"When you piss, Cordus. Does it hurt?"

"Why didn't you say? Sometimes."

The man wasn't being very helpful. Cordus was the opposite of patients who described several detailed but conflicting conditions, which also made diagnosis difficult. Yet the urine condition fitted with Galen. If the stone could be passed, it was preceded by a sharp pain between the kidneys and bladder as the hard material moved through the ureter. This was assuming, of course, that human anatomy was comparable to that of the monkeys Galen had dissected.

And yet the painful urination that Galen had called *dysuria* could be caused by other factors. Men who came to the clinic frightened by the hurt, and by a corresponding yellow discharge from their penises, eventually admitted to having been in Ravenna's brothels. He would have to examine Cordus for symptoms of gonorrhea, always an unpleasant experience.

"Has your stomach been upset lately?" Arcadia asked. "Have you vomited?"

"What?" Cordus scowled up at her as if she had demanded money from him.

"My wife trains with me," Getorius explained. "It's the next question I would have asked you."

Cordus picked nervously at the green band on his sleeve before admitting, "I…I been having pains."

"What do you like to eat?" Getorius asked.

Cordus leaned back with a smirk. "Fried pork...squid. Goose liver. Lots of cumin and pepper seasoning. I can afford it."

"Vegetables. Greens?"

"Don't like them."

"Do you take your time eating?"

"I've got my business to look after, woman," Cordus replied, evidently offended at Arcadia's question. "You can't trust slaves to do it."

When Arcadia looked at her husband, he read her thoughts. The urine sample suggested stones in the man's bladder, but his unhealthy eating habits might be exacerbating a stomach unbalance. "Cordus, the wrong food could be part of your problem," Getorius said, "yet the urine color is pretty damning."

Arcadia picked up the pitcher she had placed on the table and noticed that it was cracked near the top. "Cordus, what do you usually use this for?"

"Me? Nothing." Cordus's tone suggested he had been insulted. "That's my house slaves' wine jug. I wouldn't piss in a good one of mine."

"Wine jug?" Getorius realized what his wife was suggesting and asked, "Did you rinse it out first?" At Cordus's negative shake of the head, he poured most of the urine in the vial back into the pitcher, then dribbled the rest into the palm of one hand. He easily crushed the sandlike particles between a thumb and forefinger. "Sediment crystals from the dregs of a wine barrel. The lees are the slaves' portion."

"Some leftover red wine tinted his urine."

"Good that you noticed, Arcadia." Getorius wiped his hand and turned to Cordus. "You can thank Fortuna you haven't formed stones in your kidneys, but you must eat more slowly, and differently. My wife will give you a list of foods for your cook to prepare. And doses of boiled licorice root for those stomach pains."

Before Cordus could protest, the office door was opened and Childibert looked in. "Master, Senator Maximin is here. He...he insisted that I interrupt you."

"It's all right, I'm about through. Take the senator to my study. Arcadia, write up that dietetic regimen for Cordus, then join us."

Maximin was standing when Getorius entered the room. As the senator reached to grasp his wrist, light flashed off the carnelian stone on his ring. It was carved in the shape of a rooster, reminding Getorius of the senator's chicken farm.

"How are things at the Villa of the Red Rooster, Senator?"

"I may sell out. Prisca is disgusted at having to endure the smell of chicken droppings all the time."

"Of course." Arcadia had mentioned the all-pervading odor after she had spent a week at the villa in December. "Please, take a chair. You're feeling well, I hope? Not here for medical reasons?"

"No, no. And that tincture you prescribed for my eyes has done wonders. No, I came on another matter." Maximin looked toward the door. "Your wife isn't here?"

"She'll join us shortly."

"Fine." He polished his ring on a sleeve in a nervous gesture before asking, "Those counterfeit 'Valentinians.' Where exactly did she find them?"

My God, he knows about those too. He must be in thick with Leudovald. "Where?" Getorius repeated. "Uh...as you've probably heard, Senator, we boarded the *Cybele* without actually booking passage."

"Concealed yourselves in the hold."

"Yes. Arcadia found a pouch of the coins hidden in a bale of...well...of your wool, Senator."

"In the name of Hades!" Maximin burst out, smacking a fist against the palm of his hand. "Someone is trying to implicate me in whatever's going on."

"You mean in case the coins were accidentally discovered?"

"Exactly, Surgeon, and your wife did just that. I used my influence to have Leudovald postpone questioning her about where they were. Now I know."

"We're grateful, sir. How do you think they got inside your bales?"

"I'll be frank. It's no secret how I feel about Flavius Aetius..."

the fact that I believe he has designs on becoming Augustus one day."

"With respect, Senator—"

"Wait"—Maximin's ring flashed as he held up a hand to block the objection—"you're going to defend Aetius because he helped you when you were falsely accused. Oh, the man seems likeable enough…a trick for disarming an opponent."

"Senator, I'm not much for palace intrigues. What are you getting at?"

"An influx of counterfeit Western coins into the East would destabilize the economy. Sow confusion, suspicion."

"These are only bronzes. Perhaps if they were silver?" Getorius probed to see how much Maximin really knew about the coins.

"The mints at Siscia and Sirmium were closed decades ago," Maximin replied. "Equipment from them might have been stolen and sent to Scodra. Coins could receive a silver wash there. Attribute them to Valentinian and you have the basis for another civil war between East and West. You can see the reason I don't want to be implicated, and why Aetius needs a decoy to throw suspicion off of himself. At some point he'd have the coins discovered in my wool."

That's close enough to Arcadia's theory, Getorius thought, *and he's already decided Aetius is the guilty one.*

Arcadia entered the study. Maximin gave Getorius a furtive shake of the head for silence, and rose to greet her. "My dear, you look lovely. Your husband and I were talking about the Oriental who is staying at my villa."

"Chen? I'm afraid we made him sick at dinner, giving him too much wine."

"He did complain of feeling ill in the morning."

"How is his work with the writing material coming along?"

"He's finished his translation of the manufacturing process. I've ordered a moulding screen made to demonstrate the making of a sample sheet."

"Getorius, you haven't offered the Senator anything," Arcadia noted. "Let me call Silvia."

"No, no," Maximin refused. "I should get to my warehouses."

"Then let me walk you to the front entrance," Getorius said, just as Childibert appeared at the door again.

"Master, there is an accident at palace," he called out. "Go quickly. A person is hurt."

"Who, Childibert?"

"Guard only say a person. Asks that you come."

"What could have happened?" Arcadia wondered.

"I don't know, but bring my medical case."

"God forbid that anything has happened to the Augustus," Maximin lamented. "I'll come with you and be sure he's safe."

While Arcadia went for the case, Getorius hurried out of the door that opened onto the Vicus Caesar. Maximin followed alongside. When they reached Lauretum, no sentries were on duty at the entrance.

Strange, Getorius thought, *has there been a palace takeover? Valentinian, or Placidia, murdered? Is Maximin correct in suspecting Aetius after all?* He looked toward the end of the corridor and saw a line of men blocking access to the atrium. "The Scholarians are all up there, Senator." The palace guards had locked shields and were facing the garden. After Getorius came up behind them, he saw that the men were struggling to keep the two ostriches inside the enclosure. The neck and head of one of the desert birds appeared above the guards, bobbing frantically as it sought a way through the human barrier. When its head ducked down, he could hear the ostrich pecking at the guards' shields, or kicking at them with sickening thumps on leather-covered wood shields. Any guard could have severed the bird's neck with a sword stroke, but Getorius understood that any man who decapitated the emperor's new pet knew he was risking a punitive beheading himself.

Marcus Lucullus, the tribune who had arrested Arcadia, stood to one side, directing the men.

"What happened?" Getorius asked him. "How did the ostriches get out?"

"A keeper must have left the cage door open," he replied without looking away.

Arcadia passed Maximin, who was pressed against the door of

the closest reception room, watching from that distance. "Here's your medical case, Getorius," she said, then grasped his sleeve. "What's going on?"

"Valentinian's ostriches have gotten loose."

A guard in the line staggered back from the force of a kick, stumbled, and fell. Before the other men could pull him away and close ranks, one of the frightened birds lunged through the opening and trampled over his body as it escaped along the corridor.

Maximin hugged the doorjamb. Getorius shoved Arcadia back hard against the wall, protecting her with his body. The ostrich paused to look at them, its eyes wide in an uncomprehending stare, and its mouth open in a gasp. It hissed, then Getorius felt the massive feathered body knock him aside with the force of a bolting horse. The huge bird brushed past and strode toward daylight at the palace entrance, where its dark silhouette disappeared into the street.

Maximin and Arcadia were safe. Getorius was winded by the blow. He slowly rose to his knees, gasping for breath and grasping a gray plume, then went to watch two slaves who had come into the garden with a heavy rope net. The head of the second ostrich appeared briefly above the row of guards, before the huge bird was encased in the rope's mesh and its thrashing legs trapped.

After the guards relaxed their blocking formation, Getorius pushed through their ranks. The bird had been wrestled to the ground, still hissing defiance, and was struggling to break free.

Getorius saw a frightened boy slave, who had climbed a tree to be safe, and called up, "Can you see who was hurt?"

In answer the child pointed toward the ostrich cage. A crumpled human form, wearing a black tunic and head shawl, lay on the ground in front of the open door. Blood splotched the tunic material.

Getorius felt a reflexive shiver of dread. "Jesus, no. Don't let it be…" He ran to the body, bent down and pulled aside the dark head covering.

Still open in her battered face, Thecla's watery blue eyes stared past Getorius with the gaze of a dead person, straining for a glimpse of eternity.

"It *is* Thecla. Arcadia!" he yelled. "Where's that medical case?"

She hurried over and knelt beside him to open the cover. "Thecla? What happened?"

"She was evidently attacked by the ostriches." Getorius shook his head and gently pulled the veil back over Thecla's face. "Never mind. Nothing can help her now."

A shadow fell across the body of the dead woman. "The presbytera was feisty," a voice said. "I'll grant her that much."

Getorius looked up. Leudovald was stroking his mustache, almost smirking, as he glanced down at the battered body of his prisoner.

Chapter sixteen

What happened?" Getorius demanded, barely suppressing his anger at Leudovald's callous attitude. "How did Thecla get out here?"

"I spoke to her guard, Surgeon. He let her empty the slop-pot and walk around a bit."

"Without noticing that the ostriches' cage was open? Thecla was attacked in full daylight."

"I'll question the keeper." Leudovald pulled Getorius aside as six guards approached, struggling to carry the recaptured ostrich back to its enclosure. The enmeshed bird gasped from exhaustion, its eyes half-closed under curling lashes. "Mind the presbytera's body," he called to them.

"Mind her body, Leudovald? No, order Thecla taken to a hospital ward, where the sisters can prepare her for burial." Getorius saw that Arcadia had gone to stand by the garden retaining wall. "I'll talk to you later about what might have happened. I need to see if my wife is all right."

Leudovald followed him. When Getorius came up to Arcadia,

she handed him his medical case and wiped her eyes with a hand. "How terrible that Thecla should die like this. So…so needlessly."

"Bishop Chrysologos can decide on a burial site for the priest…the presbytera," Leudovald said in a more gentle tone.

"Why not in the Arian cemetery, next to her church?"

"Surgeon, didn't I see Senator Maximin with you?" Leudovald hedged.

"He was at my clinic when I heard about what had happened here."

"Ill?"

Getorius ignored the question and repeated his concern, "We can't let Thecla just lie there, Leudovald."

"I'll order Lucullus to have her body taken up to the hospital."

"Fine…" Getorius watched Leudovald turn away toward the tribune, then muttered, "Insensitive son of Hades."

"At least he caught himself after he called Thecla a priestess," Arcadia said. "Getorius, let's look inside her room. It's the second door on the left."

"I may have to treat that injured guard."

"They took him into the Scholarian barracks. Let their medical orderly clean him up first."

Getorius looked at the other guards. They were cheering their comrades who were trying to push the ostrich back into its cage and loosen the net without being flailed by its powerful legs. "We'll go in while the men are distracted."

Thecla's room was sparsely furnished. The Gothic Testament and writing materials she had requested were arranged on a table. A reed pen marked off one section of the codex, and a small, rolled-up papyrus was centered on the top cover.

"Arcadia, she wrote something here," Getorius said on opening the sheet.

CREDIMVS ĪN VNVM DEVM
FV̄NDATOREM OMNĪVM
BEATV̄M PATREM FILĪI
QVI EMITTIT SPIRITV̄M.

"'We believe in one God, originator of all things'," he read, "'blessed Father of the Son, who sends forth the Spirit'."

"'The Lord of the Holy Spirit'," Arcadia continued, "'Whom the Father created through the Son before all things. The Holy Spirit is obedient and subject to the Son, like the Son to the Father.' Sounds like a statement of what Thecla believed. 'The Holy Spirit...is subject to the Son like the Son to the Father.' It's probably the Arian Creed. And look, she sketched the old ιχθυc 'Sign of the Fish' at the bottom of the text."

"I wonder why?" Getorius studied the ink drawing. "It once identified secret Christians, but hasn't been necessary in decades. Thecla's is more elaborate, with an eye and cross on the side." He opened the book at the pen. "She's marked a section in her Testament."

"But neither of us reads Gothic."

"Let's see...good...the text is translated on the left side. Thecla underlined a passage in Luke."

"What does it say?"

"'People will lay their hands on you'," he read. "'You will be brought before...magistrates and put in prison. Some of you will be put to death, and all will hate you for your allegiance to me.'"

"I told you that Thecla was depressed. She picked a passage that seemed relevant to her Arian faith."

"There's a margin notation about another section." Getorius turned to a previous chapter. "Here, verse fifteen is underlined."

"Let me read it." Arcadia took up the book. "'Guard against greed in all its forms. A man may be wealthy, but his wealth does not give him life.'"

"What's the connection? Her Arian followers are anything but rich."

"She noted something else." Arcadia thumbed back to the section Getorius had read first. "'Nation will make war against nation, kingdom against kingdom.'"

"Rather gloomy selections. I can understand the one about persecution, but you'd think she would choose a more comforting psalm."

"Why, particularly, would she select Luke? There are similar passages in the other Testament writers."

"You think that's important, Arcadia?"

"Wasn't Luke a physician?"

"That's the tradition."

"Getorius, I think she's addressing these to you."

"Me? Why? And Thecla's not really telling me anything."

"Look at the creed again. I noticed abbreviation dashes over some of the letters, yet the complete word had been written out."

"Let me see." Getorius read off the designated letters, "I̅N̅... F̅V̅N̅D̅...Ī...B̅...V̅...L̅...V̅M̅—*infundibulum*. A tunnel?"

"That's what Thecla was telling you."

"But why? She certainly didn't expect to die."

"No, but she would have tried to get this to you with as many clues as she could give."

"Clues to what, Domina?" Leudovald's questioning voice came from the doorway behind Arcadia. "You two seem to be meddling in my work."

Getorius thought Leudovald sounded more curious than angry, but felt he had little choice other than to be honest with him. "Thecla noted passages in her Testament and wrote out an Arian creed. We found the word for 'tunnel' in the text as a kind of code. Look for yourself."

"Tunnel?" Leudovald spotted it immediately. "A child's cipher," he scoffed, "and not very well concealed."

"Perhaps it wasn't meant to be," Arcadia suggested. "Her guards couldn't read."

"Couldn't read. So where is this tunnel?" Leudovald looked around the small room in mock bewilderment. "Were her fellow heretics plotting to dig in here and free her?"

"Leudovald..." Getorius sucked in a long breath and exhaled, deciding to throw his dice with the investigator and trust to Fortune. "Leudovald, I don't think you much like me, but I believe you want to find out the truth as much as I do."

"The truth. Go on, Surgeon. These clues?"

"The tunnel could be in her church. Arcadia once wondered

whether Arians would have a secret escape route, in case they were attacked."

Leudovald allowed a thin smile of admiration beneath his mustache. "Surgeon, I had dismissed rumors about your part in solving the origin of a mysterious papyrus last year, but perhaps I misjudged. You and your wife may search the heretic's church with me."

※

The Basilica of the Resurrection presented a different atmosphere when entered by daylight. The dim gloom in evidence on the evening that the body of Atlos had been discovered had been replaced by warm light diffusing from alabaster window panes in the clerestory and side aisles. The clarity revealed brick sidewalls that were relieved by recessed arcades, most fronted by a limestone sarcophagus. Several burial niches in the wall were sealed with inscribed marble slabs.

A sparrow fluttered overhead on the smokestained truss beams. An irregular triangle of light, where the wood rested on the wall, betrayed the missing bricks through which the bird had entered. Droppings spotted the floor under a nest set on the beam.

"The porter that Thecla mentioned obviously hasn't kept to his task during her absence," Getorius commented.

"We'll start at the nearest memorial slab in the right aisle," Leudovald decided, striding to the wall with a mallet in his hand.

The area had the unmistakable odor of mildew and dried urine. He fingered the edges of the stone slabs to feel for any cracks that might indicate a hidden recess, then tapped the wall with the mallet for telltale hollow sounds.

"Nothing?" Getorius asked. Leudovald shook his head. "There's a stone coffin in the next arcade. The lead seal at the edge of its lid is stripped away."

Leudovald went to feel the rim. "Vandalized for the metal, but the top seems intact. I doubt there's an access from the inside that would lead to stairs beneath the floor."

Arcadia checked the next sarcophagus, a small coffin whose simple front inscription commemorated a child. "Lucinia Julia Optata," she read aloud. "Died at the age of six years, one month and six days. No cause given." It saddened her, knowing that if an infant lived past its first or second year, chances of survival were good. Little Julia might have succumbed to one of the plague epidemics brought in on galleys coming from Asian ports. The thought of the dead six-year-old was a fresh reminder of Thecla's unnecessary death.

Arcadia left the aisle to the men and went into the nave. Near the altar a dark splotch of Atlos's blood still stained the floor. *That porter has been careless.* Skirting the spot, she climbed up three stairs to the semicircular apse, wanting to explore the space behind the altar.

Two side windows gave light to the mural of the Risen Savior, which had been only dimly visible when she had first seen the painting from a distance. The figure was crudely done, without realistic model-ing, but the flat style gave Christ the aura of possessing a transcendent body. He hovered over the black rectangle of a tomb opening beneath, with arms extended to show the bloody spike wounds on his wrists. Behind him, an apricot-colored dawn sky silhouetted the scene at Golgotha, a mound that was topped by three T-shaped *Tau* crosses.

Under the mural, a lower part of the wall that had seemed to be five slabs of marble from afar turned out to be wooden panels painted to resemble the veined stone. Arcadia's first reaction surprised her—that this deception was as subtly false as Thecla's Arian creed. She walked past, noticing that adjacent panels on each side were decorated with drawings of a man, an eagle, a lion and an ox, symbols she knew represented the four Testament writers.

Arcadia stopped by the sketch of Luke, which also had the same ιχθυc symbol as was drawn on Thecla's parchment. Could she have meant it as another clue? Arcadia was about to call the men over, when Leudovald's excited voice echoed from the aisle.

"I've found it! In this last niche."

Arcadia ran down to a blind arch fronted by a pine storage cabinet, which Leudovald had pushed aside.

"I noticed an irregular outline of bricks that might indicate a sealed opening," he gloated. "As I tapped the area, I heard a hollow sound."

"We think there's an empty space behind the bricks," Getorius explained. "Should be a door to Thecla's tunnel."

"Stand back." Leudovald smashed his mallet hard against the brickwork. As the wall shattered under his blows, the opening was enlarged enough for him to look inside. After he peered in, his expression of eagerness changed to a frown. "There's an oak door about a half pace in. My mallet is too small, I'll have to bring a guard detail to batter it down. Let us go back."

"Leudovald, we'll stay here and look around some more," Arcadia said.

"For what?" he asked, his eyes narrowing in suspicion. "It's obvious that the door leads to the tunnel."

"We...we want to be sure this is the only entrance," Getorius added, thankful for his wife's quick reaction. "There might be others."

"Very well, Surgeon, but don't go inside and bar the front portal after I leave. I don't want any of Thecla's Arians coming in and seeing what I've discovered."

After the investigator was gone, Getorius slid a beam into its supporting brackets to secure the door. Arcadia led her husband back into the apse and showed him the ιχθυς drawing. "Look at that symbol. It's the same as on Thecla's papyrus. Could it be marking a tunnel entrance?"

"Leudovald thinks it's behind that door."

"These panels are wood, easier to move if you're in a hurry," she reasoned. "Feel around the edges."

Getorius felt, then pushed at each of the surfaces, but none of them moved. "Nothing, Arcadia. Let's just wait until Leudovald comes back."

"You commented on the unusual 'Ichthus' design," Arcadia recalled. "The eye and cross. Perhaps it's not just an eye. It could be pointing us to the left."

"Where do you get these ideas, Wife? It's just the old Christian fish symbol."

"Then humor me, Husband."

Getorius sighed and retested the two panels on the left side. All were securely attached to the bricks behind them. "Sorry, they're solid, and after the last one you're back in the nave again."

Arcadia looked up again at the picture of the open tomb above the center panels. "Getorius, the few murals of the Resurrection I've seen all have Christ at the entrance of a burial cave, the way the Testaments describe the scene. This one has a rectangular grave set in the ground."

"That *is* unusual." He tapped the black area with a knuckle. "Arcadia! It sounds hollow!" When he pushed hard at the bottom, the black rectangle began to swivel inwards. An immediate rush of cool air and the stench of decay came from the opening. He pulled back, covering his mouth. "Aggh! It smells like I've literally opened a tomb."

"Is it the tunnel?"

"Let me look inside." Getorius held his breath and glanced in. It was totally dark below, but light from the small opening revealed the rungs of a ladder attached to the back wall, about a pace in. He tested the swiveling wooden board and felt behind it. His hand came away wet and slippery. "Olive oil smeared on an iron rod, so the door can easily open. Thecla's followers weren't taking any chances, Arcadia—they kept this in working order."

"Where does it lead?"

"Judging from that smell, the ladder probably goes down to a sewer, or perhaps the drainage canal under the Via Armini. Stay here and tell Leudovald where I've gone."

"I'll *not* stay here, Getorius. I'm going down with you."

"That's insane, Arcadia. Who knows where the tunnel leads?"

"You're wasting time, Husband. I'll follow you in."

Getorius felt too curious to argue with her. The stench filled the immediate area now and he suppressed an urge to retch. After he had squeezed into the cramped space, he counted six ladder rungs before his feet touched solid ground. He flailed at something that brushed his hair, then realized it was Arcadia's sandal. She had not waited long to come after him, and was carrying his medical case.

Getorius helped his wife down to a low, curved passageway. A bluish glow in the distance tempered the darkness. "Let's walk toward that light. Keep your head down."

Arcadia slung the case over her shoulder and clutched the back of her husband's tunic as he hugged the curved wall. Getorius counted thirty paces before the darkness brightened and the gurgle of running water was heard.

The wall ended at right angles to a higher arched tunnel that stretched off into the distance. Small wells of light from above, at what Getorius estimated were twenty-five pace intervals, illuminated the sewer. In front of him, a stream of water almost as wide as the Via Armini swirled past. Its smell, although unpleasant, was not that of raw excrement.

"I'd guess that this is Augustus Caesar's old canal from the Padus River," Getorius said, with an eerie echo to his words. "It's a storm drain now, with a few slops tossed in through street openings, but we're lucky…it would be a lot worse if public latrines emptied into the culvert."

A narrow maintenance walkway built above the channel followed the left wall. The stones were wet, and slimy with green, moss-like growths. Getorius ducked down and went in.

"Which way do we go?" Arcadia asked, following him. "Left or right?"

"I'm not sure." After looking around, Getorius noticed a faint fish symbol scratched high on the wall, facing to the left. "This graffiti looks to be ancient. Thecla's predecessors were well prepared. If you're correct about the eye, we should go in the direction it's pointing."

Getorius started along the walkway, counting paces. After reaching the first opening overhead, he heard the rumble of carts passing on the Armini and realized it would be impossible to become lost. It *was* the ancient canal, now a sewer that went in the same straight direction as the road above. Peering through the grating, he saw a sky that was a cloudless cobalt blue. He and Arcadia would not be drenched with a deluge of rainwater from the curbs. Yet up ahead, at the next opening, a slim column of water sparkled in a brief cascade—someone was emptying a pot though the opening. *There are hazards* he thought, grasping Arcadia's hand to continue their trek.

Getorius estimated he had walked over a hundred paces when bright daylight ahead shone in from the right. The Armini sewer had intersected with another channel, a cloaca that swept wastes from the western quadrant of Ravenna into the harbor.

The mouth of the drain was a short distance away. Through the opening, Getorius caught a glimpse of galleys at anchor and some of the harbor warehouses. An iron grate over the end of the cloaca was jammed with brush, and what he realized were the bloated and decaying carcasses of small animals. There were undoubtedly human remains in the tangle of debris, possibly murder victims whose bodies had been disposed of by being jammed through street sewer openings.

"I'll have to wade across this channel, but I'll carry you," he said, giving Arcadia's hand a squeeze. "Are you all right?"

"Yes, but I can walk by mysel…" Arcadia started to protest, when a gray snake slithered past in the murky water. "Fine, carry me," she relented. "And please don't fall."

Getorius tested the bottom with a foot. It was slimy, and the water ankle-high, but he made it across, with Arcadia clinging to his back, her nose buried in his tunic to block out the stronger stench. The lateral sewer did carry latrine wastes off into the harbor.

Further on, at a point Getorius estimated was a few paces more distant than they had come, a smaller tunnel angled off to the right. He looked at it and the main sewer, which, like the Via Armini, continued on toward the Porta Anastasia in the north wall.

"Do we keep going straight or turn here?" Arcadia asked, glancing up at a grate over the intersection.

"We're somewhere in the port area. The harbor is on our right, so this side tunnel might lead to a wharf where the escapees could have boarded a galley."

"That would make sense if they were trying to escape." Arcadia looked around the well of light and spotted the incised outline of a fish on the wall to her right. "There. Another 'Ichthus.' It's pointing into the tunnel."

"Good, then we're still on the Arians' escape route." Getorius helped his wife across paving stones set in the channel to the passageway. "Watch your head again," he warned. "This tunnel is lower and darker."

Only a small patch of light shined in the distance, from above, where the passageway suddenly ended. The dim illumination revealed a wooden door set in an end wall of bricks.

"Let's find out where that leads." At the door Getorius rattled its sliding bolt, but the securing wards held fast. "Of course…locked. Look around. The Arians wouldn't have come this far without hiding a spare key somewhere close by, in case they couldn't bring one from the church."

After searching the wall in the poor light, Arcadia noticed an equal-armed Greek cross scratched on one of the bricks, less than an arm's length above eye level. "Getorius, look. This may mark something."

"Makes sense. Open my medical case, I'll try to pry the brick out with one of my larger scalpels." After Getorius had worked the bronze blade into the mortar joint he edged the brick forward in short, grating scrapes. He handed the block to Arcadia, reached inside the opening and pulled out a bronze key. The short handle was decorated with a head of Christ. "That was almost too easy, but then I don't imagine anyone but fugitives would ever be down here." Pushing the key wards up into their corresponding slots, Getorius slid the bolt loose and cautiously pulled the door open. He peered in. "Incredible luck—a room, and it's empty."

The entranceway led up three stairs, into a medium-sized area with rough brick walls and a low ceiling. Two narrow windows set high on one side lighted the space. Another larger door was at the far end.

"This looks like the basement of a house," Arcadia whispered.

He nodded. "After our eyes adjust to this light, we can see what's stored here."

It soon became evident that worktables were set against the walls, and a number of lampstands near them, that, when burning, would substantially increase the light. Getorius puzzled at an upright device, which had a long handle attached to a wooden worm screw.

"Are we in a fuller's shop? This looks like the cloth press at the one on the Vicus Caesar." Glancing around, he noticed a basket on a worktable next to the press, heaped with coin-sized bronze discs. He examined one and found it blank. "Could it be?" He ran a finger under the head of the press screw and felt a circular incised design. Directly under it, a matching depression in a block of bronze had been lined up with the center of its upper mate. Peering into the die, he recognized the reverse profile and inscription of Valentinian III. "Arcadia, this is a coin press! It's where the counterfeits are minted. Could Thecla…her Arians…be involved in a conspiracy to subvert the emperor?"

"I can't believe that. There aren't enough members, and they have enough trouble as it is. Getorius, let's go back. I'm frightened someone will find us."

"Right, and it wouldn't do for Leudovald to discover that we vanished into the ether. On the way back I'll pace off the distances down here more carefully. If I start outside at the Arian basilica and count steps north along the Armini, then to a street on the right, I probably could come close to the building where we are."

Getorius locked the door, replaced the key and brick, then led the way back to the main sewer. At the junction, he paused to lean against a wall. "I can't believe we've found the place where the counterfeit coins are being made. But what can the connection with the Arians be?"

"I don't believe there is one, or Thecla wouldn't have led us there."

"Good point. One of her congregation members might have stumbled on the room in checking out the escape route."

"And she was alluding to it in her Testament passages," Arcadia said. "She wanted us to find the place."

"I'll have to think about that later. Right now, we'd better get back before Leudovald does."

❧

Retracing and counting his steps, Getorius reached the ladder and helped Arcadia out through the access door concealed by the tomb painting. Inside the church apse, he glanced down at his boots.

"Soaking. If Leudovald notices these are wet, he'll have questions. What can I dry them with?"

"That cabinet he moved could hold Thecla's vestments. There might be towels, for the Baptistry." Arcadia ran down, opened the door, and pulled out a folded linen cloth. "Yes. Here, dry your shoes with this."

Getorius had soaked up most of the wetness by the time Leudovald pounded on the front door for admittance.

"Open it for him," Arcadia said. "I'll mop the floor with the towel and put it back."

After Getorius unbarred the portal, Leudovald stalked in with four palace guards.

"Now we'll see where this tunnel leads," he told the men. "Smash down that wall and pry the door open."

Getorius wondered if there might be two escape routes, as he watched the men hammer apart the bricks. They used a crowbar to yank the door planks off, but even before the work was finished, he had seen the blank wall behind the splintered wood. "It's a decoy, Leudovald," he said. "Wasting a pursuer's time on the niche and false door would have given the Arians more time to escape through the…through a real tunnel."

"Perhaps I've underestimated the heretics." Leudovald scowled. "Did you two find anything?"

"They say that cunning helps weak folk survive," Getorius hedged.

"Indeed. And if you hunt a fox, know his tricks. Surgeon, you said there was a porter here?"

"An old man, Thecla told me. I forget his name."

"I'll find and question him. The presbytera may have deceived us with 'clues' to a non-existent tunnel."

Arcadia shivered. "It's chilly in here. I'd like to go home, Getorius."

"Of course, *Cara*. Leudovald, you'll investigate Thecla's death and let me know what you find out?"

"Investigate to what purpose?" he retorted. "We have the girl's testimony about the slave's murder, and the perpetrator's death is an accident. I'll report those to the magistrate."

"That's all you'll do?"

"Reprimand the guard for carelessness. Yet there is still the matter of the false 'Valentinians.'"

"Well, you know where our home is. Let's go, Arcadia." *So much for trusting Leudovald,* Getorius thought as he took his wife's arm. *"Solve" the murder no matter what.* As he walked to the door, he glanced down at his damp boots. Evidently, "the little icy man" had not noticed them.

Once she was outside, Arcadia took a deep breath of spring air. "I need a bath to soak away that sewer stench."

"I'll certainly join you."

At the corner of the Via Porti, Getorius turned to look along the Armini. The tunnel underneath had run roughly north, into the heart of the harbor quarter, then the smaller one a short distance east. But to which shop, house, or apartment?

"Are you figuring out where we were?"

He nodded. "Thecla knew about that room, Arcadia, but she couldn't tell us in so many words. And it's under a building I may or may not be able to find."

"The Testament passages she marked off might be clues in locating it," Arcadia suggested.

"What, that her persecuted Arians devised an escape route?"

"The other sections, Getorius. About a man's wealth not giving him life. Nation making war against nation."

"Senator Maximin is certainly the best candidate for the first one, but how would Thecla know that the counterfeits were being smuggled in his wool bales? If that's what she's telling us."

"Nations…our two empires…would be at war with each other as a result of the coins' distribution in the East."

"Either Thecla's a prophetess, Arcadia, or she somehow found out about all this and her death wasn't an accident."

"Horrible. You thought that the power of Chen's invention could change warfare entirely."

"The Dragon's Cough. Those four crates are at the senator's villa, with Chen."

"We haven't seen him again," Arcadia recalled. "I wonder how he's doing there?"

"I don't know who it is that Maximin intends to have witness the power of the dragon, but I need to talk with Chen once more. And *soon*."

Chapter seventeen

Zhang Chen had decided that he was not happy at the Villa of the Red Rooster. For one thing, he was lonely. Ravenna did not have a community of his people, as had Pessinus, and the strangely seasoned food of the Ta-Ts'in was not to his liking. His quarters were permeated with an overwhelming stench of chicken dung that stuck in his throat day and night. In addition, this arrogant official, Sent'or, now treated him like a servant, and had not spoken of the gold coins that the eunuch priest Dio-t'r had promised he would receive for bringing samples of *chih*, his writing material, to the West.

And now that the screen for making *chih* was finished, Sent'or did not seem in much of a hurry to see a demonstration of how the writing sheets were manufactured. And after foolishly trusting As-t'us, Chen felt that the cunning healer and his wife had tricked him into revealing the Dragon's Cough by bewitching his mind with the enchanted drink that Lao-Tzu had warned against.

Although Zhang Chen did not much like Dio-t'r, he thought that it was time to talk to the womanish priest. It was the eunuch who had suggested that Chen travel to the land of the Western Emperor with his inventions, promising that he could sell them there and escape as a rich man from the repressive statutes of the new ruler of Sina. Yes, he would go see the priest whose strange goddess ordered her worshippers to turn themselves into neutered capons. Was it not well known that the eunuch court around the Sinese Emperor wielded enormous influence? Perhaps Dio-t'r could take Chen away from the stinking house of roosters, and get him his promised gold.

⅔

When Zhang Chen arrived at the gate to the temple compound of Cybele, a novice porter admitted him to Diotar's rooms. Adonis and Claudia were there, the girl dressed in her vestal robes.

"Ah, Chen." Diotar stood to greet the man. "Good, I was planning to send for you."

"You wish see Zhang Chen?"

"Yes, about…what do you call it…the cough of a Dragon?" Diotar turned to Claudia. "Child, go to your room and rest now. Adonis, stay with us."

Claudia did not reply, but, after a glance at Adonis, obediently left the room. When she was gone, Diotar motioned Chen to a couch upholstered in silk damask.

"Chen, I'm making plans for a public celebration to Cybele at the June solstice. It would be an appropriate time to honor her as Fruitful Mother. I wanted to ask you—"

"The girl is child of galleymaster?" Chen interrupted.

"Yes, Virilo's daughter."

"Why she not dress like other Ta-Ts'in?"

"The robes? Through metempsychosis, Claudia is the reincarnation of an ancient Roman Vestal priestess."

"Met-em—?"

"The rebirth of the soul after death," Diotar explained with a high-pitched giggle at Chen's confusion. "It's a Greek term, but Eastern holy men in India also teach the concept."

"In-d'a." Chen nodded. He had heard of an immense country to the southeast of Sina, beyond a river called the Gangem. It might be that the strange rebirth idea was held there, but he had seen from the recent corruption of Lao-Tzu's precepts that men tried to make others believe whatever suited their own ambitions.

"Our Cybelene cult grows day by day," Adonis boasted, standing up. "The Great Mother protected Rome from the Carthaginians once before, and we are convincing more and more citizens that she will do so again against this new invasion of Vandals."

Chen nodded politely, not really interested. He was concerned with his own well-being, not some remote conflict in which these Westerners fought each other. He voiced his complaint, "Dio-t'r, Zhang Chen not happy at house of Sen-t'or."

"Unhappy?" Diotar frowned and toyed with a medallion of Cybele hanging around his fleshy neck. "Why is that?"

"Sen-t'or strange man. Have room with many rooster statue. Bad smell in house. Bad food. And Chen not have gold you say Sen-t'or promise. Chen want bring *chih* and Dragon's Cough here."

"Here?" Diotar gave Adonis a questioning glance. What was Maximin up to? He had the process for making a writing material that would make him unimaginably wealthy. How could he be stupid or treacherous enough to balk at paying the Oriental? Might he have some other scheme in mind and be planning to betray Chen? In any case it might be advantageous to have him and his inventions here at Cybele's temple. At Pessinus he had seen the Dragon's Cough used during Sinese New Year celebrations, harmless displays of noise and smoke that had frightened children and dogs, but done no harm. It was an amusement that he thought would attract attention and add another element of interest to the solstice celebration of *Cybele*.

"Want boxes here," Chen repeated, "not at rooster house."

"Yes, if you wish," Diotar agreed, "but the Senator's villa is well-guarded. How will you bring the crates to the temple?"

"You friend of Sen-t'or," Chen snapped. "You find way."

"Indeed." Diotar thought a moment. "Adonis. Get me a list of those new members you mentioned. Perhaps one of them has access to Maximin's villa, a servant or guard. A gold coin blinds all eyes."

After Adonis left, Diotar took a key from his belt ring and opened an iron box that was bolted to the floor under a table and concealed by drapery. He took out a leather bag, selected a sapphire from inside, and put the gem in Chen's palm.

"There will be more of these for you," he murmured, closing the man's fingers over the blue stone, "along with that gold you were promised. I wanted to ask you to make a few of your sparkling dragon candles for Cybele's feast. If Senator Maximin is foolish enough not to appreciate you, Chen, know that you have friends at the temple of *Magna Mater*. Of course you may stay here."

Zhang Chen bowed in appreciation. The capon-man might be a friend after all.

⁊

Around mid-morning on May sixth, Leudovald sent word to Getorius that Bishop Chrysologos had permanently closed the Arian church, but had given permission for Thecla to be buried in the sect's cemetery. The time of burial was to be at the first hour after sunset. He added that the name of the basilica's porter was Odo, but he had not been found.

⁊

"Why is the service so late in the day?" Arcadia asked Getorius, ducking under the awning of a shop on the Via Porti as a gust of wind brought in a cold spring rain.

"This storm will keep people away and it will get dark early. Mourners won't stay at the graveside for long afterwards. No doubt the bishop intends this to be the last gasp for Thecla's Arians."

"Poor woman. To die so horribly that way."

They found the cemetery close to the west wall of the octagonal baptistery, but the narrow sides gave little protection against the rain that continued to drive in from the northeast.

In the murky light, the scarred brick building and its adjacent basilica seemed like abandoned mausolea guarding the burial ground's wooden and limestone grave markers. The leaning and toppled monuments and slabs resembled the scattered, bleached bones of some dismembered antediluvian creature that had expired there.

The few mourners who were gathered around the open grave

held squares of leather over their heads as protection against the downpour. Alongside, on a wooden pallet, Thecla's body lay wrapped in a simple winding sheet, its rain-soaked linen cloth clinging to the contours of her frail form.

Getorius recognized Leudovald and Deacon Dagalaif standing in the lee of the baptistery.

"The wolves as watchdogs," he commented to Arcadia.

"I noticed an iron grille nailed over the baptistery door," she said. "There's probably another one sealing the basilica entrance."

"Then we'll never get into that tunnel again, and I want to find out more about where those coins were being struck. Look, that's Fabius over there with his mother."

"I didn't realize they were Arian Christians."

"Neither did I. I'll talk to him about locating Thecla's porter."

A gaunt, middle-aged man, who identified himself as Deacon Maurilio, began the funeral service with a reading of the sect's creed, the same text that Thecla had used to direct Getorius to the tunnel entrance.

After a nervous glance in the direction of Leudovald and Dagalaif, Maurilio shielded the book under his cloak and began his eulogy.

"Taking the name of Blessed Thecla, Paul's companion, our presbytera served this Arian community for over thirty years," he told the assembled mourners. "She tried to follow Christ's command to love one another, but as Arians we are a hated people, persecuted for our beliefs, just as the Israelites were persecuted by their enemies. Yet, as did Blessed Paul, let us persevere in our distress, in our hardships, in the floggings and imprisonments imposed on us by our countrymen."

"Surely, he's exaggerating," Getorius whispered to Arcadia.

"I'm not so sure. Have you noticed women looking back at Leudovald from time to time? They're frightened."

"Then this Maurilio isn't helping."

"Enough falsity!" Dagalaif suddenly called out from the shelter of the baptistery. "Throw mud over the heretic, then go back to your homes."

Maurilio frowned at him and motioned for two men to approach the graveside. One was Fabius. He and his companion lifted Thecla's body and lowered it into the rectangular pit, coffinless, wrapped only in the wet shroud.

Defying Dagalaif, Maurilio announced, "These are the words that Paul wrote to those he had recently converted in Corinth. 'Not all of us shall fall asleep, but all of us are to be changed…in an instant, in the twinkling of an eye. The trumpet will sound and the dead will be raised incorruptible.'"

"Appropriate, at least," Getorius remarked. "Thecla's basilica was named for the Resurrection. I didn't know about the deacon, but I think I'll talk to him afterward. Maybe Maurilio can shed more light on that tunnel room."

As the mourners quickly began to disperse after the burial, Leudovald hurried down to the grave, where Maurilio had lingered to watch the men shovel wet earth into the opening. Getorius saw the investigator say something to the deacon, then grasp his arm and guide him across a muddy field toward the Via Porti, in the direction of the palace.

"Looks like I'll have to wait until Leudovald finishes talking to the deacon to see him."

Arcadia stifled a sob and wiped her eyes. "While you're talking to Fabius, I'll ask Felicitas about her leg. She hasn't come to the clinic lately."

"Good. See if she's following that diet we gave her."

Getorius waited until Fabius had thrown a last shovelful of muddy dirt into the open grave, then approached him. "I'm your mother's physician."

"I'm helpin' mother," Fabius said with a defensive scowl.

"Fine, but this is not about her. When Thecla called me to the basilica about the dead youth, she mentioned a porter. Do you know where he might be?"

"Odo? Nobody's seen him since then."

"The man just disappeared three weeks ago?"

Fabius shrugged and started toward Felicitas and Arcadia. "I got t' take mother home. Out of this furcin' rain." He paused, searched through his belt purse, and handed Getorius a bronze piece. "Look, I got money t' pay you. I want t' bring mother home."

"Where did you get this?" Getorius asked after seeing the coin.

"Th' 'Valentinian?' I…uh…change from a *siliqua* I gave Videric for mother's pork."

"I see." He handed the bronze back. "Here. Take your mother home now."

Getorius followed him to where Arcadia was talking to Felicitas. They both watched Fabius support his mother as she hobbled toward the Via Armini, then Getorius turned to his wife. "Fabius had one of the counterfeit coins. When I turned it to the reverse there was the RV minting location, here at Ravenna. He said he got it in change for a *siliqua.*"

"Where would he get a silver coin, Getorius? As far as we know he has no job."

"Exactly. This may connect him to the counterfeiters, although it's not impossible that some of the false coins are being circulated in Ravenna."

"Felicitas said she'd come to the clinic soon. Did her son tell you about the porter?"

"His name is Odo, but he seems to have disappeared."

"But this Odo probably would know more about that tunnel than anyone except Thecla."

"Or that deacon." Getorius sneezed and wiped water off his face. "Let's go back to the clinic, out of this downpour. My dry humor is completely out of balance."

"Do you still feel feverish?"

"A bit."

When they had almost reached the end of the Via Porti, Arcadia stopped her husband under the balcony of a tavern at the eastern corner of the palace grounds.

"Let's wait a moment," she suggested, "there's no shelter between here and the Vicus Caesar."

"We could both use hot mulsum to temper the chill. Let's go in."

The tavern was crowded with supper customers. Getorius knew the proprietor, Ageric, a florid-faced man who looked like he sampled too much of his own vintages. He escorted the couple to a small table against the wall, and then hung their wet cloaks on pegs at the back. The unheated room felt damp, but was fragrant with the smell of Ageric's food. A tan-colored dog nosed around the black and white mosaic floor, snuffling up food scraps.

Getorius ordered white wine mulled with mastic and laurel leaf, and a portion of prawn rissoles. After listening a moment, he asked his wife, "Are you catching any of the conversation around us?"

Arcadia shook her head.

"I'm picking up words like 'Vandals' and 'Carthage.' There evidently hasn't been another large grain shipment come in since the *Horus*. They're worried about a bread shortage."

"And higher prices." Arcadia continued after a moment, "Getorius, I'm really interested in setting up a clinic for women."

He looked down and feigned interest in the dog. "Yes, you've mentioned that once or twice."

"For problems with monthlies, or pregnancy, childbirth."

"You'd have trouble on your hands from midwives. You know that's their specialty."

"I'd hire some to help out....to teach me." Arcadia leaned aside to let a serving girl put down the rissoles and clay cups of steaming wine. "Perhaps the midwife we saw at Faustina's."

"I wonder how she is. No one has called us over there since we returned."

"Her midwife was Calliste," Arcadia recalled. "Greek women are the best, according to Soranus, the most free of superstitions."

Getorius took a sip of wine and reached for a rissole. He had met Arcadia when she was fifteen, after he went with Nicias to treat her uncle's fever. She later told him she had decided to marry him then and there, although it was four years until the wedding.

Before the marriage, one of the "understandings" they had

come to—coercion might be too brutal a term—was that Getorius would allow Arcadia to study medicine with him, and eventually become a medica. There was no denying that his wife was what her father called "strong-willed." Even David ben Zadok, the old rabbi in Classis, who had known Getorius's parents, observed that Arcadia seemed as determined as his mother, Blandina, had been. She too had flouted tradition, in her case to be trained in map-making.

Getorius realized that Arcadia had learned rapidly in the past five years, but the idea of opening a clinic of her own was still premature. The Oath of Hippocrates demanded ability and judgment. He had worked under Nicias for six years before the physician died, and eleven more since then. Seventeen years in all, and yet at times he still felt as incompetent as an apprentice. No. His wife would have to wait.

"Getorius? Are you thinking about what I said?"

"Yes." He looked up, touched her hand, and replied gently, "Your clinic proposal, *Cara*. I can't agree to it just now. You need more training."

Arcadia pulled her hand away, pushed her cup aside and stood up. "It's stopped raining. Let's go."

"Don't be upset."

"I'm upset at what happened to Thecla. And tired. I just want to go home."

Getorius shrugged and dropped the last rissole on the floor for the dog, left a half-*follis* on the table to pay Ageric, and retrieved their cloaks.

Arcadia walked in silence for the rest of the distance to the villa, and Getorius did not bring up the subject of her women's clinic again.

※

Childibert met the couple at the door and told them the galleymaster's daughter was waiting to see them.

"Claudia? This late?" Getorius asked in a mixture of surprise and alarm. "Has something happened?"

He hurried to the clinic, with Arcadia following. Claudia was sitting in the wicker chair. She looked pale and her eyes were red from crying.

"Did you come alone, child?" Getorius asked.

"Adonis is waiting outside."

"Atlos's twin. Is your pregnancy giving you trouble?"

"I...I feel sick." Claudia stared down at her lap a moment, then mumbled, "Father made me jump up and down to shake the baby loose."

"The bastard—"

"Getorius," Arcadia chided. "Claudia, that's terrible."

"But then he said you could give me something to...to get rid of it."

"Abort the fetus? No, I can't do that," Getorius told her. "My Oath is quite clear about protecting human life."

"I don't want a baby."

"But...you loved Atlos. It would be a part of him." When Claudia did not respond, Getorius went on, "I hope your father isn't letting you take part in any more rituals like the one we saw at Olcinium, just before the earthquake."

Claudia looked away instead of responding.

"Child," Arcadia asked softly, "why did you accuse the woman presbytera of killing Atlos?"

Claudia looked around, startled at the unexpected question. "She...she did kill him."

"But Leudovald said he found Virilo's knife next to Atlos's body. Are you trying to protect your father? Is he responsible?"

"No!" Claudia bolted up and smoothed down her tunic. "If you won't help me, I'm going back home."

"Wait"—Arcadia held her back by the arm—"first let me give you a pelvic examination. To make sure there are no complications, no vaginal bleeding from that jumping."

Claudia glared at her and shook herself free, then started for the door that led outside to the Via Honorius.

"I could get you a sedative," Getorius called after her. "You said you weren't feeling well."

"Let her go," Arcadia advised. "You don't want to bring on an epileptic attack."

"No, but I'm certainly going to talk to Virilo in the morning. He can't order his daughter to do dangerous things like that."

"He shouldn't, but, under a stupid law, he can."

Arcadia was quiet a moment before asking, "Getorius, did you notice that Claudia didn't seem quite so timid as before, when we first saw her?"

"She's worried about having the child."

"Not just that. Did you see the look on her face when she pulled free of me?"

He shook his head. "I didn't."

"It was one of pure hatred."

"So, our little girl has a temper."

"She may not be that young, Getorius."

"Oh? Claudia looks no more than seventeen. And you examined her that night, after you brought her back here from the basilica."

"Just enough to determine she was pregnant," Arcadia said. "That's why I wanted to do another examination now."

"And she wouldn't let you."

"Exactly."

"What's your point, Arcadia?"

"I'm not really sure. I probably don't have one...yet." She waited until her husband finished a bout of sneezing. "Getorius, I'm going to order Silvia to fill the bathtub with hot water. You have a long soak, then take that sedative you mentioned and get a good night's rest for a change."

"'Physician, heal thyself,'" he jested, "with the help of thine wife."

※

While her husband bathed, Arcadia went to his study with her copy of Soranus's treatise on gynecology.

"Getorius is right," she admitted to herself. "I need more experience before even thinking of opening a clinic for women. I couldn't even get a pregnant girl to agree to an examination."

There was something disturbing about Claudia, but it was probably due to physical changes brought about by her pregnancy. What did Soranus have to say on the subject? Arcadia opened his volume and went to Section XVI of Book I, about the care that should be given pregnant women.

The ancient physician had suggested three levels of concern: in the early stages, the need to preserve the injected seed; then the alleviation of subsequent physical and mental discomfort during the pregnancy; and lastly, preparation for the birth. Soranus believed the embryo could be discarded for a variety of reasons—from extreme fright, to joy, to mental upsets. These could have happened to Claudia in the amounts necessary to produce a miscarriage. The gruesome death of her lover had to have been a traumatic experience, and suspecting her father to be Atlos's murderer would have added to the emotional shock, yet if all the reasons the physician gave were valid, few women would carry a fetus to term.

Perhaps, like Galen, Soranus was mistaken in some of the medical advice he gave. He listed several other ways that women might miscarry, but, again, these were so all-inclusive as to be almost useless information. He stated that the pregnancy discomfort called *pica* began at the fortieth day, a condition marked by a craving for unusual substances, and other gastric symptoms. Claudia had passed that date, but she was also an epileptic. How would this affect her pregnancy? Maybe Hippocrates could provide an answer.

Arcadia took down her husband's volume of the Greek physician's work, and turned to Section LXX, titled, *On the Sacred Disease*. She went past the preliminary paragraphs refuting the superstitions associated with the disease, and concentrated on Hippocrates' theory that epilepsia occurred in those with an inherited phlegm imbalance.

"'This malady, then, affects phlegmatic people…and begins to be formed while the fetus is *in utero*. For the brain…is cleansed and purified as it grows before birth.'"

Hippocrates went on to explain that if the brain was improperly purged, phlegm would accumulate in the organ. Children might rid themselves of this through ulcers on the head and body, as well as the copious discharge of saliva and mucus. Otherwise, they would be susceptible to getting the disease. Most of the youngsters who did, died in childhood.

I have no way of knowing if Claudia suffered from body ulcers as a child without examining her skin more carefully. She doesn't exhibit a chronic phlegm imbalance, and Hippocrates describes other symptoms and causes that are impossible for me to know, unless I talk to whoever raised the girl.

Arcadia put down the book and closed her eyes. Claudia had accused Thecla of killing Atlos, a charge so ridiculous that someone had to have put her up to it. Leudovald kept insisting that a fisherman's knife he suspected belonged to her father was found next to the body. Perhaps Virilo had ordered his daughter to blame Thecla to divert suspicion from himself.

We weren't dreaming! That was a golden sickle in the dead youth's hand. I saw it. Getorius saw it. So why does Leudovald say he found a knife? If he did, how could it have gotten into the church after we left?

The revelation came to Arcadia despite her fatigue. *Blessed Cosmas, the sewer tunnel! Someone who knew about the passageway could have come into the church and replaced that sickle with a fishing knife. Fine, Arcadia, you may have discovered a clue, but the mystery is still as murky as an image in a cheap bronze mirror. Leudovald…even Getorius…believes that Virilo found out about Claudia's pregnancy and killed Atlos. Yet he, or whatever professional killer he hired, certainly wouldn't have been so careless as to leave the knife at the scene. Someone is trying to blame Claudia's father…*

Arcadia opened her eyes and exhaled in frustration. "I'm too tired to think straight," she muttered. "I'll make a mint and thyme valerian drink for Getorius. Perhaps in the morning I can sort out my thoughts about the girl."

Chapter eighteen

Scanning the list of cult members Adonis had recruited, Diotar discovered that one was a guard at the Villa of the Red Rooster. He also found out that Publius Maximin and his wife would be in Arminum from the sixth to the twelfth of May, celebrating the Lemuralia, an ancient Roman festival commemorating the dead. Diotar knew that it would have been too dangerous for the senator to attempt to travel to Rome to honor his ancestors. Perhaps Maximin had a branch of his Anicii family in Arminum.

He recalled seeing the rites performed last year by a few of the bolder pagan sympathizers. In the necropolis outside the Lawrence Gate, black beans had been burned on graves. The resulting unpleasant stench was believed to frighten away evil spirits, and a few participants had beaten kettles and drums to help the exorcism succeed. This time Diotar guessed that citizens' attention would be drawn to the few defiant pagans who still observed the festival, and to possible trouble from Christians opposed to the ritual. The festival would create a diversion that could be used for moving Zhang Chen's crates from Maximin's villa. With the senator away, his guards would relax, some even be absent. Gold would buy the silence of any who noticed what was happening.

Adonis had found the new cult member among the guards. His name was Malarich, a Goth. The plan was for him to arrive with a cart loaded with wine amphorae cradled in straw. After unloading the jars in the storeroom where Chen's boxes were kept, Malarich would help the Oriental hide his crates under the straw of the empty wagon bed, for the return to the temple compound.

☙

May seventh, Frigedag, according to its new Frankish name, was a market day. Arcadia and Ursina went out to purchase food supplies for the next few days. Getorius was feeling better and thought now would be a good opportunity to retrace the surface route he had plotted while in the sewer under the Via Armini. If he could find the opening of the lateral drain into the harbor, then estimate the paces he had counted from there to the underground room, he felt he might be able to find the location where the illegal coins were being minted.

☙

Getorius reached the warehouses at the end of the Via Porti and noticed the *Cybele* riding empty at her berth, while stevedores loaded nearby merchant ships. He saw that a few more galleys had finally arrived—also from the Eastern Empire, judging by the names that were close enough to read; Greek, all of them—*Arcas, Neleus,* and *Selene.* That was encouraging. Wheat imports sent from Constantinople might yet forestall the looming bread shortage in an Italy threatened by the Vandal occupation of the African provinces.

Getorius threaded his way north between workers, along the edge of the stone wharf. He counted paces until he heard a splash of water and saw bits of debris swirling from an arched sewer opening near the far end of the galley anchorages.

"One hundred twenty paces," he told himself aloud. "This is the outlet of that lateral cloaca." He looked along a canal opposite that led toward the Armini. "The intersection with the main sewer was a little past halfway to the smaller tunnel, where I found the door to the room."

He started walking west along the canal, which was stagnant with floating refuse. The houses opposite were among the oldest in Ravenna, dating from a time when many of the streets were canals. Most buildings had been cheaply made of mortared stone rubble that was held together by a timber framework. All of the house fronts still displayed some Roman god or other in a shrine niche, yet the burned-out shells of several buildings were charred testimony that the old gods had not always protected their worshippers.

Shabbily dressed, dirty children played in flat-bottomed skiffs, or floated blocks of wood in the canal filth. The sons and daughters of freemen laborers, Getorius surmised, or of slaves whose masters lived, not here, but in new homes in the quarter where Galla Placidia's mausoleum was located. He wondered if there was even a single physician to serve these people. Most of the children who had reached five years of age would have seen playmates and adult family members die of disease or in horrible accidents.

At the Via Armini, Getorius turned north and counted paces, oblivious to jostling by pedestrians on the sidewalk and imprecations by vendors selling from booths.

There should be a street somewhat beyond the distance I've counted along the wharf, and an apartment or house to the right. That distance had been twenty-two paces, he recalled, the same number as from Thecla's church to the Armini sewer. The building would not be located too far from a corner.

Sixteen paces beyond those he had measured to the drain, Getorius stopped at the Vicus Judaeorum.

"The street of the Judeans. This must be where Nathaniel took Rabbi ben Zadok when he was here last December, but is this the place that I'm looking for?"

He saw Ravenna's north wall and the Porta Anastasia a long block ahead. The Judaeorum seemed to be the last fair-sized street. From the noise and acrid smell of metalworking shops lining the narrow way, Getorius knew he was in an artisans' quarter.

He turned into the Judaeorum.

Beyond an outdoor bronze foundry and potters' kilns, an alleyway separated what appeared to be an open space on the right, surrounded by a brick wall. Continuing along the barrier, Getorius peered through a gap in the gate, and caught a glimpse of a garden and two-story villa complex beyond.

Could this be the place? Who might I ask about the people who live in there without arousing too much suspicion?

Getorius turned. The shop across the street had a sign painted on its front wall in Greek that identified it as ΑΠΟΛΛΕΙΟΝ, the Apolleion. A crude painting of a silver statue of the god was underneath, and the Latin word ARGENTARIVS. He might get information from a silversmith who spoke Latin.

Getorius crossed the Judaeorum and went to the shop's sidewalk counter. A swarthy, bearded man glanced up from his bench, then motioned to a young woman who was polishing a dish. "*Roto afton ti aftos thelo,*" he ordered her in Greek.

She came to see what Getorius wanted. "You wish to buy or commission silver work?" the woman asked in softly accented Latin. "Pharnaces gives the best price."

"Not just yet." Getorius slid a half-*follis* across the counter to her. "I was wondering who lives in the villa across the street. If it's the place I want."

She looked up from the money with a smile of scorn. "*Kirios...* sir...a half coin buys half that information."

Pharnaces had evidently heard the clink of money and his daughter's answer. He put down his engraving burin and came to the counter. When he saw the bronze, he shrugged in mock disdain and pushed it back with a forced grin.

"Ah, sir. Regretfully, the price for what you ask of Pharnaces would be a *siliqua*. Still the best bargain in Ravenna."

"Half a *siliqua* for all the information," Getorius countered, mimicking the artisan's smirking grin. He took a small silver coin from his purse and spun it on the counter.

"Done!" Pharnaces deftly scooped up the disc before it stopped turning. "You, *Kirios,* are indeed a shrewd bargainer." He pulled at the girl's sleeve. "Back to work, *kori.*" He watched his daughter return to her bench, pouting, then asked Getorius, "You perhaps have important business at the villa?"

"And will *you* pay *me* to know that?" Getorius quipped.

Pharnaces's eyes crinkled in delight as he hid a chuckle with the back of his hand. "Humor. A commodity as rare as truth these days." He leaned closer and whispered, "The house *could* be that of the galleymaster Gaius Quintus Virilo."

"Virilo?" *Unbelievable...what good luck!* "His boat is the *Cybele?*"

"Indeed, sir. Named for the infernal goddess who is worshiped by that gaggle of womanly eunuchs who also reside there."

"Eunuchs?" Getorius feigned surprise, thinking that he should not tell this artisan too much. "Gaius Virilo, you say? I've heard of him, but no, I...I was looking for someone else. I'm grateful for your help, Pharnaces."

"Of course you are," the craftsman mocked. "I was not the galleymaster you wanted, but the pleasure of telling you about him was mine. And should you desire the finest in silverwork—"

"I'll come to you for another bargain."

Getorius turned back toward the Via Armini, shaken by the implications of what he had just heard. The 'Valentinians' evidently were being counterfeited by Virilo and hidden in Maximin's wool bales. But were the coins made for the senator, or were his exports simply a convenient place for the galleymaster to smuggle them into Dalmatia? Surely not all of the bales contained leather pouches, so how would the receiver know where to find them?

Getorius visualized the wharf at Olcinium, recalling that the bales were being separated into two unequal piles. The answer struck him with the suddenness of summer lightning. *The knots! The bales were tied differently when I opened the two that we slept in on the galley. That means at least one of the customs officials at Olcinium...probably more...have to be part of this. The sapphires also must be Virilo's. The man has a complete smuggling operation going on, using the prestige of*

Maximin's senatorial position to allay suspicion and avoid much of the usual customs inspection.

⁊⁊

Arcadia had still not returned by the time Getorius got back to the clinic. No one was in the waiting room, so he went into his study.

He was making notes on a wax tablet when Arcadia entered and saw him there.

"I found some early asparagus at the market," she said. "It will be nice for supper tonight. Did any patients come in while I was gone?"

"No. Arcadia, sit down. You won't believe this."

"What is it?"

"I traced our route on the streets above the sewer. That room we found at the end, where the 'Valentinians' are being counterfeited, is probably a basement inside Virilo's house."

"Virilo? Then that definitely makes him involved in the smuggling."

"Not only that—I think Diotar's temple to Cybele is located on the property."

"How did you find that out, when Leudovald couldn't?"

"I wouldn't have, except for the hidden door you noticed in Thecla's basilica, and our odorous odyssey beneath Ravenna. It turns out that Virilo's place is in the artisans' quarter, on the Vicus Judaeorum, just east of the Armini. I bribed a Greek silversmith across the way to tell me who lived there."

"Clever, but what do we do now?"

Getorius held up his note tablet. "I've been trying to figure out the relationship between Virilo and Diotar. Even Senator Maximin...if he has a part in this."

"We did suspect that Diotar had some kind of hold on Virilo."

"Perhaps by threatening to expose his smuggling operations? If Diotar's temple is there, he may have found out about them."

"Did you see anyone at the villa?" Arcadia asked.

"No. In fact, it looked deserted."

"If it is Virilo's, that must be where Claudia lives."

"With her father and that nurse he once mentioned." Getorius stood up. "After our noon meal I'm going over to see Maros."

"The sick pigment-maker?"

"Yes. I want to make sure he's not gone back to the library and is still working with the lead."

"It's almost the sixth hour. I'll tell Ursina to serve us in the dining room."

❧

That afternoon, after her husband had gone to see Maros, Arcadia thought about what he had discovered and decided to go to the artisans' quarter. If she could locate Claudia, she might somehow convince the girl to let her help with the pregnancy. Getorius would have discouraged the idea, of course, so she did not tell him or Childibert, nor even Silvia, where she was going.

❧

Arcadia retraced the route Getorius had mentioned, and found the Vicus Judaeorum and the silversmith's shop. Now she stood outside the gate to Virilo's house. If she waited long enough, she reasoned, someone would surely come out, and she could ask about going in to see Claudia. She glanced across the street. A bearded man, who had been watching her, quickly bent back over his workbench. She had read the sign, ARGENTARIVS, on the shop's wall, and guessed he was the silversmith Getorius had mentioned.

Arcadia was about to cross over and ask him if there were specific times when those living in the compound came out, but then she heard a noise on the other side of the gate. Peering through the crack, she saw a cart being driven toward the entrance. She stepped aside as the driver got off and opened the portals, and was surprised to recognize the youth who had pretended to castrate himself at the Olcinium temple.

"Adonis?"

He was equally startled. "Th…the surgeon's wife! How…what are you doing here?"

265

"I came to see Claudia. Is she here?"

Adonis hesitated a moment before asking, "Is this about her pregnancy?"

"Yes. I'm worried about her condition. Could you persuade Claudia to let me examine her?"

"I was going somewhere," he said, closing the gate again, "but I'll take you to where she is."

Arcadia glanced into the cart as she passed, and was surprised to see the two crates of Zhang Chen's writing material that she and Getorius had witnessed in Galla Placidia's anteroom. The boxes were partially hidden by straw and several sackcloth bales placed on top of them, but the red Sinese characters on the sides were unmistakable.

"Adonis, what are you doing with Senator Maximin's crates?" she asked. "I thought they were at his villa."

"I…an…an errand for the senator," Adonis stammered. "Come with me if you want to see Claudia."

Arcadia followed the youth across an unkempt, weed-filled garden area, noticing that a pool in the center was clogged with dead leaves. Obviously Virilo did not employ a competent gardener.

The villa was arranged around three sides of a courtyard. To her left Arcadia saw that half of the two-story wing had been faced with pink marble. An entryway, flanked by Ionic columns, suggested a sacred building. *There's no inscription, but if Diotar's cult is located here, that's probably his temple to Cybele.*

Adonis led the way under the portico of a building across from the temple, knocked on a door, and then entered.

Diotar turned from a mirror, where he was combing his hair, but stopped in mid-stroke when he saw Arcadia.

"ArchGallus, I found this woman outside our gate," Adonis told him. "She wants to see Claudia."

"The wife of the surgeon. How did you find our temple?"

"I can help Claudia," Arcadia told him. "I'd like to talk with her and her father about an epilepsia treatment…about care during her pregnancy."

"Your husband sent you?"

Arcadia shook her head. "Getorius doesn't know I came." As the words slipped out of her mouth she realized her mistake in admitting that, but it was already too late.

Adonis bent down and whispered something to Diotar, who nodded and forced a smile. "Claudia may be in the temple. Adonis, we'll take...again, what is your name?"

"Arcadia."

"Yes. We'll take Arcadia to see Cybele's house. Bring Thalassius and Malarich...to prepare the temple for evening worship.

Outside, as Diotar escorted Arcadia across the garden to the temple entrance, he continued talking, his high-pitched voice amiable, "I understand your shock at first seeing Cybele's face in Olcinium...the sacred stone...but you'll see that our statue here is quite beautiful."

Inside the temple the space was gloomy, the waning afternoon sunlight diffused by the single high window. Arcadia saw that Diotar had spoken the truth. The seated image of Cybele was lovely, similar to the smaller statue in the outdoor booth that had been destroyed in the earthquake.

"The two paintings explain our cult," Diotar said, leading Arcadia to a mural on the left wall. "This one depicts Cybele and Attis rising heavenward to eternal bliss."

Intent on studying the unfamiliar imagery, Arcadia paid little attention when she heard the front door open. She glanced around to see Adonis come in with the two men Diotar had sent for, but then turned back to continue looking at the mural. Suddenly she felt a hairy arm encircle her throat. Frantic, she tried to struggle free, but a powerful grip kept her hands pinned to her sides. A cloth was stuffed into her mouth and tied roughly in place behind her hair. She winced at a sharp pain on the side of her face. One of her earrings had almost been torn off.

Arcadia went limp, realizing she would only be hurt more if she tried to fight back. She felt her feet being lifted off the floor by one of the men, while the other supported her under the arms. Together they easily carried her behind Cybele's statue, then more awkwardly down a series of steps, into a small chamber. Another flight of stairs led further downward.

Arcadia only had time to think about what a fool she had been to come alone before she felt the man at her head press his finger against the pulse in her throat, and blackness overcame her.

❦

Arcadia awoke to an unfamiliar, slightly salty taste in her mouth, and an aching head. When she became aware of her surroundings again, she found herself lying on her side, with the gag still in her mouth.

I remember passing out, but they must have rubbed opion on my gums as a quick anesthetic to keep me unconscious. Someone here knows about medicine. Arcadia looked down at her tunic. It was untorn and intact. *At least no one raped me.* Struggling to stand up, she found her feet were bound and her hands tied behind her back, but by twisting her body around she managed to get into a kneeling position on the stone floor.

Light from two small high windows gave feeble illumination to a room that looked familiar. Although Arcadia did not feel as if much time had passed, her hunger and need for urination told her that it was later in the day. After her eyes became accustomed to the dim light, she recognized the worktables she and Getorius had seen a few days earlier. The baskets of bronze coin discs were gone. The press lay on the floor, dismantled, with its parts laid out in sections. *I'm in the room we discovered at the end of that final sewer tunnel. It was under Virilo's house, and it looks like he's getting ready to leave, move his counterfeiting operation elsewhere. That silversmith must have warned him that Getorius was around, asking questions. Poor Claudia. What will happen to her now? If Cybele's temple is here, Diotar must be part of whatever's going on, and I was stupid enough to ask Adonis about Chen's crates in that cart. The priest was evidently afraid that I'd tell someone about them, but what does he and Virilo plan to do with me now?*

Arcadia shuddered on recalling that her husband believed that the galleymaster had murdered Atlos. *Getorius. He must realize I'm gone by now and be frantic. Neither he nor anyone else knows where I went. Blessed Cosmas, at least I should have had enough sense to tell Childibert!*

Chapter nineteen

What do you mean, you don't know where Arcadia went?" Getorius stormed at Silvia, shoving away the breakfast plate she had put in front of him. "Don't you keep track of your mistress better than that?"

"She di…didn't tell me wh…where she was going," Silvia sobbed.

"Nor I. And she's been gone all night…" Getorius glanced up, feeling both hope and alarm when Childibert looked into the dining room. "What is it, word about Arcadia?"

"Master, sick woman came to clinic."

"Of all times. All right. Silvia," Getorius said to her more gently, "perhaps your mistress went to her father's house. Valerianus may have come back to Ravenna from his winter villa. Take Brisios and go over there. It's near the Theodosius Gate—he knows the place."

Getorius watched her leave, then went through his study to the clinic. Childibert had admitted Felicitas, the former patient he had seen at Thecla's funeral. Her son Fabius was with her.

The woman suffered from mellitus, Getorius recalled. A few months earlier he had prescribed a vegetable diet, unsweetened wine, and vinegar rubs for her leg ulcers. Arcadia had given Felicitas the first treatment and instructed Fabius to continue them at home. It was logical that an excess of sweet be balanced with acid, hence the dry wine and vinegar washes.

Felicitas's soiled tunic reeked of urine. She was sniffling, indicating a wet humor imbalance. It was evident she had lost some weight by following the diet, but her legs were no better.

"Are you continuing the vinegar treatments, Domina?" Getorius asked gently. "Your legs—"

"Had t' bring mother here in a litter," Fabius complained, confirming what Getorius had observed about her ability to walk.

"You said I'd be dancing around the basilica on the Feast of Palms," Felicitas scolded in a tone that was more disappointed than angry.

Getorius tried to recall why he would have told her that. The woman's case was serious and he avoided giving patients false hope. "I probably meant that I'd like you to be well enough to do that, Domina. Have you been eating properly?"

Felicitas gave a non-committal shrug of her head and looked away.

"Fabius?"

"Mother wants her fried pork. She's still pissin' in bed. Tired all th' time. Thirsty. I'm workin' now and can't be with her as much."

"I understand." Arcadia had been there the first time Felicitas came in, Getorius recalled, had treated the woman's leg ulcers, and even cajoled her son into continuing the vinegar washes. He suddenly realized how much he missed his wife, how much he needed her as a partner. Felicitas's weight loss obviously was not the result of dieting. It was clear that the woman would die soon, probably before the summer solstice. The thought reminded him of what she had said about walking around the basilica, but he had meant Bishop Chrysologos's church—back then he had not known Felicitas was an Arian Christian. Perhaps she knew what happened to the porter.

"Domina, the Arian basilica. Do you—"

"We don't cause trouble," Fabius cut in, "but your bishop closed our church."

"Fabius, I'm not harassing you, I even treated your presbytera. I thought your mother might know what happened to Thecla's porter."

"I already told you that Odo's never been found."

"Do you know anything about the death of that youth in April? After Thecla found him she called me to the basilica."

Fabius shook his head. "What about mother?"

He's obviously not going to talk. "Get her on a vegetable diet... without the pork...and continue the vinegar washes as best you can. I'm sorry, that's all I can tell you that might be of help."

After the two of them left, Getorius went into his office to wait for the return of Silvia and Brisios. He wandered the room, absently touching his jars of preserved animal organs, and parts of the skeletons in his collection. The plaque of the Hippocratic Oath, which Arcadia had given him on his birthday, was still propped up on a lower shelf; he had not gotten around to having Childibert mount it to the office wall. Getorius took up the bronze plate, half-heartedly held it up in various locations, and returned it to the shelf.

He sat behind his desk and idly leafed through the Soranus volume on gynecology that Arcadia had been reading. Had he been too harsh in refusing her wishes to open a women's clinic? Claudia had asked for an abortifacient. It had been the first such request in his experience, since women usually went to midwives for such advice. Soranus had an entire section on the procedures, yet most midwives could not read, and knew only what their own teachers had taught them. Perhaps Arcadia could save the lives of both mothers and children, if women trusted her enough to ask for her services.

❧

Getorius was asleep, his head on the desk top, saliva dribbling from his mouth, when he was startled awake by Childibert's voice.

"Master. *Master!*"

"What is it?" he asked, wiping his lips on a sleeve and rubbing at the stiffness in his neck. "Was your mistress at her father's house?"

"Man from magistrate office is in atrium."

"Leudovald? What hour is it?"

271

"Ninth, Master."

"Leudovald came here?" Getorius repeated as his mind cleared of sleep. *Christ, don't let it be that he's found Arcadia's body in a canal or the harbor.* He rose and swept past his steward, half-ran into the atrium, and saw the investigator idly tossing pebble bits into the pool. "Leudovald. Is…do you have news about my wife?"

"News about your wife," he repeated in his eccentric manner. "Surgeon, I came here to interrogate her. What is this riddle?"

"No riddle. Arcadia has been missing since yesterday afternoon, and without telling me, or her house servants, where she went. I sent Silvia to her father's house, but Childibert didn't say anything just now. I presume she hasn't returned."

"You perhaps…offended her, Surgeon?"

"What?"

"It's said that women are like wasps in their anger."

"We've not had a quarrel, if that's what you're saying. Look… come into my study." Getorius led the way through the reception area and into his room, then closed the door. Leudovald chose the same stool on which he sat the first time he had questioned Getorius, three weeks earlier. "You wanted to talk to her about the counterfeit 'Valentinians'?"

"Yes, but now there seems to be a more serious problem. A missing wife."

"Leudovald, I'll be honest," Getorius told him. "I don't much like your sarcasm and insinuations, but I've already said that I believe you're sincere in wanting to find out the truth about the death of Atlos."

"A death with unfortunate consequences for the old woman. The…presbytera."

"Yes." Getorius was surprised at the investigator's soft words that did not refer to Thecla as a heretic, or belittle her ordination. The man sounded almost regretful. "Leudovald, if I'm going to find Arcadia, I probably don't have much choice but to trust you. We…accidentally discovered the 'Valentinians' hidden in wool bales aboard the *Cybele*."

"In the property of our illustrious senator."

"Publius Maximin. On impulse I told Arcadia to put a few of them in her purse."

"Three."

"One of the bronzes in the pouch had been silvered."

"Silvered. A sample," Leudovald suggested, "for an accomplice at Olcinium to imitate?"

"You already know a lot about the coins."

"Surgeon, why would one export false coins of the western emperor to the eastern empire? For what purpose?"

"We've asked ourselves that…" Getorius paused. "Can we speculate about the coins later? This isn't helping me find Arcadia."

"Where would you suggest we start, Surgeon?"

Talk of the counterfeiting had reminded Getorius of the underground room at Virilo's. He could tell Leudovald about its location, at the end of a sewer tunnel, but not necessarily that he knew it was in the galleymaster's villa.

"I haven't been completely open with you," he admitted. "That day we went to the basilica with you, Arcadia found the hidden passage that Thecla's people used to escape church authorities. We followed it through sewers."

"Through sewers to *where*, Surgeon?" Leudovald's velvet tone had hardened, and he phrased the question as a demand.

"To a location where…where we found counterfeiting equipment."

"Counterfeiting equipment. Then let us first search for your wife there."

"There? Actually, I…did tell her…" Getorius caught himself before blurting out that the press was located in a basement of Virilo's house.

"Tell her what?"

"Never mind." Getorius stood up. "Let's go to the Arian basilica and get down into that tunnel."

❧

It had begun to rain, sending rivulets of water down the street gutters to gurgle into sewer openings in swirling pools. Despite leather rain capes, by the time the two men reached the basilica they were soaking wet. Leudovald pried the grille off the door with the iron bar he brought. Getorius led him around the apse to the hidden ladder, and down along the same route he had taken with Arcadia. But this time water poured through the street openings and dropped down in drenching cascades at twenty-five-pace intervals. The Armini channel was filling up rapidly, and had now almost reached the level of the walkway.

When they reached the lateral sewer leading to the harbor, it was calf-deep with mucky water, its smell intensified by having been stirred up by the torrents of falling rainwater. The splashing sound, as it emptied into the harbor, echoed back into the tunnel arch.

Water in the main channel was nearing the level of the maintenance walk when Getorius led the way into the side tunnel that led to the underground room. He worked the brick loose with his belt knife and retrieved the key.

Leudovald grabbed it. "I'll open that door."

Getorius watched him push the wards up and slide the bolt back. Leudovald pulled the door open a crack, then stepped aside, waiting for anyone who might be in the room to investigate the intrusion. All was quiet.

He stepped in.

Getorius walked after him. The room's already minimal light had been made even dimmer by the storm, but he sensed that something was missing. "What the...? That screw press is gone!"

"You have me chasing phantoms, Surgeon?"

"Christ be my witness, there was a wooden press here, like the one fullers use. I saw the inside of the coin dies." Getorius went to the tables ranged around the walls. "The lamps and bronze slugs are gone, too...only these workbenches are still in place." After glancing around once more, Getorius's eyes caught the glisten of shiny fabric on a shelf beneath the farthest table. Goosebumps shivered down his neck as he went to kneel beside what seemed to be a lumpy bundle of cloth that was shaped somewhat like a body. "Blessed Cosmas, don't let it be..."

"Step back, Surgeon," Leudovald ordered and stooped down

to tug at the bundle. It was heavy. After he used both hands to ease it toward the edge of the shelf, he jumped back.

The stiff body of Zhang Chen, dressed in an orange silk robe, rolled out onto the floor with a dull thump.

"It's the Oriental!" Getorius exclaimed. "Zhang Chen is supposed to be staying at Maximin's villa. What is…was…he doing here?"

"What was he doing here, while our senator is away at Ariminum?" Leudovald stood up and examined the bench tops, then scooped up some particles he found on the surface of one. "Breadcrumbs among the bronze shavings. And here a candle stub, yet the dead do not eat, nor need light to see."

"Then Chen was kept here as a prisoner before he was killed."

"Or someone else, Surgeon? The crumbs are recent, otherwise mice would have left us their mementos." Leudovald tugged at the candle to loosen it from a pool of hardened beeswax holding it in place. He turned the stub over, then worked a shiny object off the bottom. He held up a small piece of jewelry. "Surgeon, is this perhaps your wife's?"

Getorius fingered a gold earring fashioned in the form of a circular serpent. "It…it is Arcadia's. I gave it to her on the ides of January…her birthday."

"A clever woman, to leave us a clue that she was here."

"But none to where Arcadia is now."

"Where are *we*, Surgeon?"

"I…I think in a basement somewhere under Virilo's house."

"Virilo's house. Then the porridge thickens. This Zhang Chen arrived in Ravenna on the *Cybele?*"

"Yes. That door on the far side of the room probably leads upstairs to Virilo's." Getorius went to run his fingers over the portal. "Solid oak, and undoubtedly barred from the other side. It will take a squad of Scholarians with a battering ram to break through."

"Break through…" Leudovald looked up through the windows. "It will be dark when we return here. By then lanterns would only show that the sewer walks were flooded over and we could not reach this room."

"His villa faces the Vicus Judaeorum."

"Vicus Judaeorum. Then let us retrace our steps, like drenched rats, and confront him at dawn."

"Dawn? No, that's too late," Getorius objected. "Something might happen to Arcadia by then. Look at Chen there."

"The Oriental was an expendable accomplice. Your wife is being held hostage for reasons we do not know. I believe the galleymaster will not harm her until he makes his demands clear."

"I hope to God you're right."

"I shall alert Tribune Lucullus. A squad of his guards will be in front of the galleymaster's gate, to await the dawn light."

⁊⊱

Getorius arrived at home as soaked as the sewer rat Leudovald had mentioned. He only nodded when Childibert told him Arcadia had not been found and went straight to the bathhouse's hot pool to steam off the chill. Concern about his wife made it hard for him to completely relax.

I could enjoy this if I weren't so worried about Arcadia, and Leudovald's hesitation. The earring proves that she was held in that room, and yet Leudovald merely doubts that she'll be harmed? I've thrown my dice down in a gamble to trust the man, yet he insists upon not going back to Virilo's until morning.

Now that I've told him where the galleymaster lives, where the counterfeiting is carried out, he still seems only minimally interested. That tribune could come for me *before dawn. If Leudovald is connected in any way to the smuggling operations, Arcadia and I could end up like poor Chen.*

Zhang Chen. Why was he at Virilo's, instead of the senator's farm? What happened to his writing materials, and to the small crates with the Dragon's Cough candles? Has Virilo seen the bursting tubes and realized their destructive potential?

"It will be a long night of waiting until it's time to go back to Virilo's and free Arcadia," Getorius muttered as he climbed out of the pool to towel himself dry.

Chapter twenty

In the morning, when Getorius arrived at the gate of Virilo's compound, a golden sun had just risen, adding a glaze of reflected color on paving stones still wet from the night's rain. No one was in the narrow street. A distant pealing of bells from the Ursiana Basilica, together with those of the more distant Holy Cross, reminded citizens that it was Sunendag, the Lord's Day.

Leudovald was already at the portal with Tribune Lucullus and ten guards from an elite Germanic palace unit. The men were lightly equipped, without helmets, and wearing black wool tunics under scarlet capes, with leather trousers tucked into heavy boots. Each man carried a spear and had a sheathed longsword attached to his belt.

Four of the men stood near two ladders they had propped against the brick wall of the compound. Lucullus peered through a crack separating the gate's double doors, trying to see if anyone was inside.

To Getorius it seemed that they expected little trouble in arresting Virilo, yet he still felt uneasy. "When are the men going in?" he asked Leudovald. "Why are you waiting?"

"Waiting. Fortunately, few crafters are at work today, and I want as little disturbance as possible. The Tribune will wait awhile to see if anyone comes out."

"How long? It seems too quiet in there, even for Sunendag."

"If no one comes soon, the guards will climb over the wall by the ladders."

Getorius looked across the street. Pharnaces's shop was shuttered, and the narrow door on one side closed. "Leudovald, that's where I found out that Virilo lives here. Perhaps the silversmith warned him, or saw someone already leave earlier this morning."

"Ask him, Surgeon."

After Getorius knocked on the door several times with the handle of his knife, a window shutter was pushed open on the second story. Pharnaces peered out, scowling at the interruption, his hair tousled and dark eyes bleary from sleep.

Getorius called up to him, "I'm the physician who was here two days ago. Did you—"

"No one in this house is ill," Pharnaces interrupted curtly. "Great Zeus! Cannot a man have peace one day in the week? You are the third idiot so far to come here this morn…" He stopped in mid-complaint after he saw the guards at Virilo's gate. "*Ti?* What is happening?"

"Was it someone from that villa who came to you?" Getorius asked. "The galleymaster? Diotar?"

"*Ohi,* no, a brazen woman and her one-armed Herakles. She demanded the silver hand that I was making to fit on a wooden arm being carved for the brute."

"A woman and a companion with a single arm?" *Giamona? Tigris? The amputation was only a week or so ago.* "Was she stocky? Short blond hair?"

"*Veveos,* and bold as an Ephesian temple whore," Pharnaces whined. "She threatened my manhood if the silver hand was not finished. Already I had not slept well, from that infernal noise during the night. Carts coming and going at the eunuch's den."

"What? Virilo has moved out?" Getorius called out to Leudovald, "He's gone!"

"I heard. Tribune, order two men up one of the ladders. Have them unbar the gate from inside."

After the retaining beam was pushed off its supports and the portals opened, Getorius ran in with the guards. He saw the doors to the residences on each side, under the porticoes, hanging open. The rooms were empty. He went into the nearest one. A few items of women's clothing, perfume flasks and empty ointment jars were scattered around the room.

"Virilo and anyone who lived in his annex have fled during the night," he yelled to Leudovald.

"Fled. Tribune, take five men and go into the main house," the investigator ordered. "The others can search inside the side room areas."

Getorius looked at a temple-like facade of pinkish marble on a building to the left, the only one whose portal was still closed. "Leudovald, that might be a shrine to Cybele. I know that Diotar and Virilo are somehow connected...Of course! Those eunuchs Pharnaces complained about...the women's clothing. Diotar's cult priests lived in those rooms. He's gone, too."

Getorius sprinted to the temple entrance and found the door unlocked. He heard Leudovald following him inside the two-story room, where a ray of morning light from a high window struck the statue of a seated woman at the opposite end. From the sculpture of the Phrygian goddess he had seen in the Olcinium temple garden, Getorius recognized an image of Cybele. "I was right. Diotar's temple is located on Virilo's property. But where have they gone, and why?" He walked closer to Cybele's statue, and then paused in sudden shock after noticing a hideous sight lying at her feet.

Diotar lay dead on the stone footstool, his sightless eyes staring up at the goddess, whose smile had been turned into a mocking smirk by a chance play of sunlight and shadow. Flies buzzed and settled around the gore staining the yellow silk of his ArchGallus robe, where his throat had been slashed by a curved, golden blade that lay on his chest.

"Th...there's your...sickle," Getorius managed to blurt out

through his horror. Leudovald, as pale as the statue's marble, did not reply. "We've got to find Arcadia," Getorius shouted, in panic now.

He searched the perimeter of the shrine's walls without discovering doors to another room, then went behind the statue. A short flight of wooden stairs led onto a platform. "Leudovald! There might be something down here."

At the bottom of the steps, jars of oil and boxes of charcoal dust and colored powders were arranged on a platform. On a nearby bench, a pair of terrified doves cowered in their wicker cage.

Leudovald came down and glanced around at the paraphernalia. "I've read that pagan priests knew how to animate statues of gods," he said in an uncharacteristically weak voice. "They made them move, speak. Produce colored fire."

"That's what these are for." Getorius looked below the platform. "More stairs. I'm going down." Leudovald followed him along steps that led to a short corridor. It ended at an oak door. "This looks like the portal we couldn't open in that underground room. It's barred, and also locked. Virilo could have imprisoned Arcadia inside again. He wouldn't dare…" Getorius stopped, recalling the body of Diotar lying at Cybele's feet. *If Virilo murdered the priest, as well as Chen, what might he have done to a witness?*

After throwing the securing beam off its brackets, Getorius broke his knife prying the lock's retaining bolt free. When he pushed at the heavy oaken door, it creaked open.

It was the same room where the counterfeiting press had been, but with more light coming through the windows. Sewage water had seeped in under the outside door and pooled on the floor. Zhang Chen's dead body still lay where it had tumbled off the bench shelf, but a movement betrayed the presence of a living person, huddled against the far corner.

"Ar…Arcadia?" Getorius stammered weakly, in the hope that it might be his wife. Muffled attempts to respond indicated the person was gagged. After Getorius came closer, he was stunned to see that it was not Arcadia, but the stocky form of Gaius Virilo. A gag was tied over his mouth. Ropes bound both his feet and hands tight. Blood clotted a gash at the side of his head. "Virilo? You're the last person

I expected to find here! I thought you had killed Chen and Diotar, then gotten away." Getorius loosened the gag and hand ropes. "What happened down here? Where's my wife?"

Virilo caught his breath and rubbed at his chafed wrists. "It...it's Claudia."

Getorius shook his shoulders. "Claudia? What do you mean?"

"I don't know what's happened to her."

"A more serious epilepsia attack?"

"No, it's...she...she and that Adonis. They looted my villa and went to the *Cybele.*"

"Nonsense," Leudovald interposed, stooping to cut Virilo's foot bonds with his dagger. "Who imprisoned you here, galleymaster? Surely not your daughter."

"Those two brute guards Adonis recruited. I can tell you, they're no eunuchs."

"Did you see what happened to Diotar?" Getorius asked.

"Diotar? No, what?"

"He's up in the temple. Murdered."

"Claudia probably turned against him, too. After all I've done for that ungrateful—"

"Where's my wife? Where's Arcadia?"

"They took her to the galley, along with what they stole from me. I don't know where that Adonis is planning to sail."

"We need to get to the wharf." Getorius pulled on Virilo's arm to help him stand. "Show me the shortest way. Leudovald, tell the tribune to send his men over there. Quickly!"

❧

Virilo hobbled through alleyways and emerged at the north end of the wharf. Getorius ran on ahead of him, until he saw the *Cybele* in the distance, a flash of morning sunlight glinting off her retracted bronze ram. The sleek brown and green hull was riding high, almost empty, standing off about ten paces from her dockside berth, and secured to a mooring dog by a single hawser. The rest of the wharf and warehouses were deserted; it was Sunendag and no stevedores worked on that day.

Once Getorius got closer, he recognized Victor and Gaius on board. Both were loading one of Chen's large crates of writing material into the hold, together with another crewman he had seen on the *Cybele* during the crossing to Olcinium. He did not recognize a fourth man. Zhang Chen's other crate and the four smaller padded boxes were set at the edge of the cargo hatch, along with the dismantled screw press from the underground room.

Virilo's cook, Maranatha, was at the bow, preparing to light its charcoal and cook breakfast. Near him, Claudia Quinta, dressed in a short, belted tunic, stood on deck next to Adonis. He was supervising the stowing of cargo below deck.

Christ, they're getting the galley ready to sail! Why is Claudia dressed like that? Getorius looked toward the helmsman's platform behind the cabins. He recognized Sigeric leaning on the steering oars, a shadowy figure under an awning that fluttered in the mild breeze.

Behind him, Arcadia stood in front of another man Getorius did not recognize.

"Thank God, my wife is alive," he murmured. "But I've never seen Claudia like that. She…she's a completely different person."

Claudia, evidently alerted by the sound of Getorius's footsteps, looked toward him. "Threaten the surgeon's wife, Malarich!" she shouted to the man holding Arcadia. The Goth grasped Arcadia around the chest with one hand, and held a dagger to her throat with the other. "Surgeon," Claudia called over with a sarcastic laugh, "how nice of you to see your wife off."

Stunned, Getorius could think of no adequate reply. *What in the name of Asclepius has happened to Claudia? Why is she threatening Arcadia? It's as if a daemon has entered and taken over her body—*

"Father!" Claudia's voice intruded on Getorius's confused thoughts as Virilo came alongside him. "Did you see how I paid back Diotar, Father? You're fortunate that Adonis talked me out of rewarding you in the same way."

"Now, Claudia," Adonis soothed, putting an arm around her shoulders. "We need to stow the rest of our supplies and row out of the harbor while the tide is with us. And we have only four oarsmen, not six."

Claudia ignored him. "This is my lover, the father of my baby," she called out to Virilo, smiling stiffly. "A grandchild you'll never see."

"Claudia…" Adonis began.

She pushed his arm off, and then looked along the wharf at a new sound. The rhythmic tramping of booted feet heralded the arrival of Lucullus and his men, with Leudovald. At the tribune's command the guards formed a semicircle around the galley, holding their spears up in throwing position.

"Malarich," Claudia called out without looking away from the men. "A little blood to get those guards to move into the warehouse portico."

Getorius saw Arcadia flinch as Malarich drew his blade lightly against her chin and blood reddened her throat. "Get them back!" he yelled to Leudovald. "He'll kill Arcadia!"

Leudovald nodded to the tribune, who ordered his men away, toward the warehouses.

"That's much better," Claudia gloated. "Father, you thought Atlos was my lover. That's what I wanted everyone to believe. Atlos found out about the 'Valentinians' and threatened Diotar. Said he'd report the ArchGallus's involvement in the smuggling, if Diotar insisted on his being castrated at the Megalensia." She gave a demented giggle. "My lover killed his twin, for Diotar, and made it look like Atlos had castrated himself. But when Adonis left the sickle in the church, I told him to go back and put your knife there instead, Father. I wanted you to be blamed."

"Leudovald, that's what confused you," Getorius muttered. "I knew I hadn't seen a fish knife. They used the tunnel to go back into Thecla's basilica."

"Surgeon," Claudia called over again, "my 'seizures' even fooled you. Oh, I had the Sacred Disease when I was younger. That neutered old fool Diotar pretended that the gods had touched me, that I was his precious Vestal Virgin. I was very good at letting him believe it until…" Claudia turned to caress Adonis's face. "My lover and I have different plans."

"Claudia, we…we need to finish loading—"

"Shut up, Adonis!" she screamed. "Gaius, come up here and open that crate. Give me a piece of what's inside." After the crewman had pried off the cover and brought Claudia a sheet of the writing material, she held it up. "Watch, Father." She tore a strip off the side, ripped it into small pieces, then threw them over the rail. The tannish bits spiraled down to float in the calm water of the harbor. "Pretty, don't you think?" she taunted. "Like flower petals."

"Claudia, you can't destroy the senator's property," Virilo yelled. "That material is worth a fortune, and a fourth of the money is mine."

"You're through ordering me around now, Father," she shot back, her face stiffened into a mask of hatred. "You never wanted anything to do with me after I got sick. Just paid that Greek bitch to feed me. Then, you let that Phrygian half-man use me in his bloody rituals. Well"—Claudia reached over and put Adonis's hand on her stomach—"not all of Diotar's priests were castrated, were they, lover?"

"Claudia...."

She ignored Adonis and ripped another strip off the sheet, then threw the rest down.

After tearing serrations into the band, Claudia fashioned it into a circle, and placed it on her head as a diadem. "I'm going to where I'll be a queen," she boasted with a hoarse laugh.

"The woman is mad," Leudovald commented. "Isn't that so, Surgeon?"

"Hippocrates has a complicated explanation for the disease," Getorius whispered to him, "but her epilepsia has affected Claudia's mind. She could do anything irrational now. I've got to get my wife off that galley."

"The *senator's* property, Father?" Claudia taunted, going back to an earlier thought. "It's mine now, and I'm taking it to Alexandria. Adonis says they make the best papyrus there, so they'll pay a ransom in gold to find out how to produce those writing sheets." She giggled again. "With all of Diotar's sapphires and his temple treasure, I'll be queen of Egypt."

"Alexandria," Getorius repeated tersely. "They're taking the

Cybele to Egypt. Can't the galley be intercepted outside the breakwater mole, Leudovald?"

"Our Adriatic war fleet has been sent toward Misenum, to help against the Vandal threat."

"A patrol galley then? Like the *Apollonaris* we encountered on the way back to Ravenna?"

"How can I alert one at Classis in time?" Leudovald asked. "And without much cargo *Cybele* could outrun it. Her crew has a sailing advantage in time, and the Etesian winds at their back."

Desperate, Getorius looked toward the harbor mouth and open sea beyond. There had to be a way to stop the galley from entering the Adriatic.

In an abrupt motion Claudia took the paper crown off her head, tore it into pieces, and flung the scraps overboard. "Adonis, I want to leave now. Get the men on the oars."

"We still have supplies to take below. And that Oriental's small crates."

"What's inside *them?*" Claudia demanded. "Something more we can sell in Egypt? Pry one open."

"Later, Claudia. We have to—"

"Open one now!" she screamed.

Adonis slipped the padded quilting off the closest box and levered the top pegs out with his knife. After lifting the cover, he saw tightly packed dark granules. "It looks like only charcoal," he said, sifting black powder through his fingers.

"Charcoal? What good is that?" Claudia scowled. "Gaius, take the crates to that cook. He's having trouble lighting his kindling. I want to leave *now*, Adonis."

"We need to finish—"

"You st...stop ordering me a...around!" Claudia screamed, stuttering. "Get th...the men to the oars!" Agitated and trembling, she pointed at Getorius. "Surgeon, p...pull that rope off th...the mooring dog." When he hesitated, she threatened, "You'll c...cast us off if you want me t...to send your wife b...back to you alive from Alexandria."

Getorius knew that would never happen once the galley had left the harbor, much less if it reached Egypt. Yet Malarich might slit Arcadia's throat now, if he did not do what Claudia ordered. And the girl was deranged enough not to make many more rational choices. With numb movements he loosened the knot on the hawser, let it go, and heard the coil splash into the water.

"Sigeric, we've been through a lot together," Virilo shouted up to the helmsman. "Why in Neptune's name are you going with them? How much are they paying you to betray me?"

Sigeric looked away and spat on the *Cybele*'s deck without answering.

Four oars poked through thole pins, and the crews' strokes began to back the vessel away from the wharf. As Getorius, helpless, watched the helmsman's deck move further away from him with Arcadia on it, he saw Malarich relax his hold on her and lower the knife. *The threat to her is lessened, but that's small consolation if the galley makes it out of port.*

The *Cybele* came to a slow stop as the backstroking of the four crewmen prepared to turn the galley about and row across the harbor toward the open sea.

As the galley paused, Malarich stepped back and began to sheath his knife. In that same instant, Getorius saw a small, irregularly shaped object arcing through the air. The shiny missile struck Malarich in the temple, on the right side of his head, with a sickening crunch of skull bone. The man dropped his blade with a stare of disbelief, made a reflexive grab for his face, then toppled back off the helmsman's platform. His body slid down to wedge in the curve of the sternpost.

Dumbfounded, Getorius looked around for the deadly projectile's source. A one-armed man and a blonde woman were standing in a skiff about twenty paces from the galley.

"T...Tigris?" he blurted. "Giamona?"

She glanced at him, but turned back and shouted, "Arcadia! Dive overboard!"

Getorius saw the curve of his wife's body arc over the edge of the stern platform and deck strake rails. As Arcadia slid into the water and began to swim, Giamona poled the skiff toward her.

Claudia, who had been intent on watching the wharf recede, heard the splash. She turned her head, saw Arcadia in the water, then gazed back at Malarich's body with a vacant, uncomprehending stare.

"Adonis, w…what happened?" she mumbled. "What happened?"

"I…I'm not sure. I wasn't looking."

Claudia stood a moment longer, then collapsed onto the deck and began to cry.

Lucullus had been observing from the warehouse and ordered his men out. A few threw lances at the retreating galley, but the arcing shafts fell into the water, well short of the stern deck.

As Giamona neared the dock with Arcadia, Getorius ran to meet them.

"The harbor chain!" Arcadia shouted to him, pushing wet hair away from her face and pointing across the harbor. "Raise the chain to stop them!"

"Of course…Leudovald!" Getorius yelled. "Have some of Lucullus's men alert the harbormaster. He can raise the chain barrier to block the *Cybele*."

"If there are slaves on duty today—"

"There's a signal pennant flying. Hades, man, send the furcing guards! They could do it!" Getorius took a scarlet cape from one of the men to put around Arcadia. As he helped his wife out of the skiff and onto the wharf, Giamona frowned up at him.

"Surgeon, you owe me the cost of a silver hand," she remarked dryly.

"Sil…silver hand? Is that what hit the crewman?"

Giamona broke into a grin. "I'm glad I took your advice back at the camp, about a cedar arm after the amputation. Right, Tigris?"

The gladiator nodded and gave Getorius a slight smile.

"Not half as glad as I am. Tigris, you saved my wife's life." Getorius noticed that salt water had started the nick in Arcadia's throat bleeding again. He dabbed at the spot with the sleeve of his tunic, then held tightly onto her.

She shook loose. "Husband, I'm all right. We've got to stop the *Cybele.*"

They were watching the galley, and the men running to the twin breakwater moles, when Publius Maximin's black carriage clattered onto the wharf.

"I was told Zhang Chen stole my crates and left the villa," he shouted to Getorius. "Do you know where they are? Or where he is?"

How could Maximin know that? One of his guards must have gone to Arminum and reported the incident. "Chen is dead, Senator," Getorius replied "Your property is on the *Cybele*, headed for Alexandria."

"Egypt? *Egypt?*" Maximin sputtered. "Leudovald. Do something to stop that galley."

Leudovald glanced at him with little emotion. "Senator, Tribune Lucullus here ordered most of his men around to try and raise the harbor chain before the *Cybele* can reach the open Adriatic."

"Tribune, they'd better get there in time," Maximin threatened, "or the least of their punishments will be reassignment to some god-forsaken Danubian garrison."

On the galley, Adonis glanced at Claudia, who was still hunched on the deck, sobbing. He had seen her milder attacks lapse into listlessness, or unexplained laughing and crying.

This seemed to be the case now, but he had problems other than trying to comfort her. The galley had hove about and was on course for the harbor mouth, in a direct line ahead, but several anchored fishing boats bobbed in her path. He could not waste time maneuvering around them.

"Bear straight on, helmsman," Adonis shouted.

"We'll ram those boats," Sigeric protested.

"You're being well paid to follow orders," Adonis yelled back. "If we don't make the open sea, a magistrate will make sure your mutinous head...and those of your crew...decorate the Ravenna lighthouse up ahead."

Adonis watched over the bow as the first boat was crunched to bright-colored shards of floating wood. The rowing crew stopped to glance over the side at the sound of an impact that had barely shaken the galley. Maranatha looked up from trying to light damp moss.

"Don't break rhythm!" Adonis shouted to the four oarsmen, "we're making headway. We'll unfurl the mainsail once clear of the harbor." He looked toward the righthand breakwater mole. Guards armed with spears had run along this shorter side and reached the end of the mole. Other men, on the harbor's longer north side, were less than halfway to the harbormaster's building. Adonis chuckled. "Fools. Do they think their lances will stop us?"

He had turned back and knelt down to soothe Claudia, when the rasping sound of winches being turned sounded from ahead.

Sigeric called down to him, "They're raising th' chain barrier!"

Adonis looked ahead from the bow. In the distance, a swirl of muddy water rose from the right side of the harbor entrance, where guards had reached the chain winch mechanism. Long strands of seaweed floated up with it, but no iron links were visible yet beneath the surface.

"Row harder, y' bilge scum," Sigeric yelled to the oarsmen. "If that chain gate catches us, it'll rip into our hull like...like a knife slicin' through goat cheese!"

Now Adonis saw the rusty top links of the barrier rising at an angle on the lighthouse side. The men at the longer north mole had not yet reached the winch, so the chain was being lifted unevenly. "Bear to port!" he yelled across the deck to Sigeric. "They haven't had time to get to the handspikes on that side."

The deadly chain was about fifty feet ahead. Adonis knew it would be close, but was confident the galley would pass over it before the winch could be tightened another turn, and the barrier raised further. "A scraping of the hull planks at worst, helmsman, but *Cybele* can survive that."

"Haul in starside oars!" Sigeric yelled, realizing the iron links could snap off the long shafts like so many dowel rods.

Gaius and Victor pulled in the dripping blades, but the uneven thrust from the two port oarsmen propelled the galley back toward the chain. Still, Sigeric knew it would be a light blow and braced himself. Glancing at the bow, where the impact would be, he saw that Maranatha had coaxed the moss into smoky flame. Part of the charcoal glowed a reddish-orange as he lifted up one of the open padded boxes with both hands.

The crew felt a slight jolt as *Cybele*'s hull glanced off the iron links. Sigeric raised his steering oars to not damage the blades. Maranatha spread his feet wider apart to steady himself, and readied to shake powdered charcoal from the box onto the red coals. As Claudia had suggested, it would intensify the weak glow of the coals.

Getorius hugged Arcadia, both mesmerized as they watched the galley outracing the chain barrier that was being raised to sink her.

The *Cybele* had veered to starside, and then yawed slightly away as she struck the chain, when suddenly there was an intensely bright flash and a cloud of black smoke engulfed her. Even before a sound louder than an overhead thunderclap reached the wharf, three more brilliant flashes erupted, followed by deafening roars. A hot, acrid wind, smelling of rotten eggs, rolled across the harbor. The wind's force capsized fishing boats out in the harbor, then struck the dock with such an impact that it sent bales of wool tumbling across the warehouse floor.

Getorius instinctively turned his back to the harbor and shielded Arcadia. A few spectators, who had arrived soon after Maximin, crouched down, or stood in open-mouthed stupor.

After a moment the clink of metal was heard. A shower of scorched bronze discs, some bent, pelted the dock. A few struck the onlookers, who, despite their fright, recovered and scrambled for the coins.

Getorius picked one up, looked at the inscription, and handed it to Arcadia. "One of the counterfeit 'Valentinians,'" he said, his voice still trembling from shock. "Not quite the gold that Jupiter showered on Danae, but this should exonerate you."

She tightened her hand around the coin then turned to look at where the *Cybele* had been. Sulfurous smoke engulfed the lighthouse. Some of the uppermost stones were dislodged and others badly scorched. On the opposite mole, corner bricks had been torn out of the harbormaster's office, and all the windows in his observation area were shattered.

Lucullus's men had been swept off the breakwater, most of them dead from the impact. A few survivors were sinking in the harbor, frantically trying to strip off boots and clothing to enable them to swim away from the scene of devastation.

The *Cybele*, with her crew and cargo, was gone. The orange flame had left only shattered pieces of charred brown and green wood, lengths of rope, and splinters of mast drifting toward the open sea. Small scorched bits of a dull tan material, which had not burned inside the remnants of the galley's hull, speckled the azure water.

Getorius recalled a passage from the Revelation of John, which described a fallen star. The force of the fall had opened a pit in the abyss and caused smoke to rise, as if from a great furnace, which darkened the sun and air around it.

Arcadia recovered enough to murmur a quote from part of a letter of Peter that the bishop recently had read at Mass. "…The heavens will be destroyed in flames, and the elements will melt away in a blaze."

Chapter twenty-one

The thunderous sound and sulfurous wind had been heard and smelled by some of the people living in the apartments and houses behind the warehouses. Now they came to peer out of windows, or ran outside to the wharf to ask about what had happened. Lucullus and the four guards he had ordered to stay behind had dropped their weapons and covered their ears against the sound. They lowered their hands and joined in gawking at the harbor entrance, where the *Cybele* had last been seen.

"My cargo," Maximin moaned, the first to speak after the cataclysm. "Everything I owned is lost."

"Cargo?" Virilo repeated numbly. "M...my daughter was on the galley."

Getorius recovered from his astonishment and turned to Leudovald. "Order those four guards into the skiff—see if they can rescue any survivors."

Only two of the men overcame their fear and agreed to take the boat out to inspect the floating wreckage.

Getorius led his wife over to the gladiator. "Tigris, Arcadia owes you her life. How were you were able to throw so accurately…and from a boat?"

Giamona replied for him, "One of our games at the camp is to throw a leather ball through a line of hoops. And, fortunately, the harbor water was calm."

"I…I'm grateful to both of you," Arcadia said. "Tigris, that silversmith must still have the mould pattern he used in casting your hand. We'll commission a replacement."

"Fine," Giamona said, "but we need to get back to camp."

"What made you come to the harbor?" Getorius asked.

"When we went to pick up Tigris's hand, we noticed the night activity at Virilo's and saw your wife. We followed them. Our…profession…has taught us to hone our instincts."

"To save your own lives, and this time, my wife's."

"Let's go, Tigris. You've repaid the surgeon."

As Getorius and Arcadia watched, Giamona led her companion toward an enclosed wagon waiting at the far end of the warehouses.

Leudovald came up to them. "Strange friends you have, Surgeon. What is this profession the woman mentioned?"

"Tigris was a patient of mine," Getorius replied with a straight face. "It's confidential…I can't tell you."

"Leudovald," Arcadia said, "Galla Placidia should be informed immediately about what just happened."

Maximin overheard. "It…it's Sunendag, the Lord's Day," he objected. "The Empress Mother will be attending Mass in the palace chapel. We…we should not disturb her devotions."

Getorius glanced at the senator. *That fox! He wants to wait and tell her what happened himself, only mentioning what he thinks she should know.* "You're right, Arcadia, Placidia should be told, but you've been through an ordeal. And you're soaking wet. Go home to change clothes…rest until I get back. Virilo, you can explain about Diotar and—"

"A moment, Surgeon," Leudovald interposed, clearly annoyed at being left out of the discussion. "Tribune, arrest the galleymaster."

"Arrest?" Virilo protested. "I was nearly killed, and those mutineers destroyed my...my life. My daughter—"

"Galleymaster"—Leudovald cut him short—"you have much to explain to me. Why the surgeon's wife was abducted and the Phrygian priest murdered in that temple on your property is only one part of the mystery."

"Diotar is...is dead?" Maximin genuinely seemed stunned. "How...when?"

"That information should stay inside the palace," Getorius murmured to Leudovald, indicating the bystanders with a nod of his head. "Bring Virilo with us to talk to Galla Placidia."

He grunted assent. "Lucullus, report to the Scholarian prefect. Have him send a guard detachment to block the Via Porti and the Longa. I want curious citizens kept away from these docks while we're at the chapel."

"Leudovald, let *me* inform the Empress Mother," Maximin insisted again. "No need for this many of us to upset her."

"We shall all go, Senator, including the surgeon's wife. This matter cannot wait."

Maximin gave Leudovald an angry scowl, but assented. "Very well, get in my carriage." He signed to Mutus, who clambered down. "Take the reins, Surgeon."

❧

Heraclius, the emperor's steward, was outside the palace chapel, sunning himself on the front stairs. When he saw Leudovald and the others approaching, the eunuch got up and stood in front of the door to block it.

"The Augustus's worship cannot be disturbed," he said, holding up pale smooth hands to block the entrance.

Maximin pushed him aside. "Out of my way, you half-man." As the five entered, a deacon looked up from reading a passage from the Revelation of John. Galla Placidia turned, along with her son and daughter-in-law, to see what had interrupted him.

"Senator Maximin?" she asked, standing up. "Leudovald? What are you doing here?"

"I tried to stop them," Heraclius whined.

Optila, Valentinian's bodyguard, drew his sword and started forward.

"Put that weapon away, man," Maximin ordered. "Empress, didn't you notice those loud sounds a short while ago?"

"We did hear roars, much like thunder. Were they a reason to interrupt this service? Surgeon, why are you here with your wife? What is going on, Senator?"

"Empress, th...this is not a good place to...to explain," Maximin stammered. "I tried to tell Leudovald."

"The house of God? You shall explain here. Deacon, we will continue later. Placidus, take Eudoxia...and your Hun...out into the garden."

Valentinian glowered at his mother's order, but motioned his wife and the guard to the front entrance.

After the door was closed, Maximin went to one of the chairs that had been brought in for the service. "Empress, if I might sit? I've just come from Arminum."

"All of you may be seated," Placidia replied. "You're drenched, Arcadia. And what happened to your throat?"

"I'm fine, thank you, Regina," she replied, taking the chair where Eudoxia had been seated.

Getorius, Leudovald, and Virilo remained standing.

"Empress," Maximin went on, "as I said, I was in Arminum for the Lemuralia, but had a...a feeling that something was wrong. Fortunately, I came back."

The man is slick, Getorius thought. *One of his guards reported Chen's absence to him. Now, instead of being reluctant for us to tell Galla Placidia about what happened, as he was on the wharf, he's taking charge.*

"Senator, stop speaking in riddles," Placidia ordered in an impatient tone. "*What* was wrong?"

Maximin dropped several blackened and bent coins into Placidia's hand. "Empress, it seems that a plot to foment discord between Valentinian...our Western Augustus...and your nephew Theodosius at Constantinople has been uncovered."

Arcadia glanced at her husband, who signaled with a headshake for her not to speak.

Placidia studied both sides of the coins. "Apparently an *aurea* of my son's, but minted of bronze. What are these, Senator?"

"The false 'Valentinians' I was investigating," Leudovald answered before Maximin could reply.

"The Empress Mother was speaking to me," Maximin said coldly. "Perhaps, Leudovald, you should escort Virilo to a prison cell now."

"This man?" Placidia asked, looking toward the galleymaster. "Virilo. Is that your name?"

"Yes, Empress. Master of the merchant galley *Cybele*, just destroyed by sorcery."

"Sorcery? Explain yourself."

"Empress, my helmsman and part of the galley's crew were bewitched. Even m…my daughter was a victim."

"Leudovald, you'll take this man to our hospital, not a cell," Placidia ordered. "A presbyter can counsel him about this sorcery, then a magistrate about your concerns. Senator, continue. Tell me what happened."

"Empress, the surgeon and his wife should go home," Maximin urged. "Arcadia has been through a terrible ordeal."

"Arcadia and my physician shall stay," Placidia retorted. "Has this also something to do with Zhang Chen's writing material?"

"The Oriental is dead. I…" Maximin caught himself. "You told me that, Surgeon."

"Yes, Regina. He has been murdered," Getorius affirmed.

"Chen murdered? *Theotokos*, Mother of God!" Placidia exclaimed. "Go, Leudovald, with the galleymaster. You others stay, but I…I want to pray for a moment."

Galla Placidia went to the apse of the chapel. In the semicircle behind the altar, a mosaic image of a youthful archangel, dressed in the sumptuous robes of a court official, held a labarum, a standard inscribed with the Chi-Rho x p monogram of Christ. Next to Michael, a blue-robed Madonna seated on a cushioned throne held the Christ Child, his small right hand extended in blessing.

Placidia knelt on the bottom one of the three stairs of the

marble altar platform, head bowed, and covered her eyes with a hand. A henna rinse had not completely covered the gray reappearing at her temples. Arcadia noticed that, in contrast to the expensive silk tunics she usually wore, the Empress had put on a plain homespun robe for the service, and did not wear a tiara. Only the gold medallion around her neck representing *Salvs Reipvblicae*, "The Health of the Republic," indicated her imperial rank.

She stayed in the position for several moments, then returned to face Maximin.

"*We* are not feeling well, Senator," she told him, emphasizing the formal pronoun. "You shall leave Us while We consult with Our physician."

"But Empress—"

"Leave Us!"

Flushed, Maximin bowed slightly and strode in anger down the length of the nave to the front entrance.

"I don't trust the man," Placidia admitted, after the door closed behind him. "Publius Maximin definitely harbors enough ambition to try to become Augustus some day."

Getorius said nothing, but recalled what the senator's mother once had said about her son's imperial aspirations.

"I noticed that he tried to get rid of you as witnesses," Placidia went on with a grim half-smile. "That way neither you nor Leudovald could contradict what he might tell me. Now, you two, unravel what you know of these mysteries. Is Flavius Aetius involved?"

"Regina, there's been no evidence of that," Getorius told her.

"What is this sorcery the galleymaster alluded to?"

"The other product that Zhang Chen brought to Ravenna from Sina. In the four small crates."

"The ones Senator Maximin tried to conceal from me?"

"Yes. They held a sorcerer's 'magic' only in the sense that its potential for destruction is beyond anything known in the West. Whatever it was, it consumed the *Cybele* as if the galley and everything on it had been smashed by a…a fiery thunderbolt. I can't explain it otherwise."

"What of these counterfeit 'Valentinians'?"

"My wife had a theory about those. Arcadia, why don't you explain?"

"I think that they were being smuggled into Dalmatia and given a silver wash somewhere. Any merchant would have spotted them as false, but legionaries in the Danube garrisons might have been fooled. For a time, at least."

"We thought that Scodra, the capital of Prevalitana, might have a mint."

"Surgeon, the Eastern Empire is my nephew's territory," Placidia remarked. "Imagine the opposite…if counterfeit coins of Theodosius had flooded the West."

"Economic collapse. A civil war could result. Legion mutinies after the men discovered they had been cheated."

Placidia nodded. "Scodra? There's a good road running from there to Viminacium, then north along the Danube. All the fort garrisons would be infested…Aquincum, Vindobona. Even Sirmium, Siscia, other towns in the interior."

"Regina, you're well informed about the area," Arcadia remarked.

"And my emperor son isn't." Placidia sighed and looked away a moment, then continued "Theodosius, at least, has been compiling a new code of laws. My son will co-sign them, but he's not really that interested. How would the 'Valentinians' get to Scodra?"

"Through Olcinium," Getorius replied, "but there's a…a more horrible dimension to the plot."

"Tell me, Surgeon."

"We discovered a temple and cult of Cybele in Ravenna. She's a Phrygian goddess—"

"Who once saved Rome during the Punic wars," Placidia interposed. "Her priests practice self-castration. I'm aware of the cult, but not that it is contaminating Ravenna."

"There was a Cybelene temple at Olcinium destroyed in an earthquake while we were there," Getorius went on. "Diotar, the ArchGallus…their high priest…was involved in the conspiracy to smuggle the coins into Dalmatia. He was counting on that story of Cybele protecting Rome from the Carthaginians to draw a parallel with the present Vandal threat. Diotar used Virilo's daughter in a pathetic hoax to recruit followers, but I believe he truly thought she had the Sacred Disease."

Placidia instinctively clutched her medallion. "These pagan cults subvert the state. None should be tolerated, as my father, Theodosius, well understood."

"They're hidden, Regina. Hard to ferret out—"

"And even the palace is vulnerable to corruption," Placidia continued, as if she had not heard Getorius, then pulled a slim volume from her sleeve and held it up. "I'm reading the 'Hippolytus' of Lucius Seneca. I'd just reached these verses." She opened the book and pointed to a section. "Read this, Surgeon, and tell me, as my physician, if it does not describe the deadly disease in my palace."

Getorius took the book from her and read, "'Fate without order rules the affairs of men, throws about her gifts with a blind hand, cherishing the worst. Violent desire defeats the virtuous, and deceit reigns sublime in the palace halls.'"

"Well, Surgeon?" Placidia demanded, "have you a cure for this abominable plague?"

"With respect, Regina, I...I haven't been there long enough to know. But the Cybelene conspiracy was smashed along with her namesake galley. Diotar was a victim of his own greed. Chen also, I'm afraid, although I think he was trying to escape from what Seneca describes."

"The Oriental's special writing material...what did we decide to call it...papir? Where is that?"

"Destroyed with the *Cybele*."

"Just as well. Maximin counseled that I hold it back for now, but he was undoubtedly planning to solicit bribes from papyrus and parchment makers' associations. They would pay handsomely to see the material destroyed and their industries protected."

"Regina, I'm more concerned about what Chen called 'Dragon's Cough.' If four small boxes of it destroyed an entire galley with hardly a trace left of it, killed guards at more than a bow-shot distant, and damaged a lighthouse hundreds of paces away, imagine what a larger amount could do to city walls."

"Indeed. Do you know how it's made?"

Getorius remembered that Chen had mentioned nitron as an ingredient, and charcoal, perhaps sulfur, were others, but decided not to pursue the subject. "Regina, he wrote down nothing about its elements of which I'm aware."

Placidia sighed, rubbed her eyes and abruptly stood up. "This has been too much for me. The threat of another civil war. Bloody rites to a statue. Alleged sorcery resulting in unbelievable destruction. I only hope that all of this plot has been uncovered."

"As do we, Regina." Getorius avoided any mention of Maximin. Placidia already knew that he was probably involved in some way that could not be proven, just as had been the case with the Gallic abbot's death months earlier.

"You cooperated with Leudovald in uncovering all of this?"

"In…in a way, Regina."

"A strange man, Leudovald, yet I believe he's not one of those deceitful evildoers that Seneca abhorred." Placidia gave the couple a tired smile. "I'll stay here in the Archangel Michael's chapel awhile. Go home, Surgeon. Take care of your wife's injury."

"I will, but Regina, as your physician, I advise rest after all this, a change of scene. Your humors are close to a serious imbalance. Get out of Ravenna. Isn't there an imperial villa at Caesena?"

Placidia nodded. "A gift to me from my late brother, Honorius." She pulled forward the gold medallion from around her neck and held up the inscription. "This is an allegory of how I am thought of as guardian of the health and well-being of the Republic. I may take your advice, Surgeon, although I'm not used to taking that from many people. Go now."

Outside, the couple saw Valentinian's zoo across from the chapel, its smell of animal offal now diluted by a lingering trace of sulfur on the morning air.

Arcadia saw that both ostriches were back in their cages, lying down, and calmer now, five days after Thecla's death. The birds stood as she approached with Getorius, blinking their stupid stares.

"We'll never know if the cage door was left open on purpose or not," she said. "Or if the keeper was bribed to let the creatures loose."

"There are a lot of unresolved questions, Arcadia. In the morning I'm going to Leudovald's office to try to find some answers, but I want to get you home now." As Getorius brushed at his wife's damp hair he noticed her single earring. "I suppose it was clever of you to leave a clue that you had been in that underground cellar, but I'm still angry because you went to Virilo's without telling anyone."

"I agree, Husband, it was foolish, but it's too late to call back yesterday. Let's just forget the matter."

"I was worried about you, *Cara*."

"Let's go home."

Outside the palace, at the corner of the Vicus Caesar and Honorius, a number of people were hurrying in the direction of the port, children running ahead of their parents.

Rumor, the swiftest traveler of all the evils on earth, Getorius thought, recalling a quotation that his tutor had made him memorize. When he and Arcadia reached the door to their villa, a woman in a shabby black tunic stopped them as they were about to enter.

"I heard people were hurt," she said. "Do you know what happened at the harbor?"

"You shouldn't go there, grandmother," Getorius warned. "Besides, the area is probably closed off by now."

"There could be dead, someone who belonged to my burial association."

"There's nothing you can do—"

"I'll decide that, young man!" the crone snapped and stalked around Getorius in a rustle of ill-smelling linen.

"Spunky old lady," he commented to Arcadia. "She…she reminds me of Thecla."

❦

At the clinic Getorius treated his wife's neck wound with an application of boiled conferva root, then ordered Silvia to prepare a tub bath for her mistress.

He sat on a stool and watched Arcadia lie back in the warm water that had been perfumed with their last flask of Gallic lavender oil. The dark bronze color of the tub contrasted with the ivory-white skin of his wife's breasts and what he could see of the softly curved valley at her navel. *Even Diana in her forest pool couldn't have looked as beautiful. No wonder Actaeon was tempted—*

"This is so unreal!" Arcadia abruptly exclaimed and sat up in a splash of scented water, shattering her husband's momentary musing. "Here I am in a bath, as if nothing happened. Claudia is dead, Getorius, and I did nothing to help her."

"Arcadia," he said softly, "the Claudia we saw at the basilica never existed. I doubt that Virilo could tell us any more than we found out from her on the *Cybele*. It's clear now that she ordered Adonis to go back and leave her father's knife at the church, hoping he would be arrested. That would make escaping with his galley much easier."

"I should have been able to talk to her."

"You went to find Claudia and almost got killed, woman! We know now that Diotar was involved in smuggling the counterfeits, and Maximin was paying Virilo for Chen's writing material, but little else. The sapphires, for example, or how many of the 'Valentinians' are already in Dalmatia..." Getorius stopped his rebuke, noticing his wife beginning to sob. "I'm sorry. Silvia!" he called, "bring a towel for your mistress. Arcadia, it's still morning, but you need to sleep. Would you like valerian to help?" She shook her head. "Hopefully, we'll get some answers from Virilo...he's the only witness we know of to all of this."

When Silvia came in with the towel, Getorius told her to help Arcadia into bed, then went into his study. Ursina brought in a plate of dried figs. Getorius munched them while looking back on the morning's events.

It's true that Virilo is the main witness to the conspiracy, but I believed...wrongly...that he murdered Chen and Diotar and was running away. That leaves Publius Maximin's involvement unanswered. He was the one who leased the galley for the Olcinium runs. Will Maximin invoke his senatorial privileges to avoid being questioned?

After sleepless nights, Getorius was so exhausted that he fell into a doze in his chair. It was an uneasy sleep; his mind troubled, remembering that during the events of the previous November and December, two witnesses just like Virilo had been found dead inside the palace itself. Galla Placidia's fear about the latent violence in the Lauretum was not misplaced.

Chapter twenty-two

By early afternoon Ravenna's citizens were to hear almost as many versions of what had happened to the *Cybele* as there were real, or imagined, eyewitnesses to the unexplained devastation.

Tribune Lucullus, who had travelled to Sicilia, likened the noise, flames, and billowing black cloud to the volcanic eruptions he had witnessed on the flanks of Mount Etna, yet he could not explain the source that destroyed the fleeing galley. One of his terrorized Germanic guards reported that he saw two gigantic serpents on either side of the galley spewing the fire and smoke that destroyed it. A more rational companion scoffed that the dark lines were the two sides of the snapped harbor chain, recoiling through the air like a gigantic broken catapult cord.

One devout witness swore that he had seen the hand of God descend inside a shaft of flame—the same fiery pillar that had guided Moses and his Israelites across the desert—to strike down the pagans aboard the galley.

Another Christian reported that an aerolith had blazed down from the sky and struck the galley. He also considered the heavenly sign an act of divine justice and retribution.

A woman slave gibbered that she had seen a bolt of lightning flash down from a clear sky, but admitted that she was unsure of whether it came from Jupiter, or the Christian God, or perhaps even the fiery sulfurous realm of Satan himself.

Hipparchus, a palace philosophy master, had not witnessed nor even heard the blast, but theorized that a spherical universe, surrounded by the central and outer fires that produce the light of day and sustain the stars, had released a flash of its all-consuming heat to destroy the *Cybele*. He confidently predicted that this chance encounter would not occur again for exactly one thousand aeons.

The most bizarre explanation, by Presbyter Gaius Tranquillus, was connected to a passage in the Hebrew Testament, but was also based on Aristotle's teaching that the sub-lunar *Antichthon*, or counter-earth, turns around Hipparchus's theoretical fires. Both are invisible from our earth, he said, yet the revolution of the nine planetary spheres produces a perfect musical harmony. This harmony can only be altered by Perfection itself, in the Person of the Creator of the Universe. Thus, Tranquillus maintained, God had momentarily suspended his own natural law and permitted a tongue of the central fire to destroy the depraved pagan followers of Cybele. God had done the same thing once before, Tranquillus concluded, in scorching the wicked cities of Sodom and Gomorrah.

※

After Getorius awoke from his fitful napping, he tried to reread Hippocrates' treatise, *On the Sacred Disease*, to understand Claudia's illness better, but found his concentration still affected by the horrific images he had seen that week.

Thecla had been brutally killed by an enraged ostrich that had, by design or accident, managed to escape from its cage.

A eunuch priest of the cult of Cybele had had his throat slashed with a ritual sickle by an epileptic girl whom he had tried to manipulate to further his ambitious schemes.

Arcadia had narrowly escaped death on the *Cybele*, before the sixty-foot galley, its crew, and some twenty guards had vanished in the twinkling of an eye, with hardly a trace of their remains left behind. Had he not seen the destructive power of the Dragon's Cough demonstrated a few days ago in his own garden, he thought he too might have found it reasonable to attribute the cataclysm to some unidentified sorcery.

⁂

Arcadia awoke from her sleep of exhaustion as the afternoon shadow of the gnomon on the garden sundial moved toward the tenth hour.

Neither she nor Getorius brought an appetite to supper, even though Ursina had prepared spring lamb roasted in a sauce of onion, savory, dates, and pepper, served with blanched asparagus tips and a pan of mustard greens.

The doors to the garden were open, admitting the cooler air that always arrived when the sun slipped below the villa's second story on the Via Honorius side. The gentle splash of the fountain was audible, a pleasant sound that mingled with the chirp of emerging night insects. A mixed scent of thyme and rosemary drifted into the dining room.

Arcadia looked out for a moment before sitting down. She toyed with a piece of lamb a moment, then pushed her plate of food aside. "I simply can't believe that Claudia had us fooled for almost a month."

"All this took planning," Getorius pointed out. "She and Adonis evidently had a lot of time to themselves, to be able to hatch that kind of plot. The crewmen they recruited could have been bringing back their own contraband from Olcinium. Adonis probably got them to join him by threatening to expose smuggling in which they would be implicated."

"And money. Payments from the Cybelene temple treasure that Claudia mentioned helped bring them over to their conspiracy."

"Leaving Ravenna was better than facing a Roman court. As I found out, Arcadia, once charged, you're pretty much presumed guilty."

"What was Senator Maximin's part in all this? He's been pretty deft at avoiding any responsibility and..." Arcadia stopped and looked toward the door, where Childibert stood. "What is it?"

307

"Mistress, the person from magistrate is here."

"Leudovald? We were going to see him in the morning. Send him in, Childibert."

"Wonder what the man wants," Getorius mumbled. He stood up when the investigator entered the dining room and decided to be civil. "Leudovald. Will you join us in some supper?"

"Supper. Yes, agreed," he replied with a trace of a smile beneath his mustache. "One tires of palace rations."

"Good." Getorius was surprised that Leudovald had accepted. He looked drawn and his blond hair was unkempt and in need of a trim. Like everyone involved, the problems of these past few weeks had undoubtedly taken their toll on the man's health, in sleeplessness and worry.

"Childibert, tell Silvia to set another place," Arcadia ordered.

"Only small portions," Leudovald cautioned. "My digestion has not been well lately."

"A little wine, then, for your stomach's sake"—Getorius pushed his untasted cup toward the man—"just as Saint Paul advises."

"A little wine."

"The first time I met Thecla she told me that her stomach was tormented by a daemon," Getorius recalled. "I prescribed a cassia purge."

Leudovald chuckled softly. "I prefer this remedy, Surgeon."

He took a sip of wine as Silvia came in and set a dish of the lamb and vegetables in front of him.

Getorius pushed over a plate of bread and watched the man eat for a moment. "Leudovald, we were just wondering about Publius Maximin's role in all this."

"Maximin. Unfortunately, any physical evidence of the senator's involvement is in pieces at the bottom of the harbor."

"How convenient," Arcadia remarked. "Did Virilo tell you anything more?"

"More? The galleymaster seems affected by his daughter's death, but has not yet fathomed the depth of her deceit…her obsession with revenge. I've postponed more questioning until tomorrow."

"We admitted to you that we accidentally discovered the counterfeit bronzes in one of Maximin's wool bales," Getorius reminded Leudovald, "but we also found bags of sapphires being smuggled into Ravenna in his pepper amphorae."

"Sapphires." Leudovald shrugged. "From a source and to a destination we shall never know. It's obvious now that the person, or persons, who operated the coin press in the cellar room entered through the Arian basilica."

"And we've never discovered who that might be."

"Wait, Getorius," Arcadia recalled, "didn't you tell me that Fabius offered you one of the false 'Valentinians' after Thecla's funeral?"

"Fabius? Of course! As an Arian he knew all about the basilica's secret escape route to the underground room. And he was evasive about the whereabouts of the old porter."

"Who is this Fabius?" Leudovald asked. "How do you know him?"

"His mother is a patient of mine. You may have seen him with her at Thecla's funeral. His temptation to steal a few of the counterfeits for himself is understandable."

"I'll send my men out to arrest this Fabius and question him."

"They'll probably have to pry his body off the grille where that lateral cloaca empties into the harbor. Adonis would have seen to that if he found out."

Leudovald drained his wine, brushed a nervous hand over his mustache, then toyed with the rim of the silver cup. "It seems that the woman presbytera—"

"Thecla," Arcadia reminded him.

"Thecla." Leudovald flushed slightly. "It seems, Domina, that she provided the clue that unraveled the weave of this conspiracy. Without her simple code we would not have been led to the cellar room."

"This is something I've wondered about," Arcadia said. "Why did Claudia want to be found with Atlos in that Arian basilica?"

"Adonis must have found out, perhaps from Fabius, that Thecla filled oil lamps at that day and hour," Getorius speculated. "Claudia lured Atlos there, where he was murdered by his twin. Then Adonis went back to Virilo's by the sewer route."

"Of course. Both knew the authorities would be summoned and hoped to confuse them by implicating a heretic who would be seen as guilty, if, somehow, Virilo wasn't blamed. Leudovald, you thought him guilty."

The investigator took a nervous swallow of wine. "The girl's false confession blamed the presbytera."

"And it cost Thecla her life."

"I regret that, Domina."

"Did you question the zookeeper about the open ostrich cage?" Getorius asked.

"A magistrate decided that this...'accident'...saved the court the trouble of a trial for a heretic who had been accused of murder."

"What do *you* think?"

"Surgeon," he parried, "without...Thecla's...help the *Cybele* would have sailed to Alexandria unsuspected and unhindered. The galleymaster would have died before he could be found. The body of the eunuch priest..." Leudovald frowned and pushed his plate away, evidently recalling the gruesome sight at the statue's base.

"The Cybelene conspiracy took on a life of its own," Arcadia commented, "like...like the organ tumors we find in animals we dissect. What began simply, Claudia's obsession with taking revenge on her father and Adonis's wish to avoid emasculation, mushroomed into a treasonous plot to compromise the Eastern Empire and initiate a civil war.

"If that 'Dragon's Cough'...what the rebel crew believed to be charcoal...had fallen into the hands of our Persian enemies," Getorius pointed out, "their armies could have destroyed the walls of say, Antioch, then taken the city as a threat of what would happen to Constantinople itself. Our Eastern Empire might have ceased to exist."

Leudovald did not comment on the possibility, but admitted without looking up, "I...I'm grateful for your help in this."

The man actually has human emotions, Arcadia thought. She re-filled his cup and put the dish with his half-eaten meal to one side. "Leudovald, why weren't you involved in my husband's arrest last December?"

"I was aware of it, but the mutilation of a corpse is a church matter. The bishop insisted on his own investigators."

"Like Dagalaif?"

He nodded. "Like the deacon. Yet, to allow churchmen as judges, in their own courts, is a dangerous precedent. Easily abused. Some day…" Leudovald took a quick sip of wine.

"We know very little about you," Arcadia said, to relieve his discomfort at not wanting to complete the thought. "How long have you been with the magistrate's office?"

"My father was a Frank, *comes*…a count…on a king's staff. After our Salian tribe was allied by treaty with the Romans, he sent me from Divodurum to be educated here."

"I suspected something like that when I first met you," Getorius said. "Do you still see your father?"

"Surgeon, he was murdered by a rival."

"I…I'm sorry."

"Our people are from a violent tribe. To die by the sword is no disgrace."

"In battle, perhaps, but to be murdered?" Getorius asked.

"Murdered." Leudovald glanced out at the garden. "Indeed, Surgeon."

"Please, after all we've gone through, call me Getorius."

Leudovald looked back at him in surprise, but nodded. "Getorius. We were speculating on the senator's role in this conspiracy. It's clear the counterfeit 'Valentinians' were intended to provoke instability in the Eastern Empire…a chaos the senator could exploit by blaming the Augustus, then recruiting Flavius Aetius to depose Valentinian and back himself as emperor."

"But Maximin tried to blame Aetius," Arcadia pointed out.

"Only, Domina, after you discovered the actual coins. I was working from rumors of their existence."

"Fabius may have boasted to Thecla about making the coins," Getorius said, "but she probably had no full idea of the counterfeiters' purpose."

"I agree that the eunuch priest was Maximin's conduit for smuggling the coins to the east," Leudovald went on. "The senator undoubtedly promised to legitimize Diotar's Cybelene cult, once the Senate declared Maximin emperor."

"Maximin would go that far?" Arcadia asked.

"I believe he would stop at nothing to gain power."

Getorius recalled, "It's only been about seventy-five years since Julian the Apostate tried to re-establish paganism in the Empire. It's clear now that Diotar had been using Claudia's illness to recruit followers, but the Vandal capture of Carthage gave him an unexpected opportunity...and believability...among desperate citizens. What will you do, Leudovald?"

"Do, Surgeon? The 'supernatural' destruction of the *Cybele* has already entered the realm of myth."

"So Publius Maximin won't be indicted?"

"Indicted? With only a few bent coins as evidence against him? His coconspirators all are dead, providentially, for him. No, when it comes to justice, our senator is slippery as a market basket of eels."

Getorius looked at his wife, shaking his head. Maximin had escaped blame from a similar plot in December, by using his senatorial position and wealth to have an abbot murdered and deny any knowledge of the Gallican League's theocratic plans.

"Leudovald, if not the senator, Virilo then?' Arcadia asked. "He must know something of the conspiracy."

"The galleymaster seemed genuinely distressed at his daughter's...his crew's...defection. However"—he ran a slender finger around the silver rim of his cup—"my assistants could undoubtedly...persuade the man to tell us what we wish to hear."

"'Deceit reigns sublime in the palace halls.'"

"What, Arcadia?"

"Getorius, I was just recalling part of what Galla Placidia had you read from Seneca. Twice now Maximin has escaped responsibility and punishment."

"Domina, the senator will continue to scheme until he succeeds in becoming Augustus," Leudovald predicted, "and yet the best mountain climber may have an unexpected fall. I shall wait patiently to catch our adventurer's plunge." He drained his wine and stood up.

"The magistrate is expecting my report. Perhaps...perhaps I could repay your dinner at one of Ravenna's better taverns?"

"There's no need—"

"Leudovald, that would be nice," Arcadia interposed with a smile. "Wouldn't it, Getorius?"

"Ah...yes, very nice."

"I'll see you out, Leudovald," she offered.

Getorius realized that the investigator had not pursued the subject of Zhang Chen's deadly invention. Yet, he must have an opinion about what destroyed the *Cybele*, other than his hint about supernatural intervention. The man was too much of a realist to believe in that.

Arcadia returned and sat down. "Leudovald seems lonely. I wonder if he could become a friend? It wouldn't hurt to have one in the magistrate's office."

"*Cara*, I don't think Leudovald would let friendship interfere with his duty as he sees it."

"Hopefully not, I suppose, for the good of Rome. You once quipped about what he'd do to his grandmother if she were found guilty of a crime." Arcadia abruptly came around the table to sit on her husband's lap. "You owe me a vacation," she said, brushing at new gray strands in his black hair. "I don't consider that impromptu odyssey to Dalmatia as being a real one."

"No. Actually, I'd like to see Constantinople."

"The Eastern capital? I was thinking more in terms of a rented villa on Lake Comum, up north, with a view of the Alps."

"Arcadia, physicians in the capital must have surgical techniques I've never even heard about. They have access to all the medical knowledge of our Asian provinces, manuscripts they may have kept secret. It would be part of my training. Yours, too."

"Many books would be in Greek and ours isn't that good."

"We're far along enough in the language to find a place to stay. We could hire a translator-scribe for the medical texts."

"Exciting." Arcadia wriggled off her husband's lap and sat next to him. "Can we afford such a faraway trip?"

"A while ago I met with Childibert about the account ledger. Last year we made about a hundred *solidi* from the clinic—"

"Including all those fish?"

"Very amusing, Arcadia. And almost half again as much from renting out the five shops and two upper rooms on the Honorius side of the house. After expenses, we had a balance of about a hundred twenty-five *solidi*."

"What about your fee as palace surgeon?"

"My fee?" Getorius gave a sardonic laugh. "Not a lonely bronze *follis* yet, Arcadia. The palace financial mill grinds very slowly."

"Constantinople. Will it be safe to go?"

"A galley to Dyrrhachium, then through Macedonia along the Via Egnatia by travel wagon. Perhaps another boat from Thessalonika to the Propontis. We'll take Brisios along to deal with our luggage. He'd have nothing to do here."

"Sounds like you've been planning this for quite awhile."

Getorius grinned at her. "Perhaps we can get Galla Placidia's authorization to stay at imperial inns on the overland stretch. She might even recommend medical contacts in Constantinople to me. After all, Emperor Theodosius is the Gothic Queen's nephew."

"Could we sail on a galley larger than the *Cybele*, one where I might not get as seasick?"

"Of course, *Cara*. Perhaps a big grain carrier, like the *Horus*."

"Exciting…" Arcadia leaned over to kiss her husband. "Getorius, let's walk out into the garden while it's still light outside. It's so peaceful there."

"And we do need some peace after all this."

They sat on a stone bench, holding hands and watching swallows swoop in graceful arcs to catch insects flitting in the twilight. Arcadia had often marveled at the birds' swift, darting antics, but now their timeless movements were reassuring that, on Nature's level at least, life still went on.

In the waning light, the oval petals of pond lilies in the fountain pool reminded Getorius of the tannish scraps that Claudia had thrown overboard. All of the writing material had been destroyed, but it could only be a matter of time before more of it was smuggled to the west. *That could be beneficial, but likewise, more of the Dragon's Cough is sure to follow. A candle-sized cylinder of it shattered a pitcher into shards. Four boxes the size of large loaves of bread destroyed an entire galley and its crew in an instant. What terrible damage would it do to the human body that I would never be able to repair?*

The thought was upsetting. "Let's go inside, *Cara,*" he said, releasing Arcadia's hand. "I've thought of a place in my office for Childibert to hang your plaque of the Oath. And there'll be sick people coming to the clinic in the morning, some probably with diseases we've not yet seen…" Getorius suddenly reached down for a pebble, got up, and flung it into the pool's water. "I feel so helpless at times! I couldn't do anything for Claudia…and Felicitas will be dead by mid-summer."

"Don't be so hard on yourself. You saved Tigris's life, and without him *I'd* be dead." Arcadia stood and looked him in the eyes. "Getorius, we've all been made caretakers of this earth, and you've chosen medicine as your particular garden."

"And yet—"

"*No 'and yets'!*" Arcadia leaned over to shush his lips with hers, then started toward the door, her arm in his. "Cicero said that every man should practice the art in which he's skilled. Yours is a surgeon's. Now show me where you wanted to put the plaque, although I'll probably find a much better place for it." She released him and went on ahead. "Oh, and if you're serious about our going to Constantinople, I'll need a few of the gold coins…that *I* just might have earned working with you…to have my seamstress make appropriate clothing for me to bring along."

"Earned?" *Is she being sarcastic? It never occurred to me to pay my wife for her help in the clinic. I mean, the woman already has everything—*

"Are you coming?" Arcadia called from the edge of the herb garden.

"Right." *Setting up Arcadia's birthday gift of the Oath might be a small step back to normalcy, toward coping with a Fate who scatters her gifts with a blind hand.* Getorius caught up with his wife and slipped an arm around her shoulders. "I'll try to see Galla Placidia tomorrow about our plan for visiting Constantinople. And wherever you want to put my plaque will be fine, *Cara*, but...but...*I'll* pay for those new clothes you want to take along on our voyage."

"Very well, Husband, I won't soil my fingers with *your* gold."

"You're not upset?"

She smiled sweetly at him. "Of course not. Now let's go mount that plaque." *But, Getorius, the day will come when I do have my women's clinic and then we'll see who buys my things!*

About the Author

Albert Noyer

With degrees in art, art education and the humanities, Albert Noyer's career includes working in commercial and fine art, teaching in the Detroit Public Schools and a private college. He lives in New Mexico, and has previously published other historical mysteries, *The Saint's Day Deaths* and *The Secundus Papyrus*.

The fonts used in this book are from the Garamond family